ELLA HARPER

The Years of
Loving You

AVON

AVON

A division of HarperCollins*Publishers*
1 London Bridge Street,
London SE1 9GF

www.harpercollins.co.uk

First published in Great Britain by HarperCollins*Publishers* in 2015

1

A catalogue record for this book is
available from the British Library

ISBN-13: 978-0-00-758184-9

Set in Sabon LT Std by Palimpsest Book Production Limited,
Falkirk, Stirlingshire

Printed and bound in Great Britain by Clays Ltd, St Ives plc

MIX
Paper from
responsible sources
FSC
www.fsc.org FSC® C007454

FSC™ is a non-profit international organisation established to promote
the responsible management of the world's forests. Products carrying the
FSC label are independently certified to assure consumers that they come
from forests that are managed to meet the social, economic and
ecological needs of present and future generations,
and other controlled sources.

Find out more about HarperCollins and the environment at
www.harpercollins.co.uk/green

This one goes to my excellent friends . . .
you know who you are.

Yours is the light by which my spirit's born: you are my sun, my moon, and all my stars.

E.E. Cummings

Now

'Great party,' Sam said, shaking Ed's hand.

'Thanks. I actually did all this myself. I reckon Saskia is re-thinking our marriage now that she knows I'm actually a girl.'

Ed gestured to the silver and white decorations adorning the walls of their local pub. There were clusters of balloons in each corner, complete with perfectly curled ribbons, there were pretty silver swathes draped between light fittings as well as glitter-dusted white bows dotted here and there. It had taken ages to put everything up and he had almost broken his elbow falling off a bar stool earlier. But Saskia wasn't really into any of this stuff and, for some reason, Ed had a feeling people were expecting great things. Probably because him getting married was a bit of a turn-up for the books, or whatever the expression was.

'Blimey.' Sam raised his eyebrows. 'I thought you were the blokiest bloke around.'

'Nope.' Ed grinned, knowing Sam was probably wetting

1

his pants on the quiet. Imagining Ed festooning balloons around a pub. Hanging bows and streamers everywhere. Emasculating and then some. 'Seriously, Sam. I'm a bird. No two ways about it. Where's Molly?' he asked, before he realised Sam was on the phone.

Ed frowned. He hadn't exactly been expecting to throw an engagement party, let alone one in the pub he usually frequented with his mates. Sometimes he went there with Saskia, but mostly it was a place Ed used for down time. He wasn't sure they would ever see him in the same way now that they knew he was behind the bows and glitter.

Not that Ed was bothered. Saskia was happy, which meant that he was happy. He was content to watch Saskia in her element, floating around the pub in a cream silk dress that showed off her tanned legs, laughing and socialising.

Was Saskia a little drunk? Ed thought she might be. Nothing wrong with that, of course. He was a tad drunk himself.

Saskia's parents were in tow, Ed noted. They were a distinguished-looking couple but they seemed somewhat bewildered to find themselves in a local pub, surrounded by a bunch of people they were mostly unacquainted with.

'Saskia's parents seem nice,' Sam commented, covering the phone with his hand, following Ed's line of vision.

'Yes. They're great, really great.'

Pressing a pint onto Sam and accepting one himself, Ed decided that he wasn't entirely sure Saskia's parents approved of him. They had been pleasant enough when he met them, but they hadn't seemed exactly thrilled about the engagement. Ed wondered if it was his job – or rather, the lack of it – that was causing concern. Being a full-time writer and having the luxury of living off his friend Boyd's shrewd investments didn't show him in the best light, he supposed. It wasn't how he had started out; it was simply the fortuitous way his life had unfolded. But Ed wasn't overly inclined to sit Harrison and Margot (for those were the names of Saskia's illustrious parents) down and explain his humble beginnings. Saskia knew some of Ed's history, but not all of it and Ed thought that was absolutely fine. A partner didn't need to know everything about a person, did they?

Molly disagreed on this point, Ed recalled, glancing self-consciously at Sam, the way he often did when his thoughts drifted to Molly – as if Sam could read his mind or something daft. Anyway, Molly had questioned him about this once and Ed had defensively justified himself. Molly was a person who felt that couples should be fully open with one another and she saw it as some sort of flaw on Ed's part that he hadn't completely opened up to Saskia, some sort of indication perhaps that they weren't fully connected. Ed suspected that the reason Molly had such strong opinions on this matter was largely down to him. But shame was the perfect foil for candidness. There were just some aspects of life that were better left unsaid, in Ed's opinion.

He took a look around the pub. He couldn't deny that it was actually quite a buzz seeing all of their friends gathered together in one place, spilling out into the beer garden. In fact, he didn't even realise he and Saskia had so many friends between them.

Strange things, weddings, Ed mused, watching Saskia

almost tripping over and shrieking with laughter as one of her friends held her up. He had never imagined he would have the remotest interest in the details, or the organisation. But Saskia, who possessed many wondrous qualities, was not the most organised of people. Nor did she seem overly interested in colour schemes and venues. But she was over the moon about the wedding; Ed was certain of that. Her reaction to his impulsive proposal had confirmed that. Ed could remember it in minute detail . . .

'Have you really finished the novel?'

'I think I actually might have finished the novel.' Ed scrolled down to the page that said 'THE END' in overly large letters. 'Yes, I really have.'

'Yay!'

Saskia jumped up and punched the air, before going behind him to drape her arms around his chest. 'I'm so proud of you! This is wonderful. We should celebrate.'

Ed put a hand on Saskia's waist, luxuriating in the warmth of her body, squashed against his neck and back. Saskia was a very affectionate girl. She was only twenty-eight, but she seemed more mature than her years. She was pretty, rather full-on in the bedroom and nothing much seemed to faze her. She had turned Ed's house into a home with what he believed were called 'feminine touches' and he was very grateful.

Saskia leant over his shoulder. 'So. What's this infamous novel about? You've always been so vague about it.'

Ed saved his work and shut his laptop down. He had very good reasons for being vague about the content of his novel as far as Saskia was concerned.

4

'It's . . . it's just about these two friends. Who keep missing their timing. Who love each other . . . who are maybe very much in love with each other.'

Saskia tightened her grasp around his shoulders for a second. 'You old romantic, you,' she teased, giving his ear a lick. 'I do love this side of you.'

'Do you? I rather like you licking my ear in that sultry fashion.'

'Then more of it you shall have . . .' Saskia gave a husky laugh and focused on Ed's ear. 'And if this gets published, you might get even more . . .'

Ed suddenly felt a wave of panic about the possibility of the book being published. Had he completely and utterly bared his soul to the world? Ed thought about the content and immediately felt naked and exposed. He had poured everything into this novel. There had been times when Ed had felt utterly raw during the writing of it. Reliving certain moments in history had been cathartic but also intensely challenging.

Writing a love story that wasn't quite a love story had been poignant and then some. But writing it was just something he had had to do.

He heard Saskia murmuring something in his ear about how much she loved being with him . . . about her loving his house . . . the garden . . . everything about it . . . everything about him. Saskia wanted more. Ed knew she wanted more. And so did he. Ed wanted more. He was ready to settle down finally. And Saskia was a lovely girl. Perfect for him.

Ed wasn't sure about the whole having children thing. Not yet, at any rate. But he could possibly see himself with Saskia long term. She was sweet, funny and loving. They got on well. They had much in common, enjoyed the same things. All of Ed's friends thought Saskia was beautiful and sweet.

'I'm going to get some champagne,' Saskia announced. 'We need to celebrate this moment. Well done,' she said, giving him a juicy kiss.

Could he do better than Saskia, Ed wondered? In realistic terms, anyway. He had gone through a number of girlfriends over the years and none of them had captivated him the way Saskia had. She was a straightforward girl, but she appealed to Ed on so many levels. Maybe what he needed in life was someone uncomplicated. Saskia had moved in shortly after they started going out and Ed now couldn't remember if she had asked or if he had given her a key unprompted, but it didn't really matter. Saskia didn't work, but she didn't need to with all the investments Boyd had put Ed's way. And Ed could hardly talk. He had worked so hard in the early years of his life, he had welcomed the years he had been able to focus on what he wanted to do – writing.

Saskia appeared in the doorway. She had shed all her clothes bar her underwear (Saskia did a fine line in underwear) and she was brandishing two flutes and an open bottle of champagne.

'Let's get drunk,' she said.

Ed caught his breath. She really was lovely. They worked. Together, they worked. 'Come here,' he said.

Saskia smiled and sashayed over. Sitting on his lap, she almost dropped the flutes. 'Ooops! We need those.'

Ed put his hands around her waist. 'Marry me, Saskia.'

'W-what?' She almost dropped the glasses again.

'Marry me.' Ed kissed her. 'Let's get married.'

Saskia stared at him. 'Do you really mean it?'

Ed panicked then pushed the feeling away. 'I really mean it.'

'Oh my God!' Still clutching the champagne and flutes, Saskia put her arms around Ed's neck and kissed him. 'I can't believe it. This is so unexpected!'

Ed grinned. It had been somewhat unexpected on his part as well. He had always thought he would plan such an occasion for months – plotting all the details the way he had learnt to do with novel-writing. He had always thought the event would have a beginning, a middle and an end, not be something he blurted out on a whim.

'You've made me so happy,' Saskia murmured against his ear. 'I just want to be with you.'

Ed kissed Saskia. No. He'd done the right thing. He had finally finished his novel and he and Saskia were getting married. Everything was slotting into place. Everything was making sense. In fact, the only thing that didn't make sense was that Ed's next thought was that he wanted to call Molly. But this was his and Saskia's moment. It was just that Molly was the first person Ed always thought of when something important happened . . .

Back in the room again, Ed bit his lip. One person was notable by their absence. Where the hell was Molly?

'Where's Molly?' Ed said to Sam again, noting that he was off the phone at last. 'She promised she'd be here.'

Sam frowned at his phone. 'No idea. She had to pop out and do something but she didn't say what. I'm sure she'll be here. Congratulations, anyway,' Sam added, tucking his phone away. 'And I really mean that.'

Of course you mean that, Ed thought to himself. Sam was hardly his biggest fan and seeing him married off would please him no end.

He met Sam's innocent-looking green eyes and something unspoken passed between them. Ed knew that Sam knew that he knew what Sam had done. All with the very best of intentions, no doubt, but still. What Sam had done might have changed the course of history. Maybe. Ed had no way of knowing for sure.

Saskia appeared at Ed's elbow. 'And this is my fiancé,' Saskia said to one of the friends Ed hadn't yet met. She was slurring.

'Charmed I'm sure,' Ed said, leaning in for kisses and pleasantries. 'Thanks so much for coming.' Christ, he sounded as though he was already at his wedding. He glanced at Saskia. She really was very drunk. Her cheeks were flushed, her hair was in disarray and she was clearly having trouble standing up.

'Are you ok?' Ed said into her ear.

'Of course!' Saskia patted his cheek and looked past him. 'I'm absolutely fine.'

'You might have had a bit too much champagne,' Ed grinned. Even plastered, Saskia was ravishing.

Saskia smiled. 'Maybe. I'm just having fun.'

'Me too.' Ed gave her a kiss. He watched her walk away from him, happy to see her enjoying herself so much.

'I'll give Molly a call,' Sam said as he took his leave. 'Chase her up. If I can't get hold of her, I'll probably call it a day and pop home.'

Ed nodded back, itching to get his phone out and chase Molly. Where on earth was she? It was his engagement party, for heaven's sakes! Ed had attended Molly's wedding and they hadn't even been speaking to one another at the time.

'Ed, lovely do.' Boyd pumped Ed's hand.

'Thanks.'

'Listen, we need to chat about some of our investments.' Boyd raked a hand through his hair. 'Sorry to do this at your party, but I'm afraid I have some bad news.'

Ed raised his eyebrows. 'Christ, I won't have to sell the house, will I? Saskia will never forgive me.'

Boyd shook his head gravely. 'I don't think it will come to that, no.'

'I was joking, Boyd!' Ed felt a jolt of shock. 'Are you saying we've lost some serious money here?'

'I'm afraid so.' Boyd was joined by two of his many children. They wrapped their arms around his legs and started whining about wanting crisps. 'As I say, apologies for the timing, but I had to warn you.'

'Er . . . thanks. I guess.'

Ed felt a tremor of anxiety. The last thing he needed was for his investments to take a turn for the worse. His life was finally getting settled. He glanced over his shoulder. Where was Saskia? She seemed to have disappeared. He decided to go in search of her; he was about to make a slushy speech and she really needed to be around to hear that.

Ed headed for the toilets but couldn't locate Saskia. About to give up, he heard a giggle coming from the kitchen area. A Saskia giggle. Hoping she was ok, Ed poked his head in. His smile faded.

Saskia was kissing one of the bar staff. With some enthusiasm. She caught sight of him and stopped.

'Ed.' She put a hand to her mouth.

The young bar chap looked extremely uncomfortable. 'Shit. Sorry. I was . . . this is . . .'

'Not what it looks?' Ed shook his head. 'Let's not be silly.' He held the door open for the boy who scuttled out, red in the face.

'Ed, I'm sorry about that.' Saskia swallowed.

'About what?' Ed was reeling. 'About me finding you snogging someone else at our engagement party?'

'Yes.' Saskia looked away. 'You make it sound terrible.'

'Er, no, Saskia. It just is terrible. I'm not sure I could articulate it in a way that doesn't sound horrendous.' Ed wondered how he was holding it all together. Clearly his world had just imploded slightly. Massively.

Saskia was pleating her skirt ferociously. She had gone from flushed to pale in a short space of time and seemed to be looking at the floor with great intent. Perhaps searching for words to explain herself.

Ed wanted to rage at her. But for some reason, he couldn't. He wanted her to tell him why he had just walked in on her kissing some other guy. Was it the first time she'd done something like this? The tenth? Had she always been unhappy? Why had she got engaged to him if she wasn't fully committed?

No words formed.

Eventually, Saskia spoke. 'I . . . Ed, I just don't think I can do this.'

'Do what?' Ed stared at her.

'This.' Saskia swallowed. 'This party. The engagement. The . . . the . . . wedding.'

'You don't think *you* can do the wedding?' Ed shook his head dumbly. 'I don't think *I* can do the wedding! Not after that.'

'No, but I was thinking that beforehand . . . not just . . . after that.'

'Is that supposed to make me feel better?' Ed put his hands on his face. What the hell was happening here?

'Probably not. But I need to explain.' Saskia was twisting her hands together and she suddenly looked absurdly young.

Ed's stomach shifted. 'Go ahead.'

'It's just all become a bit . . . serious,' Saskia said, her eyes meeting his pleadingly.

'A bit serious? Yes, I suppose weddings do feel a bit that way, don't they?' Ed wasn't sure how he was supposed to deal with this.

Saskia grabbed the edge of the kitchen counter, presumably for support. 'The whole getting married thing. I did want things to move along a bit, but I would have been happy to stay engaged, you know. For quite a while, in fact.'

Ed looked her in the eye, wanting to see the expression reflected there. All he saw was regret. 'Meaning?'

Saskia averted her eyes. 'This has all been fun, Ed. You and me . . . we have incredible fun, don't we?'

'Fun. Right.'

Ed was starting to feel like an absolute idiot. He had misread the situation between himself and Saskia. He

11

had assumed that her hints to move things along meant marriage. But no. She wanted commitment in a soft form . . . a prolonged engagement that kept the 'fun' element of their relationship alive. No wonder she hadn't been interested in the wedding itself. It was Ed who had allowed himself to get carried away with all of that. He had believed he was ready and that Saskia was the right girl.

'So you never really wanted to get married?'

Saskia grabbed his hand. 'Oh, Ed. Don't put it like that. I did want to get married. Kind of. You asked me, it felt lovely, I said yes. I just didn't realise you wanted to dash off immediately and book venues and talk about buttonholes.'

'Gosh. What a massive idiot I am.' Ed rubbed a hand over the back of his head, not sure how his life had just blown up in his face.

'You're not an idiot.' Saskia sounded upset now. 'I just got swept up with your enthusiasm. I did love you, Ed. I mean, I do.'

'Do you?' Ed turned to face her.

'Yes. This is just . . .' Saskia paused, her pretty face scrunching up. 'It just doesn't feel like fun any more, Ed. It feels way too serious. Too grown-up. Maybe that's it. Maybe I'm just too immature for all this stuff.'

Ed let out a sigh. What the hell was he supposed to say to that? Saskia was very young, admittedly. Way younger than him. But that didn't make her immature. Or it hadn't, until now.

'Stay, Saskia?' Ed asked. It was the only time he was going to ask her, but he had to give it one last shot. He

12

wasn't sure he wanted to; she had snogged someone else after all. But he did love her. And it was only a kiss. He could get past it. Probably. 'Stay and we can work things out.'

'I-I can't.' Saskia hung her head. 'I'm so sorry.' She touched his arm. 'I have to go.'

'Go?'

'Yes.' Saskia looked around vaguely. 'I need to leave. I can't be here. This is . . . too much. It's all just too much.'

Ed blinked. Was Saskia actually going to walk out of her own engagement party? Was she effectively . . . jilting him? Ed felt sick. He suddenly wished he hadn't eaten so many cocktail sausages.

'Goodbye, Ed.'

And that was that. The end of a relationship. The end of an engagement. Aghast, Ed watched Saskia walk out of the kitchen. Following her, he watched her walk right out of the pub. Her parents scurried after her, as did a couple of her closest friends.

Ed had no idea what to do. No idea whatsoever. 'I'm so sorry, everyone,' he said to the room at large. 'That was – rather unexpected. I'm afraid the wedding is off.'

There was a collective gasp.

Turning to the bar, Ed rubbed a shaky hand over his face. 'I'd like a tequila please. A large one.'

'And I'll have what he's having.' Boyd handed his children over to Helen with a mouthed apology and joined Ed at the bar. 'Let's get royally shit-faced.'

Ashen, Ed nodded and necked the first tequila of many. Molly. Where the hell was she? Ed needed Molly.

He made a quick call to Sara, Molly's best friend. Sara was on her way to the party and seemed flummoxed that Molly was absent.

Ed grimly accepted another tequila. Hurry up, Molly, he thought to himself. Hurry up. I need you.

Molly sat in silence waiting to be called in. She hadn't been kept long, but sitting in this particular waiting room was one of those occasions where time seemed to move so incredibly slowly, it was like being suspended in another realm.

Of course, there were worse things to be dealing with, Molly reasoned to herself. This wasn't the worst thing that could happen to her. She knew friends whose children were in and out of that incredible hospital in London – Great Ormond Street, was it? Children with over-sized, inoperable tumours and unusual illnesses that meant regular resuscitation and any number of other complications. Molly also had friends whose parents, both of them, were suffering from cancer or something equally hideous.

So she had no right to be acting as though her world was about to come crashing down around her. Molly realised she was gripping the edges of the chair she was sitting in so tightly that her knuckles had gone white. She let go. Her hands felt fine today, ironically. They had for the past few days, in fact. Molly wasn't sure what to make of that. Was it a brief respite? Or had whatever was wrong with her retreated for no apparent reason?

She glanced at her watch. She had missed Ed's

engagement party last week. She had sent an apologetic text to Ed to explain of course, but she hadn't heard back from him. Which might mean that he was furious with her. Molly knew she needed to speak to Ed sooner rather than later, but she just couldn't face it right now. Not until she knew for sure.

Molly shifted in her chair. She had received an immediate appointment with a consultant which was panicking the hell out of her. That didn't bode well, did it? That meant they were fairly certain she had something serious. It was usually weeks and weeks until such appointments came up.

'Mrs Bohle?' Pronouncing Molly's surname as 'Bowl-lay', a nurse appeared in the waiting room. Molly winced. Sam would go bonkers if he was here. He hated anyone who couldn't pronounce their surname properly. 'Mr Ward will see you now.'

Molly stood up, not bothering to correct the nurse. Her legs were like jelly. Was that a symptom? Or was it to be expected in the situation she was in? Frankly, Molly was fed up with all the uncertainty. It was better that she found out what was going on with her once and for all. Wasn't it?

Anxiously, she walked into the consultant's room and sat down.

'Mrs Bohle. Good of you to come in so quickly.'

'Good of you to see me.'

Mr Ward smiled politely. 'Now. Obviously you initially went to see your GP about the tremors and stiffness in your hand and it was explained that there were various things this could be attributed to. A neurological

15

movement disorder, perhaps. A few other conditions, but you haven't presented the predominant symptoms.'

Molly found that her mouth had gone completely dry, as though someone had stuffed it full of cotton wool.

'Are you feeling depressed at all?'

Molly flexed her hand. 'Only about not being able to paint properly.'

'But not in a general sense?'

'I don't think so, no.'

'But you are having trouble sleeping?'

Molly nodded. 'Not every night. But quite often, I suppose.'

'Memory loss? Confusion? Balance difficulties?'

'No.'

Molly felt panicked. She had forgotten what she had gone to the corner shop for the other day. And had suffered momentary confusion until she remembered that they had run out of milk, hence her jaunt to the shop. And she had lost her keys a few times of late. Did those incidents indicate memory loss? Was she confused? Or did most people have moments like this? Sam often went upstairs, laughed and came back down again, claiming not to have a clue what he had gone up there for. No one was saying he was ill – no one was suggesting that Sam might have something scary.

Mr Ward nodded calmly. 'But you have noticed some painful muscle contractions in your ankles and shoulders?'

'Y-yes.'

Molly was loath to admit to these symptoms but she knew she had to be brave about this. There was no point in hiding things. She had forgotten about a few things but her GP had jolted her memory the other day. It had been horrible, like pieces of a jigsaw slotting into place.

Mr Ward cleared his throat. 'A degree of numbness and tingling?'

'Very slight. But – yes. I have felt those sensations.'

'I see. And on one side of your body predominantly? The right?' Mr Ward tidied the papers on his desk. 'Well. I am going to give you my opinion, Mrs Bohle. And it's up to you if you get a second opinion, of course. I would, in fact, recommend it in this instance.'

'You – you would?'

Mr Ward sat back and regarded her. 'There is no objective test for this condition. I can't run a blood test, do a brain scan or carry out an ECG. Unfortunately. The great thing about those tests is that they give us definitive answers. What we're dealing with here is something rather more vague.'

Molly's heart sank. It was bad enough that she was waiting to hear news that could cause major shock; she didn't need to hear that she might not get a definitive answer.

'However. I have carried out a thorough neurological examination. And what I can say is that you are presenting what we call "cardinal" symptoms. Typical symptoms associated with a disease that is fairly uncommon in people of your age, but increasingly on the rise. There is a scan we might be able to run – it's not a diagnosis in itself but it could confirm that we have a movement disorder which could give us a clearer picture of what we are dealing with.'

Molly's stomach lurched. She wondered if it would be grossly inappropriate to throw up in Mr Ward's waste-paper bin.

'You are exhibiting what is known as "resting tremors" – tremors which occur when your limb isn't moving. And rigidness when it is. Typically, these symptoms – which appear gradually and increase in severity over time – begin on one side of the body and migrate to the other side later on.'

Molly suddenly wished she hadn't been silly about this. She wished she'd spoken to Ed. She hadn't even been honest with Sam about it, in case his reaction had been scathing. No, that wasn't fair. It was just Sam's way to be dismissive about illness until a firm diagnosis had been given; he had been like it with his father when he had been diagnosed with dementia some years back. Hadn't accepted the signs and symptoms until a formal diagnosis had been received.

But Molly knew she would have spoken to Ed truth-fully, for some reason. Perhaps because he wasn't married to her, because he was only a friend, he was able to be more objective than Sam.

'Mrs Bohle, my diagnosis, like that of your GP, is that you have early-onset Parkinson's disease.' Mr Ward gave her a sympathetic glance. 'Now I know that can sound like a very scary thing, but it is not – I repeat – *not* a death sentence. There are various drugs we can start you on. There are also clinical drug trials you might be inter-ested in. Once you've had a second opinion, of course.'

Early-onset Parkinson's. Early-onset Parkinson's. She had it, she actually had it. Oh my God. Molly's head was reeling. She had furtively perused the internet over the weekend and she had found that early-onset Parkinson's fitted as a possible diagnosis. She wanted to be in denial about possibly having it but nothing else fit. There had been many less-frightening conditions she could have latched on to, but Molly hadn't fully believed that they matched her symptoms.

'I have some literature here for you,' Mr Ward was saying. 'About drug trials, about support, about different symptoms and long-term prognosis. Different for everyone, of course, but it can be helpful to know what is ahead.'

'Oh God.' Molly leant over and started crying. 'This can't be happening. I'm – I'm in my thirties, for fuck's sakes. Sorry. Sorry for swearing.'

'No need. And I understand that this is very hard for you to hear. People as young as twenty-one have been diagnosed with this and it can be incredibly distressing, whatever age you are.'

'But I've read such awful things about this – about bladder and bowel problems, slow speech, the freezing thing where you seize up and can't move. Not being able to do bloody buttons up.' Molly was openly sobbing now. 'Are all of those things going to happen to me?'

'Not necessarily,' Mr Ward said soothingly. 'It affects everyone differently. Many people of your age tend to focus their energy on managing the non-motor symptoms of this disease because quality of life is the most important thing.'

Quality of life. What was her 'quality of life' going to be like now? Molly felt shock wrapping itself coldly around her body. Would she be able to drive? Dress herself? Remember her own name? Was this illness going to render her incapable of conducting a normal conversation? Was she going to turn into a manic depressive? She had read that people suffering from this disease often experienced depression – either prior to some of the motor symptoms, or later on once the diagnosis had been received.

'Get a second opinion, Mrs Bohle,' Mr Ward reiterated firmly. 'I could be wrong about this. It's one of the diseases I dislike diagnosing because of the lack of definitive testing. So as strongly inclined as I am to lean in this direction, I would genuinely like you to run this past another professional.'

Molly stood up, nodded numbly and thanked Mr Ward. Clutching the literature he had given her, she left his office and walked out of the hospital. Once outside, she gave in to the nausea and threw up down a once-pristine side wall.

Molly and Ed

September 1995
'Who's that girl, Middleford?' Ed Sutherland nudged his best friend.

'Keep your hair on. You nearly made me upend my glass of Tatt,' Middleford, otherwise known as Boyd, huffed.

Ed eyed him fondly. Boyd was such a nobber. 'It's Taittinger, as you well know. And you don't *have* to drink it. I've managed to get through the entire evening without touching a drop.' He held up his glass of beer with some pride.

'That's because it's not your mother hosting this event, is it?' Boyd went cross-eyed for no apparent reason. 'She likes me to drink champagne. Says it shows *breeding*.'

Ed gave Boyd an indulgent punch on the arm. 'Your family own this massive house on the coast,' Ed gestured outside, 'and you have a coat of arms, for feck's sakes. No one could possibly doubt that you're a toff.'

'Oh, piss off. You're lucky you're even here, you know.

My mother thinks you're a bad influence. And she says there's something dodgy about you.'

Ed fingered the packet of cigarettes in his pocket. Boyd had no idea how astute his mother was. In the first instance, Ed had learnt that mothers fell into one of two camps as far as he was concerned. Camp one (of which Boyd's mother was the archetypal, fully paid-up member) took the view that he was dangerous, a bad boy. Someone liable to lead their son – or more likely, daughter – astray.

Camp two saw him as a plaything and as such, flirted with him. Outrageously. On occasion members of camp two had been known to proposition him, despite his tender age of seventeen (just). Ed had succumbed once to such a proposition, mainly because the mother had been astonishingly beautiful and because Ed was sure she would teach him a thing or two. He hadn't been wrong about that, but he hadn't expected the stalker-ish behaviour that had followed the liaison. He had been forced to sever all ties with the friend simply to avoid the mother. Lessons learnt.

Ed edged a cigarette out of the packet and put it in his mouth. He couldn't exactly blame camp one for being wary of him. He *was* a bad boy, in the mildest of forms. And frankly it was an image he cultivated. Like many of the macho heroes he admired, Ed loved drinking, smoking and women. Especially women. Or in his case, they tended to come under the banner of 'girls'. He loved the way they looked, the way they smelt, the swell of their chests, their long, smooth legs. Their full mouths, their beautiful eyes looking at him with appreciation, or sometimes trepidation. Ed easily dealt with either response; the former fed his ego, the latter presented a challenge.

But Mrs Middleford had also worked out that there was something 'dodgy' about him – a very upper-class way of stating that he didn't fit in somehow, that her social antennae had detected a mismatch. Ed made a mental note to keep an eye on that. He could do without his secrets being revealed just as he was about to leave the school he had worked so hard to get into. He had promoted an enigmatic image for himself, one that hid his real background and, as such, he deliberately kept his friends and his home life firmly separate. Ed never took friends home. He had done it once, with disastrous results. Again, lessons learnt.

Ed cleared his throat and took the cigarette out of his mouth. 'Anyway, Middleford, pay attention. I've seen a girl I like. She's gorgeous and I want to talk to her. I need her name and some background details, please.'

Boyd let out a sigh of resignation but narrowed his eyes nonetheless. 'Which one is it? Not Gaby, surely? She's a friend of my sister's. Her nickname is "Vacuum", which probably makes you even more excited, but I wouldn't touch her with yours, quite frankly . . .'

'Not Gaby. As if, Boyd.' Ed knew exactly how Gaby had earned her nickname. 'No, that one over by the window. The one with eyes I could drown in and a body like the Venus de Milo.'

Boyd frowned. 'God, you are a massive tit. I know you want to be a writer, but honestly. Do you mean that one with the terrible hair?'

Ed rolled his eyes. The long, wild tangle of mousy curls conjured up thoughts of bare backs and exquisite shoulders, surely? Boyd, a sturdy, unimaginative fellow at the best of times, truly lacked vision.

'I think she's called Molly,' Boyd offered finally. 'Molly . . . Wilkes. Yes. Her mother is an old school friend of my mother's. Father's an Oxford Don. Older brother. Tom, perhaps. Successful architect. Ummm . . .'

'That'll do. Good work, Boyd. You are a veritable goldmine.'

Ed headed straight for the window as the girl called Molly slipped outside. He followed her, knowing he had the perfect excuse in his hand should he need it; a sneaky fag was useful in so many ways. As a result, he was taken aback when Molly turned and eyed him suspiciously.

'Are you following me?'

Ed lit his cigarette suavely but spoilt it by almost burning his fingers when he snapped his Zippo shut. 'Shit. Er, might be. Molly, isn't it?'

'You know my name.' She raised her eyebrows in a ladylike fashion. He was handsome. And he knew it. She wasn't sure if she liked that. Obviously Molly understood that everyone had a mirror – it was more that she preferred confidence that came from achievement, not looks. 'You're following me and you know my name. There are laws against that, you know.'

'I'm having an innocent cigarette and a friend told me your name just now. Hardly grounds for arrest, surely? I'm Ed, by the way.'

'Hi. I'd tell you my name but clearly you already know me.'

Close up, Ed found himself drawn to Molly's eyes. They were cat-like, shrewd. Brown. No, dark blue – an unusual shade that no doubt earned her compliments aplenty. From lesser mortals. Ed would need to come up with something more original. This was a smart, eloquent girl who looked as though she might, with impeccable manners, coolly dismiss boys who bored her.

Ed sucked on his cigarette, feeling something spark inside him. He was tired of easy girls; Molly was already challenging him.

Out of the blue, Molly smiled. Was she mocking him? Ed felt unnerved, wrong-footed. He really needed to get a grip.

'I'm not planning to get you arrested, no.' *God, but he was sexy*. Molly checked out his mouth. Kissable, definitely. Hmm. How annoying. She hadn't felt this attracted to someone at first glance before. Was this what everyone called 'chemistry'?

Molly pulled herself together and gestured to his singed fingers. 'But I do think you need to learn how to use a lighter properly. Otherwise everyone will think you're a right nobber.'

Ed let out a shout of laughter. He'd never met anyone else who used his favourite insult before. He stared at Molly. She was on the short side but perfectly proportioned. She had that irresistible blend of slender, with tantalising curves in all the right places. Ed was willing to bet Molly worried about the size of her bum constantly. Molly might be a challenge, but he was confident he knew how her mind worked. To a degree. Because Ed could modestly acknowledge that he knew a fair amount about girls. He caught sight of her bum as she began to walk away from him and almost dropped his cigarette. Delectable. Rounded. Ripe. Bloody hell. Better than he'd imagined. Hang on; where was she going?

'I'm off to do some stargazing,' Molly said, as though she had heard his thoughts. She sincerely hoped he wasn't looking at her bum. She always worried about it, stressed that it was a little on the large side. 'I think if you carry on walking in that direction, you get to the beach, right?' She began strolling but threw a glance over her shoulder. 'Aren't you coming, shadow?'

Ed watched her. It wasn't his style to chase after a girl like some sort of lap dog, but Molly was intriguing. He had a feeling about her. Whatever that meant. Ed threw his cigarette down and hurried after her, slowing his steps when he realised what a dick he must look.

Act casual, dude, he told himself sternly. She's just a girl.

Molly kicked her shoes off at the edge of the beach and carried on walking. She was glad Ed had followed her. She would have looked like a right idiot strolling off on her own. She would have followed it through for an indeterminate period of time, of course, so as not to look even more absurd – and being on a beach wasn't exactly a hardship – but she would have felt downright silly. She gestured to an area of sand edged by long grass. 'This looks good. What do you reckon?'

'Well, wherever we sit will mean sand up our—' Ed stopped. He wasn't sure Molly would be impressed with talk of 'cracks'. That was the sort of conversation he and Boyd might have. Ed squinted up at the sky, his mind rapidly flicking through some pages from . . . what,

Geography? He flipped through his memory banks until he fell upon 'Constellations'. Ah, yes. A number of them popped into his head, complete with names, historical references and relative chance of visibility. The Late Latin meaning of 'constellation' was 'set with stars'; Ed had always found that kind of romantic. He'd been blessed with a photographic memory of sorts. A valuable tool when it came to passing exams (Ed hoped to sail through his GCSEs). And when it came to impressing girls, a memory like his was invaluable.

'It's perfect,' Ed said, meeting Molly's eyes. 'The perfect spot for this. You. Me. Us.'

'Oh, you're good. Really good.' She laughed but gave him a look he couldn't fathom. Was she impressed? Did she find him amusing? Did she like him?

Molly flopped down on the sand and threw her arms above her head. 'Seriously. I'll probably fall in love with you if you carry on like that. Won't be able to help myself.' She was a bit concerned at the way her heart was racing. He had only looked at her and made a corny comment!

Don't be silly, Molly, she told herself sternly. He's just a boy.

Ed was transfixed. The way she had thrown herself down like that suggested confidence but there was a softness to her that took the edge off both her mannerisms and her comments. There was no malice present in her tone, just delight and enjoyment at the banter. He found himself staring at her bare legs, at the way they twisted together. It hit him in the groin somewhat, the sensual way her limbs moved and flowed.

God. Ed frowned. Boyd was right. He was a great big tit.

Molly lay back and closed her eyes, giving him the chance to continue his study of her. He noted that she wore several silver rings on her fingers – an assortment of slim, decorated bands. Her ears were studded with little sparkly earrings all the way from the lobe to the top, which lent her an air of bohemia. He wondered if she had a tattoo hidden away somewhere, and felt a strong urge to find out. Maybe she didn't; like him, she was only sixteen, maybe seventeen. Ed lay down next to her, wondering about his next move. She was different. So he needed to be different.

'Aren't you going to tell me about constellations and stuff?' Molly asked, turning her head towards his. He was doing an awful lot of staring. She was flattered, but she did worry that he was dissecting her looks too much. She wasn't a girl who cared overly about her appearance, not like some of her friends. She liked to look good but as soon as she was dressed, she was off and she didn't spare it another thought. 'Go on. Tell me about constellations.'

'As if. How naff would that be?'

Molly laughed. 'So naff.'

Ed inhaled. He could smell her perfume and her hair. He felt an irrational urge to bury his face in her neck but he yanked himself back into line. He reminded himself that Molly was simply a girl. And that he knew tons of girls. If this one didn't like him, he could quite simply – and easily – find another who did. Yes. Except that, even at his young age, he had figured out that some girls were special and that some just weren't. Damn Molly for being beyond special.

'They are awesome though, aren't they?' Molly pointed. One of them might as well get some constellations named. 'I mean, look at that. That's Cassiopeia, that is. From the Perseus family.'

'Is it?' Ed squinted up at the sky, captivated. 'You're very knowledgeable about this stuff. Ha. You just told me about constellations.'

'Aah, but I swot up deliberately to impress boys.'

He propped himself up on one elbow. 'Are you laughing at me again?'

'Yes.' She matched his stance, the pose bringing her face close to his. What a beautiful face he had. She found him both fascinating *and* hellishly attractive. How very dangerous. Molly wasn't used to being knocked sideways by a boy. So far – and her experience was reasonably limited – she had always been in charge, had always been the one calling the shots. She was a virgin but she wouldn't dream of telling Ed *that*. She could tell just by looking at him that he had slept with tons of girls. Which made her feel slightly queasy, but she knew she could hardly judge him for whatever he had done up until now. And boys always did stuff like that.

Molly wondered why she had gone quiet. She rarely went quiet. She forced herself to say something. 'I love stargazing. Pretentious though, isn't it?'

Ed wasn't interested in the stars. He was interested in Molly. He studied her. What a heavenly face. Those eyes . . . slanted, penetrating. A full mouth. Lips he wanted to kiss. Sublime cheekbones, a scar on her chin

– a childhood injury? – that prevented her from being conventionally good-looking. Attractive, certainly, but not in an obvious way. Which fascinated him. Molly had a face Ed was suddenly sure he would never tire of looking at.

'So, Ed. What are you going to do with your life?' Molly bestowed a lovely smile upon him that sent him all over the show. 'Aspirations, dreams, all that stuff?'

'You'll laugh at me again.'

'I really won't. I want to know. Genuinely.' She moved her bare arm next to his, her hair trailing across his shoulder. He had nice skin. He smelt nice. Basic things, but they were doing less than basic things to various, critical parts of her body.

Ed wasn't sure how on earth he was supposed to concentrate with her bare arm leaning against him that way, but he steeled himself. 'I want to be a writer.'

'Really?' She was interested now and it showed. 'What kind?'

'The best kind. Well, in my view. I want to write novels that people talk about. Novels that move people in some way.'

'That's ace. I love reading. I'm always reading. Well, apart from in the middle of the night, obviously. Although sometimes I am. And my father is . . . well, he's an Oxford Don.'

'Is he now?' Ed played dumb. 'Now that really *is* ace.'

Molly flipped over on to her front, brushing sand from her hands. 'I imagined you might want to be an actor or something. Looking like that.'

'Like what?' He turned over as well but moved his head closer to hers. 'Do you fancy me? Am I handsome?'

'Good grief. You're so arrogant!' She shook her head and her curls whipped his face. 'You're just really confident. I thought acting might be your bag. Playing on your ego and all that.'

'I'm a man of words,' Ed stated pompously. God, but he sounded like a wanker. He carried on, regardless. In for a penny and all that. 'I love words. They're my life, my passion. I plan to be very successful at it. You'd call it arrogance, I'm sure.' He grinned. 'What about you? What's your passion?'

'Art. I want to be an artist. A great, great artist.' Molly ducked her head, feeling embarrassed. 'Now *I* sound arrogant. But anyway. Uni is the plan. Lincoln,maybe.'

'No way!' Ed grinned. 'That's where I want to go. We could end up at the same uni! Imagine.'

'Gosh. We might have to talk to one another every day.'

Molly smiled again and Ed felt something expand in his chest. And in his groin. Shit. Could he be any more uncool? He just hoped he was hiding his ardour. Being on his front might start feeling uncomfortable soon.

'Tell me about your art,' he said, desperately trying to quell his urges.

Molly hadn't noticed his 'urges'. If she had, she might have felt better about what happened later. Instead, she obliged. She waxed lyrical about art for a long time and he managed to join in, despite not knowing an awful lot about the subject. But he liked hearing Molly talk about it – she was passionate, enthused. And that made him want to talk about it as well. After a while, they moved on to novels. They talked about childhood books, about classic literature and about their favourite writers. They discussed Oscar Wilde (consensus: 'nothing short of a fucking genius'), Shakespeare ('I call him Willy Shakes,' Ed told Molly. 'It's affectionate.' 'It's *rude*,' she retorted, but she laughed accordingly) and they dissected the works of Thomas Hardy (reaching a mutual agreement of 'turgid'). They talked about universities, about friends, about life and about love. They talked a lot about love – what they thought it was, what it should be, if they had experienced it (Molly, yes – Ed, no) and how long it lasted in general. They talked and talked and talked. For six hours straight.

'We've talked for six hours straight,' Ed commented, glancing at his watch. 'I am covered in sand; it's in my hair and everything. And instead of stars providing light and brilliance, we are clothed in early morning sunshine.'

'"Instead of the stars providing light and brilliance". Oh, I like that.' Molly sat up and yawned. 'Six hours? I don't think I've ever talked to anyone for six hours in my life.'

In fact she *knew* she hadn't. And they had barely paused for breath. It was astonishing. She hadn't noticed the time and if she had, she might not have cared, even though she was due home and her parents were probably worried sick. Even though she had never done anything like this in her life before. Molly shook sand from her curls.

'I am a bit special,' Ed answered. Molly had sand in her hair and goose-bumps all over her arms. And she looked stunning. Just beautiful.

'Special needs more like,' Molly chided. 'Christ. I've

caught your crap joke disease. Hey, what's Ed short for? Edmund . . . Edward . . .?'

He frowned. He was rarely asked that question. 'It's just Ed.'

'What, you came out and your mother said "That baby looks *just* like an Ed."'

'She did, actually.'

'Liar.'

'For fuck's sakes.' Ed gave Molly a sheepish smile. 'Ok then. Ed is short for Edison. Go on. Laugh yourself silly.'

She considered him. 'Edison. That's not so bad. Original at least.'

'Yeah. Original is right. Downright mortifying is the other way to look at it.'

She grinned. 'You can carry it off. You're cool enough.'

'Oooh. Careful, Molly. That right there was a compliment.'

'Goddammit. You're right. Forgive me, Edison. Won't happen again.'

Ed could practically hear the barely contained chuckle she was withholding and for some reason, it made him want to gather her up and do . . . something. She had her knees drawn to her chest, her arms clasping them, her chin resting atop her arms. It was a wistful pose. Appealing. Everything about her was appealing.

She turned as though feeling his eyes on her. His glorious mouth tilted into a smile. Molly realised she wanted to know everything about Edison. Everything. She knew an awful lot after their in-depth chat, but she had this strange feeling that however much she found out, she might never be able to find out enough.

'Are you a romantic, Ed?'

'A what?'

'A romantic. Are you one of those types?'

'I'm what I call a dirty romantic. Does that count?' He laughed self-consciously. 'Might sound a bit rude. I just mean I'm a romantic, but I try not to be too flowery about it, you know? So I do love romantic novels and all that. If I'm being honest, and I am, *Romeo and Juliet* is my favourite play by Willy Shakes. And I found E.M. Forster's *A Room with a View* achingly romantic,' he added earnestly. 'But don't tell anyone. Dirty, but yes. Romantic. I suppose I am.'

'Ok, so a dirty romantic then. Oh, I like that. I like that a lot, Edison. You are full of surprises.' Her eyes met his. 'I like being surprised.'

So did Ed. And he liked her calling him Edison. For no real reason other than that it was her doing it. Without another coherent thought, Ed took the back of her neck in his hand and drew her in. Within seconds his mouth had met hers. Gently. *God*. Her lips were exquisite, soft and full. They met his willingly. Ed experienced sensory overload; the scent of her hair, the perfume wafting from her neck, the taste of the fruity cocktail she'd been drinking hours ago, her mouth, her ripe, but somehow delicate mouth.

Molly put her hands on his face and Ed felt a shiver. He felt her rings, cold against his skin, but her palms were warm and soft. She kissed him more ardently, her tongue searching his out. A bolt of lust shot through Ed and he fought to restrain himself from hurling her to the sand and taking her.

34

Control yourself, Edison, he berated himself. He had kissed countless girls. Countless. But Molly was rocking his world and he had no idea how or why. Yes, her hands were delving into his hair. Yes, her fingertips were stroking his scalp. Yes, it was exquisite. More exquisite than he could articulate. That was the thing; he simply couldn't pinpoint what it was she was doing that made this all so incredible. It was everything put together.

Molly kissed him again. Yep. There it was. A shot of something bouncing all around her body, pinging off of every angle. Tingles, bursts, sparks. What the hell was happening to her? She was in danger of doing something really foolish in a second. She wanted to do *other things*, things she normally stopped herself doing to boys. Things she didn't normally think about when she kissed boys, but that she knew might be expected.

And though Molly was a 'good girl', she had kissed rather a lot of boys. Often in place of sleeping with them. Which made her an aficionado in some ways. And Ed was a good kisser. A very good kisser. The kind that made Molly want to lose control of herself.

Ed luxuriated in the feel of those lips on his skin. It was romantic, yet erotic. Her hands were sliding under his shirt and he could barely stand it. He rolled on top of her, needing to regain control. His arms were around her and he could feel the warmth of her skin through her clothes. He smoothed her hair away from her face, gazing into her eyes. They were alert but slightly glazed.

Molly met Ed's eyes. Was her lust for him obvious? She wasn't sure she could do anything to control the emotions and desires being reflected in her eyes.

Ed fell headlong into them. Headlong. He couldn't help himself. He kissed her again, groping for the feeling it gave him. Yes. There it was again; he wasn't mistaken. It was like coming home. A comfortable newness. No. That made it sound too cosy. It wasn't. It was an excitement that felt so right, it was bloody mind-blowing. Ed owned that feeling. He wanted her. *Badly*.

'I want you,' she murmured against his mouth. 'Badly.'

How did she seem to know what he was thinking? It was like half starting a sentence and her finishing it, but it was even spookier than that because she was in his thoughts.

Christ, he'd be going all *Wuthering Heights* in a minute.

Edison, he said to himself, smiling slightly as he remembered Molly's comments about his name, do rein yourself in. She is just a girl. This is just a kiss.

It was just a kiss, right?

Molly coiled a leg around his, drawing his body to hers. Their groins were crushed together, hard against soft, hot against hot. And it felt right. They rolled again. She was on top of him, her chest squashed against his. His breath smelt sweet as she found his mouth again. He felt amazing against her. Amazing. Molly was falling. She was bloody well falling.

Ed sank a hand into her hair, claiming her. Kissing her. Owning her. But wait. He needed to take a minute. More than a minute. This was spiralling out of control. *He* was out of control. He was in danger of being . . . inelegant. He was also aware that he was in danger of being completely and utterly done for if this went any further. But he wanted it to go further.

36

Molly took advantage of the pause to collect her thoughts. Something huge was going on and she didn't know how to control it. 'I . . . I think you're going to be . . . very important in my life,' she said, feeling the need to put some kind of label or description on what was happening. Her father always told her she over-analysed. 'Does that sound weird? It sounds weird. Sorry about that.'

'Important in your life?' Ed drew back. With an effort that was so monumental, it felt akin to unsticking something tightly glued together. 'How so?'

'I don't know.' She met his eyes. 'But . . . you are . . . this feels . . .' She faltered. 'It's just me. You're not thinking that . . .'

Ed said nothing. And cursed himself. It wasn't just her. He did feel something. He didn't know what, but something had just happened. The earth hadn't exactly moved but Ed's life had surely just shifted on its axis. Molly had rendered him dumb. Another first.

'Right.' Molly sat up a bit and slowly rubbed her hands together. Mostly to dust the sand off them. Also to give her a moment to think. 'What I mean is . . . I don't mean we're going to run off into the sunset together or anything. I mean maybe, but not now. I just think we seem to have some sort of connection. It's like . . . I think I sometimes know what you're thinking, what you're about to say.'

'Am I that predictable?' Ed frowned. He hated being predictable. But at least his mouth was working again.

'No. Not remotely. That's what I mean.' Molly looked unnerved. 'There's just something between us. Something a bit . . . freaky.'

'I guess so.' Ed knew so, but saying that would make him feel far too vulnerable. 'Maybe we're going to be friends?' He offered this as a question, testing the waters. He wanted more, far more. Perhaps not right now. Perhaps he meant later, when he'd grown up a bit. But what did Molly mean?

Her eyes were fixed on his and just for a second, he sensed a glimmer of disappointment. But it was fleeting.

'Friends,' Molly repeated. She was trying it out, seeing how it sounded. She wasn't sure if she felt somewhat disappointed. She had felt something far, far deeper than mere friendship surging between them.

But Molly was a dignified girl; she hated looking silly. 'I suppose we could be that. Yes. Good friends. Why not?'

Ed battled with himself. It was more. What had sparked between them was more. It was . . . oh, fuck. Had he been about to mentally use the expression 'soulmates'? Did he even believe in soulmates? Something had sparked between them, like a firework that had been inadvertently lit in a room, bouncing off the walls crazily, leaving delicious little scorch marks everywhere.

Ed swallowed. Could it be that true love malarkey people always banged on about? Had he and Molly got really, really lucky and at a very young age found that thing that people sometimes searched their entire lives for? Or was that just romantic nonsense for losers? He was seventeen, for fuck's sakes.

Ed released Molly and sat up. He wasn't ready to meet the love of his life yet. If that was indeed what had just happened. He had too much to do. He had responsibilities;

he had an impossible home life. He was going to try with everything he had to become a great writer, and writers needed experiences. What the hell would he write about otherwise? He was surely destined to love many women. Hundreds. He wanted to travel, to see the world, to experience everything life had to offer. If they started something now, he might hurt her. He would hurt her. And Ed didn't want to do that.

He looked down at Molly. God, but she was beautiful. And sexy. In that girl-next-door way that made him want to both cuddle her *and* tear her clothes off. He had the urge to inhale her neck, to breathe her in, to consume her, to allow her to consume him. She was different to anyone he had ever met before. He felt a connection with her he simply couldn't explain. He knew she felt it too.

So what was stopping him?

Molly sat up, leaning against him casually as if she was perfectly fine with everything. It was a knack she had, appearing fine. A useful skill that allowed her to rise above situations that had hurt her in some way. She had learnt it at a very young age when her brother had blackmailed her shamelessly after she broke the foot off an expensive china doll. She had behaved as though she was completely unmoved by the event and her brother had given up because her lack of reaction had presumably been tedious. More recently she had honed her technique when a girlfriend had done the dirty on her with a guy she had really liked. In both cases, she had been distraught, but she had developed a way of appearing haughtily indifferent. A handy gift, that.

The thing was; she had never spoken to a guy for this

long before. She had never shared so many intimate details of her life. Molly felt exposed, vulnerable. She had trusted Ed – she still did, oddly – and letting her guard down had actually felt good.

Ed put his arm around her; it was involuntary. He couldn't seem to be this close to her without touching her, wanting to coil her into his body. He had never felt so confused in his life.

Molly leant into him. He crushed her a little, but it felt so right to be held by him, she couldn't find it in herself to pull away. She knew if she was dealing with another boy right now she would stand up, disdainfully look down at him before marching off, vowing never to speak to him again. But for some reason, Molly knew she wouldn't do that with Ed. Because he was different. Because she somehow felt able to forgive him for hurting her when she wouldn't allow it from someone else. Even if she didn't quite understand why.

'The thing you need to know about me is that I am always classy, Edison,' Molly said, before he could say anything. She sensed – although she had no idea where this sixth sense came from – that he was about to justify himself, to excuse the way he had behaved. He'd acted as though he wanted her more than anything, before backing off like a frightened rabbit. She had to get in first, before he – this boy who seemed so incredibly sensitive, so eloquent and full of thought – said something thoughtless and deeply insensitive. Molly feared he was capable of such a thing, that despite declaring himself a 'girl', Ed was very much a male of the species.

'Classy?' Ed was confused.

'Maybe classy isn't the right word. Dignified, perhaps? Anyway, I rarely make a prat of myself if I can help it.' Molly wished his eyes weren't so devastating. She wanted to dive into them, but it seemed that it was not to be the case. 'And the other thing you need to know is that I don't ever chase people. If it's not mutual, it's not happening.' She smiled and she made sure it was a sunny one. 'So, friends it is.'

Molly then leant forward and kissed Ed on the forehead. On the forehead. But slowly, deliberately.

Ed felt emasculated, put in his place and aroused all at once. It was a tender, non-sexual gesture that positioned him firmly in a box, and, ironically, it made him want her even more. Whatever she was saying she had felt *was* mutual. It was. It *wa*s.

Molly hoped the languid forehead kiss had done the trick. Her friend Sara had taught her that, said it was the best way to arouse a guy (the proximity, the erotically slow action) and to put him right in his place. Molly hated playing games but she detested looking idiotic even more. Her mother always said her pride would get her into trouble one day.

Ed inwardly groaned. That kiss on the forehead. It had sealed his fate. Jesus. What had he just done? Molly was the most incredible girl he had ever met. The feeling he'd had when he first set eyes on her had been spot on. She was special. He didn't want anyone else to have her. Would he ever have this moment back again?

Molly got to her feet, grabbed his hand and clumsily

yanked him up. 'Come on,' she said. She found herself grinning in a totally spontaneous way. Whether he fancied her or not, Edison made her feel happy. 'We should go home.'

Now

'Sam. I really need to talk to you.'

Give me a sec, Molly.'

Sam sounded impatient. He was on the phone to an important client and Molly wanted to give him space. But she had also sat on her news for an entire fortnight and she felt that she needed to finally let it all out. But it was the weekend. And Sam was still working. He was conscientious like that.

Molly sank down on to the sofa. She wasn't sure how Sam was going to take the news. Sam was a practical guy, but Molly hadn't really seen how he coped with illness. They hadn't ever been challenged in this way before. Illness hadn't featured. But Sam coped with everything. He was very capable. Molly relaxed.

Sam finally finished his call. Turning his chair to face her, he gave her his full attention.

'Sorry. You wanted to talk to me.'

'Yes.' Molly took a breath. 'I've had these symptoms for a while now.'

'Symptoms?'

'Tremors. A few other things.'

'You haven't mentioned anything before now.' Sam frowned.

'I know.' Molly immediately felt guilty. She should have mentioned something before, shouldn't she? If she had, her illness would have been drip-fed as opposed to being a massive bombshell. 'I . . . I didn't think anything serious was going on.'

Sam sat forward. 'It's serious then?'

'Ummm . . . yes. It is.' Molly chewed her lip. 'I have . . .' She faltered. She didn't want to say it out loud. Saying it out loud made it real. And reality was a scary place at the moment.

'Molly.' Sam came and sat next to her. 'What's going on? What do you have?'

Molly took his hand. 'I have early-onset Parkinson's.'

Sam stared at her. 'What?'

Molly said it again.

'I heard you. I mean how . . . you're . . . I know you said early onset but Parkinson's . . . it's . . .'

'An old person's illness, right?' Molly shook her head. 'Wrong.'

'But . . .' Sam stopped. 'I just can't understand it. You're so healthy! You're fit, you look after yourself. How could this have happened?'

'Well, it's not anything I could have prevented.' Absurdly, Molly felt the need to defend herself. 'I do look after myself. It's just one of those things.'

Sam got to his feet. 'Well, it's ridiculous. I mean, it's

awful.' He began to pace. 'So. Tell me about it. What does this mean?'

Molly told him about it. A condensed version. A slightly more glamorous effort than it could have been. Which was her way of drip-feeding. Molly strongly felt that immediately blasting Sam with all the details wasn't the way to go. There was time enough for that.

A few seconds later, Molly felt that her approach was justified.

Sam stopped pacing and sat down suddenly. 'God, Molly. That's grim. I mean, grim for you. For us. What a curve ball. Ok.' His mind was clearly racing. 'So what do we do about it?'

'Do?'

'Yes. There must be some course of action. We need to do something here. There must be drug trials, something we can do to make things better, to get you well again.'

Molly stared at Sam. 'I mean . . . I'll never be well again, Sam. Not completely. This is progressive.'

'But we can manage it, right? We can slow things down.'

'I don't know.' Molly was starting to get a headache. 'We need to look into it.'

'We do.' Sam sat down at his computer again and started typing rapidly. 'We need to look this up and get to grips with it.'

'Yes.' Molly felt oddly surreal. She had dreaded telling Sam about her diagnosis. She had put it off for a fortnight because she had been trying to get her head around it. And Sam's reaction was sending her all over the place again. Mainly because he was being so practical.

Suddenly, Sam caught her off-guard. He turned in his chair, walked over to her and gathered her up in his arms.

'Molly,' he whispered. 'I'm so sorry.'

Molly burst into tears. Clutching Sam's shoulder, she sobbed hard. This was what she needed right now. A cuddle. Some sympathy. Sam was so incredibly practical and that was a great skill. A wonderful skill. But nothing beat a hug.

'But we're in this together,' Sam said, pulling back and wiping her tears away. 'You and me. We'll get through this. Together.'

Molly nodded. 'I know. Thank you. I'm so sorry.'

'Never be sorry.' Sam kissed her forehead. 'We can beat anything, you and me.' He returned to his desk and started typing again.

Molly lay back against the sofa. Whatever she and Sam did, they weren't ever going to 'beat' her Parkinson's. Surely he knew that?

Maybe the drip-feed approach had been the wrong way to go after all.

Ed

August 1997

'Edison. I've said it's fine! Stop worrying about me.'

Ed watched his mother as she moved around their tiny kitchen. She seemed normal. Together. She wore a summer dress printed with flowers. Her dark hair was held up by a scarf – it clashed but it was a cheery touch, one that showed some thought for her appearance. On closer inspection though, the dress had a tear in the seam under her armpit and the scarf was splattered with glossy white marks, as if a candle had accidentally been spilt all over it. But still.

Florrie Sutherland. A statuesque woman on days like today. Calm, composed and in control. On days like these, Ed could almost imagine bringing his friends home to meet her, but still, he wouldn't dream of it. Anything could happen. Literally anything.

'I'm fine, honestly,' Florrie reassured him, placing a

47

cup of tea in front of him. 'I have Michael now. He looks after me. I'm on top of the world right now.'

Ed gamely drank the tea, even though he only ever drank coffee. But the offer of any kind of drink was unheard of around here, so he was grateful, in principle at least. He tried to conceal a grimace. It was laden with sugar and tepid. The way his father used to drink it. Ed wasn't sure what that meant exactly.

'I want you to have this chance,' Florrie insisted, reaching out to stroke a lock of hair away from Ed's eyes. It wasn't so much a gesture of tenderness; it smacked of irritability. Florrie frowned. 'I'm not a child, Ed. I can take care of myself.'

Ed nodded. 'Right. Of course.' It really wasn't worth him disagreeing. Not when she was actually being amenable about the whole thing. He sat back in his chair and inspected the kitchen. It was small and dingy. Even when it was scrupulously clean (which only ever happened when he was around), it looked grubby. Formica work-tops in a shade of grey, garish tiles from the seventies in clashing oranges and yellows. Basic cupboards and shelves fronted with off-white MDF, all set off by a lino floor that stuck to the bottom of every shoe as though smeared with year-old jam.

Out of all the rooms in the small house they shared on the outskirts of town, far away from the likes of Boyd and Ed's school friends, the kitchen depressed him the most. It seemed to epitomise everything difficult about his life.

'So. Are any of your friends going to the same university?' Florrie removed the tea, not appearing to notice he had barely touched it. She swished it into the chipped sink, her eyes fixed on the disappearing liquid.

'Er, just Molly.'

'Who's Molly?' Florrie turned round and wagged her finger in a coquettish fashion. 'You haven't mentioned her before. Is she your girlfriend?'

'No. Absolutely not. She's just a friend.' Ed wished he'd kept his mouth shut. He never mentioned girls to his mother. She became oddly fixated, almost pushing him into serious relationships he didn't want. At other times, she seemed jealous that someone else might be taking his attention away. Besides, he was speaking the truth. Molly was just a friend. More was the pity. Ed remembered them getting their results together. Molly had been painting him while they waited for the post to arrive. She'd requested he take his shirt off and he was trying his best to keep his cool. It had all been fun and games until he'd seen what she'd done. It was, quite simply, amazing.

'I shall treasure this for ever,' Ed declared, unpinning the portrait from her easel.

'You're so sweet.'

Ed looked affronted. 'Sweet? Molls. Let me impart some knowledge to you, some wisdom. When it comes to guys, you never tell them they're sweet. Or cute. Or adorable. Have you got that?'

'Sweet, cute, adorable, never tell them. Got it.' Molly cocked an ear. 'Was that the post?'

'Crap. I hope not.'

'It was. Let's go.'

Molly grabbed Ed's hand and they headed downstairs

together. Molly snatched the envelope from the mat as her parents rushed out of the kitchen.

'Hello, Edison,' said Molly's mother Eleanor, casting her eye over him.

Ed shot a withering glance at Molly. She simply had to go around telling everyone his proper name. He had never known a girl take the piss as much as she did. Cheeky sod.

As they walked into the lounge, Ed suddenly realised why Eleanor was giving him funny looks. He hadn't put his shirt back on. Shit. What a nobber.

'Nice to see you, young man,' said Molly's father John. 'I generally wear clothes in company, but each to their own.'

'Yes. Er, sorry about that. My shirt is upstairs. Molly's been sketching me . . .'

'Quite so, quite so.' John twinkled at him. 'Well, Molls. What's the damage?'

'I got two A's and a B!' Molly shrieked, waving the sheet around. 'Two A's! In Art and Literature! I can get into Lincoln with those. Easily!' Molly was enveloped by her parents, all of them talking and laughing loudly.

Ed felt so proud of Molly. She had such devoted parents, the kind everyone should have. Ed glanced away for a second. No, he wasn't going to think about it. He hated feeling sorry for himself.

As if on cue, the phone rang and Ed's stomach shifted. He had never felt more scared in his life. He was nervous of his mother phoning, and he was utterly petrified that what she was about to tell him would mean being far away from Molly.

Eleanor picked the phone up. 'Yes, she did very well indeed . . . we're so proud. Yes, he's right here . . . I'll pass you over . . .'

Ed took the proffered phone, anxiety kicking in. 'Er, how did I do?' He listened and nodded. 'Right. Thanks for letting me know.' He put the phone back into its cradle and turned to Molly.

'Well?' She wrung her hands. 'Oh God. You've flunked them. You can't come to Lincoln . . .'

'I'm really sorry . . .' Ed started.

'Oh, Ed.' Molly's shoulders slumped. She couldn't believe how disappointed she felt. Not in Ed, as such, but on his behalf. On her behalf. Uni wouldn't be half as much fun if he wasn't coming with her.

Ed grabbed Molly's hand. 'I did it too! Somehow. An A in English Language, a B in Literature and a C in History. But hey, I hated History anyway!'

He clumsily caught Molly as she threw herself into his arms and they danced around like loons.

'We must call Tom and tell him the news. Your brother will be so pleased for you, Molly,' Eleanor said, picking up the phone again. 'John, open that champagne, would you? We need to make a toast.'

'This is brilliant,' Molly said, when they'd finally stopped jumping around. 'Just brilliant. We're going to uni together. We can share a place and everything. Well, maybe – although my friend Jody wants to get a place together. But we can hang out all the time.'

'Well done, Edison,' Eleanor said warmly. 'I'm so pleased for you. And for Molly. She so wanted to go to uni with you.'

As Eleanor hugged him, Ed felt John's watchful eyes on him. Dads were always harder to impress. Dads and their daughters, it was a special relationship. And Ed knew John was suspicious of his motives, he didn't quite buy the whole 'friends' thing. Whether or not he knew the thoughts that went through Ed's head was by the by, but either way, John was Molly's father. Which meant that he would fight to the death for her. And kill anyone who hurt her. Ed understood that. He felt irrationally protective of Molly himself.

John handed him a glass, and Ed clinked it against Molly's, dismissing the feelings of trepidation in his gut. Could he do this? Was he actually going to be allowed to go to university, to move away from home? Ed was desperate to forge some sort of life for himself.

It would be fine. Ed steeled himself. Everything would be fine. He had to go. He needed to get his degree, to have fun and to just throw off the shackles a bit. Not completely, just a bit. He watched Molly excitedly outlining university plans with her parents. He envied the easy relationship she had with them, but he liked it. He enjoyed being part of her world. It was easy and loving and something to be admired.

To be part of it was all that he really wanted . . .

Ed pulled himself back to the present and realised his mother was chattering away to him still.

'Sorry, what did you say?'

Florrie narrowed her eyes. 'God, I hate it when I talk to you and you don't bloody well listen.' She sounded like a petulant child. 'Anyway. Shouldn't you go and pack?'

Ed frowned. 'I'm not going until next week.'

'Oh, really?' Florrie looked disgruntled. 'I said Michael could use your room as an office, you sec. Sorry, I just assumed that you would be leaving sooner rather than later. No matter; it can wait.'

That was it, then. Decision made. Ed got to his feet. 'That's fine, Mum. I can go down early, find a house, meet some people.' He was shocked that his mother was moving Michael in so soon, but she was a grown woman. And at least Michael seemed like a nice guy – from the little Ed had seen of him – one who had genuine feelings for his mother. Maybe this was all going to work out after all.

'I'll go pack,' he said. 'I can be out of your hair by tomorrow morning.'

'Good, good.' Florrie sounded vague again. 'Bye then.'

'Bye, Mum,' he answered her, even though he was sure he would see her in the morning before he left.

Ed tore upstairs, feeling strangely elated. Life was looking up. Michael was moving in, which made him feel far better about leaving his mother. Maybe he was finally going to be able to live his life.

He resolved then and there to make the most of every second of university. He made a pact with himself not to rely on his memory any longer. To apply himself the way Molly did. He owed it to himself. His life was finally about to begin.

Now

'So. Tell me about the symptoms again,' Sam said, taking Molly's hands.

Molly tried not to sigh. They were currently sitting in bed going over and over the details. Again. They had done this a number of times now and Molly was feeling exhausted. She understood why Sam was doing this; it was his way of coping. He was a person who got to grips with something by gathering as much information as possible in order to make sense of it. It was all part of his process. Molly knew that Sam would spend considerable time after their discussions ordering books about early-onset Parkinson's, scouring the internet for data and immersing himself in the subject so deeply he would practically be able to take an exam on it.

'Primary motor symptoms are tremors, slowness, stiffness, balance problems.' Molly leant back against the headboard. She was beginning to feel like a broken record. 'Non-motor: changes in mood – depression being the most likely – sleep disorders, skin changes – whatever that means – problems with low blood pressure and sweating. I mean, you know this stuff, you've looked it all up.'

Molly faltered. She didn't want to move on to the possible bladder and bowel issues or the way her speech might be affected. Not yet. Sam might have already read about those symptoms, but if he had, he hadn't mentioned them.

'Well, honestly, I don't see that there is anything there we can't cope with,' Sam said confidently. 'I know this is very grim for you and a huge shock.' He put his arm around her shoulder and pulled her closer. 'But I'm here for you. We'll get through this together. You're not alone. Always know that.'

Molly started weeping again. She had done an awful lot of weeping over the past few days. Obviously it was a huge thing to deal with, but Molly had surprised herself with the volume of tears she had managed to produce. Yet oddly enough she no longer felt she was in a nightmare. Telling Sam had made everything feel extremely real. She wasn't sure if that was a good thing or not. Since she had dropped her bombshell a few days ago, she and Sam had done nothing but talk non-stop about her illness. Molly wondered what on earth they had talked about before, because it seemed that every single conversation revolved around Parkinson's in some fashion. It was overwhelming to say the least.

'We will need to get a second opinion, of course,' Sam said, reaching for his phone. 'I'll see if I can rush you through to see someone. I have a few contacts I can probably lean on.'

'I don't need any kind of special treatment,' Molly said, swinging her feet out of bed. She placed them on the floor cautiously. She wasn't sure what she was expecting, but since her diagnosis, she seemed acutely aware of all movement and motion. Being able to walk, to pick something up, to clean her teeth. Writing something down, using her phone. Each of these actions gave her relief and, at times, joy. It had only been a few days, but Molly was suddenly so appreciative of the things she had previously taken for granted.

Which was a horrendous cliché, of course. Not appreciating something until you were threatened with the loss of it. But Molly couldn't help it. Being told she might lose control of certain motor functions, that she might not be able to conduct herself in the way she always had, had been like someone throwing cold water in her face. It was a sharp shock and it had brought everything into focus.

Molly heard her phone alerting her to another text message. She glanced at it quickly. As she thought, it was Ed again. Molly really had to get back to him soon, before he got really worried.

'I wasn't thinking of any kind of special treatment,' Sam was saying mildly, already selecting a number from the address book in his phone. 'I just think it's important that we get you seen immediately. I mean, until we do, we don't actually know if we're dealing with early-onset Parkinson's. We could be looking at –' Sam turned to his iPad, predictably already open at the Michael J. Fox Foundation page '– any number of neurological disorders. We don't know anything for certain yet.'

'True.'

Molly knew Sam was clutching at straws. She would let him. It was his way. It was what he needed to do. Of course he wanted to think it might be something other than Parkinson's; it was only natural. She would feel the same in his shoes.

Molly walked to the bathroom, enjoying the sensation of thick carpet beneath the soles of her feet. 'I'm going for a shower,' she said over her shoulder.

Sam wasn't listening. He was already on the phone to his contact, whoever that was. Switching the shower on to get the water heated up and spending a fair time cleaning her teeth, Molly peeled her t-shirt over her head. Ed always used to laugh at her cleaning her teeth before she had a shower, but her argument was that she was such a clean freak, she liked to feel completely fresh and sparkling by the time she left the shower.

Ed. Molly leant her head against the cool tiles in the shower. She must speak to Ed. She had missed his engagement party and she had to explain why.

Molly hoped Ed would forgive her for missing the party. After all, he had managed to make it to her wedding, despite the way things had been between them. Molly felt a pang when she remembered that time. Christ, she had been so in love with Ed. Not at her wedding, but before . . . What she felt for Sam was completely different. Safe, secure, deep. Molly's feelings for Ed might have been passionate and romantic, but they were childish by comparison. Passion was overrated. It didn't last and it wasn't more important than friendship and companionship.

And that wasn't to say that she and Sam didn't have passion, Molly thought to herself, pushing her wet hair back from her face. It was just more measured. Not as uncontrollable and head-spinning. Although – Molly paused with her shower gel in her hand – when had they last had sex? She couldn't rightly remember. But there had been a lot going on lately. Her worry over her health, her diagnosis – and Sam had been extremely busy. Well, Sam was always busy, but he had seemed even more distracted than usual. Molly felt guilty about that. He must be finding it difficult to juggle everything now that she had ducked out of work to paint more. Molly reasoned that Sam could always hire someone else, but she knew Sam liked keeping staff to a minimum. And that he preferred to work with her.

Molly wondered if she should join Sam at work again. It would be disappointing to have to do it now that she had finally got back into her art, but if she wasn't able to paint any longer, what did it matter? She felt the now-familiar stiffening in her hand and cursed it. Bloody, *bloody* disease. She jumped as she heard the door opening and put her hand behind her back.

'I've managed to get you an appointment for tomorrow,' Sam said, poking his head into the bathroom. 'With a top guy. We'll find out if you have this once and for all. Or if it's something else. And then we'll know exactly what we're dealing with and how to plan for it.'

'Right. Great, thanks. Sam,' Molly called to him before he could walk away. 'Um. Join me?' She wasn't sure if she was after sex as such. Maybe just a cuddle. A wet one. Intimacy. Something to reassure her. Something to convince her she hadn't suddenly become the sexless being she felt she had.

Sam smiled. 'Very tempting. I wish I had time. But I have to get to the office – I have about six meetings today.'

'Can't they wait?' Molly felt exposed, vulnerable. 'It's just – I'd really like to spend a bit of time with you.'

'In the shower?' Sam grinned and glanced down at himself. 'I'm fully dressed.'

'Then come in and get wet with me. Please.' Molly hoped she didn't sound desperate. But she really needed Sam. She needed him to be with her, to comfort her, to let her know he still loved her. Not just as a wife, but as a woman.

'Molly, I'm really sorry. Can we call a rain check until tonight?' Sam looked at his watch. 'I really want to, but I have to get to the office.'

'Sure.' Molly turned away so he couldn't see her tears. She heard the shower door open and felt Sam's hand on her waist.

'Molly. I'm not freaked out, I promise. I just have to be somewhere. And I meant it about tonight.'

'But I really need you, Sam. I need you.' Molly sounded whiny. She hated it when she sounded whiny. She got out of the shower and wrapped a towel around her body.

'And I need to be somewhere else,' Sam said firmly as he walked away.

'Why do you never put me first?'

'What?' Sam stopped by the door.

'Why do you never put me first?' Molly repeated.

Sam looked furious. 'You've got to be kidding me.'

Molly shook her head. 'I'm not. It's just . . . I just some-times feel like I come second for you, after your work.'

Sam let out an impatient sound. 'Really? Are you actually saying that to me?'

'I'm actually saying that to you. And do you have to keep answering with questions?'

'You're being stupid.'

Molly stared at Sam. 'Am I? I'm being stupid because I want you to be here with me. To make me feel like I'm not just a walking disease. That you still see me. Me, as a person.'

Sam bit his lip. 'Of course I still see you, Molly. How could I not, when you're standing there yelling at me? Oh, I'm sorry, that was another question. Do forgive me.' He left and slammed the door.

Molly walked into the bedroom, sat on the edge of the bed and started to cry. Sam was trying hard to be good about her diagnosis. He was coping the only way he knew how. But she couldn't help wishing he had put work to one side. Just this once. To stay with her, to put his arms around her. To love her and let her know that nothing would change between them.

Molly knew Sam was hoping the diagnosis was wrong. She was too, obviously. But she knew it wouldn't be any different to the first opinion. It would be exactly what she had heard from Mr Ward. Molly wasn't being defeatist about it; she just knew when something made sense. She didn't blame Sam for wanting to hear some-thing else. He didn't want her to be sick – why would he? He wanted her to go back to normal. He wanted everything to be normal between them again.

But Molly knew things wouldn't be normal again. She wasn't being negative, she was being realistic. And Sam would be too. Once they had the second opinion confirmed, Molly knew Sam would be fine with the whole thing. He would be his usual practical self, sorting out a plan of action, wanting to know every type of medication available and basically taking control.

It was for the best that Sam was this way, Molly decided. After all, she was so far out of control, she needed someone to rein her in. She just hoped Sam remembered she needed love and affection as well as support. And that rows were the last thing she needed. Even though she felt she might have started the one just now.

She stood up and tiredly selected some underwear. As soon as she had the second opinion confirmed, she would go and see Ed. She was loath to pee on his bonfire when he had just got engaged, but they were best friends. If Ed had news like this, she would want to know. She would *have* to know. Molly also knew that if Ed had something like early-onset Parkinson's, she would feel as if her heart was breaking.

Molly and Ed

February 1998
'Tonight, I drink to the health of . . . of . . . Cardinal Puff, Puff, Puff.'

Molly carefully tapped the top of the table three times, then underneath the table, clicked her fingers and looked helplessly at Ed. She was drunk. Hopelessly so. And she couldn't for the life of her remember the rules of this dumb drinking game.

'Three fingers on your glass, Molls,' Ed whispered loudly, falling about laughing.

'Don't help her!' Jody, Molly's housemate nudged him indignantly. 'There are rules in drinking games, you know.'

Everyone in the lounge – a plethora of bodies that had somehow found their way back here from the student union – booed and hissed. Someone even tossed a cork coaster at Jody's head.

Ed blew Jody a kiss. 'Ignore them. I love how pedantic you are. It's endearing.'

Jody made a show of looking cross for a second before giving him a wide smile. A sexy smile. One that said, 'Fuck me later you *massive bastard*.'

Ed deliberately broke the eye contact. He had slept with Jody when he and Molly first arrived at Lincoln University, oblivious to the fact that she had just moved into a house with his friend. Molly had no doubt told him about her new living arrangements before they had even left home, but names weren't Ed's strong point. Well, remembering names of random flatmates-to-be wasn't his strong point. He hadn't acquitted himself well on the Jody front; he'd done that shitty bloke thing of collecting up his clothes and sneaking out without a word in the early hours. Ed wasn't proud of himself but he had regretted the union almost as soon as it was over and he couldn't wait to get away.

He seemed to be doing a lot of that lately. He had found university to be a veritable goldmine when it came to available, willing pretty girls and he had over-indulged somewhat in the first few months. Ed was seriously beginning to wonder if he had some sort of problem, but his old school mate Boyd had ruefully reassured him that if he possessed half of Ed's charm and good looks, he wouldn't think twice about making an absolute killing, instead of surviving on what he described as 'meagre pickings'.

Molly caught Ed's eye. She couldn't help making a bit of a dig at him every so often about Jody. They had slept together months ago and Jody had waxed lyrical about it, providing Molly with rather more detail than she might have liked. She was fascinated on the one hand, appalled on the other. Molly didn't want to visualise Ed with someone else but she found herself perversely intoxicated by the intimate details Jody had provided her with.

Molly was laughing at him again, Ed thought grumpily. She was always making references to the Jody situation, stopping short – but only just – of singing 'Ed and Jody, sitting in a tree . . .'

Ed cursed himself as he watched Molly flick her long, newly blond curls over her shoulder. He hated that she saw him as an idiot Lothario. It shouldn't matter, but it did. Of course, he was both an idiot and a Lothario, but still. Ed felt irrationally self-righteous about the unfairness of it all.

He truly wished he could control himself, especially when he was drunk. But his nether regions thought differently. The stupid thing was that his mind was consumed by thoughts of Molly – both wholesome and not so wholesome – for an absurd amount of time. But when he had a few drinks, he acted like a total and utter nobber and found himself sticking his tongue down the throat of any number of inferior girls. Sometimes he slept with them as well. Mostly because he knew Molly didn't want him that way. Probably because he kept sleeping with her friends. Jesus. He seriously was a nobber.

Ed really was a nobber, Molly thought. Why on earth did he keep sleeping with all of her friends? She didn't know if he did it on purpose to annoy her or if he had some sort of problem. Molly stole a glance at him. He looked rather drunk this evening. His hair was all over the place and his eyes had gone all sexy, the way they did when he was a bit squiffy.

Ed rubbed his eyes. God, but he had drunk too much

tonight. Some filthy cocktail in the union – just because it was half price and he knew he looked as camp as Christmas drinking it. He gazed at Molly again and felt a pang. He felt it almost every time his eyes alighted on her. Sometimes in the groin, but mostly in the heart. Fuck it. He was her best male friend. Which meant that after her father, he was sort of the number one dude in her life. Ed knew it couldn't stay that way for ever, but he couldn't think about that, couldn't think about her being with some other guy. The one thing Ed had on his side right now was that Molly was discerning. When it came to men, she was pickier than anyone he knew. He wasn't even sure if she'd slept with anyone yet, but it wasn't a subject he liked to dwell on. It made him feel as though his guts had been kicked inwards.

Finally remembering what she was supposed to be doing, Molly picked her beer up, holding it awkwardly with three fingers. She hit the table three times with the bottle, clearly searching her mind for the next bit of the drinking game. 'And, ee, once a cardinal, always a cardinal!' she exclaimed triumphantly. She drained her beer in one and twirled the empty bottle over the top of her head, beaming at Ed.

Ed punched the air, mostly to distract from the way his stomach was doing the usual fizz and slide antics that happened whenever Molly went full beam on him. And he didn't mean just in a smiley way. There were moments when she turned her full attention on him and it literally rocked his world.

'Let's make spaghetti bolognese,' Molly slurred in his direction. She stood up, hiccupped and took his hand.

'What? Why on earth—'

'I'm hungry. Come on.'

She stepped over Jody – Ed apologetically did the same and received a furious frown in return – and they made their way to the kitchen, Ed following Molly's weaving motion, mostly because it amused him.

Molly gave Ed orders bossily, demanding that onions were chopped, meat was browned, tins of tomatoes opened. She always got a bit bossy when she was drunk. Hopefully, she thought, Ed found it endearing, the way he found Jody's pedantic antics 'endearing'. She dismissed the thought. Even in her drunken state she knew she was being ridiculous.

She gave Ed a half glance. Speaking of endearing. She watched the way he sliced up an onion, his eyes all crinkled up at the corners as he tried to stop them watering all over the place. Molly wished she didn't find him such good company.

'I take it I'm sous-chef,' Ed grumbled, examining a tiny cut on his finger from an onion-related mishap. 'Ouch, Molls. I'm bleeding.'

'You're moaning. And you're everything-chef, for the record,' Molly said. She tried to focus on him, but he kept swimming out of her vision for some strange reason. 'I am in no fit state to wield a knife, my friend. Now the trick with bolognese is to use both pork *and* steak mince. Did you know this? It's the best way. The only way.'

Ed spent the next half hour doing as he was told, an unusual state of affairs, but he was not of a mind to resist Molly when she was in domineering mode. Ridiculously, he found it sexy and he couldn't stop laughing as she waved her arms around in place of actual words and coherent sentences. She did allow him to force a pint of water down her to stave off a hangover, and five minutes later she sashayed off to the bathroom to 'break the seal' as she delightfully put it.

Thoroughly distracted by her retreating form, Ed proceeded to drop an entire carton of passata down the front of his jeans.

'Oh for fuck's sakes,' he muttered. His jeans were ruined. Not sure what else to do, he peeled them off. Fuck. He'd gone commando. It wasn't a sexual thing, it was more of a: 'I haven't washed any boxers' thing. He stuffed his jeans into the washing machine and quickly looped an apron over his head to save his dignity.

'Ed.' Molly appeared in the doorway, seeming to be gripping it for support. 'I'm either more pissed than I thought I was or your arse is on show. Have you been like that all night? Surely not. I would have remembered. I know I would have remembered.'

'Don't be daft. My jeans . . . oh, it doesn't matter.'

'Nice bum, Edison.' Molly's mouth lifted mischievously. 'Seriously. I had no idea. Hey – is that some sort of invitation?'

'Begging your pardon?'

'That. On the apron.' Molly pointed. She was sobering up fast. But she was also feeling reckless tonight.

Ed glanced down at himself. 'Snog The Chef' was emblazoned across the front. He felt his breath quicken, but he reined it in. Of course Molly didn't mean anything by it. It was just that she rarely flirted. Not with him at any rate. He had watched her charm many a poor bugger practically to his knees without even trying, but she hardly ever directed her flirtation in his direction.

He looked up and pasted an amiable smile on his face. 'Absolutely. An invitation is exactly what that is.'

'Gosh.' Molly made a decision. She tested it out briefly first, as was her way, and it felt right. She was going for it. 'Rude to turn down an invitation. Right?'

She ambled towards him. Ed felt a rush of lust. Good God. What was happening here? Was she . . . was Molly going to kiss him? She was mucking about, surely. His head swam. Molly was drunk. Squiffy, at very least. He should not do this. He definitely shouldn't do this. He had never wanted to do anything so much in his life.

Molly leant against him. She wanted nothing more than to hurl herself at him and snog his face off. But she didn't want to ruin the moment. If there was about to be a moment. Molly pressed her body up against his, her hands either side of him on the counter. It felt erotic being squashed up against Ed. She could be corny about it and say their bodies slotted together perfectly but – aah, sod it, they actually did.

Ed held his breath. He had never been so turned on in his life. He met Molly's eyes, surprised to find them attentive and watchful. She put her mouth on his and kissed him. It was a sweet, exquisite kiss that seemed to ricochet around Ed's body, lighting a billion tiny bulbs along the way. He felt the same sensation as he had the first time; the familiar, thrilling buzz that felt right.

Ed kissed Molly back. How could he not? He took the back of her neck in his hand, angled her mouth to his. It fit perfectly. What was that about? He had kissed many a mouth and sure, all mouths meshed together one way or another. But hers just fit.

'You're an annoyingly good kisser, Edison,' Molly murmured against his mouth. He was. The memories of that first night came rushing back. Molly had kissed guys since Ed – not that he knew about them; discretion was her middle name – but none had made her feel the way he did. She wished that wasn't the case, but it was. Kissing Ed consumed her with lust. She had fire chasing around her body in the most disturbing places – she wanted to pull his face to hers and kiss him endlessly. Before doing all manner of things she might not have the guts to do with someone else.

'Being a good kisser is annoying?'

Ed felt Molly's hands on his bare backside and closed his eyes. Good lord. There was clearly something very wrong with him. He wasn't used to reacting like this. This is the way he tried to make girls feel. Ed aimed to give a girl the best time he possibly could. He tried to make a girl feel special, to make her feel that something awesome was happening to her. Molly was doing this to him without even trying.

'Yes, it's annoying. When it's you.' Molly paused and looked at him. His face was so achingly familiar. She wanted to kiss it all over. Slowly. She gave in to the urge. She took her time. She caressed his face as she did so, placing her lips against his cheeks, his chin, his forehead. Molly made sure the kiss to the forehead was a sexy one, a lingering kiss that couldn't be confused with the dismissive one she had given him a few years ago. She whispered stuff as she kissed his face, moving to his neck to savour the smell of him.

Ed's groin jerked. Not a twitch – a full-on jerk. The likes of which normally required physical contact of some kind. This one, however, was so sharp it damned near took his breath away. Molly's mouth on his skin, her hair under his nostrils, her warm body curved around his. It was a sensory-overload situation. But Ed welcomed it. Wanted it, craved it.

'What is that God awful song?' Ed said, trying desperately to grasp a moment to rein himself in.

'What?'

'That song. What . . . what is it?'

Molly lifted her head. 'It's that one that bangs on about showing someone heaven. Maria thingy. From that film about the cars. NASCAR racing.'

Ed was none the wiser. But it had bought him a moment. Over Molly's shoulder, he saw Jody standing in the doorway. She shot him a look – shock? Contempt? Loathing? Ed wasn't sure. But he was fairly certain Jody would never utter another word to him again, unless it was either 'fucking' or 'bastard'. He couldn't blame her. Why was he such a shit sometimes? Ed forgot about Jody two seconds later when Molly put her mouth to his ear.

'Let's go upstairs,' she whispered. 'Right now. I want your hands on me. All over me.'

Ed bit his lip. He was aroused. God, but he was aroused. He could barely see straight. He wanted Molly badly. *Badly*. Was he taking advantage of her? Could he resist? It wasn't exactly helping that he only had a ridiculous apron between his desperately rearing manhood and Molly and her warm, lovely skin.

Jeepers alive, how was a man supposed to cope with

70

such a thing? He shouldn't do this with her. She was drunk, he had to stop this . . .

'I'm not drunk,' she said. Molly could tell Ed was battling with himself, no doubt reminding himself she was drunk, that he was taking advantage of her. She had to stop him thinking that way. 'I want you. Ok?'

Molly took his hand and led him out of the kitchen. Led him up the stairs, into her bedroom. Her heart was thumping but this was right. It was right.

'Molly . . .' Ed tried to speak but her mouth was upon his again.

'I want to lose my virginity to you,' she murmured, kissing him again.

He pulled back, stunned.

Molly went bright red. 'Jesus. I can't believe I just said that! What a bloody idiot. I'm ancient and still a virgin.' She openly cringed, her fists balling tightly. She went to turn away from him, but Ed held her steady. He felt a rush of something for her but he couldn't quite identify what it was. He just knew he didn't want to let go of her.

'Molly, you don't want to do that with me.'

'Yes, I do.' She met his eyes fiercely. Something about Ed always made her feel a bit defensive. He called it her 'feistiness' and he made much of both enjoying it and inciting it, but Molly knew it was because he was the one person who was capable of exercising some sort of power over her. And in the same way, she made much of both enjoying it and inciting it.

'You've slept with tons of girls, Ed. You must be ace at this. And we're friends. I know you, you know me – almost inside and out. Who better for my first time?'

71

Molly meant it. She had made a decision downstairs in the kitchen. It had to be Ed. Had to be! Who else would she trust like this? It didn't have to mean anything heavy. Surely they were grown-ups, surely they could do this and still be friends?

Molly had no idea if that was the case. She wasn't even sure she believed it herself. Did she just want it because it was Ed? Because she so very badly wanted Ed?

Molly started to say something. But she felt too exposed, too vulnerable.

Ed took a shaky breath. Molly wanted to sleep with him because he was experienced. So that her first time was a good one. Because they were friends. Not because . . . Christ. He wanted her so much. But did he want her like this?

'This should . . . you should . . .'

Ed mentally slapped himself. He had to stop this, to nip it in the bud. He wanted Molly more than he had wanted anyone, but he wasn't going to sleep with her if it was just because she wanted a so-called 'expert' to be her first.

'Molly.' He held her by the arms, as much in his own defence as in hers. 'This is a huge moment. We're friends, very good friends, but that's not a reason for us to . . . to do this. You should . . . your first should be someone you love. If at all possible.'

'I bet yours wasn't,' she retorted.

'Well, maybe not.' Ed took that on the chin. Had to, really. His first experience had predictably been with one of the 'easy' girls at his school. He certainly hadn't been in love with her, nor had he cared about such a notion.

But this was Molly. And Ed cared about her too much to take advantage. 'I mean it, though. You should do this with someone you love, Molls. Not with me.'

Molly stared at him. For a drunk person she was holding his gaze surprisingly well. Was she drunk? Ed realised Molly was actually fairly sober now.

Molly was feeling exasperated. Enough was enough. Without saying anything, she tore off her t-shirt. Luckily, she was wearing a black bra with pretty scalloped edges. She was hopeful she was wearing the matching knickers, but, whatever. She had started this and she was going through with it regardless of her knicker situation.

Ed sucked his breath in. Her skin was luscious. Golden, smooth. The curve of her waist was exquisite. It flared in and then out again at her hips. He wanted to touch her all over. He wanted to adore every inch of her skin.

Molly swallowed. She was going to be truthful. Because otherwise Ed was never going to agree. 'Ok. I don't want you to be my first because you're experienced. I want you to be my first because I want you – *you* – to be my first.'

Ed swallowed. Now how the hell was he supposed to defend himself against *that*?

'Kiss me,' Molly said, taking his face in her hands.

Ed faltered. Resist her, he commanded himself silently. But he couldn't. He simply couldn't. He kissed her, luxuriating in her mouth, loving her hands on his face, her body crushed to his. His hands were on her waist. It felt so small. She felt tiny, in fact. She was strong-willed yet fragile in so many ways, and that combination bowled Ed right over.

'I've never wanted someone so much in my life . . .'

73

Molly whispered. And she meant it. Her eyes met his. They were seductive yet oddly innocent. 'You *are* a dirty romantic after all, Edison. You kiss like a romantic. But it's dirty too. I think that's just perfect.'

Ed came undone. He pushed Molly against the wall, kissing her with everything he had. His hands were in her hair, his body was crushed hard against hers. She was kissing him back so ardently he could barely catch his breath. He felt consumed by her. And he bloody well loved it.

Ed heard something in the distance – his name. Was that his name? But he ignored it. The way Molly was making him feel, Ed was struggling to make sense of it. He felt her hands on his bare bum again and he groaned, leaning into her. He put his hand on her shoulder, slipped her bra strap to one side. Dropped a kiss where it had been, loving the way Molly squirmed against him.

'Do. That. Again,' she said, pulling him closer by the apron. 'And then I want you naked. I want you naked and all over me.'

'Are you absolutely certain you haven't done this before?' Ed panted, tearing off the apron.

'I am absolutely certain,' Molly said slowly. She looked down. 'Well. I'm a bit speechless.'

'Can you be a bit speechless?' Ed asked, chuckling as he slid her other bra strap off her shoulder. 'Is that a thing? Is that like being a bit pregnant?' He left a trail of kisses down her neck. 'Christ, this is not a time to mention pregnancy . . .'

Molly impatiently undid her bra and let it fall to the floor. She loved all the romantic stuff, but at the same time, she was about to explode.

'Fucking hell,' Ed said. 'I am going to hurl you on to that bed and do unspeakable things to every single inch of your body. And then I'm going to—'

He paused. There it was again. His name. Someone was calling his name.

'Ed!' It was Jody yelling up the stairs. She sounded pissed at him. 'Phone call.'

Molly carried on kissing him, oblivious. 'Who would be calling you here?' she mumbled against his mouth. 'Don't stop, Ed, don't stop. Ignore it . . .'

Ed let her kiss him, just for a few seconds more. He savoured her mouth, tasted her, kissing her as if it was the very last time he might do it. As it may well be. Molly was a girl who could only be rejected – or rather, sidelined – so many times; he knew that. Ed knew it.

But he had to stop. He drew back. He was needed. He wanted to stay right here in Molly's arms, her fragrant hair under his nostrils, her warm body thrust against his. But he was needed elsewhere. There was only one person who would call him at Molly's house, only one reason such a call would be made.

'Molly. *Molly*. I need to take that call.' Summoning every vestige of strength, Ed removed Molly's arms from his waist.

She straightened, meeting his eyes. 'Who's calling you, Ed?'

'It's an emergency. I mean, it must be.' Ed dragged a hand through his hair. 'I left a number with my . . . with my mother. In case she couldn't track me down at my digs.'

Molly rubbed her fingers across her mouth. Was she already regretting what had happened?

Molly was, in fact, doing nothing of the sort. She was wondering why her mouth suddenly felt lonely.

'Your mother?'

'Yes.'

'Isn't there anyone else who can help?'

Molly felt slightly pathetic clutching at straws like this, but she couldn't shrug off the feeling that she was experiencing that first night on the beach all over again. As though something amazing that she could practically taste was being snatched away from her.

Ed's heart clenched briefly in his chest. He wanted to tell her. He really wanted to tell her. Why couldn't he bloody well tell her? Christ.

'What sort of emergency?' Molly said. She folded her arms across her chest. If anyone else had done that, Ed would have thought it was to cover a naked chest but Molly merely looked edgy. And exasperated. And gutted.

Ed hated himself. Hated this moment. Hated his mother. Only for a second, but he truly did. 'I-I can't say. I— but trust me. I have to take this.' He squeezed Molly's hand, silently pleading with her to trust him.

She held on to his hand. She didn't want to, but she did it. Because it was Ed. 'Why don't you trust me?'

'I do trust you. I do. It's just . . .'

Ed shut up. He sounded like an idiot. But he'd sound even more like an idiot if he actually told Molly the truth. It was such a shameful, wretched tale.

'I'm sorry, Molly,' he said, picking up the apron. 'I'm truly, truly sorry about this. Just know that I have to take this call. And I'll probably have to go home for a bit. It has nothing to do with . . . with this. With us.'

'Us?' Molly started to laugh but it caught in her throat. She didn't want to cry. Well, she did, but she would never forgive herself. 'Is there such a thing?' She raised her chin. 'Go, Ed. Go. Answer your call. Do what you have to do.'

Ed felt paralysed. He didn't want to leave this moment. He had a feeling that it was a very significant moment in his life. But he had no choice. He had obligations. Not able to think of a single thing to say that could smooth the waters and make Molly smile again, Ed left the room to take his call. He chucked the apron over his head before he reached the hallway and picked up the phone.

Ed could barely make sense of the voice at the other end of the line, but it didn't really matter. Something had been ruined and he had to go and sort out another mess caused by the same hand.

He put the phone down, went into the kitchen and put his cold, wet passata-stained jeans back on.

'Leaving yet another girl high and dry?' Jody sneered as he headed past her to the front door.

'Yeah,' Ed said bitterly, striding past her. 'It's what I do, Jody. It's just what I do.'

Upstairs, Molly shakily sat down on the bed. Feeling like this once was bad enough. Feeling like it twice was like a punch to the heart. So, lessons learnt. She and Ed should never get that close again. However incredible it felt in the moment, clearly they weren't meant to be.

Shattered, Ed opened the front door. He had missed a train, then been forced to get off and change to another line, and then he had walked two miles from the station as he couldn't get a cab. It was unexpectedly quiet in the house. Eerily so.

'Mum?'

There was no answer. Opening the door to the sitting room, Ed sucked his breath in. The air smelt stale and pungent. Sick? Urine? Both? The room was dimly lit, only a side lamp providing a small umbrella of light, but Ed was familiar with the scene in front of him. Chairs were overturned, glasses smashed. A picture – nothing special, just a cheap print – had been hurled across the room. It lay at an odd angle against the wall, its frame splintered, the print poking out. A curtain had been torn from its rail and hung shabbily.

Ed swallowed. He was accomplished enough at clearing up to be able to assess the room and judge how long it would take him to put it to rights. With the furniture damage, and the as yet undiscovered pool of sick somewhere, he was looking at a good three hours or more. He turned to the sofa.

There she was. Sprawled across it, her legs flopped out at an undignified angle, her skirt bearing a wet stain that to Ed was unmistakable. There was a smear of lipstick smudged from the corner of her mouth to her chin, giving her the air of a macabre, violated doll. Ed leant over and pulled a blanket over her legs. He'd deal with the urine situation later. He grabbed a tissue and wetted it with his mouth, the way a parent does for a child, carefully dabbing at the lipstick until her face looked normal again. Then he sat back on his heels and gazed at her. And here it was. The very reason Ed didn't ever bring friends – or, God forbid, girlfriends – home. The explanation for Ed's only-child status. The shameful grounds on which to lie to the person he cared about the most in the world.

His mother. The devout, committed alcoholic. She had been married to a serial cheat, a husband who had upped and left years ago, abandoning both of them without a second glance. She had fallen apart and turned to the bottle. Ed had followed her around, picking up the pieces and clearing up her mess. Keeping his guilty secret under wraps from everyone, especially anyone who meant something to him.

He remembered some school friends turning up unannounced years ago, when his father had first left. His mother had been in the throes of a horrendous drinking binge and when she saw Ed's school friends, she had danced around the garden laughing hysterically, trying to get them to join in. All with her skirt tucked in her knickers. Which was better than her stripping all of her clothes off and falling over on the patio with her legs splayed everywhere. Which she did later, in front of Ed's friends. He had never been so mortified in his life, and he swore he would never allow anyone he remotely cared for to meet his mother ever again.

Florrie stirred and opened her eyes with some difficulty. Mascara and tears had seemingly welded them together and she almost had to put a hand to her face to unstick them. Ed found it both tragic and painful to watch.

'Darling,' she slurred. 'Where *have* you been? I went out to look for you. Got a bit lost. Have you been climbing trees again?'

Ed closed his eyes. 'Mother, I'm eighteen years old.'

'Of course you are!' Florrie cackled. 'I'm forgetful;

what can I say?' She gave him a coquettish smile. 'Is your girlfriend with you? The lovely Molly? You're always talking about her.'

Ed opened his mouth to correct her then thought better of it. 'No, no, she's not,' he said finally. It never ceased to disturb him how his mother seemed to flit in and out of past and present, from vagueness to startling accuracy.

'Where is Michael?' he asked her, enunciating clearly.

'Michael?'

'Michael. The man who moved in here. Your boyfriend.'

'He's gone.' Florrie started to cry. It was a pitiful, child-like sound.

Ed put his hand on hers. 'What happened?'

'We had a fight. I had a drink.' Florrie swallowed. 'I said some things. Not very nice things. But it was all his fault.'

Ed nodded. He was well-acquainted with the down-sides of an alcoholic with a mean streak. She had once told him she wished she'd never had him, that he had ruined her life and that he could drop dead as far as she was concerned. Not a great thing to hear at the tender age of fourteen.

'He packed his stuff and he's gone,' Florrie said, her voice reaching a whiny pitch.

'Maybe he'll come back.' Ed tiredly pushed his hair out of his eyes. 'You were in such a good place, Mum. Such a good place. How did this happen?'

'I miss you,' she said, pulling her lips into a pout. 'I miss you so much, Edison. You won't leave me again, will you?' she pleaded, clawing at his hand. 'You're all I've got.'

'I'm doing a degree, Mum. I'm trying to make a better life for us.'

'But I need you here.'

Ed closed his eyes briefly. Here it came. The emotional blackmail. He could barely stand it. He had lived with it for so long now, he knew he should be used to it, but he hated it.

'Time for a sleep,' Ed told her gently. She resisted for a second, but exhaustion and alcohol soon overcame her and she relaxed against the sofa. Ed tucked the blanket more securely round her, feeling a multitude of emotions rushing into his throat – love, sympathy, resentment, responsibility. Overwhelmed, he settled down on the opposite sofa and rubbed his eyes blearily, wondering what on earth he was going to do now.

Should he leave university? He couldn't bear the thought of giving up, of not seeing Molly any more, of not making the absolute best of his life. He was responsible for his mother and he had to look after her, but did he have to give up everything that meant anything? There had to be a way. There had to be a way he could make this work.

Ed sat forward with his elbows on his knees and did what he always did when he felt bleak and hopeless. He thought about Molly. He always thought about Molly. Except this time it didn't work. Because this time all he could think about was the way she had looked at him in her bedroom, her eyes full of lust and hope and fun. About her incredible body. About the way she had made him feel. About the fact that he, Ed, had just walked out on a situation he had been aching for. Molly, kissing him senseless up against a wall. Wanting to sleep with him. Telling him what he had waited a long time to hear her say.

But he had walked out. And he hadn't even provided a good explanation. Because he couldn't. She was a friend – a good friend – and he did trust her. But Ed couldn't have her knowing his secret. He couldn't bear for her to think differently of him. He didn't want her knowing how ashamed he was. And so, as far as Molly was concerned, he had simply walked out.

Ed watched his mother breathing in, breathing out. Just like a normal person did. While she slept, he could almost believe her to be just like any other mother. The ones he was familiar with, anyway. Friends' mothers. Molly's mother. Ed felt desolate. And so incredibly trapped. He loved his mother but he hated her too. Quite vehemently, in fact. Not all of the time, but some of it. Yet he had a duty to care for her. And it meant putting her before absolutely everyone else in his life. Including Molly. It was the card he had been dealt.

Ed put his head in his hands and felt a sob coming on. No time for that. He leant back and rested his head against the sofa. He would stay awake and make sure his mother didn't choke on her own vomit in her sleep. In the morning, he would bathe her and dress her and then he would make a start on the room. After that, he would try and figure out what the hell he could do about his place at university. And he would do whatever he could to make things up to Molly.

Now

'Ed?'

'Molly? Is that you?'

Thank God. Ed felt a rush of relief. At last. Molly had come to see him. He sat up, realising he'd fallen asleep on the sofa again. And that the lounge looked like shit.

'The front door was open,' Molly called. 'Is everything alright?'

'I'm in here. Come on in. 'Scuse the mess.'

Ed raked his fingers through his hair and tossed his phone to one side, not wanting to look as though he'd been checking his messages for the millionth time. Which of course he had. To see if Saskia had been in touch. To see if Molly had been in touch.

Molly walked in and Ed caught his breath. Not in the way he usually did though, but because she looked incredibly tired, gaunt even. Beautiful, naturally, but tired. Her face was pale and her mouth was pinched and tight. Something was wrong.

Molly was thinking the same about Ed. He looked unusually dishevelled and unkempt. His clothes were crumpled – nothing unusual there – but they also looked as though he'd worn them for a few days. Which meant that something was wrong.

'What's happened?' they both asked at the same time.

'You first,' Molly insisted. She sat on the sofa and took his hand. 'I'm so sorry I missed your engagement party.'

Ed let out a short laugh. 'You will be when I tell you what happened. It was a party that will go down in history.'

'Oh dear.'

Ed squeezed her hand and told her everything. Molly's eyes widened, and she kept wanting to interrupt and ask questions, but she managed to wait until Ed had finished speaking. More or less.

'Ed. No. Saskia jilted you at your engagement party? That's hideous.'

'Right? I've had better evenings.' Ed put his head back against the sofa.

'I can imagine.' Molly joined him. 'Where's she now?'

'She's gone.'

'Where?'

'Away. For ever, I think.'

Molly's eyes widened. 'What? What reason did she have for doing this to you?'

Ed explained in more detail. The words sounded empty, even to him.

'I cannot believe she was in this for fun. And that she just got carried away.' Molly was flummoxed. And she felt horribly sorry for Ed. 'This is terrible. I can't believe

84

Saskia would do this to you. I thought she was really in love with you.'

'I don't really want to talk about this any more.' Ed no longer felt emotional; he just felt thoroughly fed up with the whole thing. He sat up. 'So, what's your news then?'

Molly swallowed. 'Oh that. Well. Christ. It's going to be a bit of a bombshell. It's such a bombshell, in fact, that I have started to afford it capital letters. The Bombshell. Like that.'

'Capital letters are all the rage around here. Go for it.'

Ed was fairly certain Molly couldn't say anything that would shock him after Saskia's unexpected departure.

'It's very likely that I have early-onset Parkinson's disease.'

Molly took Ed's hand apologetically. She had felt horrendous imparting this news so far. It was a huge thing to drop on anyone and Molly knew how awful she would feel if she heard this news about a friend or a partner or a parent. Her father had been in pieces and Molly had felt terribly guilty for having to own up to such a thing.

'No. Molly, no.' Ed felt as if he'd been hit by a bus. His stomach lurched and slid downwards, ending somewhere close to his ankles.

'I'm afraid so.'

'Oh God. Shit. Christ. Come here.' Pulling her into his arms, Ed felt a sudden urge to bawl his eyes out. *Not Molly. Not something like that. Parkinson's? At her age? It was just unfair. So fucking unfair.*

'I wanted to tell you about it, but Sam insisted I got a second opinion before I told anyone.'

Ed's mouth tightened. 'And do you have a second opinion now?'

Molly pulled back, rubbing her eyes. 'Yes. And it was the same as the first.'

Ed was shell-shocked. This was far worse than Saskia leaving. Because that could be dealt with. That had a beginning, a middle and an end. This . . . this just felt as if it had an end. A twisted, grim, unimaginable end.

Ed bit his lip as he stared at Molly. She looked tired and fragile. He wanted to hold on to her, to grip her tightly and make it all go away. He also wanted to fall to pieces. But that was selfish of him. This wasn't about him, it was about Molly. And Molly didn't deserve this. She didn't fucking well deserve it. Ed's fists tightened. He felt like punching a wall.

'Not many people know about it,' Molly was saying. 'Just Sam, my dad, you. I need to go and tell Sara as well.'

'H-how's Sam dealing with it?' Ed didn't rightly care how Sam was reacting to the news; he was more concerned about Molly. But he felt he should ask.

'Sam's being very – Sam about it.' Molly smiled. A smile Ed felt was tinged with sadness. Disappointment, maybe? 'He's been practical and logical and he'll have me on a course of proven drugs very soon. He's conducting a detailed family tree to see if he can identify a hereditary cause – not that I care remotely about that – and I'm fairly certain he'll have a new exercise and healthy eating regime sorted for me in no time.'

'Balls. No more greasy pizzas together?' Ed had no idea why he was cracking jokes.

'Well. Maybe the odd few here and there. Sam doesn't need to know.' Molly gave him a wink. She felt relieved that Ed was making jokes. It meant that he cared and it also helped remove the elephant from the room.

'Listen, I can't claim to be like Sam when it comes to this stuff,' Ed confessed. 'I'll read everything about it, I promise, but for now, please treat me like a dumb-assed novice and tell me everything. If you want to.'

Molly did want to. She painstakingly went through the same details she had outlined to Sam, but with Ed, she didn't hold back. There was no need. He wasn't going to be the one dressing her or helping her to eat later in life, so she could be completely honest about the way she could potentially disintegrate. She might not, of course. But the second neurologist she had seen had mentioned that some of her symptoms seemed to be gathering momentum. They might be slowed by medication, of course, but there was a chance that Molly's Parkinson's might be more aggressive than others'. As if having it wasn't enough of a shitter.

Ed was appalled. Not at the potential disintegration, but for Molly. 'Christ. Molly. This is grim. You're being so brave about everything.'

Ed felt as if he'd been punched hard in the gut. He genuinely thought he might be able to handle this news better if he'd been receiving it about himself. Hearing it about Molly was so incredibly painful, he could hardly stand it. Ed couldn't bear the thought of her having to go through any of this – be it pain, the loss of motor skills, or the loss of her dignity. Ed would do anything for her not to have this horrible illness.

Molly scoffed. 'Me? Brave? Don't be absurd. I've been bawling my eyes out about it ever since the first diagnosis.'

Without warning, Ed suddenly burst into tears. 'Well if you've been doing it, it's ok for me to do it too, isn't it?' He wiped his eyes self-consciously. 'I'm so sorry, Molly. What a twat. You're going through hell and I'm crying my eyes out. I just hate that you're going through something like this.'

Ed more than hated it. He wanted to run out into the garden and scream at the sky. Rage at God. Hurl flower pots over the fence. Beat the ground with his fists. He wanted to reverse time and stop Molly getting this awful illness.

'I told you I was a big girl,' Ed said, smiling weakly.

'Oh Ed, now I'm blubbing. I'm a big girl as well. Wait, I actually *am* a girl. I'm probably allowed to cry like this.'

Molly let the tears fall. It actually felt rather good. Like a proper release. All of her previous weeping had been mostly conducted in private. Sam didn't cope that well with tears so Molly tended to move somewhere else when she broke down. Which she actually preferred, most of the time. Ed was one of the only people she didn't mind crying in front of. And Sara. She was fantastic in the face of sobbing. At least, Molly hoped she was. She would find out later when she dropped The Bombshell on her other good friend.

'Anyway, you can talk, Ed. Your fiancée left you.'

Ed hiccupped and wiped his nose. 'Oh crap. I'd forgotten about all of that for a minute. You're right. I have far more to worry about. That was a joke, by the way.' He reached for Molly. 'Come here for a hug. To make me feel better, not you. It's a properly selfish hug.'

Molly went into his arms. Inhaling his neck, she closed her eyes. Ed always felt – right. But he would, wouldn't he? They had been friends for a long time; there was an unspoken familiarity between them.

Ed held her, feeling his heart contract. This couldn't be happening to her. Not to Molly. It was going to kill him seeing her go through this, but he would be there for her, in whatever capacity she needed him. She had Sam, of course, and Ed knew Sam would be fantastic. He always was. And as much as Ed had sometimes perversely wished Sam would fail and let Molly down, this was not a time he would wish for that to happen. Not in a million years. Ed wanted Sam to be there for Molly, wanted him to be the most incredibly supportive husband ever.

'I'll do whatever you need me to do,' Ed said.

He sounded choked. Molly was going to come undone in a minute.

'You mean the world to me, Molly.'

'Ditto,' Molly said, her voice muffled by Ed's shoulder. She pulled back at last, not because she wanted to, but because someone's phone was ringing. 'Whose phone is that going off?'

'Mine. It's Boyd. He won't leave me alone. Some of our investments have gone tits up.'

Molly stood up. 'I'm sure you'll be ok. You're one of those people who always comes up smelling of roses. Always. Despite your current situation, you're one lucky sod most of the time.'

Ed shook his head. He wasn't feeling particularly lucky today.

'Listen. I need to go. I have to speak to Sara. Are you going to be ok?'

'Of course,' he said. 'I'll call you later.'

Molly kissed the top of Ed's head. 'Ok. And I'm truly sorry about Saskia.'

'And I'm sorry about your Parkinson's.' The words caught in his throat as he said them and Ed fought hard not to start crying again. But he knew Molly would want him to be upfront about it.

After she left, Ed decided to put Boyd out of his misery. It was a call that in any other circumstances would have carried the worst news possible.

They had lost everything. Pretty much everything. Someone Boyd had trusted implicitly had run off with all their money. An investigation was being carried out, but Boyd was doubtful they would get any of it back. He was apologetic – excruciatingly so, even though he was going through the same thing himself – but there was nothing he could do. Their portfolios had more or less been wiped.

Ed ended the call. Saskia had left him. Molly had early-onset Parkinson's. And now he was penniless. As days went, it was a bit of a crapper. But he'd give all his remaining money just to make Molly well again.

Ed went downstairs and opened a bottle of wine. Pushing aside the thought that he was turning into his mother, he filled a glass to the brim and prepared to get thoroughly plastered.

Molly and Ed

April 2000

'So, my dad got you an interview. With a newspaper.'

Molly propped herself up on her elbows, cupping her face with her hands. She wanted to witness Ed's reaction.

They were lying on Maplethorpe Beach, in their favourite spot just to the right of the first beach hut. They were stretched out on a checked blanket wearing shades; Ed in Ray-Bans, Molly in a funky red-rimmed pair of no particular origin. Ed wore a crumpled linen shirt in a shade of blue that was known as 'Oxford', teamed with cut-off denim shorts and deck shoes. He knew it was the uniform of posh twats but it helped him cultivate his pseudo-posh image.

Molly wore a white cotton sun top that made the most of her golden shoulders, and a long, floaty skirt thing in a vivid shade of purple, which clung to her slender legs yet concealed them from thigh to ankle. Ed had initially been rather disturbed by the way the skirt had moulded itself around her, but he told himself to grow up and stop being a perv. Although his shades did mean that his perving went largely unnoticed.

In proper student fashion, they were sharing a large bottle of cider and a tube of Pringles. Ed wondered if Molly might actually prefer a good Shiraz and some breadsticks, but she had assured him that Pringles were her favourite. And she regularly drank cider. Ed had meant to bring some plastic tumblers but he'd forgotten. Still, it was deliciously intimate, swigging from the same bottle.

Ed refocused his mind and flipped his well-thumbed copy of *The Picture of Dorian Gray* over. He had an interview. With a newspaper.

'Are you serious? That's awesome, Molls. I'll phone John later to thank him.'

'No need for that. Just turn up, you know?' Molly fixed him with a pointed stare. She supposed she could say that they had some trust issues going on. Had done for some time. 'Dad's gone to a lot of trouble with this and I promised him you wouldn't let him down.'

Ed looked away. He deserved that, obviously. Over the past two and a half years he had consistently let Molly down. His mother had spiralled into a hideous depression since Michael had left; Ed found himself constantly called upon. He had spent almost every weekend at home, plus any number of evenings, which meant that he had missed out on a multitude of social connections. Not that he cared about those, particularly. He cared about the time with Molly he had lost and could never get back. Parties, dinners, drinks and just hanging out. Talking. Having fun. Maybe more. But no. Ed checked the resolute set of Molly's chin. That ship had well and truly sailed.

Molly felt Ed's gaze on her, but she pretended not to notice. Ed often stared at her. She didn't take it seriously. There was no point. Ever since that night when he had walked out on her after his mysterious phone call, things had been strained between them. She had lost her virginity to a guy named Toby in the end, some six months after the spaghetti bolognese incident. Toby had been a conventionally good-looking and extremely gentlemanly guy on Ed's course. It had been rather a polite coupling, all very considerate and respectful. Molly supposed that was entirely appropriate for her first time and as such she had been extremely annoyed with herself that flashes of Ed inappropriately thrusting her up against a wall and messing her hair up with his hands had popped into her head now and again, even at highly inopportune moments.

Molly turned her face as she heard a familiar voice. How strange. There was Toby, strolling past them, his arm around a pretty girl. Molly raised a hand – Toby was hot on manners. She felt a pang. She had kept the details of her tryst with Toby mostly to herself, confiding in only Jody and her friend Sara from back home, but she hadn't mentioned much about it to Ed. Toby had chased her for months after it had happened and Molly had dated him for a short time. But she had to admit to herself that he didn't really set her on fire. She hoped the new girl in his life felt differently, because Toby was a really sweet guy – he just lacked charisma.

Molly had come to realise that while chemistry wasn't everything when it came to guys, it was definitely something.

Something fairly important. Molly glanced at Ed then looked away quickly. Well, in most cases.

Ed frowned as he watched Toby walk past. Christ. There he was. Smug bastard. Not that he knew the details of his thing with Molly. Molly barely referenced it, airily referring to it as 'that night', and he had been glad that she had kept the details to herself. But part of him wanted to hear it, to hear it all, from start to finish. The self-destructive part of him wanted to torment himself with how, how often and in what positions. But in reality, he didn't want to know. The thought of another guy's hands on her made Ed want to heave slightly.

There had been other guys for Molly since Toby, Ed knew that, but there had only been a few, and thankfully no one serious. Molly was picky. And Ed thanked his lucky stars that this was the case. It would have killed him otherwise. He could hardly knock her though; he had dated a fair few girls himself over the last couple of years.

Well, dated was an exaggeration, Ed thought ruefully. He wasn't around enough to strike up anything serious with anyone, should he even have had the inclination. Which he didn't. His liaisons had been casual and firmly moored in the sexual arena. Mostly while drunk. Not drunk the way his mother did it, but tipsy, up for it and full of bravado. Ed had no desire for anything other than that; there really wasn't any point when he felt the way he did. Unmoored. Unable to commit. Weighed down with responsibility.

Ed glanced at Molly again, watched her adjust her sunglasses. Her proximity still disturbed him in every

94

way. He wanted to look at her constantly, drink in her eyes, that lovely mouth. It irked him the way she disturbed him. He both revelled in it and resisted it in equal measure. Ed sometimes wondered if he was obsessed, if perhaps Molly was simply his physical ideal and that was why he found it hard to stop thinking about her in a sexual— no, Ed corrected himself. What he felt for Molly went far deeper than a mere sexual connection.

They weren't best friends as such. 'Good friends' covered it more appropriately, especially with the problems his other responsibilities created, but Ed just enjoyed being around Molly. She was the epitome of everything he thought a girl should be. He longed for another girl to waltz along and smash this viewpoint, if only for his own sanity.

He had to make it to this interview Molly had arranged, he simply had to. He didn't want her to give up on him. Not completely, at any rate. He was aware he didn't have the best track record when it came to reliability, but Ed worked hard at being a good friend to Molly. Even if she didn't realise it.

Ed sat up and lit a cigarette. 'So, how's your work experience thingy going?'

'My work experience position? It's going really well, thanks.'

Molly sat up and mimicked his stance, but declined a cigarette. She had the occasional puff, but she preferred menthols and Ed drew the line at those. 'I've started working on Saturdays as well now. Might as well. You're never around.' She nudged his leg with her bare foot.

'Yes. I'm sorry about that. Home stuff.'

Ed knew he sounded vague. But what else could he do in the circumstances? He rubbed a hand over the battered face of Oscar Wilde on the back of his novel. A weird-looking chap, but hey-ho. He was a genius.

Ed glanced at Molly again. He had done his level best to spend quality time with her when he could. But it was quality time spent in short, punchy bursts. Once a fortnight they ate greasy pizza and mouth-wincingly pungent garlic bread washed down with very rough red wine. They hung out at the library now and again and Ed visited her at her work experience place – a design company above a bakery. It smelt like heaven and it was run by some slick-looking workaholic who reeked of money and success. Ed could never remember his name. Mostly, he decided, on purpose. He didn't like the way the guy looked at Molly.

'So how many assignments do you have left?' Molly shifted to lie on her back, turning her face towards the sunshine.

'Three. You know, nothing to worry about.'

Ed felt a mild thread of panic weave around the already present knot in his stomach. Three assignments to do before he even sat his finals. Three. He was working on two of them but he hadn't touched the third. He did much of his writing on trains these days, as he travelled between uni and home. Sometimes he wished the journey was longer so he could really get stuck into his coursework. But at least he was able to get home quickly.

'Ah, you'll have those done in no time. You're on a roll. So, do you think you'll go straight into journalism?'

'Maybe. I don't know. I still have this yearning to write a novel.'

'You have a yearning to be Oscar Wilde.'

'I do not. I have no wish to indulge in the joys of bottom sex, nor do I wish to do hard labour in prison. I am far too beautiful to do the latter, because the former would no doubt then be forced upon me.'

Molly frowned disapprovingly. 'I do believe we can attribute far greater achievements than bottom sex and imprisonment to the great Oscar Wilde. And, as you well know, I meant that you have always wanted to be seen as a great writer.' Molly's eyes danced. 'Far too beautiful indeed. Darling Ed. You are absurdly pretty, it has to be said.'

Ed cocked an eyebrow. 'Pretty? Yes, all men like to be seen as pretty. For fuck's sakes, Molls. I'm wasted on you, utterly wasted. I do believe I brought this to your attention some years ago. Boys are neither cute, nor pretty. You seriously must refrain from using such language around the male of the species.'

He gave an elaborate sigh, but he was amused. Molly was forever poking fun at him. He loved it; no other girl did this with him. It also put him slightly off-kilter. He was never really sure if she was mocking him or if she meant what she said when a compliment occasionally slid out.

'You really are pretty though,' Molly said, reaching out to grab his chin for a second. She was surprised at herself; she kept physical contact with Ed at a minimum, but now and again her guard slipped and she gave in to what felt natural. 'And anyway, I like pretty boys.' She let go of his chin.

'Do you now . . .' Without thinking, Ed took her hand and caressed it with his thumb.

'I do.' She smiled, but her stomach was flipping over. 'Do stop flirting with me, Edison. I might fall for you if you carry on like that.'

He stared at her. Did she mean it? Was she toying with him? Surely not. Molly was the most upstanding person he knew. Decent, honest, loyal, principled. Always principled. Molly had staged many a peaceful sit-in over various issues she felt strongly about. She stopped short of being strident, but when she felt passionately about something, she had no compunction about making a stand.

'Well, hello there. Am I interrupting something?'

'Sam!'

Molly yanked her hand out of Ed's and sat up.

Ed squinted as a face danced in and out of the sunlight. He took his sunglasses off and shaded his eyes with his hand instead. He instantly wished he hadn't and he inwardly scowled. Blimey, if it wasn't bad enough that Toby was strolling around the beach aimlessly, now that dude from the design company had rocked up. What was his bloody name again?

'Sam Bohle,' Sam said obligingly, holding his hand out to Ed.

Sam Bohle. That was it. Pronounced 'bowl', by all accounts. In a snide fashion, Ed wondered if this was Sam acting like Hyacinth Bouquet off that programme from the nineties. What was it? *Keeping Up Appearances*, that was it. Most likely he wasn't at all pretentious and simply had a name people mispronounced, but you know. Ed was feeling uncharitable.

He shook Sam's hand and was affronted when Sam

pumped it with unnecessary force. God, some men just felt the need to overly grip a hand.

'Nice to see you again, Sam,' Ed said with a genial smile. He put the surname issue aside and considered the name Sam. A name for a dog, perhaps? Or was he being uncharitable again? Maybe it was a name for an all-round good guy who was attractive, suave and well-dressed. Ed was fascinated by names and their meanings – the pompous affectation of a would-be writer, no doubt – he spent inordinate amounts of time weighing up the relative qualities of Wayne versus Henry.

Noting Sam's smart jeans and purple-and-white striped shirt, Ed suddenly felt gauche in his crumpled attire. And gauche did not sit well with him. Nor did being wrong-footed.

Molly was beaming at Sam in a way that Ed found inexplicably offensive. What was so bloody fascinating? Ed scrutinised him. Up close, Sam had wide green eyes and brown hair. Very clean-looking hair and a smooth jaw line. Ed rubbed a hand over his own, somewhat stubbly chin. He remembered Molly once professing an 'immature, short-lived' obsession with green eyes. Great. This was all just great.

'You look lovely,' Sam said to Molly. 'Very summery.'

Stop looking at Molly like that, Ed thought, irritated. He understood why Sam couldn't take his eyes off her, naturally. Molly was beautiful. That mouth, those eyes, her smile. Ed found it hard to tear his own eyes away at times. But he didn't like watching some other dude leering at her. No siree. It made him want to put his fist in the guy's handsome face. And, in a properly childish fashion, give him a wedgie.

'Having a picnic?' Sam gestured to the crisps and alcohol.

'Something like that.' Molly pulled a face. She didn't have the first idea why but she didn't like the idea of Sam thinking she was a bit naff. 'Not very sophisticated.'

'Oh, I don't know.' Sam helped himself to a crisp. Gamely, Ed thought.

'My choice,' he offered, leaping to Molly's defence. 'I'm a proper heathen when it comes to these things.'

Molly shot him a grateful glance. How incredibly sweet of Ed to say it was him. She was more of a heathen than he was most of the time.

Ed smiled then faltered. Molly was pleased he had covered for her. In front of this Sam bloke. Balls. What did that mean? He put his sunglasses on. He wanted to watch this exchange carefully.

'So Molly tells me you want to be a writer.'

Ed nodded, blinded by Sam's genial smile.

'What sort?'

'An author – a novelist. I want to write books.'

'Oh, great. Which genre? Crime, fantasy, romance?'

Ed's eyes narrowed behind his Ray-Bans. Was Sam taking the piss? He was smiling pleasantly enough but . . .

'Oh, definitely romance. I'm a romantic. A dirty romantic, if we're being specific.' Take *that*, suave, good-looking guy who may or may not be taking the massive piss and who clearly has intentions to get in Molly's underwear. A private joke between Ed and Molly – oh yes.

Molly frowned. She remembered the last time she and Ed had talked about the dirty romantic thing. It had been that night in her bedroom. Memories came rushing back and she quickly pushed them away.

Ed bit his lip. Molly was looking pissed – really angry. Then he remembered. Of course, they had talked about the dirty romantic thing under the stars the night they first met, but Molly had also referenced it the night they'd kissed in her bedroom. When he'd run out on her. Fuck. Ed cringed. What on earth was the matter with him? He was being an absolute nobber. In front of someone he really didn't want to be nobbish in front of.

Molly returned her gaze to Sam. She assumed he must be utterly perplexed by the conversation but if he was, he was hiding it well. Sam was quite attractive. Not in the way that Ed was – Sam was rather more clean-cut – but he had a very nice manner. And he was so self-assured.

'I see. Well, all the best with that, Ed. I'm afraid I'm terrible with words. Art is my thing. Me and Molly could bore for Britain about it when we get together.'

Pow! An uppercut to the chin. No, to the stomach. Ed felt that hit like a physical blow. Sam and Molly had things in common, things they could wax lyrical about, things that would baffle Ed with his silly words and dirty romantic nonsense. Oh, he was good. Ed felt a grudging respect. But he still wanted to give the guy a wedgie.

'He's right,' Molly nodded earnestly. 'We are *so* dull when we start talking about art and design.' She wondered why Ed was looking at her so antagonistically. She talked endlessly about art with him as well, but she and Sam were able to get rather more technical.

Sam straightened up. 'Anyway. It was lovely to bump into you but I'll leave you to it now.' He gestured behind him to a gaggle of equally attractive-looking people who were playing beach-rounders and chaffing wine from plastic glasses with stems. 'I'll see you tomorrow, Molly, and great to meet you, Ed.'

Ed watched him strolling away. And hoped one of Sam's splendid friends lobbed the rounders ball into his chiselled face.

'Isn't he *nice*?' Molly sighed, lying down again. She always felt very relaxed around Sam. She never worried that he would do anything unpredictable.

'Yes,' Ed replied. 'Wonderful. You know he fancies the fuck out of you, don't you?'

There was a pause. 'Don't be ridiculous, Ed. You say that about everyone.'

'Well, yes, that's because pretty much everyone does fancy you – they're not blind.' Ed felt exasperated. 'But him – that Sam dude – he's got it bad.'

Molly put her hands behind her head and considered him. 'Do you really think so?' She turned her head in Sam's direction. She hadn't ever thought of him in that way. Not Sam. He was a bit older than her and very much in control of himself. Molly wasn't sure Ed had it right. But she felt strangely flattered. 'Well, you know I walk around with my eyes shut when it comes to such things. But you're a veritable expert. And a man. So I'll take your word for it. How very intriguing, Ed. Thanks for letting me know.'

Ed tersely swigged cider from the bottle, spilling it down his already crappy shirt. What a monumental bell-end he was. He had alerted Molly to Sam's obvious infatuation, a fact that might have flown under the radar for ever if he'd kept his mouth shut. Christ. He might as well have just invited Sam over to Molly's and told him how she liked to be kissed. That she had a particularly sensitive spot around her hip area. Jesus.

Molly noted that Ed looked aggravated. Did he dislike the idea of Sam fancying her? Surely he wasn't bothered? Ed had girls coming out of his ears. She was simply the one that got away; that was all. Molly was sure of it. If Ed had *had* her already, Molly was in no doubt he would have moved on and forgotten about her by now. She was the only girl he was good friends with, and Molly was utterly convinced that it was because they hadn't actually sealed the deal.

Feeling the need to placate Ed for some reason, she reached out and briefly covered his hand with hers.

'Read to me?' she said. 'It is an afternoon for Oscar Wilde's gorgeous words and for your mellifluous voice. And word of the day for *that*, methinks. Right, Edison?'

Ed felt briefly mollified.

'But promise me you won't miss that interview?'

'I won't miss the interview. I promise.'

'*Dorian Gray*, please.'

Ed reached for the novel but felt troubled deep in the pit of his stomach. And he felt fairly sure it wasn't because of the interview.

Now

'So.' Sara shook her dark fringe out of her eyes. 'Hit me with it. What's going on?'

They had taken a day off to go shopping. Molly had told Sara that she had news to impart and that it would be best delivered after the copious use of credit cards. Either that, or later, over the champagne they usually consumed on such days. Sara worked in investments. Whatever that meant. She had a good job and she rarely took days off. She had done so because she knew Molly had something serious to say.

Molly gave Sara the low-down. She had become somewhat of an expert at summarising her illness in the form of bullet points. It probably sounded rather blunt and unemotional, but that somehow helped her remain on an even keel and prevented the rush of tears that listing her symptoms out loud might otherwise have caused.

Not that it mattered if she cried in front of her oldest friend. Sara had been there when Molly had fallen over and sprained her ankle at primary school. When someone had spilt yellow paint water all over her skirt and everyone had pointed and said she had wet herself. Best friends – old friends – had an unspoken agreement that tears, swearing, and basically anything that might be deemed inappropriate by others was perfectly acceptable.

'What the fucking fuck?' Sara said, proving this point. 'Sorry,' she muttered, realising some people passing them had children. 'Molly, you can't just hurl that at me when we're out shopping for shoes.'

'When should I hurl it at you?' Molly asked reasonably. 'Would it have been any better over a curry? Coffee? At our Pilates class?'

Sara raked her fingers through her hair. 'No. I guess not. I just can't take this in. You've got Parkinson's, you said? That's . . . you're too young for that, Molly. I don't get it.'

Molly ushered her into a posh shoe shop. They sat down on some padded seats. 'It's early-onset Parkinson's. The clue is in the title.'

'Well, what the hell does it mean?' Sara said belligerently.

Sara always became aggressive when she was feeling emotional. Molly sighed. 'It means that it's perfectly legitimate that I have it at this age. I'm in my thirties, but it can catch people in their twenties sometimes.'

'Bloody hell.' Sara rubbed her face. 'That's just . . . that's just shit, Molls.'

'It is a bit. But there are far worse things out there, believe me.'

'Yes, but this is still grim and it's happening to you

and it shouldn't be.' Uncharacteristically, Sara burst into tears.

Molly put her arm round Sara. She had become accustomed to placating others when she delivered her news. It was par for the course, however strong the other person might be. Molly decided it was simply down to the shock factor. It was just that no one knew what to say. They all thought it was terribly unfair – that often came across – but apart from that, what does one say to someone who basically cannot avoid physical and mental deterioration of a fairly embarrassing nature?

'Stop looking after me,' Sara hissed, wiping away her tears. 'I don't need cuddles, you do.' She put her arms around Molly's neck and hugged her. 'I'm really sorry, Molls. It's pants and honestly, I don't know what to say.' She took a breath. 'But you're right. There are worse things. It's obviously not a death sentence. Some of those symptoms sound horrible, but they are probably a way off, right?'

'Probably. Possibly. Maybe. But they could come sooner rather than later. Mine seems to be rather progressive.'

'Ok. Also pants.' Sara processed this information. 'But there are things that can be done. There must be. Drug trials, ways to manage those symptoms. Research.'

'Yes, yes and yes. All of those things.' Molly picked up a black stiletto. 'Crikey. These are seven hundred pounds. Three hundred and fifty pounds per shoe. That's some serious footwear.'

'How has Sam reacted to the news?' Sara asked.

Molly considered her answer. Sara had never been Sam's biggest fan for some reason. Which was strange because everyone warmed to Sam sooner or later. He was just one of those people who had such an amiable nature, most people found him utterly lovely.

But, oddly, Sara seemed to harbour some silly notion that Molly and Ed should have got together at some point. Lord only knew why. They had such a ridiculously chequered past, Molly wasn't sure at what point their timelines should have merged. Sara also knew that Ed had hurt her beyond measure in previous years, but she remained unfazed by that, stoically believing that real love hurt and that it was all part of the journey. Molly took that with a pinch of salt. Sara was dating but not in an actual relationship, hadn't been for a while. Molly wondered if she had perhaps forgotten what real love was and what that involved.

'Sam is upset, obviously, but he's being very practical.'

Sara raised an eyebrow briefly, but then shrugged. 'I guess maybe practical is good in this situation. You probably need someone being very matter-of-fact and grounded about this.'

'Yes,' Molly agreed. 'Practical is good.' But was it?

'And what about Ed?' Sara asked, picking up a red shoe. 'Would I ever wear red shoes?' She glanced at Molly.

'Red shoes, no knickers!' they said together, bursting into laughter. It was a childish joke.

'Red shoes go with lots of things,' Molly said reasonably. 'Red underwear, for starters.'

'Indeed, indeed.' Sara put the red shoe down. 'So. How did Ed react?'

Molly bit her lip. 'He was devastated. And I mean, really gutted. He cried, of course.'

'Of course.' Sara smiled. 'He's a girl in disguise. A very good disguise, to be fair. But anyway, we'll let him off of that one, this is emotive news. Surely even Sam blubbed a bit?'

'Er, yes.' Molly couldn't rightly remember, but she supposed Sam must have cried at some point over her news. He just wasn't a particularly emotional person – on the outside at least. Ed and Sam were complete opposites in that way. In many other ways too. Which had always baffled Molly, although she chose not to think about it too much.

'I think I'd rather have hugs and stuff than someone being practical,' Sara commented. 'But that's just me. And Sam being that way is probably for the best.'

'Listen, in Sam's defence, he's very stressed right now.' Molly picked a nude patent shoe up and shoved her foot into it. 'We're hosting this party soon to celebrate new business coming in, which is great, but we actually made a huge loss some months back. It shook him to the core. Sam is all about security. He can't cope when he feels unsafe, as if we might lose the business.'

Sara admired the shoe. 'You should buy those. Jimmy Choo? Cor, I would.' She picked up a suede boot. 'Fair enough about Sam. But this is separate, isn't it? You and the business? He should love you more than he loves the business. And this isn't about him. This is about you and what you need.'

'Of course. And it doesn't mean he loves the business more than he loves me.' Molly laughed, but there was an edge to her laughter. She heard it and caught herself. She always felt defensive about Sam when she was with

Sara. When a close friend disapproved of a husband on any level it was natural to want to boost him.

'I take your point,' Sara said quietly. 'And it is good that Sam is being sensible. After all, you must have people falling apart all around you right now.'

'Something like that. My poor dad took the news really hard.'

Molly didn't even want to think about the way her dad had reacted. He had literally clung to her for dear life. Molly understood. He had suffered one major loss; he saw this as another, even though she wasn't going anywhere anytime soon. Her brother Tom had also had a bit of a weep over the phone, but he had hidden it well. Molly had decided to take the overwhelming wave of tears from all and sundry as a positive thing. Presumably everyone was crying because they cared about her. That was one thing about having an illness like this. It was kind of like seeing one's funeral in advance; people's reactions were a clear affirmation of how they felt about her. Every cloud and all that.

'Actually, Ed has some serious stuff of his own going on,' Molly said, realising Sara didn't know anything about Ed's dramas. She gave her a rundown.

'Good God.' Sara was shocked. 'Poor Ed. He must have been reeling after all of that, let alone your diagnosis. I feel compelled to invite him out with us and get him drunk.'

'He'd love that. You know how much he likes girl time.'

'We'll get him out later, then. Cheer him up. So, anyway. Forgive me for asking this, but what symptoms do you actually have right now?' Sara said. 'If you don't mind talking about it, I really want to know.'

'Of course.'

Molly steeled herself and gave Sara an outline. This was the bit she hated. Everyone wanted to know what she was going through, how the changes were affecting her life. It was human nature, but Molly struggled with it every single time. It was basically a case of her listing everything she hated about the way her life was changing. But it was a question she would ask. Without fail. If Sara was going through this, if Ed was, she would ask that question. Molly would want to know everything. All the details – good, bad and ugly.

'Ok. Ok.' Sara stood up and started pacing restlessly around the shoe shop. 'Tremors. Stiffness. You're not sleeping very well. It's affecting your painting.' She stared at Molly. 'Oh God, I just want to hug you again.'

'Please don't. I'll cry and then I'll have to do my make-up again and I'll look awful. Honestly, you'd think I'd have taken to wearing waterproof mascara every day now, wouldn't you?'

'It probably would be the sensible thing to do, yes.' Sara sat down next to Molly again. 'I'm really sorry to drag all of those details out of you. I just want to understand what you're going through. I want to do anything I can to help you. Even if it's giving you the name of the best sleeping tablets on the market. Because I can confidently tell you that I do actually know which ones are the best.'

'That would be great. Thank you.'

Sara glanced at the Jimmy Choo on Molly's foot. 'So. Are you buying those?'

'They are . . .' Molly turned one over and gasped. 'Very expensive. How can I justify the cost of those?'

'Well.' Sara held one of the shoes up. 'They are nude patent. They'll go with everything. They are classically beautiful and will be a staple in your wardrobe for years to come. They are your size and you have silly, child-sized feet. So it's meant to be. You are meant to buy these shoes.'

Molly smiled. 'Excellent reasoning.'

'Aside from that, you have received some very shit news. And you are being very brave about it,' Sara said, with tears in her eyes, 'but I know deep down you are shitting it. Because I would be, anyone would be. And that's ok.' She sniffed. 'And so, you deserve these shoes. Because if you're going to do anything daft in front of people, you might as well be wearing beautiful shoes.'

Molly laughed and cried at the same time. 'Sold. I'm buying these shoes right now. There are too many amazing reasons to have them and I can't come up with a single reason to not buy them.'

'Good.' Sara gathered up their handbags. 'And just to warn you, I plan to make you spend an awful lot more money today. Because when the proverbial hits the fan, we go shopping. And we spend money. And we get drunk on champagne. By the way, I'm paying for those.'

'You are not.' Molly fished her purse out of her handbag.

'Too late.' Sara handed her card over to the girl behind the till. 'It's my pleasure. Because even though those things are superficial and they don't make all the difficult stuff go away, they put a plaster on. Just for a while. Ok?'

'They do. And thank you.' Molly kissed Sara on the cheek. 'One good thing about this bastard Parkinson's is that I have been made so aware of what great friendships I have. How many people around me care. I . . . I really appreciate that.'

'Ok, pack it in now. We sound like something out of a girls' film. I can only be slushy for so long. Let's find some shoes for me. The only condition is that they have to be incredibly, shockingly expensive, ok?'

'You don't have Parkinson's, you know.'

'I know.' Sara shrugged. 'Any excuse.'

Molly and Ed

'You can't leave, Ed. You can't leave me!'

'I have to, Mum. I can't let Molly down. I have an interview.'

'Oh, but you can let me down?' She sounded petulant.

Ed wished he had the rights a parent had with a child, but he wasn't sure slapping his mother around the legs was really going to cut it. She was drunk and in a mean mood.

Ed felt some tightness in his chest, akin to someone standing on it. He was trapped. He had no escape. Heading through the French windows into the sunlit garden, he took out a cigarette.

Florrie followed him, clutching a tumbler of vodka. Embarrassingly, she had tried to tell him it was water earlier. Ed found her clumsy attempts at deception excruciating. But he was also so well-acquainted with the characteristics of an alcoholic that he knew it was par

113

for the course. Lies, deceit, sly cunning were all to be expected. That and so much more.

'I tried to kill myself, Edison,' Florrie said in a wheedling tone. 'Remember? I took a whole bottle of pills and I drank some vodka.'

'Of course I remember,' Ed bit back. 'I came straight home when I got the call. And now I'm here. I'm looking after you twenty-four seven. I just want a few hours off to do an interview. That's all. I'm not abandoning you.' He felt a pang. He didn't want his mother to feel abandoned; they had both suffered enough of that over the years.

Yet Ed wasn't convinced his mother's suicide attempt had been genuine. Or a cry for help. She had taken the pills before staggering next door and flopping down in a spectacular fashion on their front porch. There had been a dramatic dash in an ambulance and an undignified stomach pump.

Ed had smoothed over the incident with his appalled neighbours by offering so many apologies and platitudes, he was of a mind to join the diplomatic corps. And he wouldn't dream of saying such a thing to his mother after the horrible episode, but he couldn't shake off the feeling that it had all been a calculated attempt to get him back home.

And that hadn't been the only 'attempt' at suicide. There had been several others since, and each one left Ed more on edge than before.

Obviously his mother was lonely. Ed understood that. But he also feared she had developed such a high level of dependency on him that he now had no choice but to perform the role of full-time carer. At the age of twenty-one.

Ed wearily leant against the wall. He felt like his shoulders could barely take the crushing weight of responsibility. He lit his cigarette and drew on it heavily.

'Mum. Have you thought any more about joining AA?'

'I don't need car breakdown cover, thank you.'

Ed ignored her stock petulant response. 'I realise that. You haven't driven a car in around a decade. I'm talking about Alcoholics Anonymous, as you well know.'

'What, my name's Florrie and I'm an alcoholic?' Florrie sneered. 'Pah. What's the point? I know I'm an alcoholic. Standing up and making a big song and dance about it isn't going to change that fact.'

'Of course not.' Ed felt so frustrated he could barely articulate what he wanted to say. 'Giving up booze is what's going to change that fact. You don't go to meetings to make speeches, you go to share your experiences with other people who are going through the same thing you are. You encourage each other and you all try and give up together.'

'*You all try and give up together*,' Florrie mimicked in a sing-song voice. 'Edison, may I remind you that I'm your mother. I'm a grown woman and I don't need you to tell me what to do or how to live my life.'

Ed drew hard on his cigarette. He wished his mother would remember that she was a grown woman when she had wet herself like a child for the umpteenth time. Of late, Ed had begun to detest her voice. She spoke with relative eloquence at times, but her voice was slurred and thick and it often turned whiny. He could barely remember what she sounded like when she was fully sober.

'And you know I don't like you smoking,' Florrie said sharply.

Ed snapped his lighter shut in disbelief. Was she really telling him off for smoking?

Florrie sat heavily on a garden bench. 'Anything could happen if you leave me. Anything. I might get all depressed again and . . . and . . . take more tablets.' She wrung her hands. 'I can't cope on my own. I can't.'

Ed irritably snapped his lighter open and shut. She looked wretched. He felt sorry for her. But he also felt suffocated. Was this really how his life was going to be from now on?

'Please don't leave me,' Florrie said, bursting into noisy sobs. 'I-I don't want to be alone. I can't cope. I can't.'

'I know, Mum. It's ok.' Ed threw his cigarette down. Kneeling down, he drew her into his arms. She smelt unclean and her hair scratched his face like aged candy floss. He bathed her every morning, but somehow she never remained fresh. Ed felt both repulsed and over-protective. In a rush, he gave in. 'I won't go, ok? I won't do the interview.'

'Thank you,' she wept into his shoulder. Then, abruptly, she pulled herself together and yanked her body out of his arms. 'I wish you didn't let me down so much, but now and again, you come up trumps.' She eyed him coldly.

Let her down so much? Ed stood up. Wow. He knew he shouldn't be surprised by anything that came out of his mother's mouth, but she still managed to flabbergast him on occasion.

Seconds later, he was glad he had moved out of her way. Florrie leant over and without warning, vomited all over her shoes. Just liquid, no solids.

Ed's nostrils registered the pungently sour smell and he stared out across the tiny patch of garden that was badly in need of a tidy up. He'd tackle it later, perhaps, once he had jet-washed the patio and put his mother's shoes in the washing machine. He had long since given up trying to clean anything of hers by hand. If she ruined an article of clothing, he simply went to a charity shop and purchased something similar. His mother had never noticed the difference.

Yes, the garden was the best project to get on with now that he wasn't attending the interview that could have changed his entire life for the better. And so, he was about to let Molly down again. As was his way.

Ed made sure his mother wasn't going to fall off the bench into the pool of vomit at her feet while he went inside, then prepared himself for a difficult, damaging phone call.

As he picked up the phone, Ed made a decision then and there not to have children of his own. He would never make a kid feel the way he did right now.

Now

'So. How are you feeling?'

Molly swallowed a sigh. Sam asked her this question a few hundred times a day now and it was beginning to get on her nerves. He cared, and she knew that, but it was tough to be reminded of her illness all day long.

Molly welcomed her painting time even more these days. Not because she wanted to paint – far from it. She constantly felt disappointed by her inability to capture her vision on the canvas. But at least being in her studio gave her some respite from Sam's caring. Molly had a chance to breathe and deal with her symptoms. And they were worsening. Not quite by the day, as such, but it was petrifying how much momentum they seemed to be gathering. The hand tremors were definitely on the increase. There were some balance issues. And as for her memory – Molly was quite frankly terrified about that aspect. She was doing a canny job of hiding some of the things she had forgotten, but she wasn't sure how long she could keep it up for.

'I'm absolutely fine, Sam. The same as I was when you asked me twenty minutes ago.'

'God, sorry. Was it really only that long ago?' Sam looked contrite. 'I'm just worried about you, Molly. But I've been reading up on this drug trial you might want to consider. It's had some really good results and it's using this new drug they developed in the States. It contains . . .'

Molly tuned out. She loved that Sam was so involved in her illness. It proved that he loved her. But she needed a break from it. It had only been a few weeks since the second opinion, but it felt like far longer.

Molly got up and walked slowly to the window. She walked more slowly now to avoid losing her balance in front of Sam. Molly didn't want him to become even more focused on how quickly she was deteriorating. She sometimes wondered if everything was speeding up because she barely had a second that didn't remind her of what was happening to her. Didn't people always say that whatever you focused upon caused you to create more of it in your life? Something like that, anyway.

Molly placed a hand on the cool window, watching the haze outside. It was sunny and hot and she had the urge to be in the sunshine, feel it nourishing her skin. She glanced at her bare arms. She hadn't suffered any of the skin changes that Parkinson's sometimes caused. Obviously she might later on, but for now, she seemed safe on that front. A small consolation.

Molly felt a shot of panic like a snake curling its venomous body through her chest. Why did some people get diagnosed with Parkinson's and manage not to notice too much difference in their lives? Why was the form she had so . . . so *angry*?

'Aren't you interested in this drug trial?' Sam asked, joining her at the window.

'Yes. Yes of course I am. It's just – it's just a lot to take in.' Molly forced a smile and put her hand on Sam's arm. 'Thank you for doing so much research. I really appreciate it.'

'It's the least I can do.' Sam frowned and looked down.

Molly saw her hand trembling on Sam's arm. Of course. She had rested it there for a moment; her arm often felt the need to move of its own accord in such a state. She snatched it away.

'Sorry. Sorry about that.'

'Don't be silly.' Sam turned away but not before Molly saw tears in his eyes. 'You can't help it. It's just hard, isn't it, this? You've always been so capable.'

'I'm still capable,' Molly protested. 'I can still do everything. More or less everything.' She was struggling to paint, but that was a personal thing. That wasn't a run of the mill, normal thing that most people did every day. It was a passion, something she loved. Which made it all the more hateful that she wasn't able to do it.

Sam nodded kindly. 'I know, Molly. You are. You're very capable still.' He turned away and went back to his desk.

Christ. It sometimes felt as though Molly was propping Sam up. He didn't mean to do it, she was sure of that, but it did often feel as though she kept having to step in and make him feel better.

He is too close to my illness, that's all it is, Molly told herself soothingly. And Sam was a problem solver. He wanted to solve her and fix her and he couldn't handle the fact that he couldn't. Molly wondered if Sam would be better equipped to deal with something like cancer. Cancer at least had some sort of plan. Chemo, perhaps, followed by surgery in some cases, with a course of radiation therapy to finish off. Sam would be reassured by such a plan. It had a beginning, a middle and a (hopefully) positive end. Whereas this – Parkinson's – didn't. It stretched out in front of them painfully – yawning widely into the future with no happy ending in sight.

Molly had reminded Sam that Michael J. Fox, who had famously brought early-onset Parkinson's into the limelight, had continued for many years before anyone worked out what was going on. And he still acted now. But Sam hadn't seemed particularly cheered by the Michael J. Fox story.

Bloody hell. If she wasn't careful, she may well need a good old blub herself. Which meant that she needed to see Ed. Ed always made her laugh. She sent him a quick text to see where he was. He replied, saying he was on the beach. Molly decided to join him.

'I need some fresh air,' she said to Sam as she swept past him. Kissing the top of his head, she noticed that he barely looked up. He was staring at something on his desk, but Molly didn't stop to find out if it was work or more Parkinson's stuff. She just needed some space from it all.

Molly and Ed

December 2000

'So, what do you think?'

Sam stood back and admired his handiwork.

'Beautiful. Really, Sam. That looks amazing.' Molly smiled. His work was astonishing. She was full of admiration for it and, by association, for him. 'You certainly have a flair for this stuff.'

'Well, I should do really. It is my company, after all. My offer is still on the table, by the way. You're incredibly talented. And you just scored a first. That will look fantastic on my books.'

'Ha. Well, thank you. I'll think about it.'

She really was thinking about it, had thought of nothing else since Sam had made the offer. Off the back of her part-time job and the first she had just pulled off, Sam had offered her a partnership. Not just a job – a partnership. It was an amazing offer. And they worked really well together. But the fact remained that Sam offered design services to companies. It was art, but it was commercial art. It wasn't painting, it wasn't the 'soul' of art, as Molly saw it. She was worried that instead of feeding her soul by taking up Sam's offer, she might be selling it instead.

Molly glanced around Sam's stylish, well-lit studio. There were some tasteful Christmas decorations strung up around the windows – silver and purple garlands with some funky, oversized baubles at carefully measured points. An aroma of croissants and freshly baked bread from the bakery downstairs permeated the air, making Molly's stomach rumble, and she realised what a pleasing space the studio was.

But her ambition in life was to be known as a great artist – the naïve-sounding plans she and Ed had outlined that starry night still stood fast, as far as she was concerned. Sam insisted that if she took up his offer she would still have time to paint, but Molly wasn't so sure. Sam's company was successful, fast-paced, growing rapidly. He had a solid portfolio, he had recently attracted several high-profile clients and he was courting many more. He worked long hours and Molly knew she'd end up doing the same. But at least she would be earning a salary.

Picking up a design board Sam had put together for Transdale, his biggest client, Molly remembered the conversation with Ed all those years ago. He was going to be a great writer, she a great artist. But Ed had dropped out of uni and he was still living at home doing whatever it was he did at home. Molly was fairly certain it didn't involve much novel-writing. She had tried to guess at what Ed might be up to, but she hadn't been able to fathom it. As for the novel-writing, Ed claimed to have an idea for a novel but if he was telling the truth about that, as ever, he was keeping it to himself.

'Have you sold any more paintings?' Sam asked, ignoring the phone that was ringing non-stop on his desk. He switched it to answer phone.

'Only one,' Molly admitted. 'That gallery down the road put my work up for a while and I had a flurry of sales, but it's all died a death now.'

'Surely not? Your paintings are incredible.'

'Yes. Apparently they are "beautiful", "haunting", "poignant" and "thought-provoking". But commercial? Not so much.'

Molly knew she sounded bitter. But it had been hard to take the lack of huge sales. It was early days, of course, but it felt like failure. She was mocking Ed for not writing his novel and what was she doing? Not much better, even though she was maybe trying harder to make things work.

'And what is it you're always saying about commercial, Sam? Commercial equals profitable, saleable and marketable.'

'Well.' Sam looked slightly uncomfortable with his own words being repeated back to him. 'I was talking about my company, Molly. Not your paintings.'

Molly shrugged. 'It's all the same thing though, isn't it? I achieved a first and it doesn't seem to mean much in the real world.'

'It's only been a few months,' Sam protested with a laugh. 'I'm not sure you can say your first counts for nothing just yet.'

Molly stared past him. Sam was probably right. But she felt disillusioned. This wasn't how she had imagined post-uni life to be. She felt as though something marvellous should have happened by now. She'd had all these dreams and aspirations, she had been so sure, so positive everything would work out the way she had planned. Molly wished she could speak to Ed about that, because she knew he would have a take on it. Probably a truthful one with a humorous angle, but regardless, it was something she would eventually wrap her head around.

But she and Ed had hardly spent any time together since he'd missed the interview her father had arranged. Not because she had been cold-shouldering him (Molly knew Ed well enough to know that something had been hideously wrong that day), but because Ed had quite simply been more or less missing in action ever since.

Sam glanced at her as they strolled to what Molly jokingly called 'the staff room' – the joke based on the fact that it resembled a high end, open plan loft space rather than the usual poky rooms allocated to workers. Sam only employed two other people – an accountant and another designer. He preferred to handle the bulk of the work himself. Ed described this as control-freakery, but Sam always said he liked getting his hands dirty. Molly suspected both had a point, but she wasn't sure why Ed, who was, except in jest, notoriously non-critical as a general rule, seemed so judgemental of Sam.

'Hey. Are you ok, Molly? You don't seem yourself today.'

Molly smiled. 'Yes, thanks. Just a bit tired.'

'Late night?'

'Something like that.' Molly curled up on a nearby

sofa and pulled a charcoal-grey cushion to her chest. 'I finished with Alex last night. Late last night. Not so much an acrimonious ending as a damp squib.'

'Really?' Sam fired up the coffee machine. 'I thought you were really happy with him. I mean, I know you were only with him for a few months but you seemed fairly into him.'

'Hmm. I just didn't feel that buzz. Do you know what I mean?'

'I certainly do.' Sam made two very frothy lattes. 'It's not the be all and end all, but it's pretty significant, that buzz. When it comes to lasting happiness.'

Molly frowned and chewed her thumbnail. 'Indeed. Ed always bangs on about this stuff but I tend to tell him to shut up.'

'How is Ed?' Sam placed their lattes on coasters and sat opposite her.

'Don't pretend to care,' Molly said caustically. She reached for her latte. 'I know you're not his biggest fan.'

'That's not fair,' Sam asserted. 'Ok, ok. If I'm being honest, I worry that he lets you down a bit. It just seems as though you're always checking on him and worrying about him and in return, he's somewhat flighty.'

'Flighty?' Molly raised her eyebrows. 'I can just see Ed's face if you ever told him that.'

Sam downed his latte and checked his phone. 'Seventeen messages. How can that be? Well, I'm not going to say it to his face, am I? I don't generally go around asking for my nose to be broken.'

'Ed wouldn't punch you. He's a pacifist.'

'Is that girl talk for wimp?'

'Good lord. You really are Ed-bashing today.'

Molly realised that the angst Ed harboured towards Sam was entirely mutual. She wasn't arrogant enough to think it had anything to do with her; she put it down to a personality clash.

Molly stole a glance at Sam. He really was quite lovely. Molly could . . . could what? See herself with him? Maybe. Maybe she could. She wasn't entirely sure how Sam felt about her. Well, not exactly. But Sam seemed like a real prospect. Serious. Not like Alex or the other idiots she'd been dating. Molly just had this slight reservation. She wasn't sure what it was and it was only minor. Maybe it was because Sam didn't like Ed. Shouldn't he like Ed just because Ed was her friend?

Molly smiled to herself. That was ridiculous. Sam was entitled to his opinion.

'I'm only joking about Ed.' Sam stood up. 'Listen. He's good-looking, clearly intelligent and I can't deny that he's extremely charming. But all I'm saying is, is he that great a friend to you?' He gave her a gentle smile. 'I just care about you, Molly. I don't want you to get hurt.'

'Well, Ed wouldn't dream of hurting me so you don't need to worry.'

Molly felt compelled to say that. Despite the fact that Ed had actually hurt her a great deal. More than anyone else she knew, in fact. She glanced at Sam. He really did have lovely eyes. A cool shade of green – unusual and rather mesmerising. Molly remembered telling Ed once that she had gone through a phase of being obsessed with guys with green eyes. Perhaps she wasn't quite out

127

of that phase. Or, more accurately, perhaps she could get back into that phase.

'Fair enough. I'm popping downstairs to the bakery. Would you like anything?'

'No, thanks. My bum is quite big enough as it is.'

Sam rolled his eyes in amusement, but said nothing as he strolled to the stairs. Molly immediately felt contrite. Sam was lovely. He was kind and generous and loyal and she had an inkling that Ed might be right – maybe Sam had a thing for her. She wasn't sure how she felt about that. She was attracted to him, for sure, and she had a feeling he would look after her. Put her first. Be faithful and caring and wonderful. He ticked many boxes.

How about that? She hadn't really properly thought about Sam that way. Maybe it was because she had finished with Alex, maybe she was allowing herself to see Sam as a possible relationship person.

Molly cast her eyes down as her mind refocused on Ed. Was it because she cared about him so much that he had the capacity to hurt her more than others did? Molly wasn't sure. She just knew she wanted to spend time with him – craved it, sometimes – and he was rarely around. He was the person she always wanted to turn to for advice. Even if his musings were useless, he always made her laugh. He always had a take on something. Ed was so opinionated about almost every aspect of life, he couldn't help but express his views. He even had a strong reaction to tomato ketchup. *The work of the Devil*, was his impassioned claim. And no one should ever get him started on the topic of Marmite.

Molly wandered to the window. Not turning up for

the interview her father had arranged had caused some serious damage to their friendship. Molly accepted that Ed must have had a good reason for missing such an incredible opportunity because he had *promised*. He had devoutly promised that he would attend the interview, that nothing, not even his 'responsibilities' at home, would keep him away. But Ed had proved himself to be predictably unpredictable. Right at the last minute he had bailed. Molly's father had fumed. But mostly he had been disappointed. Molly had ranted at Ed for a few seconds before she realised that he was utterly devastated. And one thing Molly could say about Ed was that he wasn't disingenuous. Enigmatic, yes, but he was not insincere by nature.

Molly turned as she heard Sam coming back upstairs.

'Now. Stop talking about your bum and have a slice of coffee cake. I know you can't resist it.'

Molly grinned. Ed had very strong thoughts on coffee being in cakes as well. Along with fruit being served with meat, and condiments of any kind, not just ketchup. But Sam was right. Coffee cake was indeed the cake she couldn't walk past in any shop.

'How incredibly sweet and thoughtful of you. I'll eat it on the go,' Molly said, helping herself to a slice. 'I have some errands to run.'

'Don't forget what I said about the partnership,' Sam called as she headed for the stairs. 'I want you on board.'

'I'm thinking about it,' she mumbled, dropping some cake as she left. 'I'm seriously thinking about it.' Maybe it was time to grow up. To stop living in cloud cuckoo land. To start earning a decent crust. And spending time with Sam wasn't exactly a hardship either.

Molly and Ed

December 2000

Molly staggered out of bed. What time was it? She grabbed her bedside clock. It was two o'clock in the morning. Whoever was banging on her door at this time of night was going to get an absolute mouthful. She shrugged her arms into her silky kimono, tugging it down over her bottom. She slept in just underwear, even in the winter. She got too hot in bed, even sleeping alone. Previous boyfriends had moaned excessively about this, comparing her to an extremely hot hot water bottle, but Molly couldn't do much about it. She decided she really should invest in one of those unflattering woolly dressing gowns for moments like this. Not that she had many moments like this.

Squinting through the spy hole in the door, Molly couldn't see anything. She tried again. Ah, right. Whoever it was had their head up against the spy hole. She made out a tuft of brown hair and the penny dropped. Ed.

'I'm about to open the door,' she called, giving him a chance to move. He either didn't hear her or he was incapable of moving because as soon as she opened the door, he fell through it.

'Molls!' He looked briefly delighted then landed face first in the carpet.

'Jesus! What the hell are you doing, you idiot?' Molly bent down and tried to pull Ed to his feet. Which was practically impossible. He wasn't remotely helping and he was more or less a dead weight.

'You're going to have to help me,' Molly wheezed as she tried again. 'Ed, you reek of booze.'

'I do *not*.' His voice was muffled, indignant. 'I am not even the teeniest bit drunk. I've had one Bailey's. With ice. And that is *all*.'

'Rubbish. You hate Bailey's. Good God, man. You weigh a ton.'

'Ooh! How *rude*.'

Ed started making noises like something out of a *Carry On* film; Molly half-expected him to call her matron. He finally made an effort and between them, he was on his feet again. In a manner of speaking.

'Nice Christmas tree,' Ed commented. 'And I do like those lights.'

'Thank you. We're not on a home makeover show, Ed. Right. You need some fresh air, some water and some coffee. To counter-balance that one Bailey's you've had.'

'Don't forget the ice.' Ed giggled then abruptly stopped. 'I feel a bit funny.'

Molly put his arm around her shoulder and half-carried him to the kitchen. Risking dropping Ed on the floor again, she grabbed the door and flung it open. 'Ed. You're walking up some stairs. Help me out here.'

He obliged, singing something nonsensical as he tripped up the wrought iron staircase. 'Oh. It's your roof terry. Terrace. Your roofy terrace.'

'Yes. Isn't it enchanting? Do have a seat.' She tipped him on to a pile of outdoor cushions. Luckily, it hadn't rained for a few days.

'It's fecking freezing, woman. Why have you brought me out here? What are you trying to do to me?' Ed stuck his bottom lip out.

'Sober you up.' Molly snapped the outside heater on, trying not to smile at how cute Ed looked. 'There you go. Stop being such a girl. What's happened?'

Shockingly, Ed suddenly started to cry. He put his face in his hands and Molly immediately knelt down. Ed cried at many things – soppy adverts and films, songs that moved him, and absolutely anything relating to children or animals. But he rarely burst into tears without a visual prompt. Horrified, she put her arms around him, feeling him soaking her shoulder through the thin silk of her kimono.

'Ed. Talk to me, please. What's happened? Something has happened.'

'My . . . my mother . . .' Ed could hardly talk for heaving. 'She's not well. She's really not well. I feel so guilty but I had to get away . . . had to . . . couldn't breathe . . . just couldn't do it. I needed a break . . . but I shouldn't be here . . .'

Molly pulled away so she could look at his face. 'Your mother? What's wrong with her?'

132

Ed shook his head and wiped his nose. 'I can't talk about it. I've said too much. Shhhh.' He put his finger to his lips and looked at her. Tried to look at her. But he kept going cross-eyed.

'What can't you talk about? It's me, Ed. Molly. Your friend. Who you apparently trust with your life.' Molly felt a stab of guilt. Was she taking advantage of him? He was drunk, he was rambling and she knew he might slip up and tell her something he didn't mean to. And she didn't want that. If he was going to confide in her, Molly would prefer it if he did it sober, so she was sure he properly trusted her. That he wanted to open up about whatever the hell was going on with his mother.

She was intrigued though. Ed didn't speak about his parents. He never mentioned his father. Molly wasn't sure if Ed's father was dead, if he had run off or what. But she assumed he wasn't around because Ed hadn't ever uttered a word about him. And there was obviously something wrong with his mother.

Ed rubbed his eyes. 'I'm so sorry, Molls. If I could tell anyone about it, I would tell you. I promise.'

'Don't worry about it, Ed. It's fine. You don't have to say anything.' Molly stood up, yanking the kimono down again. 'Now, behave. I'll be two seconds.'

'You have lovely legs,' Ed slurred. 'You have a lovely . . . everything.'

'Shut up.' Molly disappeared briefly and reappeared with a tray. 'Headache pills. Water – two pints. Hot coffee. Drink, please.'

Ed did as he was told, sitting up to take the tablets and to down a pint of water. Then he wrapped his hands around the mug of coffee and hunched over it. Molly joined him on the cushions.

'Feeling any better?'

'Marginally. Bit embarrassed. Did I just cry?'

'Only a little bit.'

Ed knew Molly would try and make him feel better, that she would perhaps gloss over his cringe-worthy moment with a reference to it being macho or something.

'Nothing to worry about,' Molly said breezily. 'They were very manly tears.'

'I'm sure,' Ed smiled. He loved that he knew her so well, that they seemed to mimic one another's minds on so many occasions. 'Manly tears. You are lovely, Molls.' He caught her eye and he knew she understood what he was getting at.

'I am, aren't I?' She stroked his fringe into place and Ed found it an oddly erotic gesture. Molly had beautiful hands – small and elegant. He fought the urge to hold one in his own.

'Now.' Molly looked him in the eye. 'What's all this about? Or rather, what are you doing here?'

Ed took a deep breath. He wanted to tell her. He wanted to tell her so much. He shuddered and hoped to God he wasn't going to start bawling again. It had all just been incredibly stressful recently. His mother had tried to kill herself again – twice – and with much more serious intentions than the previous attempts. At the hospital they had been keen to have her sectioned. Ed wished they had, even though such an idea made him feel guilty. He worried he simply couldn't look after his mother any more. Not on his own.

Earlier today she had got extremely drunk, despite him getting rid of every single drop of booze in the house, again, and she had turned nasty. They had had a tremendous row, one that involved her spitting at him once again that he had ruined her life, that he had destroyed her body. Towards the end, she had confused him with his father, slapping his face hard and calling him a philandering bastard.

Finding himself in his own version of ironic self-destruct, Ed had decided to get royally pissed, spectacularly so, in fact, which was fairly stupid in the circumstances. A drunk in charge of a drunk. Brilliant.

It was not one of his finest moves, but it had been the only way he could think of to escape. He didn't do drugs, had never touched them. Ed hated the idea of being out of control to that degree. He was daring but he didn't have a death wish. So booze had been the obvious – but extremely crass – choice. When he saw that his mother had passed out in bed, he had turned her on her side, put a bucket by her bed and made an executive decision that it would be better if he simply made himself scarce until he sobered up.

In truth, Ed needed sanctuary. And Molly, among many other things, was his sanctuary.

Gazing at Ed and seeing several emotions flitting across his face at once, Molly realised he needed to feel safe. That it was why he had turned up on her doorstep. He didn't need interrogation and accusations. She took pity on him.

'Let's look at the stars. They're amazing tonight. Let's be all pretentious and see if we can spot Cassiopeia.' She shuffled so she was sitting between his legs, leaning on his knees.

Ed moved closer and rested his chin on her shoulder.

'Can you see it, Ed?'

'What?'

'Cassiopeia.'

'Oh, right. No. I mean, yes. I only ever see that when I'm with you. Fact.'

'Is that so? Well. I thought you swotted up on this stuff to impress girls.'

'The only girl I ever want to impress is you.' Ed realised his comment had sounded somewhat serious. It had been truthful, but he hated making Molly feel uncomfortable. 'Anyway, you always know far more than I do about everything.'

'This is true,' Molly agreed, leaning back a bit. 'Not that you're ignorant, Edison. I'm just super-smart. Ha.'

Ed could hear her smiling. He loved that. The scent of her hair drifted under his nose. He had that sensation again, the one he always had when he was with Molly – excitement mixed with comfort and familiarity. She was the only person in the room he wanted to be with – even when there were hundreds of other people there.

God, but he was a bit wet sometimes. Ed decided it was time to put a few things right. He would do the same when he got home and spoke to his mother, but right now, it was Molly's turn.

'Listen, Molls. I just wanted to say that I'm sorry. About a lot of things. Especially when it comes to you.' As a natural reflex, Ed put his hands around her waist.

'Don't be silly.' Molly squeezed his knee. She wasn't

sure how she felt about his hands on her waist. It was a tender gesture. And when Ed went all tender on her, she tended to unravel slightly. Change the subject, that was the best way to deflect such a thing. 'I've decided to take that job with Sam, by the way. For the time being. I mean, I still want to paint, but I need to earn some money, you know?'

Ed let out a breath. He knew what Molly meant about earning money. He needed to do the same. He was writing every day, albeit in the early hours of the morning when his mother had passed out. He was writing a novel. A novel he didn't want to tell Molly about yet. And Ed had a good feeling about it. He thought it might actually be worth something. But in the meantime, he wasn't earning any money. His mother seemed to have a small, mysterious income – he wondered if his father perhaps sent money she didn't want to talk about – but it was barely enough. If he'd been able to get a good job with a newspaper or something he might have been able to afford to pay for a decent nurse to look after his mother twenty-four seven. But obviously, she had put paid to that.

Ed frowned. He was bothered by Molly's admission that she was going to work for Sam. It made him feel sick. Right down in the pit of his stomach. Because Sam wanted Molly. Ed sensed it. He knew it and he hated it.

Years later, Ed would wonder if his trepidation about Sam taking Molly away from him prompted his next move – a knee-jerk reaction. Years after that, however, Ed acknowledged ruefully that Sam was a mere fraction of the reason behind what happened that night.

'Good for you, Molly,' he said finally, realising he had been silent for a while. 'That sounds eminently sensible.'

Molly turned and gave him a scathing look. 'Oh piss off. You know I hate it when you call me sensible. It makes me sound properly boring and sad and I don't like it one bit.'

'You can't be properly boring when you're feisty and ace,' Ed returned. 'In fact you're verging on strident. Which can't ever be boring, if you think about it.'

'Strident,' Molly tutted. 'Hang on; this will finish you off – I'm moving, too. Next week. Closer to Sam's office to cut down on the commute.'

Ed moodily watched the twinkling lights of the city over Molly's shoulder. He liked Molly's flat. It had character, and it was miles away from Sam's office. Not that he wanted Molly to waste time travelling, but he did detest the idea of Sam being right there on Molly's doorstep since he also lived literally minutes from his office.

Ed made a pact with himself then and there to visit Molly as much as he could when she started working with Sam full-time. He would turn up unannounced with her favourite lunch. Sod that, he would *cook* her lunch – Molly loved it when he cooked for her. Not that he did it that often, but he cooked all the time at home, mostly for himself. Alcoholics often waved food aside for booze, apart from breakfast, which tended to be a carb fest.

Ed focused his mind again and changed the subject back to what he'd been saying before. He was searching for accurate thoughts but in his befuddled, still drunken state, he knew he had something he needed to say.

'Look. I'm not being silly about all of this, you know.

I really am fed up with letting you down. With not being able to be honest with you. You're too important to me to be treated this way.'

'Ed.' Molly sounded upset but she was facing the other way again. She squeezed his hand. 'You don't need to feel that way. I'm your friend. I'm glad I'm important to you – I had bloody well better be, because you fill my mind far more than you should.'

'I do?'

She nudged his knee. 'Because I worry about you constantly.'

'Oh.' Not what he'd been hoping for.

Molly's curls moved momentarily as she registered his impatience at her comment. 'Look, I just hate the thought of you constantly beating yourself up about all this stuff. Please stop.'

Without thinking, Ed dropped a kiss on to Molly's bare shoulder. There was a minute gap where her kimono had slipped away from her, but he found it. 'Ok, Molls. I'll try.' He stared at the stars. The sky was suitably inky but there were a few clouds masking the beauty of the stars. 'Why is it that when I'm with you, I always feel calm; I always feel right? I can't fathom it. But it's true. It's just something that's lodged in me in the same way the stars perennially stud the sky.'

Molly turned. 'That was beautiful. Drink turns you into a poet, Ed.'

'Does it?' Ed gazed at her, his eyes roaming over her exquisite features. Those eyes, that quirky mouth. 'I'm pretty sober now, as it happens. Maybe I have some talent as a writer, after all.'

'Of course you do.' She met his eyes earnestly. 'You write like a dream. And you speak like a poet – your eloquence is one of the things I love most about you. Your words often reduce me to a wibbly plate of jelly.' She laughed. 'Now, *that*, my friend, is the very personification of eloquence.'

Ed reached out and touched a curl. His heart appeared to be thumping erratically in his chest. 'I meant every word of that, Molly. And I mean every word of this.' He hesitated, but only for a second. He knew how he felt. He had known for a very long time.

'I will never tire of drinking you in. Your face, your hair, your scent, your body, your soul. You are, without a shadow of a doubt, the most beautiful person I know. Both inside and out. But it's the inside that matters the most. Inside, you radiate brilliance. Like . . . like those stars we're always looking at.'

'Careful.' Molly's tone was light but she looked shell-shocked. 'You sound as though you have feelings . . .'

'Feelings? I've always had feelings. For you, at any rate.'

Molly turned to face him more squarely. 'Have you now? And what are they exactly, Ed?' Her tone sounded mocking but it was a defensive trait Ed was familiar with.

'I can't . . . I can't really describe what I feel for you.' Ed frowned. Inadequate. He was a writer, for fuck's sakes. He searched and stumbled for the words he knew were somewhere inside him.

'What I . . . what I feel for you, Molly, is something intense. It's a feeling I carry with me, endlessly. You're

140

in my thoughts and in my mind. In my heart, in fact. It's like wherever I am, you're with me. Do you see? You're with me. Beside me, inside me, next to me.'

Molly's eyes didn't leave his. She wasn't smiling, but her breath had quickened.

Ed found he couldn't stop talking. It was like that night they first met when he had rambled on incessantly about Oscar Wilde and William Shakespeare and his stupid plans to become a world-famous writer. Except that this time he appeared to be on the verge of exposing his soul.

'I mean, I can't look at anything without thinking, "I wonder what Molly would think of that? Would she like it? Would she make a joke?" I see everything with my eyes and then with yours. I . . . I don't even really understand that myself.' He dipped his face, breaking the eye contact.

Molly paused, considering her words. 'I feel that,' she said, her voice breaking. 'I feel that . . . the way you do. I didn't realise it, but I do it too. I wonder what you will think about something and I can sometimes hear an echo of you, laughing or making a sarcastic comment. It's . . . it's because we're so close. Isn't it? That's what it is.'

'Is it?'

Ed raised his chin. Her mouth was so close to his. So close. If he just leant forwards, their faces would touch. His mouth would find hers. They would kiss. Their mouths would mould together in perfect symmetry, the way they had before. They would taste one another, reach for one another, fall into one another . . .

Molly's breath was ragged, her chest rising and falling rapidly. 'What else can it be, Ed? What else?'

He gazed at her. Shook his head.

'I feel it here,' Molly said, pointing at her chest. 'What can that be?'

'Heartburn?' Ed offered, feeling his own chest responding in kind. 'Indigestion? Or is that usually in the stomach?'

'I have no idea.'

'Thing is, I feel that too. It's like an ache. Right here in my chest cavity.'

'The chest cavity. That contains the heart, I believe.'

'So it does. Well, that's it then.' Ed put a hand on Molly's cheek. 'It's my goddamned heart. It feels something for you.'

'Well. If that's the case, I'm afraid I have to do this.'

Molly kissed him. Hard. Then softly. She sank her hands into his hair and snogged him. Ed let out a groan. God, the taste of her mouth. The feel of her face against his. He yanked her towards him and she put her legs over his. Their groins met and Ed placed one hand in the small of Molly's back, pulling her mouth to his. He held her neck possessively, hungrily kissing her. They kissed. And kissed. Just for the sake of it. Just because it felt amazing.

Ed clasped Molly and turned her over on to her back. Her kimono fell partly open and Ed caught his breath. She wore black underwear. Simple, classic, with some lace edging. God, but she was beautiful. He wanted her, all of her. Ed had a feeling that even if he was able to have all of Molly, it would never be enough. He wanted to own her. And for the first time in his life, he wanted someone to own him back.

'I'm going to kiss every inch of you,' he told her carefully. His voice sounded strange to his ears but he was sober. 'Every inch. I am going to adore and inhale your skin from every angle until you can't take it any more.'

Molly gave him a half smile, her hand trailing down his arm. 'Gosh.' Oddly brazen but blushing furiously, she undid her kimono and opened it properly for him.

'Shit, Molls. I've lost my train of thought.' Ed couldn't take his eyes off her. 'But . . . but I will do whatever I can to make you gasp. With my hands and my mouth and . . . and . . . with everything I have in me.'

Molly reached for him. She held his mouth close to hers. 'Ed. If you do all of that glorious stuff, I . . . I have a feeling that once you've finished, I will be incapable of speech. So I'll ask you now. When you have done all of that, will you please, please, for the love of God, with everything you have, make me lose myself in you? Until I'm in a state of complete erotic and romantic disrepair.'

It was Ed's turn to catch his breath. 'I thought I was the poet around here.' He put a hand on her waist and leant forward to kiss her smooth, flat stomach. 'You will never, never have to ask me that twice, Molly. And I fear it is I who will be in a state of erotic and romantic disrepair.'

Now

'Thank you, yes, it's been an exceptionally good year. Help yourself to a drink . . .' Sam smiled and greeted another guest.

'You're very convincing,' Molly said in his ear as she slipped her arm through his.

Sam grimaced and squeezed her hand. 'I wish we hadn't gone ahead with this party. But we had to, didn't we? Cancelling it would have looked bad, considering the people we've invited.'

'Very true. And smoke and mirrors are always good.' Molly smiled brightly at a client. 'Lovely to see you. Do have some champagne. And it was only one loss, Sam. We're not on our knees or anything.'

'I know that, Molly.' Sam accepted a drink from a waiter. 'It's just that I've built this company up from scratch, from absolutely nothing. That was a large loss. Only the one, but it was significant. It's seriously damaged our five-year plan.'

Molly nodded. 'I know. I'm sorry. I was trying to see the positive side of it.'

Sam sighed. 'And so you should. You're right to do that as well. I just can't help worrying about money, Molly. It's the way I am.'

Molly sipped her champagne. It was true that Sam had always been concerned about money. She had put him in a box labelled 'workaholic' from day one, but it wasn't strictly true. Sam came from a poor background. An only child to parents who constantly lived on the breadline, Sam had always had to fight for everything. He had experienced real hunger and deprivation as a child and as a result, he simply couldn't handle his personal finances taking a hit. Or being at a level he felt was unacceptable in terms of savings and investments. Sam wasn't stingy by any means, it was all about security.

Molly just wished he could be more balanced about it. He spent so much time worrying about losing money that he rarely seemed to enjoy the fact that he had a huge amount of it already. He didn't buy flashy cars, they didn't ever go on holiday and they lived a fairly frugal existence. Molly had always thought it was a shame, but it was just the way Sam was and the way he always had been.

'Nice of Ed to lend us his garden for the afternoon,' Molly commented, mostly to change the subject.

'Yes.' Sam frowned. 'Surely he has a gardener or something? I can't imagine Ed on his hands and knees with a trowel somehow.'

'I have no idea. He's never been green-fingered in the past, but you never know . . .'

'Hmm.' Sam looked sceptical.

Molly could see why. Ed's garden really had come into its own recently. Always pretty, it appeared to have had a complete overhaul, with nicely shaped flower beds stuffed full of flowers, the colours artfully complementing one another. There were magnolia trees in random places across the lawn and every area had been tended to. It was unlikely Ed had managed this himself, but Molly felt compelled to defend him. She wasn't sure how long the garden would look nice for, mind. Ed's chocolate Lab, Fingal, was running amok, chasing imaginary rabbits, digging up imaginary bones and generally causing havoc.

Sam squared his shoulders. 'Right. I'm off to do some more of that smoke and mirror stuff you were talking about.'

'Ok. I'll do some more after I've had a quick chat with my dad.' Molly saw her father arriving and joined him at the back gate.

'Hey. I'm so glad you came. Lovely day for it.'

John gripped her in a warm hug. 'It certainly is.' He pulled back and looked into her eyes. And didn't ask how she was. He didn't need to because she could see how much he cared for her just with a glance. 'So, the garden looks lovely, Molly. I assume Ed has a gardener?'

'Let's go and find him and ask, shall we? Everyone seems to want to know about Ed's garden and who looks after it.'

Molly was amused, but she was also grateful not to be talking about her illness for once. And to be fair, Ed's garden did look astonishingly beautiful.

'Ed!' She called him over. 'Now, everyone wants to know about your garden. As in, who looks after it. I defended you to Sam and pretended that you might have done it yourself.'

'Hello, John. Great to see you.' Ed shook John's hand and pulled a face. 'Me, do the garden? As if, Molls. You know I kill most living things without even trying. Of course I have a gardener. Sheesh. I wouldn't have even suggested you having your party here if my chap hadn't been round twice a week over the past month.' He put his mouth to Molly's ear. 'He's an old guy, more or less does it because he loves it, wouldn't be able to stomach the expense right now otherwise.'

Molly winced. Was everyone worrying about money at the moment? 'Dad, will you have some champagne?'

'Don't mind if I do,' John said, accepting a glass.

'So, your money woes,' Molly said, turning back to Ed. 'I can't believe it. Everything else you and Boyd invested in turned to gold, didn't it?'

'Pretty much.' They all strolled towards a wooden bench that sat in a most likely ill-advised spot beneath a crab apple tree. 'Just one of those things, I guess. Bad luck. Very bad luck. Don't worry about me though; I'll be ok.' Ed gestured for Molly and John to sit down. He scrutinised Molly. She looked pale and a bit thin. 'Do you know what might do you good, Molly? A holiday. A really long holiday. Somewhere amazing. With lots of sunshine. Nourishes the soul, you know.'

'God, I would love a holiday,' Molly groaned. 'But you know Sam. He . . . he won't take the time off work.' She could hardly say Sam wouldn't dream of a holiday right now because of the money issue. She had promised him she would keep it under wraps from everyone.

'I think Ed is absolutely right,' John said. 'A holiday would do you the world of good right now, Molly. Some sunshine and relaxation. Some time to process what's going on.' He jumped as an apple fell precariously close to him. 'And more to the point, it would do you good to be away from here. Sometimes a change is as good as a rest, as they say.'

'Sam really won't do that at the moment,' Molly said, her heart sinking. If her father and Ed talked about a holiday any more, she was worried she might cry. A holiday would be wonderful. To feel sunshine on her skin, a warm breeze. To do nothing but read a book and decide what cocktail to have. Britain was actually in the throes of a fairly good summer, but it was nothing like the sunshine that could be experienced abroad.

Ed looked perplexed. 'Surely Sam can take a few weeks off work! For you . . . to help you . . .'

Molly didn't know what to say. Sam just wasn't into holidays. He might possibly take the time off work but he wouldn't spend money like that right now. Not when he was so stressed about it.

Ed glanced at Molly's hand. She looked down at it and saw that it was trembling slightly. All on its own. Mortifying. Molly felt her cheeks colour slightly. About to snatch it away, she was moved when Ed quickly scooped her hand up. Drawing it to his mouth, he tenderly kissed it, then discreetly held it by his side until it stopped trembling. And only then did he let go.

Molly swallowed and stared at him gratefully.

Ed shook his head imperceptibly.

'Now. I don't know about you, John, but I could really do with another drink. What can I get you? I have a very nice pear cider indoors.'

'That would be great, thanks,' John said. 'Champagne makes me gassy.'

'Me too,' Ed smiled. 'I'll be back in a minute.'

John studied Molly thoughtfully. 'Now, is the problem Sam taking time off work or is it a money thing?'

Molly couldn't help laughing. 'Am I that transparent, Dad? I was trying to keep that whole money thing under wraps for Sam's sake.'

John shrugged. 'I know you. Sometimes it's not what you say, it's what you don't say.'

'I honestly don't think he'd take the time off anyway.'

'Right. Well, I'm going to take one of his excuses away. I'm paying for a really big, expensive holiday for the pair of you.' John's mouth set resolutely. 'And I'm not taking no for an answer. I made a packet selling the house, Molly. I'm giving some to Sam for a holiday.'

Molly put her arm around her father's shoulder. 'You make me want to cry, Dad. You're so sweet.'

'I'm not. I'm a grumpy old man who just wants to do something nice for his daughter.' John dropped a kiss on to Molly's head. 'You're my girl,' he added gruffly. 'Do anything for you, I would.'

Molly was lost for words. This illness seemed to be bringing out the best in everyone else, even if it was bringing out the worst in her. She gripped her hand to stop it shaking involuntarily again and closed her eyes. God. And this was just the tip of the iceberg.

'Good lord. Is that—?' Molly frowned. No, surely not. She hadn't seen her for years.

Across the lawn, Ed was striding up to the new guest. 'Jody?'

'Hi, Ed.' Jody came through the back gate. 'Hope it's ok to come round but there was no answer at the front door . . .' Seeing all the people milling around Ed's garden, Jody faltered. Then blushed. 'You're having a party. I'm so sorry.'

'Don't be daft.' Ed went straight over to her and kissed her warmly on both cheeks. 'Come on in. It's not actually my party, it's Molly and Sam's . . .'

Jody looked completely different to how she had when he had last seen her some – what, seven years ago? Her hair was shorter, her face more gaunt. She looked all American-ised. Or was it Canadian-ised? Ed couldn't quite remember where she had taken a job all those years ago; he just knew she had disappeared off the face of the earth to follow her dream and no one had really heard from her since, not even Molly.

'And who's this?' Ed caught sight of someone peeking out from behind Jody's skirt.

'This . . . this is Jake,' Jody mumbled.

Ed smiled at the child. He was probably about six. Or seven – maybe nine. Or ten, even. Ed was always vague about the age of children, having put his foot in it with various friends in the past. Some kids resembled teenagers and turned out to be under ten; others looked fresh-faced and child-like and were far older than expected. Ed had absolutely no idea how old Boyd's kids were, so he didn't ever reference their ages.

150

This Jake was one nice-looking kid, Ed decided. Big, innocent brown eyes, tufty brown hair. Slight in frame, but fairly tall.

'Is he your son?' Ed asked. Silly question. He must be. Jody would hardly be gallivanting around with some other person's child.

Jody put her arm around the boy's shoulders. 'Yes.'

'Charmed, I'm sure,' Ed said. 'And how old are you, Jake?'

Jake lifted timid eyes to meet Ed's. 'I'm six. And a bit.'

'Six and a bit.' Ed beamed. 'Excellent. I do love the way children are so precise about their ages. Now, can I get you both a drink? Lordy, not sure what I have in the way of kiddie drinks, but I might be able to rustle up a pineapple juice. Or a coke. Anything that comes under the banner of mixer.'

'That would be lovely, thank you.' Jody looked sheepish. 'I can't apologise enough for barging in like this.'

'Stop saying sorry. Molly, look who it is.' Ed beckoned Molly over. 'It's only Jody. And her son Jake.'

Molly was already walking over. 'Jody! It's been too long. How are you?' She hugged her old housemate and glanced at Jake. 'And a son! Wow. Hello, Jake. Lovely to meet you.' Molly put her hand out for a formal shake.

'You're pretty,' Jake said, going red when he shook her hand.

'Why, thank you. Your mum has taught you some beautiful manners.' Molly met Jody's eyes. 'Did Jake's dad come too?'

'Er, no.' Jody accepted a glass of champagne from Ed.

'Just a sip. I'm driving. No, I'm here alone. I mean, just with Jake.'

'For a fleeting visit or a long one?' Ed asked, handing Jake a glass of coke. 'That'll put hairs on your chest. Or send you hyper, one of the two.'

Jody shrugged. 'I'm not sure yet. It all depends.'

'On job stuff?' Molly asked with a smile. Without thinking, she reached out to ruffle Jake's hair and, oddly, he let her. He really was a cute kid.

'On . . . a few things.'

Ed raised his eyebrows, but nothing more was said.

Jody raised her glass. 'Well. Cheers. It's lovely to see you both.'

'And you,' Molly and Ed said together.

As Ed and Jody started chatting about Jody's life in Canada, Molly stole a discreet glance at Jake. That was one good-looking, charming little boy. Molly's stomach shifted a fraction. No, that was insane. And frankly, impossible. She met Ed's eye briefly and looked away. What was she thinking? It must be the illness.

Ed

December 2000 (The morning after the night before)
Ed opened his eyes sleepily. Felt a warm body draped around his. Molly. He opened his eyes properly. *Molly.* The night flashed before him like a movie replay. An explicit one. An achingly romantic one. The kissing on the roof terrace, under the stars. The exquisite, lengthy exploration of each other's bodies. The languid removal of clothes that had become frantic and passionate. The nakedness. The incredible, *incredible* sex. Which had taken place on the roof terrace, in the kitchen and in Molly's bedroom. On cushions, up against the wall, on the floor, rolling around in the bed. Gasps and sighs, whispered ramblings, yelps and swearing. It had been fun and funny and sexy. It had been serious. Achingly tender. Indescribably sensual. Ed had been floored, literally and figuratively. And that had never happened to him before. Ever.

He carefully turned on to his side, propping himself

up on his elbow to get a proper look at Molly. Her arms, now that he had extricated himself, were wrapped around her pillow for dear life and her face was scrunched into it. Her blond curls were obscuring her eyes, but Ed knew they were shut; her breathing was deep and regular. He trailed a finger down her arm gently, needing to feel her skin again. Yes. This felt right. Molly felt right.

Ed swung his legs out of the bed and placed his feet on the floor. He felt the need to ground himself, for some reason. He didn't know why, because he felt blissed out, complete. Then he remembered something from last night – the phone ringing relentlessly. Molly had whispered to him ignore it, not to worry, and conscious of the last time he had run out on such proceedings, Ed had done just that. He had ignored the calls, told himself that Molly's phone ringing on and off all night was nothing to do with him.

He pulled his boxers and jumper on and padded to the kitchen. He was tempted to get Molly's coffee machine working but he decided against it on the basis of noise. Staring at a beautiful print of a lotus flower hanging on the wall, he made himself a cup of instant and took it up to the roof terrace. They'd left the heater on all night. About to turn it off, Ed realised it was freezing and instead, he pulled one of Molly's fold-up chairs in front of the heater and sat down.

The roof terrace had an air of innocence about it this morning. The pile of cushions looked artfully arranged rather than bearing evidence of one of the most earth-shattering experiences Ed had encountered in his life. He cradled his coffee cup. He felt different. Something had happened to him. Last night had changed him. He put his coffee cup down and stared out across the city.

What the hell was going on? He had this feeling in the pit of his stomach. It was a confusing blend of hot and cold. The hot sensation felt oddly heavenly. Like real happiness exploding inside. Like one of those shooting stars he and Molly were always banging on about. It was tangible. It was the kind of euphoria Ed often felt around Molly. But the other thing, the coldness, felt very much like . . . like what? Like fear? Ed normally laughed in the face of fear. But this was . . . he was . . . was he . . .? Oh fuck. Ed almost dropped his coffee cup.

He was in love with her! He was in love with Molly. Had been for as long as he could remember, if he was going to be brutally frank. And now they had slept together. And it had been gorgeous. He was done for. Utterly done for.

'Edison. How are you this fine morning?'

Ed turned. Molly had the bed sheet wrapped around her and Ed immediately felt a kick in the groin. 'Chilly, madam. Yourself?'

'Fine and dandy.' She looked at him and screwed her nose up. 'Actually, I feel a bit strange. I mean, we're friends and now we've done the dirty. Do I come and hug you? Give you a kiss?'

'I would suggest that a massive kiss might be in order. But . . . do you have morning breath?' He looked at her sternly. 'Because if you do, I'm outta here.'

'Aah, shut it.' She shuffled towards him in the bed sheet and fell into his arms. 'God, how corny. Come on, give me that mouth.' She gave him a juicy kiss.

155

Ed kissed her back and fell for her all over again. The terror in his gut subsided. He had nothing to be scared of. This was the best thing that had ever happened to him.

'This is right,' he mumbled against her ear. 'This is so, so right.'

She grinned and looked up at him. 'Thank fuck for that. I had this horrible, niggly feeling you might have run out on me.'

Ed felt hurt, but he knew Molly wasn't being nasty. He hardly had a good track record. But he would never run out on her. Never. Why on earth would he do such a thing? He wanted to be near her – he had always wanted to be near her – and now he knew he wouldn't be able to stay away.

Molly slid her arms around his waist. 'Sorry, Ed. It's just that . . . it's . . . maybe it's what you do when you get scared. And this . . . I don't know. I figured it might have scared the living shit out of you.'

'How *dare* you.' Ed pulled an indignant expression then laughed. 'God, you know me so well. Ok, I'll admit to a wobble. Just for a few seconds.'

'Aha! See. You are nothing if not predictable, my friend.'

Ed pulled her closer and positioned his mouth against hers. 'I'm still here, aren't I?'

'That you are.'

'You are always where I want to be, Molly. You have to believe that.'

Molly broke into a smile. The kind that knocked Ed sideways. 'I think I actually do believe you. Gosh. I'm so incredibly happy.'

'Me too.'

She kissed him again.

'Hey, what's that lotus flower print in the kitchen? I haven't seen it before.'

'The print? Gorgeous, isn't it? I just like lotus flowers. I thought it could be my signature thing.' Molly shrugged. 'Company logo. Focus of my paintings. Tattoo on my backside maybe.'

'Cor. I'm liking the sound of that. I can't keep my hands off your backside as it is but if you have a tattoo there . . . phew . . .'

'Perv. Hey, have you phoned home yet?'

'God. No.'

Ed felt stricken. Guilty. He and his mother had parted on terrible terms last night. The awful row, the things that had been said. Since leaving uni, Ed had hardly spent a night away from home. He breathed in some air. He enjoyed the feeling of liberation, but the suffocating weight of responsibility was never far away.

'Phone home. You'll feel better.' Molly picked his coffee up and took a swig. 'Good lord.' She pulled a face. 'This tastes like syrup. I can't even taste the coffee for the sugar . . .'

'Whinge, whinge, moan, moan . . .' Ed headed inside to make his phone call. It rang for ages. Then someone answered it. Someone who wasn't his mother. Ed's heart plummeted through his body. He listened. He felt screaming pain in his chest then numbness. Then screaming pain again. He nodded, not able to answer, then he carefully put the phone down.

'Ed?' Molly was halfway down the stairs in her bed

sheet, clutching something in her hands. 'What's going on? You're all pale and weird.'

Ed started to shake. 'I have to go. Where . . . where are my jeans please?'

'Here.' She handed them over, looking anxious. 'Can I do anything?'

'No. I don't know. Probably not.' Ed shoved his feet into his shoes without bothering to find his socks. He grabbed his jacket. He couldn't look at Molly. Those phone calls – he had been wrong to ignore them. And Molly had been wrong to stop him from taking them. 'I'll call you, ok? I'll call you.' He turned and left.

Molly stared after him and twisted the sheet in her hands. She had no idea at that moment that she wouldn't clap eyes on Ed again for at least six months.

Now

Molly stretched out on her sun lounger. What a glorious feeling. Sunshine on her skin. Complete relaxation. Cocktails on tap. Mexico. It was a gift. Quite literally. From her father. She knew it, but Sam didn't know she knew that her father had paid for it. That was the arrangement. Molly wouldn't let on and Sam would simply act as though he had decided to do this off his own back.

Molly turned to Sam's lounger. He had gone again – maybe for a walk. Sam couldn't seem to sit still for more than five minutes. She hadn't even heard him get up. Perhaps she had dozed off for a minute.

Molly rolled over on to her front. She was wearing a purple bikini that had fitted her when she had bought it a year ago, but it wasn't terribly flattering now that she had got so thin. Molly hoped she'd start putting weight on again soon; she was certainly eating enough.

At least Sam had agreed to the break, even if he hadn't paid for it. He had seen how much she had been struggling with her diagnosis and how tired she was and he had booked Mexico. Somewhere she had always wanted to visit because Ed had talked about it so glowingly. And it was certainly living up to expectations.

They had explored the world of the ancient Maya at Chichen Itza, the most well-known of the Yucatán Maya archaeological sites and one of the Seven Wonders of the World. They had wandered around tall temples looking in awe at the sculpted faces of the Mayan gods, and they had ended up on Cozumel, an island with a history going back to the Mayan civilisation. Molly had been amazed at the archaeological ruins, the remnants of small pyramids and the quaint little villages that were dotted around the main sites. It also boasted beautiful beaches with turquoise seas. Molly had been keen to spend a bit more time there, but Sam wanted to get back to the hotel because he had some work to follow up on.

Molly sipped her mojito. She felt different away from home. Better. There was something incredible about being able to kick back and just – be. Was that the expression? Being away from home had given her the opportunity to step back from her disease (she hated calling it that) and she felt almost detached from it.

Not that any of her symptoms had changed, obviously. In fact, she was perhaps noticing them more in such opulent, lush surroundings. But somehow being away from home, a place Molly associated so acutely with her illness, had given her a level of peace. Not being able to sleep at home was one thing; Molly tended to head downstairs for a cup of tea and some very strange television programmes (who knew that such things were transmitted at 4 a.m.?) but here, she was more inclined to go and sit on the balcony so as not to wake Sam up. She had been reading more as a result – books about painting, mostly. Which she found oddly soothing. She was still struggling to paint with the combination of tremors and stiffening in her hands (she had even tried painting with her left hand – disastrous) but reading about it still kept her connected to the thing she loved.

'Would you like another cocktail, madam?'

Molly looked up and smiled at the pretty waitress. Ed's eyes would have been popping out of his head if he could've seen her. 'I don't mind if I do, thank you.'

Molly thought about Ed. They had been in touch almost daily for the past three weeks of her holiday, and they had seen each other every few days while she had still been in England.

'There you are!' she said as Sam appeared. 'I didn't hear you get up.'

'I know.' He sat down on his lounger and stroked her arm. 'You've got an amazing colour going on.'

'I never realised I would tan like this,' Molly said, glancing down at herself. 'You've caught the sun a bit too.'

She glanced at him. Sam looked good. Handsome, suave and fairly chilled. Sam didn't really do 'casual', as a rule – he was far more at home in a suit; he wore them to the office every day, even at the weekend – but he was wearing a pair of plain navy shorts and a white shirt. Which for Sam was casual and then some.

'Still spending a bit too much time at the laptop,' Sam said rather guiltily. 'Sorry, Molly. I can switch off; I just need to make sure everything is straight at home.'

Molly shook her head. 'I don't mind. I'm just happy we're here.' In truth, she would prefer it if Sam could step away from his laptop more. But she had long ago accepted that this was just the way he was. Molly could hardly expect to marry a workaholic and then believe he might change further down the line. Once a workaholic, always a workaholic. Molly felt guilty calling Sam a workaholic and she often defended him and said he wasn't. But Sam lived and breathed for work; it was like a drug to him.

'So how are you feeling today?'

And there it was again. That reminder of her illness. The evidence that her disease was never far from Sam's mind.

'I'm fine, Sam. The same as yesterday and the day before, really.' Molly wasn't sure why Sam's questions bothered her so much. He was just being caring. Surely it was better that he asked her how she was – better than him treading on eggshells, avoiding the elephant in the room? Even if it was several times a day. It was just that Ed never seemed to ask her about her Parkinson's. He just had accepted that she had it, that it was something that was going to get worse and that if she wanted to talk about it, she would. However, Ed was her friend, and perhaps it was the different dynamic of the relationship that afforded him the right to either make jokes about her condition, or to pretty much ignore it, albeit in a very sweet fashion.

Molly took the mojito from the tray the waitress was

offering. Her hand seized up and she slopped sticky liquid all over her lounger.

'Oh God, I'm so sorry.' She leapt up and started mopping at it with a towel.

'Not to worry,' the waitress smiled, using some napkins from her tray to clean the mess up.

Looking embarrassed, Sam put his sunglasses on and gazed out towards the sea. Molly frowned at him, annoyed. Why was he reacting like that? She couldn't help spilling her drink, for heaven's sakes! She might have done that even if she hadn't had Parkinson's. She was relatively clumsy at the best of times. And there were far worse things to come; how was Sam going to cope?

She wondered how Ed would have reacted in the scenario that had just happened. Not that it mattered; it was pointless contemplating such a thing, but she couldn't help thinking Ed would probably have joked with the waitress about Molly having one too many mojitos and please don't bring her any more because she's clearly a lightweight.

'Sam – I couldn't help that. It was just one of those things. I used to spill drinks even when I was in full control of my faculties. You know that.'

'Of course.' He turned to her and smiled brightly. He put his hand on her leg. 'And I spilt my coffee last night at dinner.'

'So you did.' Molly leant over and kissed him. 'We're both clumsy buggers.' She put her hand on his shoulder. 'We should have an early night tonight. Take advantage of my ridiculous insomnia.'

Sam laughed. 'That sounds like a plan. I'll make sure

all of my work is out of the way and then you will have my undivided attention.' He pulled her closer.

'I can't wait, Sam. Looking forward to it already.'

And she was. She had hoped to spend more intimate time with Sam since they had been on holiday, but he had still seemed rather preoccupied. Paranoid that her illness was a turn-off for Sam, Molly had cautiously spoken to him about it one night, but Sam had insisted that it was work and work alone that was stopping him from doing more of that kind of thing, which Molly did understand. But she needed Sam right now – in all sorts of different ways. And, oddly, making love was one of them. It was just another way of feeling cared for and secure, she supposed.

Molly lay down on her lounger again, feeling a wave of peace wash over her. She was being silly worrying about Sam. He loved her and he just wanted her to be alright. And they were a dream team – that was what Sam always called them. 'Together, we're invincible,' he was always saying. Mostly in a business sense, but Molly knew he meant as a couple as well. And the thought that Sam was finally going to connect with her on that level again was great.

She still fancied him, even after all these years of marriage, and it was reassuring to know that he felt the same way about her. Especially since the Parkinson's. No disease was sexy but Molly was sometimes concerned that Sam saw her symptoms as particularly off-putting. And while she knew that not everyone was like Ed, who was like a dog on heat most of the time, by all accounts, she would still like to get back on track in that area.

'I'm off to get that work out of the way,' Sam said close to her ear.

She nodded and settled again. Her sleep patterns were all over the place at the moment, so if she felt sleepy, she went with it. And what could be better than sleeping on a sun lounger on a beach in Mexico, knowing she was going to have an incredibly sexy time with her husband later?

Ed

After leaving his incredible night with Molly, Ed had arrived home to find his house full of people. He had never seen so many people in his home before – it was usually so quiet and empty. The peace and tranquillity were occasionally interrupted by his mother's shrieking or crazed cackling, but it was usually short-lived. Today, there was a hum, a drone of talking and activity. It was discreet, but at the same time, Ed felt it like a shrill, disorientating whistling in his ear.

He sat down on the sofa and a paramedic sat down opposite him. 'Please tell me what happened,' Ed said, sounding absurdly polite.

The paramedic did so. It seemed that his mother had woken up and tried to find him. She had wrecked Ed's empty bedroom. She had found Molly's phone number on Ed's notice board and she had phoned it repeatedly.

Ed had no idea how she had dialled the number correctly; surely she had been drunk? The paramedics weren't sure if she had been at that point. Apparently she had then gone next door, banging on their front door and windows, screaming for Ed, wanting to know where he had gone, mumbling mostly incoherently, but the neighbour distinctly remembered her mentioning Molly.

Before the neighbour made it to the front door, Florrie had gone back inside the house, and locked all the doors and windows. During this time, Florrie had taken two bottles of pills. Unaware of this, the neighbour called the police who then called an ambulance, but by the time it arrived, it had been too late. No one knew where Florrie had got the pills from as the medical staff had found Ed's safety deposit box of painkillers and household medicaments under his bed, fully intact. Florrie had washed the pills down with a bottle of scotch. She never drank scotch. It was a strangely unsettling fact to Ed that she had switched to a drink she despised to end her life. It smacked of self-loathing, of a desire for complete and utter self-annihilation.

'But I . . .' Ed's voice was hoarse. He could feel hysteria rising in his chest. 'But that means it's my fault. I wasn't here. If I had been here, this wouldn't have happened . . . she'd be alive . . .'

'You can't think like that,' the paramedic said, reaching over to gently take his hand.

'But I was with Molly.' Guilt weighed heavily on Ed's shoulders. It was so immense, in fact, that he felt quite crushed by it. 'The phone was ringing and I didn't answer it. I should have answered it. I might have been able to stop her.'

The paramedic shook her head. 'Ifs and buts. It's just the way it goes. You might have saved her tonight and she could have succeeded tomorrow. Trust me, I see this all the time and the guilt simply isn't worth it. But I do understand.'

Ed absently thought that the paramedic was exactly the right person for the job she was in. He felt calmer just hearing her voice; she was so matter-of-fact. However, it didn't change how sick he felt inside.

The paramedic tried again. 'Your mother was an alcoholic but she was still responsible for herself. You mustn't blame yourself.'

'I do. How can I not?' Ed started to cry, great tears racking his body. *Oh God, oh God, oh God.* He had let his mother down in the worst way possible. He had been selfish, he had thought about himself instead of her. He had run away, just when she needed him the most, and she had taken her own life. And worst of all, she had called him and he had ignored the calls. Molly had *told* him to ignore the calls. And so he had. Ed felt a flash of resentment towards Molly, even though he knew it wasn't really her fault. But if she hadn't stopped him from taking those calls, if he hadn't let her, would his mother still be alive?

Inwardly, Ed raged at himself. His mother had attempted suicide before. He knew this. Why had he left her on her own? Why on earth had he thought she might be safe? If he was honest with himself, he hadn't thought much about anything when he had fled to be with Molly. He had simply needed to get away. Ed wrung his hands, wondering if deep down he had known something bad might happen if he left for the night. He hadn't left his mother alone overnight for months and months. What on earth had possessed him to do it now?

'You really must not do this to yourself,' the paramedic said in a firm voice. 'You're a full-time carer and these things happen. Everyone needs a break now and again.'

Ed felt sick. He couldn't be sick. He tried to draw on some words, to put them in some semblance of order. But they wouldn't come. He wanted to say sorry. To his mother. For not being there, for making a mistake. For needing some space, for needing Molly. For ignoring those calls. For letting her down. The one thing he had tried so hard over the years not to do.

Ed felt an ache in his heart that his mother was no longer here – no longer in his life. And God forgive him, Ed felt awash with relief. Relief that he was finally free.

Feeling like a child, Ed put his face in his hands and wept. He wept noisily and messily and with complete abandon. Until he had nothing left. He wanted Molly. He needed her. He needed her arms around him, her voice telling him to stop being such a girl. Even though he couldn't help blaming her a bit.

God. Ed had never felt so alone in his entire life. When he raised his head, the paramedic was standing by the door talking to someone, but then the silence prevailed once more. Perversely, Ed wished for noise and bustle to break the eerie tension.

He rubbed his arm across his eyes and stood up. His legs felt wobbly and unstable, but he knew he had to pull himself together. Thanking the paramedic, he did his best to listen to instructions about death certificates and potential funeral arrangements. He was bewildered. He didn't have the first idea how to go about arranging such a thing.

Heading upstairs, he paused outside his mother's bedroom. Engulfed by an enormous sense of loss, he rested his head on the door momentarily. She was gone. His mother was gone. She had been like a bright, dangerous flame – compelling but volatile. Liable to cause untold damage to anyone who got too close. And he had been too close. Always too close.

Ed assumed his mother was finally at peace, but it didn't surprise him that, as ever, she had left utter carnage in her wake. He felt a rush of hatred. He had spent a beautiful, incredible night with Molly and now it felt sullied, dirtied by his mother's final insult. How on earth was he going to be with Molly after this? How on earth would he be able to stop himself from feeling guilty in her presence? While they had been doing exquisite things to each other – things Ed believed he may well be doing for the rest of his life, and with sheer happiness – his mother had been ending her life. And he might have been able to stop it; that was the worst thing. He felt so torn. And so bloody angry. He didn't know who he was more annoyed at – his mother, Molly, or himself.

Ed was suddenly hit by a wave of claustrophobia. The house felt as if it might close in on him and he knew he couldn't ever sleep here again, not after this. He would have to sell it. The ghost of his mother would hang heavily in every room – unhappy memories, echoes of horrible arguments, smells that no longer prevailed but somehow still managed to permeate wallpaper and fabric.

Where could he go? What could he do? Ed thought

hard and quick. Molly. He should go to Molly. He could tell her everything now. He could explain and she would understand and it would all be alright. But he was angry with her. Probably without just cause, but he was. But he could get past it. Could he get past it?

Ed went into his bedroom. Stuffed clothes into a bag, his passport, driving licence, birth certificate and the like. All the things he'd need. Because he never wanted to set foot in this house again. He had kept them in another locked box, worried his mother might destroy them in an irrational rage or something similar. Taking the small sum of money he had squirrelled away, Ed headed downstairs, locked the house and headed to his car. He stopped in town to grab some cigarettes, with no fixed plan in his mind other than to drive.

'Ed!' It was Boyd, his old school friend.

'Boyd. Hey.' Ed shook Boyd's hand tiredly. 'How are you?'

'Better than you, my friend.' Boyd frowned. 'You look terrible. What's happened?'

Ed told him everything. Including what had happened with Molly. It was a strange relief to finally let everything about his mother out to someone. It was a relief to discuss how he felt about Molly, because he never talked about Molly to anyone. Ed was aware he was gushing about her, waxing lyrical about what had happened, no doubt making Boyd feel desperately uncomfortable as he rambled on about their 'spirtual connection' and other turgid stuff. He also mentioned the phone-call incident and Boyd made sympathetic noises.

'That's awful, Ed. Where are you planning to go now then?'

'Not really sure. Maybe to see Molly. Thought I'd tell her everything.'

Boyd raised his eyebrows. 'Really? Not sure that's a good idea. Quite a lot to throw at someone, isn't it? I mean, this is huge. And you're feeling pretty angsty towards her about that phone-call thing, aren't you?'

Ed faltered. Was Boyd right? Surely Molly would be able to cope? She would understand; Ed was sure of it. The phone-call thing, yes, that was an issue.

'Oh, I wasn't saying don't tell her about it,' Boyd reassured, trying to read Ed's expression. 'I just meant . . . maybe not immediately. You're emotional. You're in shock. Why don't you come to my parents' house for a drink and we can talk things over calmly? You have a lot to sort out.'

'Do I?' Ed suddenly felt rather bewildered, without the first idea of the best course of action.

'You do. Come with me. My car is parked round the corner. Follow me back and we'll talk things over.'

Ed did as he was told. He felt rather child-like all of a sudden, as though the rug had been pulled out from under him. He wasn't quite sure what Boyd was doing home; as far as Ed understood it Boyd had a job doing something complicated with hedge funds, something Ed had no comprehension of, other than that it earned Boyd an immense salary.

'In between girlfriends,' Boyd explained, as he ushered Ed into his parents' palatial home. 'Once I'm getting my leg over full-time, my mother won't see me for dust. But shh, don't tell her that.'

'Wouldn't dream of it,' Ed said, following Boyd into the kitchen.

'Tea? Coffee? Tatt?' Boyd smiled but it faded almost straight away. 'Fucking hell, Ed. You must be in a right old state.'

'I guess so. The thing is, it's a relief to be honest about everything now. I mean, you should know that I'm not remotely posh. Or rich,' Ed added for good measure. 'I won a scholarship to that fancy school we went to and made sure no one found out.' He shrugged. 'That's why I didn't invite you to my house. Not so much because it's tiny and squalid, but because my mother might have puked on you or wet herself while we had a cup of tea. Or stripped off naked. And I'm not joking.'

Boyd listened without interrupting. Ed had never appreciated his stoic nature more than he did right now. The last thing he needed was judgement or overt sympathy. Ed couldn't have handled either of those things at the moment.

Boyd put the kettle on and took out some mugs. 'Right. Coffee it is. That's horrendous – not the Molly stuff, but the stuff about your mum. I'd give you a hug, but we're men and we don't do that shit.'

Ed smiled briefly.

'But do accept my deepest sympathies,' Boyd added, giving him a clap on the shoulder, like a stiff-upper-lipped character from an Enid Blyton book. 'I can't imagine what you've been through over the years. Why didn't you tell me about it? I'm sure I could have helped. My mother has some excellent contacts. She might come across as a posh so-and-so, but she actually does an awful lot of work for charities. Including one for alcoholics. Her father was an alcoholic, you see. So she really wanted to help other people dealing with that kind of addiction.'

Ed cursed himself for his silence. Help had been right under his nose and he had been so hell-bent on caring for his mother himself that he hadn't spoken to anyone about her. To be fair, his mother hadn't wanted anyone else involved, but still.

'Ok. Well, that doesn't matter. Hindsight is a wonderful thing as they say.' Boyd made two strong coffees. 'What to do now, that's the issue.' He regarded Ed seriously. 'Fancy getting away for a bit?'

'Away? Where?'

'My parents have a place in Bermuda,' Boyd said, pointing to a photograph on the kitchen wall. It depicted a ravishing, opulent building with pillars and ornate stone work. 'I know, I know – terribly middle class. But a great place to go if you need to escape. And you, my friend, need to escape.'

'I couldn't . . . I don't have any . . .'

'I'll get you a flight,' Boyd said, waving a hand. 'I have tons of air miles. And you can stay there for free, certainly for a few weeks. I think my parents are due to fly out shortly so you'd have to bugger off then. I was thinking more along the lines of you going travelling for a bit. You know, meeting up with some people, seeing a bit of the world.'

Ed was about to tell Boyd that his idea was the dumbest thing he had ever heard, but he stopped for a second. Maybe it wasn't such a dumb idea. Maybe it was the perfect thing for him to do. He could get his head together, he could put his guilt to one side and just live a little. A few weeks away and he would feel better about his mother's death. About not taking her calls. About Molly's part in that. Molly. But what would Molly think about him leaving like this?

'What about Molly?' Ed asked, suddenly sure it was a bad idea. 'This is going to sound crazy, but I feel . . . tainted by what's happened with my mum. I feel awful. Like I might mess everything up if I go and see Molly now. Do you know what I mean?'

'I do, I do.' Boyd thought for a second. 'Write her a letter,' he suggested. 'A beautiful, heartfelt letter, the kind a big poofter like you can easily write. Explain that you had to get away, that you are sorting out your head. Tell her your mother died, but you don't want to tell her anything else right now. It's probably better to tell her face to face anyway. Or tell her the whole shebang, if it floats your boat to do so. Either way, leave it with me and I will make sure Molly gets the letter.'

A letter. Ed quite liked that idea. He could write a superb letter to Molly. Sensitive, emotional, eloquent. He could tell her exactly how he felt and she would understand why he needed to leave. Only for a short time, of course, and then he would be back. And everything could go back to how it was before, because the hideousness of his mother's death would have been more or less erased.

'Boyd. You really are the most excellent friend. I could maybe send Molly some tickets. She could join me out there in a few days.'

'You romantic sod.' Boyd grinned. 'But that's a great idea. I could arrange all of that for you.'

Ed came back down to earth. 'Balls. I have to . . .'

'. . . sell the house. Of course. Leave it with me. Seriously. No hassle at all. I have contacts, well, Dad has.' Boyd looked shame-faced for a second. 'Christ, listen to me. I really *am* a posh so-and-so. But anyway, I'll use those contacts, get you a good price. I can put the money in your bank account and you'll be all set by the time you get back. I'll check it all out with my dad. You might have to make me executor of the will or something, not sure. Either way, we'll sort it.'

Ed let out a shaky sigh. Life suddenly didn't seem so terrible. He had a plan. He had something he could cling to and he would make things right with Molly. He would arrange his mother's funeral and as soon as it was over, he would make sure Molly got his letter and then he would leave. For a month or so. And by the time Molly came to meet him he'd be healed, ready to accept her love. And when he came back, he could start living properly – the way he had always wanted to. He would get a job, he would impress Molly with how sensible he could be, now that he was free.

Ed almost wanted to cry again, but he held back. He had cried enough. He had things to do, and although his heart felt crushed by what had happened, he knew it was time to get himself together.

Now

'I'm sorry, Molly.' Sam looked devastated. But the words coming out of his mouth were even more devastating. 'I just can't do this any more.'

'You-you can't do what?' Molly swallowed. 'Mexico?'

Sam shook his head. 'I'm not talking about Mexico.'

Molly tightened the belt of her dressing gown. This had to have something to do with the other night. She and Sam had had an early dinner and had headed back to their room. They had started kissing, and it had felt good. But when Molly had pushed Sam towards the bed, he had changed. He seemed to want to slow everything down – to talk. Which Molly hadn't minded. So they had talked. They had talked about when they first met and about their relationship back then. Sam's tone had been animated as he had discussed the way he felt about her in the early years, about the way Molly had energised the business – and him.

Molly had been faintly confused by all this talk of the

past, but she had joined in, assuming that Sam needed to do this for some reason. It had actually been lovely, talking about the old days. It was as though they had both remembered why they had fallen in love with one another. Molly had started kissing Sam again but he had seemed tender with her rather than passionate and they had ended up curled around one another, falling asleep in each other's arms. Not so bad, although not the evening of intimacy and frenzied lovemaking Molly had envisaged.

But the following morning, Sam had been distant – detached. Something had shifted and it didn't feel good. In fact, Molly felt rather like her marriage was slipping through her fingers and she couldn't gather it up again, however hard she tried.

I'm being dramatic, I'm being dramatic, I'm being dramatic, she had told herself. Her marriage was fine. Well, it had been shaken slightly, but it was just a bad patch. Sam was simply adjusting to the news about her Parkinson's, but he would be ok. Because Sam was always ok. He was a coper, he was practical, he made plans and created strategies. He had done this for most of his life. Molly having Parkinson's was hardly going to make him run away.

Sam was dependable and loyal – the one thing Molly didn't need to worry about when it came to Sam, was his being flaky. Ed, yes – Sam, no.

'Our marriage, Molly.' Sam put his head in his hands. 'That's what I can't do any more.'

'W-what?' Molly stared at him. 'You can't mean that.'

Sam looked distraught. 'I feel horrible saying it. But it's true. I can't do this. I just can't. I know I can't.'

Molly panicked. 'Listen, I know you're out of your comfort zone here, Sam. You hate holidays and we've been away for ages. Once we're back home again, you'll feel normal.'

'How can I feel normal when you've got Parkinson's, Molly?' Sam lifted his head.

'How can *you* feel normal?' Molly felt a spark of anger, but she tried to suppress it. 'I don't know, Sam. I guess we both need to adjust. I don't feel particularly normal either. But I'm trying to. I'm really trying to.'

Sam let out a jerky breath. 'I know you are. And it's not your fault. You're doing amazingly well with this. It's not you. I'm not coping. It's me. I'm just not able to deal with this.'

'Did you just say it's not you, it's me?' Molly rubbed a hand over her face. Not the time for jokes. 'Look, Sam. It's not easy, this diagnosis. I'm still reeling from it, so I can understand you feeling the way you're feeling. You're scared. Neither of us knows what's going to happen.'

'That's the problem, Molly.' Sam wrung his hands. 'We do know what's going to happen. I've looked it all up on the internet and I've read around ten books on the subject. I know what's ahead. For you – and for me.'

Molly bit her lip. 'And you don't like the way the future looks.' She stood up and walked to the balcony. 'You're already embarrassed by me knocking my drinks over and losing my balance. You hate my insomnia and you've noticed that I keep forgetting things.'

'It's not that I don't like the way the future looks,' Sam protested. 'It's more that I just feel I'm not the right person to deal with it.' He rubbed his hands on his legs as though they were sweaty or dirty. 'My head is all over the place, Molly. I'm worried about the business – we suffered that big loss. I know I can claw it back but I need to focus. I can't focus right now. Not while you have this.'

'But . . . I'll always have this.' Molly knew her voice sounded small.

Sam nodded slowly. 'I know. That's the problem.'

'Sam, I can't make it go away for a while so that you feel alright. So that you can go off and make things right in the business. I can't help that I have this.'

'Of course you can't.' Sam met her eyes earnestly. 'I don't blame you, Molly. I don't. I just feel that everything is slipping through my fingers right now. You, the business, all of our savings. I just need to . . . to get some control back.'

Molly felt sick suddenly. She had always thought she was the centre of Sam's universe. But it seemed that wasn't the case. Sam's business was the centre of his world. Molly was just part of Sam's world, not the core. She worked as a wife if she *worked*. If everything was functioning, if she was ok, if she fitted. Now that she didn't, Sam needed to go back to his roots and get his beloved business back on track. Which meant losing Molly.

'I'm second best.' Molly's voice was flat, emotionless. 'The business – money – comes first, and then it's me.'

'No. No, Molly. Don't say that.' Sam looked confused. 'It's not that the business comes first. I just . . . I just need to get some . . .'

'Control. You need to get some control.'

180

Molly wished she could cry. Surely she should be crying at this point? But her heart felt numb. She felt let down. So badly let down that she could barely breathe. But she felt nothing much else. Not yet, at least.

'And I am beyond your control now, aren't I, Sam?' Molly met his eyes accusingly. 'You're thinking "Christ, soon she'll be flicking her legs out like a pony while watching TV, she'll be getting all depressed and she'll start slurring her words until everyone starts thinking she's got a drink problem."'

'Molly. Stop . . .'

'And because you've looked into it so much, you're worried about – well, good lord, let's see. My ability to multi-task going out of the window. Behavioural stuff like binge eating, gambling, excessive shopping. Bladder and bowel issues. Oh, and possible dementia.'

Molly forced Sam to meet her eye. 'That's about the size of it, isn't it? You can't face any of that.'

Sam looked stricken. 'It's just – Christ, I wish I could, Molly. It's because I love you so much. I can't stand the thought of this happening to you. Not you.' He broke down and started crying like a baby.

Molly felt tears coming into her eyes, but she felt extraordinarily impassive at this point. It was because Sam loved her too much, was it? How ridiculous. If he loved her, he wouldn't be letting her down like this. He would be sticking by her and he would be prepared to deal with everything that was coming in the future. Even if it was challenging.

'Oh, do stop howling, Sam.' Molly hardened herself inside. This was horrendous. Sam was falling at what was essentially the first hurdle. She was only showing a few symptoms and they weren't even scary ones.

'I can't help it.' Sam sniffed and lifted his head. 'I love you so much, Molly. I do. I just can't stand the thought of having to sit and watch you deteriorate.'

'It's not that you can't stand the thought of it, it's that you don't want to do it,' Molly pointed out reasonably. 'I believe that you love me, but perhaps not enough. I'm not going to throw marriage vows in your face, because I think that's pointless, but I can't believe you're ducking out of this. So early on. I'm just at the start here. And you're going to leave me. Leave me to deal with this alone.'

Molly's voice cracked as she fully faced up to what Sam was doing to her. She had early-onset Parkinson's and she was going to deteriorate alone. All alone. Who would want to take her on with this horrible illness looming? What man could cope if Sam couldn't?

Sam rubbed the tears from his face and leant against the headboard of the bed they hadn't rocked off its hinges once in nearly a month. 'But this is going to affect every aspect of our lives, Molly. Every aspect.'

'Yes,' Molly agreed. She felt utterly hopeless. 'It is. But I am on medication and I am looking into one of those drug trials you mentioned. And even though my symptoms are escalating more quickly than we might have thought, I'm not doing that badly, Sam. I'm really not.' She started crying finally. But it didn't feel like a release. It just felt like pain. The stabbing kind that didn't let up.

Sam shook his head and sobbed. 'I know. I know. I hate myself for this. But I've been thinking about it since we've been away. And I know I can't do it. I can't support you through this. I thought I could but I can't.'

'So you're leaving me?' Molly's voice was small and about as fragile as she felt on the inside.

'I think I have to.'

Sam was sticking to his guns. There really was no hope. Where there had been peaceful floods washing over her only a few days earlier, all Molly could feel now were waves of desolation. They crashed over her like massive, surf-worthy waves and threatened to drown her. Sam was leaving her. Her husband was leaving her. When she had been diagnosed with Parkinson's disease. This was the lowest of the low. This was the worst thing Sam could possibly do to her. All these years of marriage meant nothing to him – the shit had hit the fan and Sam was running away. He was letting her down spectacularly. He was sorry but not sorry enough to stay.

'That's why you don't want to sleep with me any more,' Molly said suddenly. 'Parkinson's is a bit of a turn-off, right?'

'It shouldn't be. And you're beautiful, Molly. I'm still attracted to you. I can't even explain it.' Sam looked like a lost little boy.

'Parkinson's isn't sexy. I get it.'

Sam sighed. 'You're making this sound awful, Molly.'

She let out a small, bitter laugh. Was he joking?

'I'll fly home,' Sam said decisively. 'I'll fly home first thing tomorrow and I'll move out. I'll find somewhere else to live and you can have the house.'

'How very kind of you, Sam.' Molly wondered if the insomnia had pushed her into so deep a sleep that she was unable to tug herself out of what was very clearly a nightmare. 'Because having to find a house after you letting me down like this really would be a terrible thing. Truly. What a shocker finding another house would be when my world has just gone tits up.'

'Do you know what, Molly? Sometimes you sound just like Ed.' Sam got up and started angrily yanking his suitcase out of the cupboard.

'Do I?'

Molly wasn't sure that was such a bad thing. Ed had let her down once, very badly. But it hadn't felt like this. Her heart had broken into little pieces when Ed had gone travelling, but this – this felt like a major betrayal of the worst kind. This felt like everything she had believed in, had held dear and that had any significance in her life, had been a farce.

Molly stared at Sam as he took his clothes out of the wardrobe and folded them into the suitcase. She had been drawn to Sam initially because he had made her feel safe and secure. She knew he was loyal and faithful. She hadn't imagined he would ever cheat on her or treat her badly. It was as though the Labrador had turned into a Rottweiler. Or perhaps just one of those silly little Yorkshire Terriers Ed disliked so much, one who kept barking and whinging, but didn't actually amount to much.

'And I thought Ed was the flighty one,' Molly said before she could stop herself.

'Oh really?' Sam threw his toiletries into the suitcase. 'You think Ed could handle this better than me? You're living in cloud cuckoo land if you think that, Molly!' He scoffed. 'Ed can't cope with anything. He always runs away. It's his thing – his *modus operandi*. He's the most unreliable person either of us knows.'

'You cannot be standing in front of me saying that when you've just decided to walk away from a wife who's been diagnosed with Parkinson's.'

She scrutinised Sam's face. How hadn't she seen this coming? Surely at some point Sam had given himself away? Had she missed the signs? Or was it only now that his mask had slipped? Molly cursed herself. She had invested everything – *everything* – in this man. Her emotions, her love, her career, her life. Sam had been her person – he had made her whole.

'Look, I'm sorry, ok, Molly? I guess I'm just not the man you thought I was.'

'No. No, you're really not. I just wish I'd realised it sooner.'

Sam held her gaze for a second then seemed unable to keep looking her in the eye. Shaking his head, he carried on packing. Molly decamped to the balcony for some sanctuary. She'd sleep out here if she needed to. There was no point in being around Sam any more.

Molly put her head on her knees. Her phone rang and she quickly checked it. It was Ed. She wanted to speak to him but she couldn't face it right now.

Molly ignored the call. She needed to cry. It was possible she might cry rather a lot.

Molly

'So, where has he gone then?'

'I have absolutely no idea.'

Sam contemplated Molly's rigid back. 'He must have contacted you before he left.'

'Nope.'

'So how do you know he went travelling?'

'Because I phoned his house and spoke to a school friend of his. I mean, he's a friend of mine too, kind of. Boyd.' Molly paused. 'Apparently Ed's mother died. I don't know when exactly. But she died and Ed left.'

Sam nodded. 'I see. So . . . maybe he needed to get away or something?'

'Maybe.'

Molly's heart contracted and she was grateful her back was to Sam. She didn't want to look him in the eye right now. She couldn't deal with his pity or his sympathy. Not when it came to Ed. Molly didn't want anyone to talk to her about Ed. Not with the way he had disappeared after they'd spent the night together. The next day, Molly had been in a state of sheer panic, not knowing what had happened or how Ed was. She had left it around five days before she had phoned his house – through pride or terror, she couldn't exactly say. Molly had spoken to Boyd who had been helpful and informative, but only to a point. He seemed confused that she didn't know what was going on or where Ed was. He had started to say something a few times, but had stopped himself and Molly had eventually hung up, flummoxed as to what was going on.

And Ed hadn't come back. And therefore he hadn't explained anything. Molly was none the wiser apart from assuming that Ed was in a bad way after the death of his mother. But surely a phone call, a note, *something* to communicate to her – as a good friend, apart from anything else – that he cared, that he would be in touch, that he was simply off dealing with his grief, or whatever was happening.

But nothing. Nothing. Not a word. Molly had waited. And waited. And she had believed in Ed. She had had faith. She was sure, certain, he wouldn't let her down this time. That he would get in touch and that everything would become clear. They would re-connect as soon as they had spoken and they would get back on track.

Was Ed freaked out about the night they'd spent together? Assuming his mother had died the night he had been with her, Molly guessed perhaps Ed was feeling some sort of negative association. Either way,

Molly had slowly come to the conclusion that Ed saw what had happened between them as a mistake. That he wished it hadn't happened. That he had been feeling emotional for whatever reason, but that he hadn't intended to cross the line with her. That he regretted it and had no wish to even be friends with her, let alone anything else.

The realisation poleaxed her – and that was an understatement. Molly fought hard to push down a hysterical sob that had risen in her throat. She hated feeling like this. And she hated Ed for making her feel this way.

'Molly . . .' Sam had moved closer to her, clearly concerned.

Molly moved away, pretending to assess the work on her design board. 'What do you think, Sam? It's for that beauty campaign.'

Sam stood behind her. 'It's great. You have such a talent for this – you've shown that by grabbing three new contracts since you arrived. I knew my hunch about you was right.' Evidently realising she wasn't keen to talk about Ed, he pointed to the tagline. 'That needs to be in a different colour, though. It doesn't stand out enough.'

Molly tutted. 'You're so right. Why didn't I see that? Still. What a team, eh?'

Sam smiled. 'Well. That's good to hear. I was worried you missed painting.'

'Oh, I do miss painting.' Molly turned on her swivel stool. Painting wasn't the only thing she missed. Her heart clenched. The pain was indescribable. She steeled herself with an immense physical and emotional effort.

'I'm working such long hours that I barely have time to put brush to paper, pencil to paper. Even that would be better than nothing.'

Sam leant against the desk. Studied Molly. She was beautiful. Undeniably so. Molly was one of those people with an almost hypnotic quality about her. She was attractive, absorbing, captivating. But she had lost weight; her curves were more defined than womanly these days. Her face was drawn and, worst of all, her eyes radiated sadness. And Sam knew exactly who had put that acute pain in Molly's heart. If Ed was here right now, Sam would do the thing he had once said he wouldn't do. He would tell Ed to his face that he was flighty. And a shit. And a massive, massive bastard. And Sam would then proceed to break Ed's nose and anything else he could break before someone bodily removed him from Ed's bloody carcass.

Sam unclenched his fists and focused on Molly's painting issue, because it was safer. And it didn't make him want to put his fist through a wall.

'Would you like some time off? We could arrange something. Say, every other Friday you leave at lunchtime? How about that? You could get some painting done, drawing, whatever you want.'

Molly swallowed. 'That's . . . that's really kind of you. Thank you, Sam. Maybe. But no. Maybe not. Honestly . . .' She paused, seeming embarrassed that her eyes had filled with tears. 'Honestly, work is helping me right now. I . . . I need to focus. I need to be busy. I love painting but it reminds me of . . . I can't really . . .'

'You don't need to explain anything to me,' Sam

189

interrupted, putting his hand on her shoulder. Rather than gripping it, he held her as gently as he could. 'Whatever you want to do is fine with me. And I mean that, Molly.'

She looked at him and her lip trembled. Suddenly, she stood up and put her arms around him. Sam hesitated then slid his arms around her. Tightened his grip. Molly responded, squeezing him with her hands. She relaxed, curved her body into his.

'You're so kind, Sam. You're . . . you're just what I need right now.'

Sam sucked his breath in. Placing his chin on Molly's head, he thought carefully about his next words.

'Molly. Can I ask you something?'

'Yup.' Her voice was muffled against his shirt.

'Do you . . . do you want to hear from Ed? Right now, if you could hear from him, would you want to?'

Sam felt her stiffen in his arms. He regretted ruining the intimate moment they had just shared but it was a question he had to ask. It was something he had to know. In fact, Sam felt there was probably an awful lot riding on Molly's answer.

Molly drew back. Released her arms. And then she shut down. The way she did whenever Ed's name was mentioned. It was as though she flinched internally, as if every organ and blood vessel reacted to his memory.

Sam had spent New Year's Eve with Molly. They had attended a huge party, hosted by friends of his and he had invited Molly and a whole group of her friends. They had dressed up, the men in black tie, the women in cocktail dresses. Molly had worn a deep-red strapless

190

gown, her blond curls clipped up with glittery combs, a hairstyle courtesy of her friend Jody, apparently. Molly had drifted around the room looking beautiful but broken, not eating or drinking or speaking to any of her friends beyond the odd, polite word. Sam had found her just before midnight, sobbing her heart out on the balcony, mumbling something about a star formation with a funny name. He hadn't been able to make any sense of what she was babbling on about, but he guessed it was something to do with Ed. Anything that made Molly cry seemed to lead back to Ed somehow. She had held her hands to her chest as if her heart was close to exploding and Sam had felt so overprotective of her, he didn't quite know what to do with himself.

Sam wasn't a man of words, he was a man of action. And he knew that night what he needed to do for Molly, what she needed from him. Molly needed a shoulder. A shoulder to lean on, to cry into, to punch if need be. And Sam was going to be there for her; he decided then and there. And he had been. He had been there for her all night, and ever since. As a friend, as someone who would do anything in his power to make her forget. And that was just one of the reasons Sam had to know if Molly wanted to hear from Ed.

'No, Sam,' Molly replied. She took her seat again, turning away. Her shoulders were set, but her breathing was ragged. 'No. I do not want to hear from Ed.' She picked a pen up. 'In fact, if you want me to be really honest, I don't ever want to speak to Ed again for as long as I live.' Her voice cracked. 'I'd be happy if I never heard his voice, saw his face or . . .' She had been about to say 'felt his hands on me again' but found she literally could not get the words out loud. Because the memories that assailed her when she thought about Ed's hands on her threatened to overwhelm her to the point of no return.

Thoughtfully, Sam edged away from Molly and left her to it.

Some time later, Molly looked up from her work. Noticing a box behind her handbag on her desk, she opened it curiously and found a large slice of coffee cake inside it with a note attached. Molly slowly read it. 'To my favourite star, love Sam.'

Slowly, Molly closed the box, carefully fixing the lid in place. Sam was a lovely guy. Pure, genuine and kind. Loyal. Reliable. Safe. Handsome, hard-working and yes, sexy. And yet . . .

Molly placed her hands on top of the box. She wondered when she would feel normal again. Because since Ed had left, Molly had felt disorientated and wrong, just wrong. The way she used to feel when she hadn't seen him for a while, but the feeling was multiplied by a thousand because of that night. Because of being mouth to mouth, skin to skin, soul to soul. Because she had let Ed own her that night. In a good way. And he had. Mind, heart and soul. He had told her that she had owned him right back. And she had believed him. But then he had gone and he taken the best parts of her with him.

Molly started crying. Gently at first – sad tears that tore at her, clawing at her, opening a barely closed wound and dousing it in salt. Sobs followed, bloody great huge ones that crashed through her chest, ripping into her heart and making it bleed. Or perhaps just breaking it in two. Either way, it hurt like hell.

Molly hoped Ed never came back from his travels. Because she knew she would never recover from this for as long as she lived. And her only hope of getting up each morning and dealing with life was if she never clapped eyes on Ed again.

Now

Ed frowned at his laptop. He was editing his novel. He hated editing with a passion. But he had to do it. He had to somehow get this novel in shape and shipped off to an agent. And Ed was well aware that if he was lucky enough to secure an agent, he would most likely be editing again, and if he managed to get a publisher, yet more editing would await him. So he might as well get on with it.

Trouble was, he couldn't stop worrying about Molly. *Molly, Molly, Molly.* Ed felt bleak. What a shitty thing to happen to her, getting Parkinson's. She didn't deserve this. No one did, of course, but Molly really didn't. She was like this bright, bright spark; she shone from the inside – she positively radiated from within. Ed couldn't bear the thought that some of her spark might be slowly extinguished, that she might no longer be the Molly he had known for so many years. He couldn't bear the thought that the Molly he had loved for so long might gradually fade.

Ed supposed it wasn't his problem, exactly. Molly wasn't his *person*. In terms of his heart, she was, but in a practical sense, she was Sam's person. And Sam was the most practical person in the world, so Ed had no qualms about him being able to cope. And for that Ed was truly grateful. Even if it made him feel somewhat redundant.

He turned back to his laptop and wondered if he needed to make a brutal cull to the section he was writing.

'There have to be easier jobs,' Ed muttered under his breath.

'First sign of madness, that.'

Ed jumped out of his skin. 'Jody!' He put a hand on his chest. 'Jesus. I nearly . . . well, it would be ungentlemanly of me to say what that nearly made me do.'

Jody smiled briefly. 'Sorry. I just meant that you shouldn't talk to yourself like that. It's not healthy.'

Ed stood up. 'Oh, I'm way past worrying about that. I reckon all writers talk to themselves. It's a very solitary thing, this writing lark. Tea?'

'That would be nice.' Jody followed him into the kitchen. 'This is a lovely house.'

'Thanks.' Ed busied himself making the tea. It was nice to see Jody and he always welcomed interruptions to his editing schedule, but she was making him feel slightly edgy for some reason. She seemed uncomfortable. 'Molly always takes the piss, saying it's my little slice of suburbia.'

'I know what she means,' Jody said. 'It's rather grown up.'

'Well, so am I these days.' Ed handed Jody a mug of

tea and gestured for her to go into the conservatory. 'I have a selection of biscuits and everything. Fancy one?'

'I'm fine, thanks.' Jody took a seat and sipped her tea.

Ed sat back. 'So, is this just a visit to say hi or . . .?'

'Not as such.' Jody set her tea down carefully on the coffee table. 'I . . . this is a bit tricky.'

Ed started to get a sliding feeling in his stomach. Later, he would claim to Molly that he had had an inkling of what Jody was about to say to him, but in truth, he didn't have a clue what was about to happen. He just had a sense that it was going to be important.

'It's . . .' Jody started, then stopped again. 'Ok. I don't know how to say this.'

Ed chewed his lip.

'Jake's your son,' she blurted out.

'W-what?' Ed sat up suddenly and squealed as he chucked hot tea all over his jeans.

'I'm sorry.' Jody looked apologetic. 'I didn't mean to say it like that.'

Ed shakily put his tea down. He straightened and met Jody's eyes. He saw guilt there. And deep, deep apology. He started to hyperventilate. This couldn't be happening.

'I have a son. Jake is my son.' Ed swallowed. 'Christ, Jody. Don't you think you should have mentioned this to me before now?'

Jody pulled a face. 'Good question. And the answer is, that I didn't actually realise I was pregnant for ages. By the time I knew, I was in Canada.' She pulled a face. 'I was one of those stupid women who didn't recognise the symptoms for about five months. Seriously. I just thought I was stressed out, hence the periods stopping.

I just thought I'd put on a bit of weight. It's happened before, especially when I'm doing something new with my life.'

'Ok.' Ed wasn't sure this was enough of an explanation. 'But that only accounts for the first few months, Jody. What about the rest of the time? You know, all those years since he was born? I mean, you knew where I was – you could have easily contacted me to let me know.' He raked his hands through his hair, feeling completely overwhelmed. A son? Him, who hadn't ever wanted children?

'I know.' Jody stared at her hands guiltily. 'It's just that it took me ages to get my head round it. I was in Canada, alone. I had started a new job and I was pregnant. I didn't know what to do.' She faltered. 'I considered having him aborted. I should tell you that, even though that makes me sound terrible.'

Ed shook his head. 'No. I get that. And no one wants to make that kind of decision, do they? But if you're alone and having a baby – well, it can't have been easy. Shit.' He picked his tea up and tried to drink it without splashing his jeans again. Not easy when his hands were shaking all over the place.

'It wasn't.' Jody's eyes filled with tears. 'It was so hard, Ed. I almost lost my job juggling childcare – let's just say they weren't best pleased that I turned up preggers and needing time off. But I got through it. It was the toughest thing I've ever done, but I managed it. Thank God I was so well-paid out there; childcare is extortionate. I had to hire a full-time nanny and I spent most of the time feeling guilty about it.'

'I really admire you for holding it together so well,' Ed said honestly. Somewhere inside him, he felt compassion for Jody, despite his shock. 'I don't think I could have coped.'

'Sure you could. You'd have just got on with it the way I did.'

'You say that . . .' Ed wasn't so sure. The situation with his mum had tested him beyond all reason, but having a child and bringing it up alone was a whole different ball game.

Jody shrugged. 'Well, we'll never know. But I didn't even think about the dad situation for a good few years. I just got on with it. I'd made the decision to go it alone so I did it. I-I guess I didn't think about how it might affect Jake. About how it might affect you not knowing Jake for all those years.'

'What made you come back?'

'I looked at Jake one day. Really looked at him. And – I saw you.' Jody's mouth twisted. 'I looked into his eyes and I saw you reflected back at me. And I suddenly realised how selfish I'd been. That you had missed out, that he had missed out. Here, I have some photos.' She took an album out of her handbag and pushed it across the coffee table.

Ed hesitated. Then he took it and leafed through it. Jake really was an adorable baby. And Ed was saying that from a detached point of view. Some babies – Christ, they were downright ugly. Ed shuddered. One of Boyd's kids – a girl, in fact – had been so strange looking, even the nurses had seemed rather taken-aback. The child had improved with age, as most of them did, of course, but she had been one frightening little bugger when she had first come out.

Was Jake definitely his? Ed was loath to ask the question. Was that not akin to suggesting that Jody was loose in some fashion? If she had had sex with another guy at around about the same time? Looking at the odds, Jody would have had to have sex with some other dude within a fortnight of sleeping with Ed. Which if she had, didn't make her a slut by any means, but it wasn't necessarily a nice thing to suggest to a lady.

'This is a great photo.'

Ed found himself beaming at a picture of Jake in a spider costume for Halloween. It was the cutest thing ever and Ed felt his heart swell slightly. Was that weird? He didn't even know if the little guy was his or not.

'God, he hated that costume!' Jody smiled. 'He kept ripping those bloody arms off and I gave up in the end. Told everyone he was a scarab beetle instead. Even though they have legs of some sort. Just not as many as spiders have.'

Ed laughed. 'I wonder why kids hate wearing these costumes so much? Boyd is always telling me about his lot tearing off princess costumes and pirate outfits.'

Remembering Boyd, Ed decided to leave the issue of paternity for a moment. He also thought it wouldn't hurt to check Jody's reaction to his recent news. She looked as though she was more than capable of taking care of both herself and Jake and Ed was sure she wasn't here for money. But it was best to be honest about his situation. 'I should tell you that Boyd and I have lost a vast amount of money recently.'

'Oh no, really? Bad investments?' Jody looked genuinely concerned.

'Something like that.' Ed filled her in quickly. 'It's horrendous. I have this house but not much else. I'll need to get a job. And I will. I always used to work so it will be fine. But I'd really like to earn some money from writing. Hence me finally writing this novel.'

'In the meantime, you could always approach all the newspapers,' Jody pointed out reasonably. 'Local and otherwise. You could work from home. Get some articles together and fire them off.'

Jody made it sound so easy, and Ed guessed that, like writing a novel, it was simply a case of getting on with it. One of Boyd's friends worked for some newspaper or other – not necessarily a respectable one but it might be a good place to start. He had told Ed that journalism was all about 'voice and opinion'. Which made sense, of course, but Ed wasn't sure he knew where to start exactly. Perhaps a piece about belatedly finding out he was a dad? Ed decided to run with that one for starters. Might be a goer.

'So. Would you like to see Jake again at some point? I left him with my mum for this. She's over the moon to see him for the first time – can't tear him away from her.' Jody slipped the photograph album back into her handbag. 'But obviously if you want to see him . . .'

Ed bit his lip then nodded. It wouldn't hurt to meet the kid again. Suss out whether he thought the boy could be his. And once he'd done that, surely it would be easier to broach the subject of paternity with Jody? Ed was sure it would be better to do things that way.

'Maybe some football on the beach?'

Jody looked pleased. 'Jake loves football.'

Ed's expression was rueful. 'I'm shit at playing football, you know that, right?'

'I do. I remember our student days.' Jody put her hand on Ed's and her shoulders relaxed. 'I'm so glad it's you,' she added out of the blue. 'So glad you're Jake's dad.'

Ed gave her a smile. 'Er, yeah, me too.' He would get on to the issue of paternity soon enough. He needed to be sure. The kid looked a bit like him, that was without question, but Ed needed proof. He'd see Jake first, get to know him a bit, and then he'd get the test done.

Watching Jody over the rim of his mug, Ed tried to absorb the shock of her news. A son. He possibly had a son. Molly had early-onset Parkinson's and he might have a son. What the hell had happened to them?

When Jody left later, Ed tried to phone Molly. Her phone rang and rang and then it went straight to voicemail. Not wanting to leave his bombshell in a message, Ed decided to call again later.

He did, but Molly wasn't picking up. Which wasn't like her. Something was wrong. Ed was itching to tell her about Jake, but he also wanted to know why she wasn't picking up. The last time she'd gone AWOL, she'd had terrible news to impart. Ed just hoped this wasn't more of the same.

Ed

Ed made his way through the crowds. He kept his wallet stuffed down the front of his boxers so no one was getting near his cash without getting seriously intimate with his parts first. It was half chastity belt, half DIY safe box.

Ed felt rather bewildered and overawed, his senses assailed all at once. He was at the Samba Schools Parade – a highlight of the carnival. The colours, the noise, the smells. Just the visual was enough to send his brain into overdrive. The floats, the dancing, the costumes. Vivid blues, vibrant yellows, garish oranges. Feathers, so many feathers. Apparently there was fierce competition between the Rio samba schools and they were assessed by judges who sat in special booths along the Samba Avenue. The schools were judged on continuity of beat of the music, the artistic credentials of the lyrics contained in the samba song and 'the visual expression of the theme'. Among other things.

Ed wondered what Molly would think of the costumes. She would love the rich, intense colours and the glitter and the outrageous wings and feathers, and she would most likely make some sort of amused comment about the metal bras and the jiggling breasts and the . . .

Ed caught himself. How long had that taken? For Molly to slip to the forefront of his mind. For him to see the parade through her eyes. To wonder how she would feel, what she would think and what she might say.

'So what do you think?'

Ed turned to find an attractive woman, possibly in her early thirties, eyeing him appreciatively.

'It's great.'

'Isn't it?' The woman gave him another hot look. 'Fancy heading off for a drink?'

Ed looked at her properly. She was a good-looking woman. She had a great body. She smelt amazing. She was clearly after more than a drink with him. This wasn't Ed being arrogant, he had simply been with enough women in his time to know when a woman was coming on to him with serious intent.

He could feel the music pounding through his body. He had had a few drinks so his senses were blurred. He was a red-blooded male. Who loved women. Everything about women.

'Thanks for the offer,' he told her politely. 'But I'm afraid I can't.'

'You can't?' She raised her eyebrows. She looked disbelieving rather than offended.

Ed understood. He exuded confidence. He looked like a guy who was up for it, who rarely turned women down.

'I can't,' he repeated. 'But I am very flattered by the offer.'

She shrugged and moved on.

Ed let out a breath. Deciding that the noise was suddenly getting to him, he shouldered his way through the crowds, heading to the fringes of the carnival. He found a quiet-looking bar, ducked inside and ordered a beer. Sitting at a table at the back, he leant his head against the wall. In a way, travelling had been the best experience. Cathartic and distracting.

Ed had more or less made peace with himself over his mother's tragic death. A part of him would always blame himself for not being there when she took her own life. But he also reasoned that she could have done it when he had been there, asleep in the house. If she had truly wanted to kill herself, she would have done. It was the only way Ed could reconcile himself to what had happened.

He had met various people on his travels and he, like they, had talked about why he was there, what had prompted him to go abroad and get away from everything at home. It seemed that everyone had a story, whether it related to illness, relationship traumas or some kind of tragedy. The odd person appeared to be there just for the sheer fun of it, but that was rare.

Ed had learnt an awful lot about himself since he'd been away. He'd learnt an awful lot about other people, too. He had had some incredible experiences and he had eaten the most bizarre and delicious food. The one thing he hadn't stopped doing was thinking about Molly. About why she hadn't called him. About what had made her turn her back on him after that night. That night . . .

Ed's hand shook and he wrapped it around his beer glass to stop it. That night. The whole time, all he'd been able to think was *Wow. This is it. This is what people talk about in the movies. This is what people search their whole lives for. This is the real deal, the whole shebang.* This wasn't the eighty per cent most people settled for because they feared walking away from something secure but unfulfilling. This was the one hundred per cent that made people whole. That made hearts sing every day.

Ed had sent Molly a heartfelt letter that had made him cry when he wrote it, because he had poured his heart out. He had sent her tickets as well, an invitation to join him, details of a meeting place. A beach he had thought she would love, one that reminded him of Maplethorpe Beach. It had been a romantic gesture of sorts; the one thing he thought might convince Molly that he loved her.

But there had been nothing in response to his 'come and see me' gesture. No answer, no phone call. Ed had gone to the meeting place at the arranged time, hardly daring to hope that Molly might just suddenly appear. But of course she hadn't. Ed's heart had suffered a hairline fracture and he had left, feeling horrendously rejected and confused.

Ed had called Boyd to see if he had heard anything from Molly. Boyd had started saying something but they had been cut off. Seventeen times. Ed had tried calling again every few days, but their calls hadn't lasted more than a few seconds. Finally, he had given up. If Molly wanted to speak to him, she would have called him. She would have left a message. She would have done something to let him know she cared about him, that she wanted him back.

And so he had stayed away. He had stayed away because he couldn't bear the thought that Molly regretted their night together. To him, it had been everything. He had thought she felt the same. But maybe he'd misread the situation. If so, he had never been more wrong in his life.

Ed drained his beer but shook his head when asked if he wanted another. He was keeping an eye on his alcohol intake. The last thing he wanted was to end up like his mother. Even though he longed to escape into the fuzzy, softened world alcohol offered him, he refused to succumb. Even on the days when the pain was so unbearable he wanted nothing more than to step into oblivion.

Leaving the bar, he headed out into the fray again. It was amazing how alone and empty he felt when he was surrounded by so many lively people, when music and smells were making life so vivid and colourful. A girl walked past and Ed stopped dead. Was it Molly? No way. It couldn't be. But it looked like her. The blond curls, the height. The figure. It could be her. It really could. Not stopping to think, Ed tore after the girl. As he wove in and out of the crowd, he could see glimpses of her, of her purple skirt – Molly had a purple skirt, it was her, it was. She was there, then she slipped from sight . . . back into view again . . . obscured by people.

Ed wasn't about to let her go and he quickened his

pace. Rushing up behind her, he put his hand on her shoulder and spun her round.

'Hey!' the girl cried. She looked surprised, then annoyed.

'Sorry.' Ed cringed when the girl backed away. 'I'm so sorry. I-I thought you were someone else.'

'Ok.' She smoothed her top down and flipped her hair. 'Fair enough. Christ. You've clearly got it bad.'

Ed watched her walk away, amazed he had thought the girl was Molly. She wasn't nearly beautiful enough. Her body wasn't anywhere near as exquisite as Molly's. Her eyes had been brown, not that lovely blue colour.

But the girl had been right about something. Ed had it bad. He had it really, really bad. Not realising people were impatiently elbowing past him, he sat down heavily on the edge of the pavement. And he cried. He cried his eyes out over a girl he had fallen in love with a long time ago. A girl he had given his soul to and who clearly didn't feel the same way he did. Ed knew he would never fall in love again for as long as he lived. Because if that night wasn't what he thought it was, nothing really mattered. All that had ever mattered was Molly. But she hadn't felt what he had. She had taken his soul, but she had kept hold of her own.

He had been right first time, Ed realised. Casual sex was the way to go. If he had been running true to type, he would be shagging his way round the world right now. Perhaps drawing up a card with different countries on it and devising a complicated scoring system he could share with other travellers in bars to demonstrate his prowess. He could, perhaps, award the winner with a prize – a trophy painted with the colours of the relevant flag. Or he could wear boxer shorts in those colours and dance down the beach in them.

Except he didn't want to do that. He had no interest. All he wanted was Molly. And Ed couldn't imagine how he was ever going to feel any different. Not even caring what he looked like, Ed blubbed. Good and proper. What a bloody loser he was.

He vowed to stay away from Molly for as long as he possibly could.

Now

'So. Do I need to teach you the rules of football?' Ed asked Jake.

'No!' Jake laughed. 'I play all the time. Do I need to teach you the rules?'

'Actually, you probably do,' Ed admitted, looking shamefaced. 'I'm a bit pants at this, if I'm honest.'

'I can show you,' Jake said. 'Come on.'

Ed followed Jake, and for the next half hour, they kicked a football around the beach in a fairly haphazard fashion, watched by Jody.

Ed soon found himself out of breath and he flopped down next to Jody. Jake raced to the water's edge and tore off his shoes. 'Blimey! Kids are exhausting.'

'You have no idea,' Jody smiled. 'You should get up in the night with them fifteen times and then go into work and do a ten-hour shift.'

Ed shuddered. 'You deserve a medal, Jody. I mean that.' He met her eyes. 'As shocking as this is for me, I do admire you for doing the whole single-mum thing. It must have been really tough.'

Jody shrugged. 'All of my own doing. I'm not going to whine about it. Jake's the best thing that ever happened to me.'

Ed followed her line of vision and watched Jake frolicking in the water. He could understand that. He hadn't ever seen the point of children before. Well, that was probably not strictly true. He'd never seen the point of children in *his* life. Boyd seemed to find his children an utter joy (which was presumably why he kept having them every five minutes), but Ed had always found them noisy and feral.

But Jake seemed different. Ed wasn't sure if he was biased because Jake might be his, but he just seemed to be a really sweet kid. Polite, well-mannered, easy to talk to. Ed was sure he could be an utter pain in the arse like other kids, but so far, he seemed to be really chilled.

'Could we have an ice cream please?' Jake panted as he joined them on the blanket.

'Sure.' Jody stood up and brushed sand from her trousers. 'Ninety-nines all round?'

'Here, take some money,' Ed offered, pulling out his wallet.

Jody waved it away. 'Don't be silly. I'll get these. You and Jake carry on discussing football or whatever.' She strode away, leaving them to it.

'So. What else are you into?' Ed asked Jake. 'I know you could play for . . . for Arsenal—'

'Man United,' Jake interrupted, looking horrified.

'Man United,' Ed corrected himself. 'But what else do you like?

'*Star Wars*, Lego, cars . . .' Once Jake got started, he was seemingly unstoppable.

Ed didn't mind. He was fascinated. He had no idea of the many reasons Boba Fett was way cooler than Luke Skywalker, or why a certain type of Lego was brilliant and another was pants. It was a whole new world. A world Ed was finding surprisingly interesting.

While Jake was talking, Ed had a proper look at him. He had tufty hair that didn't seem to sit flat. Rather like Ed's, in fact. Brown eyes that darted around when Jake was talking, reflecting his mind as it raced over various topics. Ed had no idea if his eyes did the same when he talked, but Molly used to make comments about his eyes all the time.

He and Jake carried on chatting, with Jake talking the most, as Ed's knowledge of Lego was fairly limited. He had had some Lego as a kid but it seemed as though it had all moved on – there was Technics and all sorts of other stuff he was clueless about. If Jake turned out to be his, Ed was going to have to up his game as far as toys were concerned.

'Here you go.' Jody returned with ice creams and handed them out.

'Cor.' Jake grabbed his and started licking it with gusto.

Ed smiled. One thing he had noticed about kids is that they had a delightful way of reminding you how brilliant little things were. Kicking a ball around, eating an ice cream on the beach. Talking about Lego.

'So, what have you two been talking about?'

'Lego,' Jake and Ed said at the same time.

'Right.' Jody looked amused. 'Was that interesting?'

'Yes,' they both answered seriously.

Jody burst out laughing. 'Oh, Jake, you must be loving having a bloke to talk to. I'm rubbish when it comes to all this stuff.'

'She is a bit,' Jake said to Ed in an undertone. 'She's the best mummy in the world, but she knows nothing about Lego. Or *Star Wars*. But don't tell her I said that.'

'Your secret is safe with me,' Ed commented, grinning at Jake. He really was an endearing kid. He met Jody's eyes over the top of Jake's head. She had ice cream on her chin and was beaming, presumably elated that he and Jake had bonded so well. Ed didn't have the heart to bring up the issue of a DNA test. It would spoil the moment completely.

He could only imagine what Molly would say if he said he was holding off on the test (and she would be right), but there would be time for that later. Not that Molly knew anything about it. She had been ignoring his calls for ages now. Where the hell was she? This was the biggest news of his life and he couldn't share it with her.

He just hoped she was ok. Despite the fact that he had all but given up on getting through to her, he tried again and left another voicemail message. He had to speak to her.

Molly and Ed

Molly gazed out of the window. She had never seen the city look so beautiful before. But then she hadn't ever been taken to a restaurant like this before. One that had views that stretched far and wide, with twinkling lights and shiny roof tops.

'How's your steak?'

Molly pulled her gaze back. 'My steak?' She let out a short laugh. 'I'd forgotten about it for a second. Sorry. The view distracted me. But it's perfect. Everything is perfect.'

'Perfect? Well, that's praise indeed.' Sam smiled at her. 'And I'm happy to hear you laugh again.'

'Laugh? Did I just laugh?'

'You did. And it sounded great.'

Molly ducked her head. 'Is that a polite way of saying I've been a miserable cow for some time now?'

'No. It's my way of saying that I like your laugh. I've

213

missed it.' Sam raised his champagne to hers. 'And congratulations on winning that big account. I've been chasing that company for months and you just waltz in there and bowl them over.'

Molly chinked glasses. 'It wasn't quite as simple as that,' she protested.

'I'd like to blame it on your fabulous legs but it was actually down to the impassioned speech you delivered.'

'You're very sweet.' Molly shrugged the compliment off.

Sam threw her a look. 'I'm not trying to be sweet, Molly. Far from it. And you do know that calling a guy sweet is nothing short of emasculation?'

Molly let out a proper laugh. 'Yes, sorry about that. Cute, sweet, adorable – all words that should never be used when talking to guys . . .' Her voice trailed away. She had managed to get to the second course of her meal without the thought of Ed coming into her head. It was better than she had managed during previous meals, but still. Not great.

Molly sipped her champagne. For the first time in months, she felt vaguely human. Vaguely human was better than not feeling present at all. And since Ed had left, Molly had felt broken. She had lost him as a friend. Even just saying that phrase in her head overwhelmed her.

It wasn't just that Ed had slept with her, she mused. It was that he had slept with her *like that*. Molly hadn't been with many men. Granted, more than Ed was aware of – she was a classy girl, discretion was her thing – but she had been with enough to know the difference between a shag and making love.

She gulped down some more champagne, gazing at the view again. It was in the way she had been kissed. Oh God, the way she had been kissed. Rudely, sweetly, passionately – every possible way. It was in the hand placement, and in Molly's limited experience, this was crucial. It sorted the men from the boys. Some men knew how to hold a woman, some didn't. And Ed did. He had this way of putting his hands on her waist . . . around her ribs . . . behind her knee.

It was in the tenderness, the eye contact, the sensuality. It was a billion tiny things that had signalled something to Molly. Tiny, beautiful imprints all over her body. On her soul, for heaven's sakes.

Molly cut a piece of steak and ate it. It really was perfectly cooked. The trouble was, she wasn't like Ed. Ed was a man-whore. She didn't dislike him for this, it was simply a fact. Like him hating ketchup with a passion, or loving Oscar Wilde. But presumably it meant that he had acquired skills along the way. Ed clearly had developed a way of making a girl feel special. Like she was the only girl in the world. Like she was the best person Ed could ever had been with. Molly had been utterly convinced in the moment – and beyond – that Ed had meant every word. That what had happened between them had been exquisite, exclusive, exceptional.

'More champagne?' The waiter hovered beside her.

'Yes please,' Molly said automatically.

She had to accept that she had been wrong about Ed. In fact she had never been more wrong about anyone in her life. And that was galling. Humiliating. Molly prided herself on being a good judge of character and she wouldn't have been such good friends with Ed if she didn't think he was a brilliant person. But Ed had let her down. It was simply something she was going to have to deal with.

It had been four months since Ed had left. Molly's heart still hurt. She still missed him every single day. Her body still yearned for him. She woke in the night sometimes, sweating, tangled in the sheets, wishing he was wrapped around her body. They had only slept together once but she craved his touch, his hands on her body, in her hair. His mouth on hers. But it had to stop. Molly couldn't carry on this way. The double blow of losing Ed's friendship as well as him cruelly snatching away their chance of romance had left her breathless.

But Molly knew she had to move on with her life. Ed had gone. He didn't seem to be coming back anytime soon. Which was for the best. It really was.

'Dessert?' Sam said.

Molly realised her plate had been removed. She had been so lost in her thoughts, she hadn't even noticed. She re-focused her attention.

'Not for me,' she replied. 'I've been eating far too much coffee cake recently. My hips are protesting.'

'Don't be silly,' Sam frowned. 'You look incredible. You'd look incredible if you were twenty stone.'

Molly scoffed. 'Now you're being silly! Twenty stone . . . tsk . . .'

'I'd still fancy you,' Sam said, lifting his champagne glass to his mouth. He took a slow sip.

'You . . . would still fancy me . . .?'

'If you were twenty stone. Yes. Yes, I would.' Sam

shook his head at the waiter hovering for a possible dessert order. 'In fact, I think I'd probably fancy you in any situation whatsoever.'

'Oh. Right.'

Molly wanted to look out of the window again, to buy herself a few seconds of panic-stricken time, but she steeled herself. That would seem inappropriate, impolite even.

'I thought it was important to say that.' He looked annoyed with himself. 'Actually, I didn't think that at all. I just said it.'

'I see.'

Molly wasn't sure how to play this. Sam had been gently flirting with her over the past month or so. It hadn't gone unnoticed, but so far, it had gone unreciprocated. Molly wasn't in any position to respond to anyone right now. Ed had destroyed her confidence and he had given her trust issues that hadn't existed beforehand. And while Molly trusted Sam more than she probably trusted anyone else, other than her parents, she still couldn't bring herself to respond in kind.

'Molly.' Sam reached across the table and took her hand. His eyes were earnest. 'I know you've been hurt. And I understand what that does to a person; I do. The thing is . . . I want to make you happy. I think I can make you happy.'

Molly was lost for words. She felt Sam squeeze her hand and she found herself squeezing back.

Sam started again. 'What I'm trying to say is . . . if you would consider spending time with me . . . as . . . more than a friend, I would devote myself to trying to do that. To making you happy, I mean. I would give it . . . you . . . everything I have. Because to me, you are incredible.'

Molly was stunned. She was sure her face must be showing just how stunned she was. She should say something. She really should say something. But she didn't have a clue what.

Sam rushed to fill the gap. 'You don't have to say anything now. I didn't mean to blurt any of that out. Really, I didn't. The last thing I wanted to do was make you feel uncomfortable.' He removed his hand from hers.

Molly stared at her empty hand. It felt oddly bereft. Sam's hand had made her feel safe and secure for those few seconds. It felt good for someone to be holding her hand, caring about her, saying lovely things. Molly suddenly realised how much she needed some loveliness in her life. Some calmness. Some security. How much she needed an anchor.

Molly looked at Sam properly and examined his face. She looked into his eyes. They were wide and sincere. Molly was fairly certain she could trust those eyes. She glanced at his mouth. It was kind of sexy. She could kiss that mouth. Maybe. Yes.

Sam was settling the bill and leaving a tip. He collected their coats and signalled for Molly to stand up as he helped her into her thin jacket. She followed him outside. It was a sunny, spring evening with just a slight breeze in the air.

They started strolling and Molly slipped her hand through Sam's arm. Abruptly, he stopped and faced her.

'Molly, about the stuff I said before . . . I'm sorry

about that. I genuinely didn't mean to dump any of that on you today.'

'Sam. Stop.' Molly reached her hand out and placed it on Sam's cheek. It felt warm beneath her touch. Safe. 'I think . . . I think I liked you saying those things.'

'You . . . you did?'

Molly nodded. 'Yes. I didn't know how to react, that was all. I didn't know what to say. No one has ever said those . . .'

She faltered. That wasn't true. Someone *had* said those things to her before. More than those things. And in a very eloquent, romantic fashion that had made her heart race and her mind flood with hope. But what good had that done her? None whatsoever. Ed had showered her with wonderful words and actions and then he had taken himself out of her life without a second thought. But Sam wasn't like that. Sam meant those words. Sam wouldn't let her down.

Molly made a decision. She wasn't prone to taking risks when it came to men. Especially not after Ed. But Sam wasn't a risk. Molly was certain of that. She leant forward and kissed him. On the mouth. She pressed her lips to his and kissed him again. Sam started. Then he responded. And kissed her back.

Molly's mind raced. Her first thought was that this kiss wasn't a patch on the ones she had with Ed. But that it wasn't bad. It wasn't bad at all. And what did it matter about Ed? Molly kissed Sam more ardently. He kissed her back more ardently and slid his hands around her waist.

It felt different. It all felt different. Different to kissing Ed. Different to the way he had made her feel. Her body wasn't sparking off haphazardly, sending deliciously chaotic charges to every inch. Her insides weren't melting. And she didn't feel the urge to thrust Sam against a wall and snog the hell out of him. But even in those few short minutes, Molly felt safe. Cherished. Adored. In capable, reliable, romantic hands. With someone who would put her first. Who wouldn't let her down.

Sam paused, took her face in his hands. 'Molly. Are you sure about this?'

Molly took a breath. 'Yes, Sam. I've never been more sure about anything in my life.'

'Then you've made me the happiest guy in the world.' Sam kissed her again.

And Molly let him. And shortly afterwards, she let go of any stupid notion that Ed was her soulmate. That he might one day come back for her and make her feel the way he had made her feel that night for the rest of her life.

No, Molly was certain now. Ed was her past and Sam was her future. Life had never been clearer.

Ed

October 2001

Ed sank down on to a rock. He felt tired. And desperately lonely, if he was honest. Travelling had its benefits; he felt completely disconnected from home and everything relating to it. But it also had its downsides. He felt completely disconnected from home and everything relating to it. Yes. Swings and roundabouts.

Ed lit a cigarette, enjoying the combined aroma of tobacco and the coconut oil from his fingers. Barbados. What a place. A heady mix of affluent, lush hotels and poverty-stricken shanty towns, lending the island an unusual, confused air. On the one hand there were friendly smiles, beautiful vistas and aromatic food. On the other, a suggestion of opportunistic danger, an edge that meant evenings had to be played out safely. The daytime was full of such sunny wonder it was hard to believe that in certain quarters there was another side to the island, a menacing underbelly that had to be seen to be believed.

That said, Ed had had a wonderful time in Barbados. He had burnt his tongue on a delicious Pepperpot stew and he had drunk more rum-based cocktails than he could remember. And the beaches were breathtaking. Pale, fine sand and shallow, turquoise waters that stretched out to nothingness. He had bought a stunning painting by a local artist which captured the very essence of Barbados; an unbeatable, gloriously bohemian vibe.

In the spirit of cliché, he had met some amazing people and he had made some friends for life. Mostly couples, strangely enough, but the odd single guy and girl. Not that Ed was remotely interested in any of the girls. He'd tried to be, he'd tried really hard. But it hadn't worked. Nothing had worked.

Ed blew smoke into the air. Why on earth was he thinking of home all the time? He was basking in sunshine. He had money in his account, courtesy of Boyd selling his mother's house. He had no job to rush back to. He was free. So why did he keep on thinking about rainy old England? And a roof-top terrace with fairy lights, over-sized floor cushions and a heater that didn't work properly?

The thing about travelling was that it distracted the mind. Took a person away from whatever it was they might be running away from, or needed distance from, as one attractive girl had corrected him once over cock-tails. Going travelling wasn't always about running away, apparently. It was about 'creating distance', so that what-ever was left at home could be confronted at a later date. Whether it be a job, a situation, or a person.

But in Ed's case, it was no longer working. He had

travelled from one corner of the world to another. He had gone down the backpacking route for a while, mainly because of the lack of available funds. Ed had told himself that such an experience would be humbling, but it hadn't really felt that way. Sleeping on camp beds and in hostels was hardly the same as working in hospitals or spending time in a shelter. Both of which he had done, searching in vain for . . . something. So, as money had arrived in his account, Ed had decided he would indulge himself a bit and stay in some cool hotels. He had enjoyed luxury, ostentation and splendour. There had been some iconic moments, most often inspired by literary heroes. Raffles Hotel in Singapore where he had immersed himself in the infamous bar favoured by Ernest Hemingway, Rudyard Kipling and Alfred Hitchcock. The Plaza in New York, off the beaten track for most travellers, but F. Scott Fitzgerald had lived there once. Ed had no idea if Fitzgerald and his beau, Zelda, actually had frolicked at midnight in the hotel's fountain, but he liked to think they had.

But Ed was done with distraction. It was avoidance at its absolute best and he had done it to death. His mother was gone and his guilt had lifted fractionally. And even though Molly's silence had hurt him deeply, Ed wanted to see her again. He felt like a junkie, craving her presence. Even as a friend. Clearly she wanted nothing more from him than that and Ed was finally in a place to accept it. To put himself out there again and see if they could get their friendship back on track.

Grinding his cigarette out on the rock he was sitting on, Ed disposed of it in a nearby bin. He had grown up considerably. He thought more about his actions. About other people. He had seen poverty at its shocking worst and he had witnessed such lavish wealth, it had taken his breath away. He had lain on incredible beaches, climbed mountains and waded through seas and streams in the name of 'experience'. All of which had been marvellous, but the journey had come to an end.

It was time to go home. It was time to lay some ghosts to rest and to resurrect some others, if he could. Heading back to his hotel, he booked himself on to a flight, packed his belongings and collected his passport from the safe.

In the airport Ed began to feel rather sick. How would Molly react to seeing him? Would she care either way? Ed had no idea. But he wasn't going back on what he had decided to do. He missed Molly too damned much to stay away any longer. No matter what she felt or didn't feel towards him.

On the plane he stuck his headphones in and half watched several films all the way home.

Setting his feet on English soil felt good – the absence of rain helped. Ed realised he was of no fixed abode, so he headed to Boyd's house. Boyd was at work but Mrs Middleford was in situ and she seemed surprisingly pleased to see him.

'Edison! You're back! What a delight. Do come in.' Mrs Middleford opened the door wide and stood aside to accommodate him.

Wrong-footed, Ed did as he was asked. He followed her into the kitchen, taken aback when she waved a bottle of white wine at him.

'Have a drink with me?' she said with a smile.

Her good mood explained, Ed accepted, even though he was feeling eminently British and was gasping for a cup of builders' brew tea. In a mug. Mrs Middleford probably didn't own any mugs.

'So, how were your travels?' she asked, offering him a seat and taking one uncomfortably close to him. 'Do tell me all about it.'

Ed did so, giving her the potted version, the highlights he assumed she would like to hear. 'And then I ended up in Barbados,' he finished. 'Lovely place. Stunning. But you wouldn't wander around at night on your own, if you get my drift.'

'I certainly do,' Mrs Middleford agreed. 'I found Thailand the same, even though we were staying at a wonderful hotel.' She name dropped some celebrities who had stayed there and topped up Ed's wine glass. 'Oh, you have some post,' she said, gesturing vaguely to a cupboard. 'Boyd has been to collect it every so often.'

Ed got up and pulled the post out of the cupboard. It was a huge pile; but then he had been away for months. He leafed through it as Mrs Middleford wittered on about security issues in the Seychelles and Jamaica, discarding most as irrelevant. Pausing at a thick cream envelope with his name scrawled across it in elaborate script, Ed put everything else down and opened it. As he pulled out an embossed card, his stomach dropped.

It was an invitation. To a wedding. With swirly writing and some rather incongruous lotus flowers printed all around the edges. The flowers screamed out shrilly at Ed more than the actual names on the card.

'Oh, did you get one too?' Mrs Middleford trilled. 'How lovely. Isn't it wonderful news? I do love a wedding. Not long now, either. All a bit of a whirlwind romance from what I understand . . .'

Ed sat down heavily. Surely there was some kind of mistake. This couldn't be happening. He re-read the invitation. It was happening. In a week's time. In a week's time, Molly – his Molly – was getting married. To Sam.

Ed had never felt so poleaxed in his life. Draining his wine and holding his glass out for a refill that caused chirps of delight from Boyd's mother, Ed made another big decision then and there. He would avoid this wedding like the plague. It would be hurtful and traumatic and he wouldn't be able to stand the sight of Molly looking gorgeous and marrying that idiot Sam.

He abruptly changed his mind. He would attend the wedding. He would be appropriately suited and booted and he would assume a nonchalant stance. He would kiss the bride's cheek and he would shake the groom's hand and he would do it all with style and aplomb. It was what he was going to have to do.

'Chin, chin!' Mrs Middleford sang.

'Chin, chin,' Ed echoed, doing his best to smile as he felt his world implode.

Now

Molly arrived home from Mexico at lunchtime. She let herself into the house, braced for what she was going to find. Or rather, for what was going to be missing. There was plenty missing. Sam had cleared his things out in a most thorough manner – just like him to do things properly, but it was tough for Molly to take.

Bookcases were missing books. There was the odd space where a photograph had been. Sam's cupboards and drawers were completely empty. The bathroom cabinet only had a few remnants of him left – a nearly-finished can of shaving foam, an aftershave he hadn't much liked. For some reason, Molly found this irksome. She grabbed the items and tossed them in the bin. If Sam wanted to be gone from her life, he might as well go. Without leaving a trace.

She sank down on to the bed. She had spent the last few days wandering around in a dream. She had cried at the most inappropriate times – at breakfast alone, lying on her lounger. On one of the days, she had cried so uncontrollably, she had almost been sick. She had felt hysterical and she knew people were staring at her but she couldn't seem to stop. Presumably she was going through a form of grief. And part of her panic related to an intense feeling of loneliness. Not just the actual aloneness she was physically experiencing now, but the realisation that she could potentially be alone for the rest of her life. Alone with her Parkinson's. Who would want to take that – her – on? She was hardly going to be a good catch for someone, not now.

Molly had then spent the days hating Sam. Really hating him. With intense venom and violence. If he'd still been around her, she would have punched him really hard in the face. Because she was so vulnerable right now. She really, really needed someone. No, that wasn't true. She needed Sam. And he had let her down. He had let her down so badly Molly knew that even if he came back to her with his tail between his legs, she wouldn't ever be able to see him in the same way. She would no longer be able to look at him and see the Sam she had always known. He was a different person to her now – a stranger. She would never have believed him capable of treating her this way. Not in a million years.

Molly wandered around the rest of the house, acquainting herself with the strangeness that Sam's leaving had caused. She felt angry and bereft. How could he do this to her? She paused in the kitchen, noticing that Sam had removed the coffee maker she had bought for his birthday. It was only right that he took it – she only drank de-caff and he used it every day – but for some reason, it incensed her. Pausing, Molly looked down at her leg. It was trembling, the way her hand often did. Jesus. Jesus. That was all she needed. Molly gripped the edge of the nearest bit of kitchen counter and grimaced.

Fuck Sam. If he wanted to be gone, he could be gone. She strode around the house rearranging things. She moved books around to cover the gaps Sam's books had left. She moved ornaments to different places so the photographs he had swiped weren't noticeable. She even went up into the loft and retrieved some bright green cushions Sam had detested and put them on the lounge sofa, discarding the more sedate ones that had resided there for some years.

In the kitchen, Molly moved the toaster to the empty spot the coffee machine had occupied. She tidied up the fridge, binned some photographs. She felt a pang as she dropped them into the bin, but she knew it was the right thing to do. She wasn't being callous, she just needed to change things around – to make sure she could cope in a Sam-free zone.

Finally, she went upstairs and shoved a load of things Sam had missed into dustbin sacks. She found a box of paperwork under his office desk and she added that to the pile. As she set the box down, an envelope fell out. Picking it up, she was about to toss it back in when she noticed that it was addressed in Ed's handwriting. Why on earth would Sam have a letter addressed to her, in Ed's handwriting?

Molly chewed her lip. She could just pull the contents out of the envelope and read it. The letter, or whatever it was, was addressed to her, after all. But she had a strong feeling about it. A feeling that reading whatever was contained inside might be too much for her right now. She had no idea why she felt that way, but she couldn't do it. She had too much going on in her head already.

With Ed on her mind, Molly called him. Not about the letter, just to hear his voice. He didn't answer and his phone went straight to voicemail. She left a message. She had missed Ed. She had really, really missed him.

Ed let himself back into the house. He had spent the entire day with Jake and he felt jubilant. They had spent some time at the beach while Jody did some work, they had had lunch in a café, sharing a huge plate of chips (Jake hated condiments too), and they had spent the afternoon at the house Jody had rented playing with a Playstation Ed had bought for Jake. He wasn't sure if it was the right thing to do (too extravagant?) but Jody had seemed really pleased and Jake had lost the plot he was so excited.

It had been an excellent day. One of the best Ed had ever had, in fact. Which seemed odd. Surely there were better ways to spend a day than in the company of a child? He'd never enjoyed being with children before. But there was just something about Jake. He was such a great kid.

Ed chucked his keys on the table. He still hadn't spoken to Jody about the paternity test. He knew he had to do it, but he was having such a great time with Jake, he couldn't quite bring himself to do it.

Trouble was, Ed had already seen a brilliant Lego set

he thought Jake would like. There were books he wanted to read with Jake. He wanted to get better at football so he could play properly with Jake and not be such a nobber at it. Ed just wanted to spend as much time as he possibly could with Jake.

On the way home Ed had even started to think about a future with Jake. Having Jake properly in his life. Which he knew he shouldn't do because he didn't know for sure that Jake was his. But there was really no denying it. They'd bonded so easily. And look at the boy! It was like looking at pictures of himself when he was that age. It was impossible to think that Jake wasn't his.

Ed picked his phone up. He had a voicemail. From Molly. He hadn't even noticed it. He quickly called her back.

'Molly! Where have you been? Are you ok? Can we meet?' Ed paused, listening to Molly. She sounded terrible. Something had happened. 'Ok. I'll see you tomorrow. I have to do something in the morning, but I'll be back after lunchtime. Meet me at mine?'

Ed ended the call with some trepidation. Something was wrong. Was it something to do with her illness? Christ. He raked his hair back. What had happened to them both? Life used to be so simple.

Ed took his coat off and threw himself into a chair. He wasn't sure he could cope with anything else going wrong for Molly.

Molly

October 2001

Molly took a sip of champagne and winced as the wedding planner pulled her corset tighter.

'Almost done . . .'

'No problem,' Molly said, breathing in. Jess, the wedding planner, had been superb from the day she had been booked, but she was proving herself to be oddly incompetent when it came to lacing up corsets.

Molly took another glug of champagne. She felt oddly calm and she had no idea why. Her relationship with Sam had been a whirlwind since they had got together back in April. They had slept together the night they had gone out to dinner and it had been unexpected. Fireworks hadn't gone off as such, but something else had happened. She had let go. She had calmed down. She had allowed herself to be happy. Molly knew she needed looking after. And Sam had proved himself to be more than capable of looking after her.

Everything seemed to slot in place from that point for Molly. Her relationship with Sam had flourished and their business had taken off accordingly, almost as though it were responding to their new-found energy as a couple. Life suddenly seemed to make sense.

'Are you happy with the flowers?'

Molly glanced at them. 'They're beautiful, Jess,' she smiled. They were. A clashing mix of cerise and orange roses, tangled up with birch and seasonal berries. Neatly tied with orange ribbon, the bouquet was very autumnal. Sam had been keen on the idea of a Christmas wedding, but she had baulked at that for some reason. It just felt a bit . . . much. But autumn was fine. Autumn seemed to suit them.

Molly moved to the window. She could see guests arriving. Many, many guests, far more than she had envisaged inviting, but Sam had been in charge of the guest list. Among other things. Sam had, in fact, taken care of much of the wedding, albeit not the more feminine details. Those he had happily handed over to her. Flowers, favours and invitations. Oh, and her dress, naturally. Molly had ended up in a structured corset with a straight skirt instead of the floaty 1930s effort she had originally had in mind. She wasn't sure how or why but when she had put the silk corset on, it had seemed right. Appropriate. She hoped Sam would find it beautiful.

Molly watched women with coiffed hair and professionally applied make-up tripping up the stone path in uncomfortable-looking high heels, holding on to the arms of men in pristine suits, who were already fingering the collars of their stiff shirts, thoughts of tie removal at the forefront of their minds.

Was this how she had imagined her wedding? Molly wasn't sure. She wasn't a girly girl with teenage visions of wedding dresses, but perhaps she had thought of this day on and off. Something more bohemian, maybe? Something smaller, more intimate. Less formal. A sun-drenched garden, perhaps. Wild flowers and handfuls of pansies in jam jars. But this was what Sam wanted. And oddly, it hadn't seemed important enough for Molly to protest. She felt relaxed about the arrangements, keen to go with the flow and do whatever made Sam happy. And he seemed equally chilled about the details that she felt were key.

'You seem very relaxed,' Jess commented. 'I haven't seen many brides this laid back on their wedding day.'

'Really?' Molly shrugged. She had nothing to be nervous about. This was Sam. They had only been together for around six months but she had felt comfortable with him from the day they had met. Molly fleetingly wondered if she should feel more anxious. More excited. Would she feel differently if . . .

No, Molly told herself. She wouldn't do that. She wouldn't think about him today. Against her better judgement and somewhat in a fit of pique, she had sent him an invitation via the Middleford family, but it had been a safe act of defiance. Ed was still abroad as far as she knew and therefore unlikely to put in an appearance. The mere thought of such a thing made her feel bilious, but Molly was certain Ed would be absent today. Even if by some freak chance he was back in the country, not even he would have the audacity to rock up at a wedding he clearly shouldn't be a part of.

'Are you ready to go down?' Jess checked her watch. 'We're right on track.'

'Excellent.'

Molly drained her champagne and picked her straight skirt up to her knees. It was tight around her legs, she was glad she didn't have to get in and out of a fancy Bentley in it. Sam had been all for them arriving at the stately home they had hired in such a fashion but Molly had gently talked him out of it. She was a reasonably flamboyant girl at times but dramatic entrances weren't her bag. It was enough that there were some two hundred guests in evidence.

Molly squared her shoulders. She was doing this. She was marrying Sam. And it felt right.

Ed was late. He hadn't intended to be late, he couldn't believe he was late, but he was. It hadn't been deliberate, in fact he had been up at the crack of dawn. Half because the new flat he was renting was positioned above a noisy supermarket whose deliveries arrived at silly o'clock, and half because the thought of Molly marrying Sam had kept him awake ever since Ed had first clapped eyes on the tasteful, slightly bohemian invitation.

Ed adjusted his tie and made sure his cuffs were showing. It shouldn't matter what he looked like in the scheme of things – Ed liked to think he had grown out of his immature, vain phase – but today, it mattered. A crumpled linen shirt and jeans wasn't going to cut it. He was wearing a navy suit that fit like a glove. Tight trousers, slightly too tight, truth be told. Ed wasn't sure they would withstand the Macarena, but his tailor had told him it was the fashion these days. A crisp white shirt, a navy silk tie with a tie pin, a starched white handkerchief in his top pocket. And a beautifully cut waistcoat. It was, quite simply, the most incredible suit Ed had ever worn. The only thing that prevented the suit from sitting perfectly was the small box in the left-hand pocket. A wedding gift of sorts. A stupid gift, no doubt.

Ed glanced down at himself. It was possible he might look more like the groom than the actual groom, but that wasn't the point. He just wanted to show Molly that he was capable of making an effort. Of being appropriate. Even though she had ignored his heartfelt letter. Even though they hadn't spoken in months. But being late hadn't been part of the plan.

He dashed into the stately home his taxi driver had apparently had such trouble finding. It was hardly small or discreet. It was opulent and lavish. Not what he would have imagined Molly choosing in a million years. If asked to outline Molly's ideal wedding plans, he probably would have offered up an idea of an outdoor summer affair with a slightly hippyish vibe. Garlands and headdresses made from wild flowers. Homemade centrepieces and cute wedding favours designed to make guests grin. A cool live band to dance to in a makeshift marquee as the sun went down and an unconventional first dance involving laughter and some deliberately uncool dance moves.

Ed shrugged off the thought as he headed inside. He clearly didn't know Molly as well as he thought, but then he had been abroad for around ten months. He had experienced all sorts of different things and Ed assumed the same had happened to Molly. Grabbing a cream buttonhole from a basket on a table in the hallway, Ed tucked it into his jacket lapel and asked for directions.

'Oh, but you've missed the ceremony!' a young girl in a white shirt and black skirt exclaimed. 'It was lovely but the guests are in the Whitmore Suite now, the bride and groom are having some photos taken.' She smiled at him. 'Grab yourself a winter Pimms and go for a mingle. Hopefully no one will notice how late you are.'

Ed felt a rush of relief. His tardiness hadn't been ideal, but he couldn't help feeling that watching Molly gazing adoringly at Sam as she said her vows might have been excruciating. Horribly so. Ed grabbed a winter Pimms as he slipped into the room and winced as he sipped it. He hated Pimms and he rather thought Molly did too. Maybe she didn't any more.

He hugged Molly's parents, Eleanor and John, and had a chat with them about his travels. He greeted Jody, Molly's ex-flatmate, with caution, but she seemed relatively pleased to see him, so he relaxed.

'Nice tan,' Jody said with a flirtatious wink as she sashayed away from him. She had lost weight. She looked pretty good.

'Christ, you're late!' Boyd clapped Ed on the shoulder. 'Why didn't you take us up on that lift?'

'Because I'm an arse.' Ed gave Boyd an affectionate hug, noticing a girl standing shyly behind him. 'And who's this?'

'My girlfriend,' Boyd said proudly. 'Helen, come and meet Ed. He's a terrible reprobate, don't fall in love with him, will you?'

'Don't be silly.' Helen blushed and nudged Boyd. 'Nice to meet you, Ed. Bride or groom? I mean, who are you here for?'

'Oh, most definitely the bride,' Ed said, catching Boyd's eye. 'Where is she?'

Boyd jerked his head in the direction of the window. 'Outside.' He lowered his voice as Ed made for the window. 'She looks bloody stunning, mate. Brace yourself.'

Ed grimaced. Of course Molly looked stunning. Molly wasn't capable of looking anything but. Even in scruffy joggers and a t-shirt she rocked it. But he was glad of the warning from Boyd. His heart was positively thumping at the thought of seeing Molly again. Pausing by the window, he caught his breath. Christ. She was dressed in a long ivory dress with some corset affair going on. She looked sexy and classy and breathtaking. Utterly breathtaking. Her hair was lighter than he remembered, caught up in sparkly combs, strands trailing down her neck. She wore a fur cape thingy around her shoulders and she looked relaxed. And happy. A serene happiness. Rightness.

Ed's heart clenched. And he hated himself for it. He wanted Molly to be happy. He did. He just hadn't seen this coming. Molly and Sam. Sam and Molly. Their names fit, but they also jarred. It had always been Ed and Molly in his head. Molly and Ed. Molly. He bit his lip. She was walking towards him, well, towards the building. He should move away, slink to a dark corner. He shouldn't be the first person she bumped into. In spite of all of this, Ed remained rooted to the spot, his feet seemingly made of clay.

Molly pushed the door open, ducking her head as guests cheered and clapped. Raising her eyes, she came face to face with Ed.

'Fuck,' she said, clearly forgetting that there were children in attendance.

'Yes,' Ed said. He stepped back to let her come in properly. He knew he only had a second to drink her in before Sam arrived and he made the most of it. He took in her intensely blue eyes. Her lovely skin. Her mouth, quivering as she examined him.

'Ed.' Sam arrived behind Molly. 'What a surprise. I . . . we . . . weren't expecting you.'

Ed hoped the wince he suffered internally wasn't evident on the outside. *We*. That hurt.

'Well.' Ed cleared his throat and gathered his thoughts. 'I came back from my trip last week and saw the invitation to your nuptials. I . . . I thought it would be good to see you again. Both of you,' he added, feeling his insides seizing up.

'Excellent,' Sam smiled, sliding his hand around Molly's waist.

Ed forced himself to look away from the proprietorial gesture. He could hardly bear the sight of Sam's hand on Molly's waist. And the thought of Sam's hands being everywhere else.

'What a lovely thought,' Sam added.

Molly's lip curled. 'Especially since we haven't heard a single word from you since you left. Not once in the months and months you have been away.'

Her gaze alighted on Ed again and he felt something fire in his direction. Anger? Fury, even? Surely not! What on earth was Molly angry with him for? If anyone should be angry, he should be. What on earth was going on?

Hang on. Ed met Sam's eye and suddenly everything slotted into place. Sam had intercepted his letter. Ed kept his eyes on Sam's. Read the message there accurately. He was to say nothing to Molly. He should not let on that there was a letter and plane tickets, not tell her that he had tried to contact her as soon as he had left. For Molly's sake, if he felt anything for her at all, he should keep quiet and allow her to think badly of him.

Ed had never felt so much like hitting someone in his life before. As if it wasn't bad enough that Sam was holding smugly on to Molly as if he . . . as if he fucking well *deserved* her, he had destroyed Ed's letter. He had let Molly think that he, Ed, was a bastard. Because he wanted her for himself? Because he was trying to protect her? Ed guessed he would never know.

The fucking, *fucking* smug arsehole. Sam knew that Ed's feelings for Molly ran so deep that he couldn't possibly drop this bombshell on her. Not on her wedding day – nor on any other day. And Ed hated him for that.

'About that,' Ed began haltingly. 'About . . . not making contact.' He met Sam's eyes once more and gave an imperceptible nod. 'I can't apologise enough about that. I'm afraid I was suffering from head up arse-itus and then I got so carried away with my travels, it just . . .' His voice dried up.

'Very understandable,' Sam said, reaching a hand out to grab Ed's. He pumped it several times. Gratefully. 'Well, I hope you had a fantastic time.'

240

'I did,' Ed said weakly, staring at Molly. She hated him; he could see it in her eyes. And he couldn't blame her. As far as she knew, he had shagged her and then he had callously buggered off without explanation or apology. And he had continued, in Molly's eyes, to be a complete and utter shit for the entire time he had stayed away. Ed felt destroyed.

'Sam! Sam, we need you over here!' One of his friends was beckoning him over, and with some reluctance, Sam let go of Molly and headed in their direction.

Molly turned to Ed. 'I can't believe you're here.'

'A mistake, perhaps.' Ed swallowed. 'But I wanted to see you. I . . . had to come.'

'Did you? Did you really, Ed?' Tears flooded into Molly's eyes and she frantically brushed at them.

'Shit, Molly, please don't cry.' Ed yanked the handkerchief out of his pocket and thrust the hard little square into her hand. 'I can't bear it when you cry.'

Molly scoffed into the handkerchief. 'Don't be ridiculous, Ed! If you can't bear it when I cry, you wouldn't make me do it so often!'

Ouch. Ed wasn't sure who was dishing out the best body blows today, Sam or Molly.

'I don't ever mean to make you cry,' he said honestly. 'Not ever. If I have, then I am truly, truly sorry, Molls. You are – and you always will be – my . . . my very good friend. The best person I know.'

Molly shook her head, her eyes full of agony.

'It's true.' Ed took her hand. 'And I mean that emphatically. And I know you won't want to be my friend ever again, but that doesn't mean I don't care for you deeply.

Even if you want to hate me for the rest of our lives, I will always . . .' He stopped and bit his lip. Not the time or the place to tell Molly he loved her. There would probably never be a right time now that she had married Sam. Ed's heart suffered another puncture.

'I will,' he said, starting again, 'always be here for you. No matter what happens. I might not have been in the past but I most certainly will be from now on.'

'Oh, Ed.' Molly dropped her eyes. 'Why did you have to do this today?' she whispered. 'Why today?'

Ed realised people were coming over wanting to speak to Molly. 'I don't know. Bad timing is my bag, I guess.' He quickly took the box he'd brought with him out of his pocket. 'Don't open it now,' he said quickly. 'It's nothing, just a silly trinket from my travels. A "I saw this and thought of you" moment.'

Molly stared at the box as though she wanted to hurl it back in his face but she slipped it into the small silk bag she was carrying. Abruptly, she pulled Ed into a hug. He wrapped his arms around her and put his chin on the top of her head.

'I . . . I'm glad you're happy,' he managed. 'It's all I have ever, ever wanted for you.'

Molly said nothing, but she clutched him tightly.

'Do you want me to leave?' he asked, moving his mouth to her ear.

Molly paused then shook her head. 'No. No. Stay, Ed. Please.'

Ed nodded. He didn't want to let her go but he was aware that people were watching. He released her, feeling the wrench acutely. He then stood back and let Molly and Sam enjoy the rest of their wedding. He ate some delicious food, got chatted up by a bridesmaid who turned out to be Sam's sister – good lord, no – and even managed a few dances with Molly's mother and a gaggle of girls who kept complimenting him on his suit and his dance moves simultaneously.

But at the point Molly and Sam hit the dance floor for their first dance, Ed decided enough was enough. The song was, luckily, one he wasn't familiar with. A bonus, since he never wanted to hear it again. Calling a cab, Ed slipped outside to wait for it.

He was surprised when Jody rushed out after him.

'Hey. Fancy a nightcap?' Brandishing a bottle of vodka, Jody sat down with a thump and gestured for him to join her. 'Come on. Let's get pissed.'

Ed took the bottle and downed an indecent quantity. He felt the warmth flood through him and he drank some more for good measure.

'Leave some for me,' Jody huffed. 'Listen. Help me make a decision, would you? I've been offered this job and I don't know what to do about it.'

'What's the problem with it?'

'It's in Canada. And I have to give them an answer in a few days' time otherwise they'll offer it to someone else.'

'Crikey.'

Ed's vodka-fuddled brain considered this. He would rather like to bugger off to Canada himself. Well, anywhere, actually. There was something very appealing about being able to start again somewhere else. It must be like being a different person – someone without a past, without baggage, without preconception. But he had only just got back from his travels. It would look pretty daft if he headed off again, however much he wanted to.

'I think you should go for it,' Ed replied finally. 'What could be better than starting again? Meeting new people. Earning lots of money. I assume there is lots of money involved?'

'Oodles,' Jody nodded. She took of gulp of vodka, her eyes shining with excitement. 'You're right, Ed. I should do it, shouldn't I?'

'You should.'

Ed drank some more vodka and rubbed a hand over his eyes.

Jody frowned. 'You ok?'

Ed shook his head. 'Nope.'

'Molly?'

Ed nodded, feeling tears pricking at his eyes.

Jody took a breath and put her head on his shoulder. 'I don't know what she's thinking. Sam's great and all that but you, you're lovely, you.'

'No I'm not.' Ed took another swig from the bottle. 'I'm a fucking idiot.'

Jody took the bottle from his hands and turned his face to hers. 'I have a thing for fucking idiots.' Clumsily, she leant into him. Her mouth found his and she kissed him.

Ed found himself kissing her back. Not because he wanted to, but because she was there. Because Molly didn't want him.

'Shall I come back to yours?' Jody whispered. 'Take your mind off things?'

Ed looked at Jody. Maybe this was what he needed. To revert back to his ways of old. A casual shag to obliterate reality. Anything to get rid of the tormenting issues of Sam and Molly rolling around together in a romantic four-poster bed. But he shouldn't use Jody like that.

'I really, really want to do this with you, Ed,' Jody said, finding his mouth again. 'I want you. Please let me have you. The cab is here.'

Too drunk and wretched to do much else but agree, Ed staggered to the cab with Jody and got in. He was fairly certain the excruciating pain in his heart couldn't be alleviated, but he was damned well going to let Jody have a try.

Watching them from the window of the honeymoon suite, Molly's heart sank. Well, what had she expected? Ed to return home from his travels a changed man? And Jody had always had a thing for Ed, so it stood to reason she would make a play for him as soon as he reappeared. Jody didn't know how Molly felt about Ed and she certainly wouldn't think Molly had feelings now – not on the day she was marrying Sam.

She took the gift Ed had given her out of her handbag. She wanted to put it in the bin – she didn't want anything from Ed – but something made her open the box.

Inside was a pair of silver earrings shaped like lotus flowers. Molly burst into tears. What the hell was wrong with her? Sam had given her a pair of beautiful, teardrop-shaped diamond earrings and she hadn't burst into tears over those. And here she was, sobbing over a pair of pretty earrings that cost far less, from a man who had let her down and made her sadder than anyone had ever made her.

Hearing the door opening and knowing Sam must be looking for her, Molly stuffed the earrings into her handbag and wiped her eyes. It was her wedding day. And she had married a wonderful man who was going to make her very happy. She had wasted enough time thinking about Ed. But one thing was for sure, whatever Ed had said earlier, Molly was fairly certain they would never be friends again. Her heart simply couldn't take it.

Now

Molly drove to Ed's house. It looked empty but, as ever, the door was unlocked. She went in, tutting. Ed really had no concept of public safety.

'Ed! It's Molly. If you're naked, put some clothes on please!'

Nothing. No answer. In fact it seemed unlikely Ed was there at all, as he usually had music on. Molly wandered around Ed's house. It was surprisingly tidy. Saskia had kept the place spotless when she had been around, but Ed was rather more male in that respect. Tidy but not necessarily that focused on cleanliness. Out of habit, Molly started cleaning up a bit, tidying piles of books and magazines, scouring the kitchen.

She gazed out of the window. This house really did have a lovely garden. She remembered the client party they had held at Ed's house, the one Sam had been so stressed at.

Molly sighed. That was one thing she and Sam had

compromised on when they bought their house; very little outside space. Sam had been happy with the small patio area for his barbecue and space enough for a table and two chairs. Molly had wanted more, but she had been content to compromise, mainly because of the great studio space.

I'm selling the house, she thought to herself. What was the point of keeping it? It wasn't what she wanted and she no longer needed to consider the views of Sam – or anyone else – which was kind of liberating. Molly switched Ed's iPod on, turned it up and busied herself with cleaning and tidying. It was therapeutic.

Ed's office was the messiest room in the house. There was paper everywhere, notebooks full of his terrible handwriting and a collection of mugs emblazoned with jokey messages containing sludgy-looking cold coffee. Molly collected them all up and put them in the dish-washer. She was loath to mess with Ed's work too much, but she tidied everything into neat piles and polished the desk.

Putting some unused notebooks in a drawer, Molly found Ed's manuscript. It was entitled 'The Years of Loving You', with 'By Ed Sutherland' typed beneath it in large letters. It all looked very professional. Molly glanced over her shoulder nervously. She had no idea where Ed was. He might walk in at any minute and find her nosing around in his desk. But it was Ed's novel. The novel he had been working on all these years – the one he rarely talked about. Maybe just a quick peek. Ed would never know.

Molly turned the front page over and started reading.

The characters were called James and Emma. She read the first few pages, a broad smile on her face. As she continued reading, the smile faded. She couldn't believe what she was reading. It was about her and Ed. About the night they first met.

'Are you a romantic, James?'

'A what?'

'A romantic. Are you one of those types?'

'I'm what I call a dirty romantic. Does that count?' He laughed self-consciously. 'Might sound a bit rude. I just mean I'm a romantic, but I try not to be too flowery about it, you know? So I do love romantic novels and all that. If I'm being honest, and I am, Romeo and Juliet is my favourite play by Willy Shakes. And I found E.M. Forster's A Room with a View achingly romantic,' he added earnestly. 'But don't tell anyone. Dirty, but yes. Romantic. I suppose I am.'

'OK, so a dirty romantic then. Oh, I like that. I like that a lot, James. You are full of surprises.' Her eyes met his. 'I like being surprised.'

Without another coherent thought, James took the back of her neck in his hand and drew her in. Within seconds his mouth had met hers. Gently. God. Her lips were exquisite, soft and full. They met his willingly. James experienced sensory overload; the scent of her hair, the perfume wafting from her neck, the taste of the fruity cocktail she'd been drinking hours ago, her mouth, her ripe, but somehow delicate mouth.

Emma put her hands on his face and James felt a shiver. He felt her rings, cold against his skin, but her palms were warm and soft. She kissed him more ardently,

249

her tongue searching his out. A bolt of lust shot through
James and he fought to restrain himself from hurling her
to the sand and taking her.

My God. Was that how Ed felt about the night they
first met? Molly was instantly transported back in time;
assailed by memories and sensations. The beginning of
their friendship – of what had turned out to be a lifelong
relationship of sorts.

Molly rushed through the next few pages. Ed's book
seemed to be an account of their lives, both together and
apart. Molly started crying. It felt like re-living key
moments in her life, moments she had shared with Ed.
But this time, she was able to re-live those flashes of time
from his perspective. Molly could feel the emotions he
had experienced – and she saw herself through his eyes.

She took the manuscript to an armchair and curled up
with it. She couldn't stop reading it. Obviously it was
more compelling for her because it was essentially about
her and Ed, but Molly was genuinely transfixed by Ed's
writing. There was so much emotion in it, so much heartfelt sentiment and passion. She knew that any woman
would read this novel and wish they had someone in their
life who felt about them the way Ed felt about her.

Molly found herself alternating between laughing and
crying as she read. Happy moments between herself and
Ed, devastating ones too. Molly was exhausted as she
neared the end of her skim-read, but moved beyond
reason.

Hearing Ed coming in, Molly put the manuscript down,
just short of reading the very end. Overwhelmed, she wiped
tears from her cheeks. She had retained so much hurt over

the way he had walked out on her after the night they spent together, her heart had never fully recovered, but now that she knew how Ed had truly felt at every moment of their history together, she realised how much time they had wasted slipping in and out of each other's lives.

But one thing was for sure: Molly loved Ed. Molly had always loved Ed. It just remained to be seen if Ed still loved Molly. She hurriedly tucked the manuscript under the chair.

'Molls?'

'In here.'

'Hey.' Ed bent down and kissed her. He sat in the chair next to her, chucking his keys on the table. 'You ok?'

Molly nodded. 'You smell of the outdoors. Have you been to the beach or something?'

Ed nodded. 'I'll tell you about that in a minute.' He leant forward. 'What's going on, Molls? I haven't been able to get hold of you for ages.'

'Oh yes. That.' Molly fell silent. She wanted to tell Ed about Sam but now it had come to the crunch, the words were failing her somewhat.

'How was the holiday?' Ed frowned. 'Was it . . . successful?'

Molly considered. 'Was the holiday successful? Hmm. It depends on your viewpoint. I had a lovely time relaxing and catching the sun, as you can see. Sam did lots of work and got embarrassed about me knocking drinks over and stuff. And then he left me.'

'He what?' Ed sat up incredulously. 'You're not serious, Molly.'

'I am. Said he couldn't cope with my illness. Said he

tried, but he just couldn't get his head round it, couldn't face the future he knew was coming.'

'Fucking hell.' Ed looked staggered. 'I can't believe it. Not reliable Sam. I never thought he was capable of such a thing.'

'Me neither.' Molly's voice was dull. 'I mean, he's worried about money, about the business. I guess he just couldn't cope with both. It was me or the business and that's all there is to it.'

'God, come here.' Ed pulled Molly on to his lap and kissed the top of her head. 'He's a fucking tool. How could he do this to you?'

'I don't know,' Molly said, starting to weep. 'He just said he couldn't do it any more. I guess he just doesn't find my Parkinson's very sexy.'

'He's a fucking idiot. You could never be un-sexy, whatever happened to you. Not you. You're the epitome of sexiness.' Ed knew he sounded earnest but he meant every word.

'Oh, Ed. You're saying that because you don't know anything about Parkinson's and what it does to you.'

'I bloody well do,' Ed protested. And he did. He had researched every aspect of Parkinson's disease since Molly had been diagnosed, both early onset and the normal kind. Ed knew exactly what was in store for Molly. And it hadn't fazed him one bit. Why had it fazed Sam?

'Right. Look, it doesn't matter,' Molly said impatiently. She was fairly sure Ed didn't have the first idea about her Parkinson's or how bleak the future looked. She struggled to get off his lap. 'I need to tell—'

Ed wouldn't let her and he held her there. 'What, you

think I don't know about the behavioural changes, the sleep difficulties, the possible depression and the way this might affect your speech eventually? The memory problems, the balance issues and dizziness? The constipation and/or going to the toilet constantly? Blood pressure? Blurry vision?'

Molly blinked and bit her lip. 'Ok, so you've read up on it. But so did Sam. And he still walked. But—'

'Well, I'm not going to.' Ed rubbed her back absently as Molly tried to turn to face him. 'I do, however, have some other news to update you on.'

'Oh?'

'Yes. Jody's son, Jake? He might be mine.'

'What?' Molly almost leapt off of Ed's lap. 'You're joking.'

'Hardly, Molls,' Ed replied wryly. 'I know my humour can be inappropriate at times, but still.'

'You have a son?' Molly was taken-aback, despite having a fleeting thought that Jake might have been Ed's when she first met him.

'I might have,' Ed corrected her. 'I don't know definitively if he's mine yet.'

'Have you . . . when did . . . how has this even . . .' Molly had a million questions but she couldn't articulate them. She suddenly realised something. 'You and Jody? I mean . . . you said you weren't even into her years ago.'

'I wasn't,' Ed agreed. 'That is, I always liked her as a friend. There was just this one night . . .' He averted his eyes.

'What night?' Molly lifted Ed's chin. 'What night, Ed?'

'Your wedding night.' Ed met her eyes. 'The last time I slept with Jody was your wedding night.'

253

'Oh.'

'Yeah. I felt a bit shitty. About you. And Jody was there.' Ed looked guilty. 'And I know that sounds terrible. But she assured me I wasn't taking advantage. That she wanted it to happen.'

Molly got off of Ed's lap. 'Well, of course she did. She always had a thing for you.'

'Well, I don't know about that. But anyway, that must have been the night it happened. If it happened. I mean it happened, but if . . .'

'Jake was conceived. Yes, I'm there on that point.'

Molly felt a stab of jealousy. Ed and Jody. She had no right to feel it, but it hurt her that they had slept together again after their student days. And on her wedding night, that felt especially horrible. Molly understood Ed was telling the truth, that he had felt awful that night and that Jody had been there. There to make Ed feel better, to take his pain away and to make him him forget about her, perhaps.

'He's an exceptional kid,' Ed said, interrupting Molly's thoughts. 'I've been spending a bit of time with him recently and I can't tell you what an ace little boy he is.'

Molly turned and faced Ed. 'You've totally fallen for him.'

'I have.' Ed didn't bother to deny it. Not to Molly. There was no point. 'I didn't mean to, but I've fallen head over heels for him. He's the cutest kid, so funny, so intelligent. I never thought I'd feel like this about a person. Certainly not a child.'

Molly felt yet another stab of jealousy. An even more irrational one. Honestly! She was being ridiculous.

'Is . . . is Jake definitely yours?' she asked.

'That's the thing. I don't know yet.' Ed looked rueful. 'I need to do a DNA test.'

'You haven't done one yet?' Molly was stunned. Surely that was the first thing Ed needed to do? Before bonding with him, before spending all this time with him. She said as much.

'I know, I know.' Ed stood up and starting pacing around the room. 'I'm an idiot, Molly. But you should see him – you can't really doubt it. And Jody is so sure.'

Hearing Ed mention Jody, Molly felt a flicker of panic. Did Ed have feelings for Jody? Tons of men fell in love with the mother of their child, suddenly felt more for them because they had carried a baby, given birth to it, nurtured it. It could bring feelings out in even the least sensitive of men, and Ed fell into the category of being an extremely emotional, sensitive guy.

Molly had sudden visions of Ed, Jody and Jake together, a little family unit. On the beach together, eating dinner together. Having fun, laughing at things only they understood, doing all manner of family-type things together. The thought of it physically hurt. Absurdly, it seemed to hurt even more than Sam leaving her. Deep down Molly had always wanted children at some point. Sam had never seemed keen, but Molly had always been hopeful that the subject would raise its head again when the time was right. Now, however, it seemed that the time would never be right. It was a sobering, painful thought.

'Anyway, enough of my problems. Come here.' Impulsively, Ed pulled Molly into his arms and buried his face in her hair. 'We're both going through it, aren't we?' Molly always made him feel better.

She closed her eyes. Never before had Ed's arms around her felt so right. But never before had she felt more insecure about his feelings. The novel he had written seemed to suggest a love that was undying, significant, everlasting. But it was possible that everything had changed now that Jake had appeared. Jake *and* Jody.

'I'll leave you to it,' Molly managed, pulling free of Ed's embrace.

'Of course.' Ed understood. It was Molly's process to retreat when things went wrong. She backed away, licked her wounds, got her head clear then emerged for support.

'Speak soon,' Molly said, heading for the door. She felt too choked to manage anything more.

Ed

Ed lit a cigarette and gazed out to sea. Maplethorpe Beach. Long, flat and sandy, it boasted a narrow strip of sand dunes and a whole host of activities for families. Not that Ed was interested in that side of things, he just found beaches peaceful and thought-provoking. Ever since his travels abroad he had been drawn to beaches, both in the surrounding area and further afield. Of course, nothing beat the likes of Barbados and Cuba, but still, where there was sand, there was sea and sea air and space. And he could sit there in a pair of shorts and a crumpled shirt and just be. A spiritual guru had taught him that on his travels. He had no idea what it meant exactly, but he enjoyed just sitting and staring out to sea.

Ed blew smoke into the air. The past eighteen months or so had floated by uneventfully. He had bought a flat in the centre of Lincoln, far enough away from Molly and Sam's office that he didn't bump into them – not often, at any rate – but close enough that he didn't feel estranged from that part of his life. He had written some articles he hoped to get published, but so far, no luck on that front. Ed had thought they were rather pithy and informative, but seemingly the national papers had no need for his inner thoughts and musings. Nor did the local rags. Or any magazines.

Ed couldn't help feeling disillusioned. Of course, he hadn't completed his degree, but was his university pedigree really of interest to newspapers and magazines? Did they care if he had letters after his name – or was it more important that he could actually pen a few paragraphs that people wanted to read? That might spark off a debate, get people thinking, cause some kind of personal development. Well, the latter was perhaps a stretch, but Ed had hoped to at very least get something published.

Maybe he wasn't controversial enough for journalism? Ed had no idea. All he knew was that his dream career of becoming a writer was eluding him. And now he didn't know what to do next. He had thoughts about writing a novel again – it had been his original dream – but he didn't have a clue what to write about. 'Write about what you know' so the cliché went, but what did Ed know about? Fuck all, it seemed. But he supposed he should get a proper job of sorts to appear credible. Ed didn't need money as much now that he had his mother's inheritance, but it wouldn't last for ever. He wanted to work. He had always worked.

Perhaps he should just get a job in a bank and be done with it. Ed sighed. He would be earning money, providing a service and he would have something to occupy his mind with. Which would stop him from thinking about Molly. Ed tossed his cigarette away and thought about Molly. Since her wedding, Molly had been distant. And Ed had allowed her to be. He wanted to give her space. He wanted her to live her life with Sam without him popping up every two seconds.

Naturally he hadn't been able to stay away from her completely. He had always been drawn to Molly and as much as he wanted to keep his distance, he needed her in his life. Which was very selfish of him, he knew that. So he limited his visits to once or twice a month. But in any event, their friendship was damaged. Their conversations were stilted. Nothing was the same and Ed had no idea how to get things back on track or what might bring Molly's walls down. But considering how she felt about him and what she thought he had done, Ed knew he was fighting a losing battle. Following Sam's silent request for him to keep quiet about his letter had driven such a huge wedge between Ed and Molly, like a gigantic splinter, it seemed impossible to ease it out.

And now he needed to see Molly again. Which was a bit silly, because Ed had actually started dating a very sweet girl called Nicki and he should probably be going to see her rather than Molly. But Molly was who he always turned to when he was mentally struggling with something, so Ed decided not to battle with himself over it.

Sloping off the beach, Ed climbed into his car – a battered, cream MG he had treated himself to with his mother's inheritance (his only other indulgence in fact; the rest of the money was now tied up in some astute investments Boyd had advised him on) – and drove to Molly's office. Sam's office, Ed corrected himself. Although Molly had certainly put her stamp on it. It was still slick and professional-looking, but there were feminine touches. Accent colours, Ed thought they were called, and also, vases and photographs and books and artwork. Company artwork framed and mounted on the walls.

Breathing in the familiar smell of fresh bread from the bakery below, Ed entered the office. It was seemingly empty, but he could hear noise from the staff room at the back.

'Ed!' Molly emerged cradling a coffee. She took a second to compose herself, the way she always did when she was around Ed. Especially when he turned up unexpectedly.

'What a nice surprise,' she added, feeling she should say something positive. She was being truthful though; it was a nice surprise. Even though their friendship wasn't what it had been, Molly always liked seeing Ed. And her feelings of hurt had diminished over time. Well, sort of.

Ed looked annoyingly good, she decided. Relaxed, healthy and he had a light tan. Probably because he bummed around on beaches instead of earning a living, she thought, before berating herself for being unchari-table.

Ed stared at Molly. She looked different. She had ever since she married Sam, actually, now Ed came to think about it. She was groomed, polished. Her tangle of blond hair was now tamed into a sleek ponytail, she wore more make-up than she used to and her clothes were trendier, less bohemian. She rather resembled her office backdrop, in fact.

Ed kissed Molly's cheek. They had established a good

enough rapport over the past eighteen months to be able to be like this, but it wasn't great that he couldn't just hug her and laugh with her and speak freely the way they used to.

'Is . . .'

'Sam here? Nope. You've just got me today.'

'Great. Well, I mean . . .'

'I know exactly what you mean.'

Molly pulled a face. It grated on her nerves that Sam and Ed didn't seem to like each other. They were two of her favourite people and each clearly thought the other was a dickhead. She could understand it on Sam's side – Ed had hardly acquitted himself well over recent years – but she was baffled by Ed's apparent dislike of Sam.

Ed immediately felt guilty. He had tried so hard to keep his feelings for Sam private, but it seemed they had filtered out. Ed would probably always have felt some sort of animosity towards Sam for being the man Molly had chosen to spend her life with, but the incident with the letter had sealed the deal.

'Coffee?' Molly held up her mug. 'It's the real thing, not instant.'

'No, thanks. I just wanted to run something past you.'

Molly led him to the staff room and curled up on the sofa. Gesturing for him to sit down, she looked at him expectantly. 'Shoot.'

Ed put his hands behind his head and tried to relax. 'Well. I want to write a novel.'

'You've always wanted to write a novel. What's new?'

'I know. But it's just how to get started. How to structure it . . .'

'What to actually write about?' Molly said, raising her eyebrows.

'Yes, that.' Ed was glad they hadn't lost their apparent ability to read one another's minds.

'Well, that's your biggest problem,' Molly promptly replied. 'And I'm stating the obvious deliberately. I mean, worry about how to start and how to structure once you figure out what the hell you want to bang on about.'

Ed let out an almighty sigh. 'I know, I know. It's stupid. I want to write articles, but it seems I have nothing to say. I want to write a novel, but I can't think what to write about. I don't bloody *know* anything, so I can't write about what I know.'

'Such a defeatist. What about your travels?' Molly's mouth tightened the way it always seemed to whenever she mentioned Ed's trip, but she forced herself to smile. 'Couldn't you write about those?'

'Well, I thought about that, but I wrote a blog at the time, and I really enjoyed it, but would it be enough for a whole book? And I want to write an actual novel, not a travel guide.'

Molly thought for a second. Perhaps it would be bitchy of her to suggest such a thing but . . .

'Could you possibly turn your experiences during your trip into a novel? I mean, you must have had some adventures during those months? You might have a romantic bonk-buster-type thing right there for the taking.'

Ed met her eyes. On the surface they were innocent, but there was a glint underneath, and Ed knew exactly what Molly was getting at. She wasn't to know that he had practically lived like a monk during his travels because his mind had been so full of her. But Ed wasn't about to enlighten Molly about that. He'd look like a right tool.

'Well, yes. That's one idea,' he agreed. 'But not really what I had in mind.'

'But you're such a romantic.' Molly knew she was trying to wind Ed up but she couldn't seem to help it. 'A dirty romantic, wasn't it? You must have a wealth of experience to draw on.' She sipped her coffee and winced. It had gone cold. Rather like her feelings right now. 'What about Jody? Couldn't she help?'

'Jody?' Ed sat up, flummoxed. How random. What on earth was Molly talking about Jody for? 'I don't see how she could possibly help me.' He decided to change the subject. 'Enough of that. I'll have a think. So, how's business?'

'Business is good,' Molly smiled briefly. 'If anything, it's a little too busy. We don't seem to have time for much else.'

'You probably need a holiday.'

'I'd kill for a holiday. We haven't been away since our honeymoon.'

Ed was surprised. Molly had always been a girl who wanted to run on the beach, who knew the benefit of stepping away from work.

'When did you last paint?'

Molly shook her head and appeared to think for a second. 'I can't even remember.'

'That's a shame, Molls. You love painting. It's who you are.'

'Sam says jobs don't define us as human beings.' Molly knew she sounded snippy. Sometimes Ed put her back up these days. 'Sam's right, I guess. I'm not actually a painter, Ed. I'm just a person who enjoys painting.'

'You very much wanted to be a painter.'

Ed frowned. He didn't like it when Molly quoted Sam at him. It was as though she'd been brainwashed or something. Ed wasn't stupid; he understood what Sam was getting at. He wasn't 'a writer', he was a person who wanted to write, but for some reason, he bloody well couldn't. He clenched his fist.

Molly put her mug down on the table sharply. 'I did. But it didn't earn me any money. This . . .' she gestured with her hand, 'this earns money.'

'Well, that's alright then,' Ed said lightly.

Molly shot him a glance. Sometimes she felt an irrational urge to slap Ed very hard around the face. Who was he to take the piss out of her for actually knuckling down and earning some money? He might have an inheritance to live off for the time being but the rest of them needed to pay mortgages and bills.

'Was there anything else you wanted to talk to me about?' Molly said, standing up.

Ed bit his lip. He had annoyed her. He always seemed to annoy her these days. Their friendship was fucked. Why on earth had he come here?

'Er, no. No thank you. Sorry to take up your time. I'll let you get on with it.' He got to his feet.

'Ok.'

Molly's stomach did a strange flip-flop thing. She had dismissed Ed and he had dismissed her. He passed by

264

her and she sensed rather than saw his fingers instinctively reach out to her. Molly bit her lip and moved out of the way.

Ed's head dropped; that hurt. He hadn't even meant to do it, he just sometimes let his guard down when he was that close to her. But that rejection stung like a bitch.

Ed decided then and there to stay well away from Molly for a while. He was dating a girl, he should focus on that for a while. He also realised what he knew about. What he could write about. He knew so much about a particular situation he was damned sure he had an entire novel about it in him.

Molly watched Ed leave the office and felt sick. She hated herself for the way she was around him. But it was called self-preservation. It was called survival. Because Molly knew for a fact that if she allowed herself to get close to Ed again, she would be a mess.

Forcing Ed out of her mind, Molly wondered where the hell Sam had got to and returned to work.

Now

Home alone, Molly was feeling seriously messed up. Not only had Sam left her, Ed's revelation about Jake had sent her reeling. The thought of Ed having a son – especially when he had always said he didn't want kids – was shocking. And the way Ed had fallen for Jake was both lovely and terrifying.

Molly inwardly cursed Jody. How could she do this to Ed? How could she turn up like this, all these years later and just announce that Ed might be a father? That there was a ready-made kid right here if Ed wanted to step up and take responsibility?

And what about Jody? Molly gazed out of the window. Did she have feelings for Ed? Is that why she had turned up out of the blue like this? Was she hoping that if Ed connected with Jake enough, he might want her, Jody, in his life as well? Molly hated thinking this way about Jody. They had been friends, although they had lost touch since Jody went to Canada. They emailed sporadically, but nothing more than that.

But Jody had always had a thing for Ed. Always. She had held such a huge torch for him that Molly had sometimes wondered how she managed to hold it aloft for so long. She didn't blame Jody, how could she? Molly had always been in love with Ed. Even when she was at the height of her relationship with Sam, Molly's thoughts and feelings had drifted to Ed. She hadn't done it on purpose, it was just something she hadn't been able to help. Molly had always blamed it on their deep friendship. But now she wasn't so sure. Now she was facing up to the fact that it was quite possibly something far more than that.

Molly put her hand on the window. How could she do anything about this right now? She was about to go through a divorce and Ed was going through the biggest upheaval of his life. And he might have feelings for Jody. The thought of Ed and Jody together made her feel sick. She suddenly realised that if Ed genuinely had been in love with her all those years ago, seeing her marrying Sam must have almost annihilated him. No wonder he had sought solace in Jody's arms that night. Molly could completely understand it. She hated it, but she understood it.

The fact of the matter was, Molly wanted Ed to be happy. And if that was with Jake – and with Jody – well, Molly couldn't stand in his way. She wouldn't. It was time to step back and let Ed find out about Jake and figure out how he felt about Jody.

*　　*　　*

Ed fixed himself a drink, mulling over Molly's strange behaviour. As he sat down he noticed something under the cushion in the other armchair. Getting up, he tugged it out. It was his manuscript. He sat down slowly. Molly had read his novel. Had it upset her? Is that why she had run off so quickly? Ed flipped through the pages. Christ. It was like some sort of open love letter to her. He had laid himself bare on these pages. He had confessed all, been totally honest. It must have shocked the hell out of Molly. Made her want to run a mile from him. Or had it finally convinced her that he had deep, deep feelings for her?

Time to put this ghost to rest once and for all.

Molly and Ed

October 2005

Molly put her arm around her father's shoulders and drew him in. She couldn't believe what was happening. This couldn't be happening.

'God. She's going to make it, isn't she?' Molly's father John asked a passing nurse despairingly.

'We're doing our very best,' the nurse replied automatically, although in the kindest of tones, as she hurried past.

Molly fought a fierce urge to shake the nurse. Obviously they had to be diplomatic, but what the hell did that mean? Of course they were doing their very best, that was their bloody job. But it wasn't the nurse's fault, she wasn't even assigned to her mother's case, she was simply passing by on her way to another emergency.

'Christ, Molly.' John slumped into a chair. 'This is horrendous.'

Molly nodded. She had received a phone call from her father at eleven a.m. informing her in a very shaky voice

269

that her mother was suffering from peritonitis and that she had been dashed to hospital. Molly had immediately shut the office and driven to the hospital, meeting her father there. Molly's mother was now in theatre undergoing surgery and they had been told to expect the worst. Apparently the infection was the result of a split stomach ulcer. Why on earth hadn't her mother told anyone she was in such pain? She must have been keeping silent for months and months, and now it could be fatal.

Molly had Googled peritonitis at the office. Apparently if the infection spread too rapidly through the body, it could move from the bloodstream to the major organs, resulting in septic shock. She kept this nugget of information to herself. Her father simply did not need to hear such a thing.

'I don't know what I would do without her,' John was saying into his hands. 'She can't die, Molly. She simply can't die. She's my . . . she's my life.'

Molly squeezed his hand and started to cry. She had always known her parents were devoted to one another, that they had been lucky enough to find 'the one', but she had really felt the truth of it over the past twenty-four hours.

Making sure her father had a handful of tissues, Molly headed to one of the reception areas to use her phone again. She couldn't track Sam down and it was driving her crazy. She needed him. He was out with a client somewhere and he was notoriously neglectful of his phone when engrossed in work. But she had left fourteen messages. Surely he had noticed? Surely he must know something was seriously wrong?

Molly started pacing. Sam was generally very reliable. He rarely let her down. He had become more work-focused recently, but he was courting some huge clients right now, ones that could potentially set them – and their company – on fire. Molly couldn't blame Sam for wanting to safeguard their future. They might have kids to think about; a legacy to leave behind. Molly felt excited about the idea. She wanted kids at some point, but Sam didn't seem keen, at least not now – he thought they should put everything into work and worry about kids in five years' time. Molly was worried Sam might never want children, but she supposed she had time to talk him round. She wasn't *that* old and women were having kids much later these days.

She tried Sam again. Straight to voicemail. Christ! Where was he? Molly felt panicked. She needed him. Ed flashed into her head. Should she call him? No. Probably not. They had barely spoken in the past two years. He had started a serious relationship with someone called Nicki and Molly had left him to it. To be fair, he had also left her to it. He'd kept his distance, staying in touch through the odd text and phone call rather than visiting in person. All Molly knew was that Ed had made a start on his novel, but had abandoned it to help Nicki with some business venture she was struggling with. What Ed knew about business was anyone's guess, but that was up to him.

Molly wondered if it was time to bury the hatchet. Life had moved on. It had been years since he had hurt her and she was over it. She wanted their friendship back. She thought she could now be in the same room as Ed without wanting to touch him in some way – either rudely or with some anger involved.

But Molly was at a loss as to how to broach the subject of rekindling their friendship. If Ed didn't want to see her – and clearly he didn't – she wasn't sure what she could do about it. Pride had always been her greatest downfall, and Molly had built up so many walls around herself, she didn't know how to tear them down. Not without getting hurt again.

'Molly.'

Molly turned at the sound of her father's quivering voice. Saw the surgeon remove his hat as he started speaking. Molly rushed towards her father. She heard the words *did all we could*. Shaking her head in disbelief, Molly held her father, almost dropping him as he collapsed against her, his full weight on her body as shock engulfed him.

The surgeon kindly explained everything: unforeseen difficulties; unable to stem the infection; cardiac arrest. Someone was going to come and see them soon and talk them through the process. The surgeon gave each of their shoulders a brisk but sympathetic squeeze then promptly got called away to another emergency.

Oh God. Molly sank down on to a chair, hoisting her father into the one next to her. She was gone. Her lovely mum was gone. Molly couldn't get her head around it. Yesterday she had been absolutely fine. They had spoken on the phone; they spoke almost every day. But not any more. Molly broke down, clutching her father.

Her phone rang abruptly and she snatched it up without looking at it.

'Sam?'

'It's Ed.'

Molly burst into a fresh bout of tears. 'Oh, Ed.'

'What's wrong? Where are you?'

'I'm at the hospital. My mum just died.'

'Molls. Stay right there. I'm on my way.'

The call ended.

'Where's Sam?' John asked as he tried to tidy his face up with a handkerchief to no avail; more tears fell immediately afterwards.

'I have no idea,' Molly said, feeling a flash of anger. 'But Ed is on his way.'

John nodded vaguely. 'Ah, Ed. I always liked Ed.'

'Me too, Dad,' Molly agreed. 'Me too.'

'We haven't seen him around for a while, your mother and me,' John commented, blowing his nose with an almighty noise. 'We weren't sure you and he were still friends.'

'We went through a difficult patch. We're still going through it, as a matter of fact.'

Molly wished she could stop crying. She couldn't bear the thought of her mum on the operating table. Were they supposed to be doing something, taking some sort of action?

John snorted in an attempt to stop crying. 'We always thought you and Ed would end up together, you know.'

'Did you?' Molly wasn't sure she wanted to hear this right now.

'We did. Always thought you were made for each other. Rather like me and your mother.' Having almost halted the flow, John unashamedly burst into tears again.

Ed arrived and found Molly propping up her father, and clearly in an utter mess herself.

'Right.' Pulling John to his feet, Ed gave him a tender hug. He stepped back and wiped away John's tears with his hand. 'John. It's Ed. This is a really shit time, but I'm here to help you, ok? I'm going to get someone to come and tell us what's going on and we'll get everything sorted. It will all be alright.'

John nodded and allowed Ed to sit him down again. Ed turned to Molly.

'Oh, Molls. Come here.'

He pulled her into his arms and held her. She looked bloody terrible. She was in pieces and he wanted to put her back together again. Ed had no idea where Sam was, he must be on his way, but in the meantime, Ed was going to do whatever he could to get Molly and her father straight.

Resisting the urge to kiss Molly's tears away, Ed wiped them the way he had her father's and handed her a crumpled tissue from his pocket that he thought was relatively clean. Then he took control of everything. Finding a nurse, Ed made sure that John was looked after. He tracked down someone who knew all about Eleanor's case and found out exactly what had happened and what needed to be done next. And once he had all the practical stuff out of the way, he took Molly to the hospital café and bought her a horrible cup of tea.

Sitting down next to her, he put his arm round her. 'How are you feeling?' he asked. He rolled his eyes. 'Dumb question. You feel like shit. Like your world has imploded and will never feel the same again. And every so often, you feel ok for a few seconds and then it creeps over you again and engulfs you and suddenly you're bawling your eyes out like a child again.'

'Wow.' Molly coughed into her tissue. 'You really do know what this feels like.'

Ed gave her a sideways glance. 'Yeah. I really do. I'm so sorry, Molls. This is horrible for you. So out of the blue as well.'

'I'm so bloody angry with her! She must have been in pain for a while . . . she must have been. Why didn't she say anything?'

Ed let out a breath. 'Who knows. Sometimes people try to be brave, I guess. And she probably didn't realise it was as serious as this.'

Molly scrunched her tissue up. 'It's just . . . I hate it when things just don't need to happen the way they do. When just talking about something, being open, could change everything. It's people being selfish that causes all manner of crap in other people's lives.'

She faltered, realising what she was saying might sound intensely personal to their situation. It was how she felt about Ed all those years ago. But she had been talking about her mother. Initially.

Ed's arm around Molly's shoulders stiffened momentarily. Was Molly talking about what had happened with them? He guessed she was probably just referring to her mother, but the words fit for him. Shit. He hated the thought of Molly feeling that way about him, thinking he was selfish. Believing that he had deliberately caused her pain.

Ed raked his hand through his hair. Christ, he wanted to throw Sam under a bloody bus! Telling Molly about the letter would undoubtedly change the way she felt about him. It would change her ugly perception of him. It could even . . . well, no. Ed caught sight of Molly's wedding ring. Molly was married to Sam now. It was too late for them. Even if she knew that Ed hadn't been a complete and utter tool back then, it would hardly change how she felt, would it? Molly was a loyal girl and she loved someone else now – if she had ever loved Ed, that moment had well and truly passed.

Grudgingly, Ed also felt that he shouldn't ruin Molly's view of Sam. Sam was Molly's husband. The last thing she needed to know was that Sam had concealed something from her, something that might possibly have changed the course of her life.

Molly felt Ed's arm relax around her shoulders and, realising she had been holding her breath, let a jerky one out. She really wished Ed would explain why he had left her. Molly had no idea why it mattered any more, but somehow it did. If there was a reason, a good explanation for the way he had behaved, Molly knew her heart would heal and that she would at least feel as if she was partly-mended. It hadn't been right since that moment and she had been struggling to get past it ever since. If Ed could just redeem himself on that front, she might even . . .

Molly pulled herself up. She might even . . . what? Leave Sam? Good God. As if. She and Sam were solid. Solid as a rock, as the saying went. No, it wasn't that. It was just that Molly wanted to see Ed differently. She wanted to see him as the person she had always thought he was.

Ed cleared his throat. 'Well. I'm sure your mum wasn't being selfish, Molly. People rarely mean to cause hurt.

Sometimes it just happens. And I'm certain your mum would apologise profusely for doing this to you if she could. Because no one would ever want to make you sad.'

He squeezed Molly's shoulder, wishing he could say more.

I want to say more, he told her silently, sadly. So much more. I want to tell you that I was in love with you when I left to go on my travels, that I thought of nothing else but you while I was away. For nearly every bloody second. That I still love you now, even though you're married to some other guy.

Molly bit her lip. Suddenly, everything with Ed seemed silly. It was all so long ago. He had hurt her, she had moved on and she was with Sam now. They had been good friends once. And they could be again.

Feeling emotional, Molly tried to compose herself. It was just too much; her mum dying and Ed being here with her. She finally felt like she could let him back in her life.

Ed sat up and turned Molly to face him. 'Molls. Do you think you could possibly see your way to being my friend again? Being properly in my life and all that?'

Molly's heart leapt. What was this thing between them? It was like they were connected, in sync.

Ed scrunched his face up. 'God, I sound pathetic! Be my friend again,' he mimicked in a whiny voice. He laughed then stopped. 'But I mean it, Molly. I just . . . I just miss you too much.'

'Me too,' Molly croaked.

Ed smiled for a second then stopped. 'And I respect your marriage to Sam, I promise. I don't want to start joining you on the sofa or double-dating or anything.

Just . . . I thought maybe we could chat on the phone and stuff. Meet for coffee or dinner now and again. Cheap pizza and cider, that kind of thing. Just like the good old days.'

Molly laughed and started crying again. 'Cheap pizza and cider sounds great.'

'Well, blimey, if it's going to make you bloody cry, we won't bother . . .' Ed gathered Molly into his arms again, fiercely. 'It's going to be alright,' he said into her hair. 'Everything is going to be alright. I promise.'

A wave of familiarity washed over him. She smelt the same. Not the same shampoo or anything, but just a Molly smell. And he had missed her. Fuck, but he had missed her.

Molly believed Ed. Everything would be alright. Her mother had gone and she was going to have to support her father, but she felt able to cope. Ed was back. She had forgiven him and he was back in her life. It didn't make up for all the bad stuff, but it was a start.

'So. How come you didn't make it to Boyd's wedding?' Ed said, deciding it was time for some distracting small talk.

Molly pulled a face. 'Working, of course. We were in Manchester for a conference then we headed straight down to Devon to see Sam's parents. They have a place down there. I did send a gift though and some big apologies.'

'Shame,' Ed mused. 'Lovely do. Mrs Middleford fair near did herself a mischief arranging those nuptials. Boyd looked as though he was going to burst, marrying Helen. It was great to see him looking so happy.'

'Bless him. I do love Boyd. And Helen is absolutely perfect for him.'

Ed glanced at her. 'Do you mean no one else would have him?'

Molly chuckled. 'Stop it. I didn't say anything of the sort. They're just perfectly suited.' Remembering what her father had said about herself and Ed, and about her mother, Molly went quiet for a second. She stopped herself from crying by biting down very hard on her lip and leant her head against Ed's shoulder. 'So, you mentioned double-dating. How are things going with . . . is it Nicki still?'

'Yes, it's still Nicki.' Ed gave her a nudge. 'I'm really not a complete whore, you know. Not these days.' He rubbed his cheek distractedly. 'We're ok, I guess. Not amazing, but we're kicking along nicely enough.'

'Sounds thrilling.' Molly nudged him back. 'And not the sort of thing that could keep you happy for long, if you don't mind me saying so.'

'Hmm.' Ed didn't really want to get into his relationship with Nicki. Not with Molly. She was happily married and he was not-so-happily cohabiting. It was pleasant but it certainly wasn't setting his world on fire any more. In fact, they were rather like flatmates and not much more, Ed reflected with some surprise. Christ. How had he ended up in a relationship like that?

'Molly! I'm so sorry. I got here as soon as I could.' Sam arrived at their table.

Ed released Molly. He stood up and proffered his hand to Sam. 'Hey. I just happened to call Molly and I came straight here.'

'Ed.' Sam shook his hand. 'Well I'm glad Molly had someone here to take care of her.' He turned to Molly. 'I can't apologise enough. I was in a meeting, I had no phone signal . . .' Sam looked mortified. 'I can't believe what's happened. Come here.'

Molly fell into his arms, sobbing again.

Ed stepped back. His heart clenched for a second, but he was done feeling sorry for himself. He and Molly were friends again and he was going to be there for her as much as he could be. He wouldn't step on Sam's toes, but Ed wanted to be around Molly. And she wanted him around too.

'I'll call you, Molls,' he said, touching her hand. 'Let me know if I can help with any arrangements or anything.'

'I'll be dealing with all of that,' Sam said, putting his arm firmly around Molly's shoulders. 'But thank you, Ed. For the offer and for being here when I wasn't.'

'Complete chance is all,' Ed replied with a genial smile. 'I'll see you both soon. And Molly, I'm really sorry about your mum. Eleanor was such a wonderful woman.'

Molly nodded, her face streaked with tears. *Thank you*, she mouthed at Ed. She turned back to Sam.

Ed took his leave, realising he needed a cigarette. It was awful about Eleanor. Poor John and poor Molly. They had a tough time ahead of them.

Ed forced himself to focus on the positives. He and Molly were friends again. At last.

Now

'So. What friends are coming over later?'

'George and Harry,' Jake said, looking mildly exasperated. 'I told you all of this before.'

'I know you did. But I like asking you about this stuff. It makes me feel like a proper dad. Are they connected to royalty, these boys?'

Jake giggled. 'No. Don't be silly. And you are a proper dad, aren't you?'

Ed picked up Jake's homework. 'I don't think so, fella. I haven't a clue how to help you with your maths. What *are* all these numbers? I'm sure I didn't have to do all this stuff in my day.'

'They used abacuses in your day, that's why,' Jake said, his eyes innocent.

'Is that so?' Ed screamed with laughter. 'I'm not *that* old. Besides, I used to sneak a calculator in to all of my exams, even when we weren't allowed to use them.'

'Great,' Jody said, shaking her head as Jake sloped off towards the TV. 'Teaching him bad stuff.'

'Ah, just showing him I was a bit of a rogue in my day. As he thinks I'm some sort of crusty old man.'

'Hardly.' Jody joined him at the table. 'You really are brilliant with him.'

Ed grinned, feeling himself puff up with pride. 'Thanks. I don't know if I am, but if you think that as his mum, I must be doing something right, I guess.'

Jody collected up Jake's homework. 'Well, I haven't seen him take to anyone the way he has with you. You definitely have a great connection.'

'He's not exactly difficult to get on with,' Ed commented truthfully. 'And I probably haven't seen him at his worst.'

Jody cocked an eyebrow. 'Oh my God. You're absolutely spot-on there. If you'd been around when he was three . . .'

'Three? I thought it was two that was the horrific time? Terrible twos – isn't that what they say?'

'Troublesome threes are just as bad, trust me,' Jody said emphatically. 'A friend of mine described children of this age as "three-nagers" and it's so accurate. Strops, attitude and answering back. Classic teenager behaviour, in the body of a little person. Dreadful.'

'Christ.' Ed shuddered. He packed Jake's school bag, picking up the rest of his books. 'Listen – and please don't take this the wrong way, Jody – but do you think me and Jake are such good mates because, well, because I wasn't around for that stage of his life? As in, I've never really had to discipline him or anything like that?'

'Difficult to say,' Jody shrugged. 'I don't think so, no.

And I'm sure there'll be plenty of time to discipline him in the future.'

She looked the way she always did when Ed referenced the time he had missed out on: guilty and remorseful. Ed could understand that and he did his best not to comment on it. It did, however, highlight the issue of the paternity test. He still hadn't pushed Jody on this and Ed knew he had to do something about it. He had relaxed when Jody had talked so much about Jake starting at the local junior school because he was sure it meant that Jake and Jody were staying in England. Which for some reason made Ed feel that the paternity test wasn't as urgent as he had previously thought. But Ed guessed he had to know, once and for all.

'That paternity test. We should do it.'

Jody's mouth twisted momentarily. 'I thought you'd forgotten about that.'

'Well, I had to be honest. But it's just a formality, isn't it?' Ed was sure his rational argument would win Jody over. But even if it didn't, Ed needed to go ahead and get this done. Just to tick a box.

'That's what I mean. I'm not sure why we need to do this.' Jody looked panicked.

'We need to know for sure. Even if it's just to tick a box.' Ed frowned. Something about this wasn't adding up. 'Jody, did you sleep with anyone else around the time you and I slept together? It's just that every time I mention this, you have some sort of seizure.'

Jody started shaking her head but seeing the look in Ed's eyes, she took a glance over her shoulder at Jake and lowered her voice. 'Ok. Look. There – there was someone. In Canada. But it was – the dates wouldn't work. It was just after I got there. I went out with the girls from work and got a bit tipsy.' She flushed. 'God, I must sound like a horrendous slut. I genuinely do not do this sort of thing much. There was just one other guy. But it can't be him.'

'Why not? Why can't it be him?' Ed felt his stomach slide.

'It's just . . . he can't be. It's not possible. I don't think it's possible.' Jody stared at him soberly. 'It's you. It must be you.'

'Jesus, Jody. You just want it to be me. Don't you?'

She started crying. 'No. No. It's not that. I do think you're Jake's father. I always have done.'

Ed got up. He felt incredibly sick. 'I'm doing the test, Jody. I've looked it up online and I know how to do it. It takes approximately five days to get the results. So by the end of the week, we'll know.'

Jody nodded, her face white and pinched. 'Right.' Her voice lowered to a whisper. 'I won't be able to bear it if you're not his father, Ed.'

'You're not the only one,' Ed mumbled. Stalking past her, he stopped at the doorway to the lounge. 'See you later, fella. I've got to go home now, I have some work to do.'

'Aww. Why can't you stay?' Jake looked downcast.

Ed literally felt the tug on his heartstrings. God, this was killing him. 'Sorry, little man. I wish I could. But I'll see you soon.'

'But when?'

Jake sounded whiny but he came over and hugged Ed.

Tightly. Ed hugged him back, inhaling the smell of his hair. He'd never thought he had it in him to feel love like he felt for Jake. It was a whole different thing to any other love he had experienced before.

God, I hope he's mine, Ed thought to himself. 'I'll arrange a time with your mum, ok?' he told Jake. 'But I promise I'll see you soon.'

He left and spent a fitful night not sleeping. The following morning, he organised a DNA test. It required swabs to be taken from his cheeks and Jake's, so he took the test round to Jody's so he could do it when Jake came in from school. It wasn't that he didn't trust Jody, but Ed had to know that it had been done correctly and that there was no chance of any mistakes. Jake seemed to find it all highly amusing, which Ed was relieved about – he didn't want Jake to be scared. Ed then sent the kit off as outlined, requesting that the results be sent to him by email.

While he was doing that, he fired off some copies of his novel to literary agents. It was a painstaking process. Using the *Writers' & Artists' Yearbook*, he followed each agent's submission requests to the letter, giving some one chapter, some three chapters, some a six-page synopsis, others a synopsis that was basically a paragraph in length. The only thing Ed patently ignored was any agent that said he could only approach them and no one else. He didn't want to be disrespectful but if an agent took months to get back to him, he might waste valuable time when other agents could be reading the novel. He found a couple who preferred emails and he sent them a copy as an afterthought. They weren't necessarily the right agents for his book, but, well, an email cost nothing. It was worth a try.

The following day, Ed spoke to Jody.

'Can I take Jake out to the beach on Saturday? Well, you can come too, of course.'

Jody had a pained expression in her eyes. 'No, that's fine. You take him on your own. You're trying to arrange a last day, aren't you? In case it's a last day.'

Ed looked away. 'Shit. I suppose I am.' He turned back to Jody with tears in his eyes. 'I really want to be his dad, Jody.'

'I know. I want that too.'

Jody started crying and Ed pulled her into his arms. 'Look, it will all be alright. Ok? We'll know soon and we'll take it from there.'

Jody nodded. 'Yes. I just hope Jake's going to be ok.'

'Me too. I'll be over on Saturday to pick Jake up.'

Jody gave him a watery smile. 'Ok. I'll see you then.'

Ed left the house feeling anxious and bleakly despondent. He really wished he could speak to Molly. But somehow he knew he needed to sort this one out on his own.

Molly and Ed

New Year's Eve, 2007
'This is *such* a bad party.'
   'Dreadful.'
   'Almost as bad as your birthday party.'
   'Molls, pack it in. I had about two hours to organise that and I was also ill with man flu . . .'
   'Oh stop making excuses. It was crap and you know it. Good lord, Edison. Look at that girl's *hair*.'
   'And that *dress*. It's making my eyes go funny.' Ed flapped a hand in a camp fashion. 'Did she even look in the mirror before she came out, girlfriend?'
   He glanced at Molly. She, on the other hand, looked sensational. She had her blond hair clipped up, rather like her wedding hairstyle but messier, and she was wearing a ruby-red dress in some velvet-type stuff that left her shoulders bare and which clung to her in a somewhat indecent fashion. Ed was having slight trouble resisting the urge to drop kisses on Molly's exquisite

287

shoulders, so he kept imagining her slapping him soundly round the face if he indulged himself, which was just about doing the trick. He had a suspicion she might be wearing stockings, but he literally couldn't think about that.

Molly giggled. 'We're such bitches.'

'Speak for yourself. I am a mere man and therefore cannot be described in such a manner.'

'You can when you're my plus one girlfriend for the night.'

'True. Is it because we're very, very drunk, do you think?'

Molly considered, almost going cross-eyed with the effort. 'Nope. I think we're just evil whether we've had a few of these or not.' She held up her glass of champagne.

'At least there's plenty of booze,' Ed agreed. 'Otherwise we'd have to leave and see midnight in elsewhere.'

'Thanks for stepping in at the last minute,' Molly said. 'Typical of Sam to have to dash off and do work stuff on New Year's Eve.'

'You're very welcome.' Ed saluted her wonkily. 'Nicki's the same, she's working tonight, but she did say she might pop along later.'

Molly said nothing. She wasn't altogether sure Ed's girlfriend liked her that much, and she had no idea why. Obviously some girls were threatened by their boyfriends having a female friend, but Nicki knew Molly was married. Not only that, but Molly and Ed only saw each other once a week, more or less, and only for drinks or dinner. They didn't rock up drunk or stay out late or anything.

'Right. I'm off for a slash,' Ed said, putting his champagne flute down very carefully with the air of a person who is so pissed they are sure they will smash something. 'I shall enjoy piddling in a ten-grand toilet.'

'If the toilet paper is silver lamé, bring me a sheet,' Molly called.

She threw herself into a chair. They were at a party hosted by one of Sam's friends, Nigel. Nigel was a barrister who wore starched shirts, trousers belted in so tightly at the waist that his bottom cheeks resembled wide, plump cushions. His hair was smoothed down with old-fashioned pomade that made Molly long to shove him under the shower and wash it all out.

That said, Nigel and his wife, Sukie, lived in a beautiful Georgian house on the outskirts of Lincoln. Seven bedrooms, five reception rooms, character features, acres of land and a very self-consciously added conservatory that boasted rolls of ceiling blinds, which looked like wicker slugs and probably cost almost as much as the downstairs bathroom, Molly thought. She knew Sam had aspirations to live in a house like this, but he was so careful with money, he couldn't quite bring himself to go through with it.

Their house was stunning, anyway – not quite seven-bedrooms-and-five-reception-rooms stunning, but perfectly lovely. Molly struggled to keep on top of the housework but refused to get the cleaner Sam kept going on about. Surely she should be able to keep her own house clean and tidy? Even if she worked. Plenty of women did that all over the country and most of them probably had children.

Molly finished her champagne. Children. Still a bone

of contention with Sam. Molly wasn't sure if he thought kids might interfere with his deadlines or if he was scared they might take her away from him. Molly had read about men who felt very pushed out when babies came along and she had done her best to reassure Sam, but he was still resisting the whole idea.

'Who's that girl over there?'

Molly turned and had a look. 'The blonde? No idea. Why? Your type?'

'Don't know.' Ed shrugged. 'She's just really pretty.'

'What about Nicki?'

'Not sure.'

'Really?' Molly was surprised. Despite what he'd said, she had thought Nicki was a permanent fixture. 'Ooh, watch out. That girl is coming over.'

Ed straightened his shirt and stood up. 'Hi. We haven't met, have we? I'm Ed.'

'Saskia,' the girl replied, smiling.

'I'm Molly,' Molly said, shaking Saskia's hand in a rather formal manner. She gave Saskia a quick once over. She was a very pretty girl close up, willowy and fairly tall. She had those delicate features that painters found intriguing, and wide, friendly eyes. Molly suspected Saskia was Ed's type to a tee.

'Great party,' Saskia commented. 'Nigel and Sukie always throw lovely parties.'

Molly and Ed exchanged a quick glance, conscious that they had been slagging the party off moments earlier.

'Absolutely,' Molly enthused.

'Didn't I read about you in the paper recently?' Saskia asked, looking at Molly. 'About your business?'

Molly cringed. A local rag had wanted to run a story on her and Sam and, against their better judgement, they had agreed. Or rather, Sam had agreed. And Molly had gone along with it. It was all very cheesy and they had looked distinctly odd in the photograph that had accompanied the piece, all big, glossy hair and shiny suits. Awful.

'Er, yes, maybe.' Molly didn't really want to talk about it.

'Is your husband here tonight?'

Molly shook her head. 'He's working.'

'Gosh.' Saskia looked sympathetic. 'That's not great on New Year's Eve.'

'No.' Molly frowned. She didn't need anyone under-lining how annoying it was that Sam was working tonight.

'So, what do you do?' Saskia said, turning to Ed.

'I . . .' About to say that he helped Nicki out with her business, Ed thought better of it, loath to talk about Nicki. 'I'm writing a novel.'

'Oh not this again.' Molly sloshed more champagne into their glasses. 'He's writing his memoirs, Saskia. Bonkers, right? Well, bonk-a-thon, more like.'

'Oh do shut up,' Ed snapped crossly. 'I never said I was writing my bloody memoirs.'

He wished Molly would stop winding him up about his novel. Granted, he had been writing it for, well, a number of years now, but novels took time to craft. He knew she was only joking when she made her occasional digs, but it seriously wound him up. If only she knew what he *was* writing about.

'A novel?' Saskia looked beyond impressed. 'That's amazing.'

'I think so,' Ed said, pulling a face at Molly.

'It's amazing, he's been writing it for about a decade,' Molly said, giving Ed an overly sweet smile.

Saskia didn't seem to notice their snippy exchange. 'Well, I guess it takes time to write a whole book,' she commented reasonably, tucking a silky lock of hair behind her ear.

'Indeed,' Ed said pompously.

Molly rolled her eyes. 'It's nearly midnight, Ed. Do try not to bore poor Saskia to death by the time the clock starts chiming.'

'Aah, bugger off,' Ed grimaced, turning to Saskia to give her his full attention. 'Now. My novel. Loosely speaking, it's about . . .'

Molly moodily drank champagne. She had no idea what was going on with her tonight, but she was in the mood to get well and truly trousered. Ed was doing her head in, but Molly had no idea why. He had actually looked rather handsome this evening. He was wearing suit trousers, possibly the ones he had worn to her wedding. Had they been navy? Molly couldn't remember. They had been dark and very tight around his thighs, that was the most she could recall. He had teamed them with a white shirt with the cuffs folded back and his hair was in disarray, the way it always looked when he'd had a few.

'*Come on and do the conga!*' Nigel shouted, dancing into the kitchen with his starched shirt unbuttoned to the waist and his face red and sweaty from drink. '*Do-do-do* . . . Come on, you lot, join in!'

'Oh good God, no,' Molly said, laughing as someone grabbed her hand and drew her in. 'Ed, help!'

Ed jumped behind her and grabbed her around the waist. '*Choo-choo-choo, a train across the flo*or . . .' he sang loudly into her ear. He turned to see if Saskia had joined them but she was lost in the throng of people crowding round.

'We've lost Saskia!' Ed shouted as the train moved outside.

'Ok!' Molly shouted back. Was this song on repeat? It was going on for ever. 'Ed, what the hell are we doing?' Molly giggled as they kicked their legs out at the same time as everyone else.

'Having fun!' yelled Ed as he enthusiastically swung his hips. 'Ooh crikey, I've done myself a mischief! Ooh!' Aware that he sounded like an old lady, Ed was nonetheless certain he might have put one of his balls out of action. He broke away from the chain and whirled off in the direction of a large shed that was about the size of his flat. Sinking down with his hands wrapped around his genitals, Ed couldn't stop laughing at the ridiculousness of the whole thing.

'Wait for me!' Molly called, managing to disengage herself to boos and cries of 'Spoilsport!' She sank down next to Ed. 'Bloody hell. The conga. I haven't done that for years.' She pointed to his hand. 'What have you done to yourself, you silly bastard? Or are you just having a cheeky fondle?'

'Yes, Molls. I thought I'd just stop dancing around like a sap and feel myself up, just for the sheer hell of it.' Ed rolled his eyes. 'Take me seriously, can't you? I think I've pulled a muscle. Or maybe I've dislocated a bollock or something.'

Molly slumped against him, shaking with mirth. 'Can you dislocate a bollock? Is that even a thing?'

'Oh, I don't know.' Ed let out a pitiful moan. 'Rub it better, can't you?'

'Edison! I can't believe you asked me such a thing.'

'Medicinal purposes only, I can assure you.'

Molly snorted. 'Yes, of course. It has nothing to do with the fact that you're a horny idiot who loves being felt up.'

'Well.' Ed lay back, one hand still on his groin. He glanced at her, loving the fact that she had the ability to irk him at the same time as managing to make him smile. 'That's the annoying thing about you, isn't it? You know me far too well. Let's just say it would be doubly beneficial. Both medicinal *and* arousing.'

'Oh, Ed.' Molly flopped down next to him, meeting his eyes affectionately. 'You don't ever give up, do you?'

'Not as far as you're concerned.' Ed knew he sounded sober all of a sudden. 'As far as you're concerned, I'll never give up trying. You should know that by now.'

'Yeah, yeah.' Molly turned her head and met his eyes. 'No one holds a torch for that long.'

'Well, I do.' Ed pushed gingerly at his groin and winced.

Molly rolled on to her side. 'Oh, stop it. I'm married to Sam.'

'Doesn't change the way I feel about you. Nothing will.' Ed reached out and tucked a strand of hair behind her ear. 'And that's a fact.'

'I don't believe you.' Molly's tone reflected the shock she felt at Ed's words.

'Believe it.'

Ed fixed his eyes on hers. He had no idea where he was going with this, but he couldn't quite stop himself now. *She's married, she's married, she's married*, he intoned in his head, in angelic mode. *But I want her, I crave her, I love her,* answered the devil unhelpfully.

Oh crap, Ed thought to himself. If he didn't get a handle on himself soon, he was going to bugger everything up and kiss Molly.

Molly stared into Ed's eyes. What was happening to her? She was having urges. Bad ones. Ones a married person shouldn't have. Ed was her best friend. And he had let her down unforgivably, But still, for some reason, he seemed to give her some kind of inner tremor no other man had ever managed to pull off.

No. Molly sat up and got control of herself. She was married to Sam. And she couldn't do this to him. 'I should go,' she said.

'I don't want you to,' Ed said, grabbing her hand.

'I have to go . . .' Her phone was ringing. It was Sam. He was calling her because it was four minutes to midnight.

'It's Sam,' she said, holding her phone up.

'Right.' Ed's heart sank. 'Take it. You must.'

Molly felt like crying. She wanted to curl up in a ball and sob her heart out. But she was doing the right thing. Wasn't she? She was committed to Sam. And whatever she felt for Ed, whatever she had always felt for Ed, was just one of those ironies of life. It just wasn't meant to be. It was never, ever going to happen for them. Not now. Molly's heart suffered a slight crack. Another, to add to the others lodged there with Ed's name all over them.

'Bye, Ed.'

'Bye, Molly.'

Ed watched her walk away with her phone to her ear. He wasn't sure his heart could take any more of this.

'Hey.'

Turning, Ed found Saskia, the girl he'd met earlier, at his elbow.

'Fancy seeing in the New Year together?' She gave him a pretty smile. Flirtatious, fun.

'I think I do,' Ed said, shuffling up to make a space for her. He was certain his relationship with Nicki was over. And as for Molly . . .

'As soon as I clapped eyes on you, I decided you looked eminently kissable,' Saskia said, sitting close to him.

'Did you?' Ed was flattered. Saskia was an incredibly beautiful girl. Rather like a breath of fresh air. Exactly what he probably needed.

'I did. Oh, there it is. Midnight. Come here.' Saskia took his chin and kissed him. Sweetly, then sexily.

And Ed let her. Nicki wasn't for him and he and Molly weren't ever going to be anything more than friends. So he might as well start afresh. He kissed Saskia back and knew he was starting a whole new chapter.

Now

Maplethorpe Beach

'Here, catch!'

Ed threw the tennis ball to Jake and it sailed over his head.

'You're almost as bad at this as you are at football,' Jake panted, having retrieved the ball from the far end of the beach.

'You really are cheeky. I was pretty good at cricket, as it happens.'

'Really?' Jake looked sceptical. 'You can't throw for toffee.'

Ed put his hands on his hips. 'Ok, well I used to be better at batting. Has anyone ever told you it's rude to tell someone they're pants at something?'

'Sorry, Dad.' Jake put his hand to his mouth. 'Sorry. About calling you dad.'

Ed walked over and pulled Jake into his armpit. 'Don't be sorry, dude. A slip of the tongue. If it makes you feel

297

any better, I properly feel like your dad, ok? But we'll just have to wait and see.' He gestured to the blanket he'd laid out on the sand. 'Here, let's take a break. Sit for a bit.'

Jake obliged. 'I'm starving.'

'Here.'

Ed opened the picnic bag he'd brought with them. He wasn't quite up to making sandwiches and all of that, but he had relieved his local supermarket of cocktail sausages, sausage rolls, savoury eggs and some of those brightly coloured cartons of drink Jody would tell him off about later.

'Ace.' Jake got stuck in.

Ed watched him affectionately. He was glad Jake had a good appetite; a fussy eater would have irked him immensely. He let out a contented breath. Who would have thought that spending time with a kid could be so much fun? The beach wasn't at its best today; the sand was rather wet from a recent downpour and some flotsam and jetsam had been washed up nearby. Ed was loath to go near it for fear of condoms and syringes, but as a potential father, he had conducted a brief inspection and there appeared to be nothing dangerous in the pile of rubbish.

Apart from that, the day had been glorious so far. Sunny with a light breeze – perfect kite-flying weather, actually. Ed made a mental note to get one. If he needed to get one.

Ed checked his emails on his phone. He had no idea when the results were due but the online centre he had used had said three to five days, so he guessed it could be soon. Nothing yet. He tucked it away and helped himself to some sausage rolls.

'So, what do you miss about Canada?' he asked Jake.

Jake shrugged. 'My friends, I suppose. But I have some new friends here now, so that's cool.'

'How about your school? Better here or over there?'

Jake shot him a sideways glance. 'About the same.'

Ed nodded. 'The weather?'

Jake shook his head. 'I don't know. Do you want me to like Canada more or something?'

Ed liked Jake's accent. 'Not really. Well, no, actually. Not at all. But I'm just interested in your life, really.'

'So why are you asking me about the weather?'

'No idea. Mostly because I'm an idiot I should imagine.'

'You're not an idiot.' Jake grinned at him, his mouth full of pastry. 'You're alright.'

'So are you,' Ed said, giving Jake a shove with his shoulder. 'Do you want one of these horrible drinks?'

'Yes, please. Mum will kill you for giving me that. Says I bounce off the walls after one of these.'

'Excellent. Look forward to that.'

Ed watched Jake drain the carton before restlessly getting up and heading to the water's edge. Jake then proceeded to hurl around thirty stones of varying sizes into the water. Not with a view to skimming them, just for the sheer hell of chucking them into the water. Ed sat back and watched him. He was sure Jake had been a pain in the arse when he was younger, the way Jody described – she would hardly make such tales up – and

Ed could imagine that there were tough times ahead as Jake hit puberty, but for now, he really did seem to be a delightful kid. Happy, carefree and fairly well-behaved.

God, was he going to get to experience Jake as a teenager? Ed had no idea. He had to keep thinking that he was, because otherwise, he felt so desolate, he didn't know what to do with himself.

'Come and skim stones,' Jake called out.

Ed brushed crumbs off his jeans and confidently stood up. Now here was something Jake couldn't say he was pants at. Ed was a stone-skimmer extraordinaire.

They spent the rest of the afternoon hurling stones, chucking the tennis ball back and forth to one another, inspecting flotsam, eating ice creams and drinking more drinks rammed with E numbers. It was a simple affair, but Ed wasn't sure when he'd last felt as happy. Even though his gut was twisting over the test result. It had been an afternoon of utter perfection.

As Jake threw himself down on the blanket and started raiding the picnic bag again, Ed checked his messages. And there it was. His stomach dropped. The email results had arrived. Ed felt panic tearing through him. This email had the ability to either destroy his world or make him the happiest guy – dad – alive.

'What's the matter?' Jake asked.

'Er, nothing. Might just call your mum and see if she wants to join us.'

Jake shrugged.

Ed made the call. Jody, her voice full of alarm, said she would drive straight down. Ed sat next to Jake and let him chatter on until Jody arrived. She was wearing jeans and a t-shirt – she had clearly just walked out of her house and into her car. She was going to freeze. Ed tore off his jumper and handed it to her as she reached the blanket.

'I'm ok,' she said with chattering teeth.

'Don't be silly,' Ed said, pulling it over her head.

'I've had loads of E numbers,' Jake announced unnecessarily.

'Great,' Jody said. She turned to Ed. 'Have you looked at it yet?'

Ed shook his head. 'No. Haven't had the courage. Also, I thought we should do it together.'

Jody nodded, rubbing her hands on her arms.

'What's going on?' Jake asked.

'Nothing, dude,' Ed said cheerily. 'Why don't you show your mum how well you can skim stones now? He learnt at the feet of the master,' he told Jody, a wide smile fixed on his face.

'Great,' Jody said, seemingly incapable of articulating anything more complicated.

Jake wandered down to the sea front again and Ed took out his phone. His hand was shaking like anything.

'Christ. I can't do it. I don't want to look.' He bit his lip and met Jody's eyes. 'Why don't I just delete it? And then we never need know.'

'You could.' Jody pleated the bottom of Ed's jumper. 'And I really, really want you to. Because then we could just live in this joyful little bubble and we'd never need to confront it and Jake would be so happy.'

'Yes. Yes, let's do that.' Ed clung to it like a frond of seaweed on some driftwood.

Jody wiped a tear away. 'But we both know we have to do this. We have to be brave and we have to find out the truth. Because if we don't, we'll always wonder. And that's not fair on any of us, is it? Especially not Jake.'

'Watch me, Mum, watch me!' Jake skimmed a stone beautifully and it bounced once, twice, seven times across the water.

Ed swallowed. 'No. I guess it's not.'

'Do you want me to read it?'

'I can do it. I can do this.' Ed opened his emails. He took one last, lingering look at Jake and turned back to his phone. Opening the relevant mail, he scanned it quickly.

'Cor, that was a belter!' Jake shouted.

Ed and Jody both cheered on cue. Ed felt a pang in his heart on hearing Jake using his expressions.

'Well? What does it say?' Jody looked petrified.

Ed's legs buckled and he sat down on the blanket. 'I'm not Jake's father.'

'Oh no!' Jody burst into tears. 'Oh, Ed. I'm so sorry.' She sat down next to him with a thump.

Ed put his arm round her. He knew he had to comfort Jody, but he wasn't sure he was capable of it. His heart had just shattered. His heart would never feel the same again. For it had swelled almost to bursting, with enjoyment, contentment, pride, love – such overwhelming love – that it would now inevitably deflate and feel empty.

'We should have done this in the first place,' Jody wept. 'I'm so sorry. I can't believe I put you through this – put Jake through this. I was so sure, I was so, so sure.'

How could you be, Jody? Ed thought to himself. How could you be sure I was the father when you knew you'd slept with someone else?

'I'm so selfish,' Jody gasped, fishing a tissue out of her trouser pocket. 'I wanted the father to be you – so I told myself it was you. I was convinced. Please don't hate me, Ed. Please.'

Ed tightened his grip on Jody's shoulder. 'Of course I don't hate you. I know you wanted me to be Jake's dad. It's just that I never knew how much I wanted something until you showed it to me, you know?'

Jody nodded and wept even harder. 'I can't believe this. I just can't believe it. The test . . . you . . .'

'I did it properly,' Ed confirmed sadly. 'I know I did. I'm just not Jake's dad and that's that.'

'What?'

Ed looked up. Jake was standing in front of them and they hadn't even realised.

'Y-you're not my dad?' Jake's lip was trembling.

'Oh God. Come here.' Ed let go of Jody and went to Jake. Jake fell into his arms, sobbing. Ed joined him. There was little point in trying to stop himself in the circumstances.

'I want you to be my dad,' Jake gulped. 'Why can't you be my dad? What does that test matter?'

Ed was lost for words. In some ways, Jake was right. Did the test really matter? He had bonded so well with Jake – they had an amazing relationship. Ed could see himself parenting Jake until he was in his late teens – well, for as long as he needed a dad. For ever, in fact. And that life had been shown to him, then cruelly snatched away. Ed was heartbroken. And judging by Jake's shaking shoulders, so was he.

'I feel so guilty,' Jody sniffed, looking agonised as she watched them. 'I shouldn't have come here. I should have done a DNA test in Canada first. I was just so convinced it was you, Ed. So convinced. God.'

Ed tightened his grip on Jake. He didn't blame Jody for wanting a happy ending for her son, but he did wish he hadn't got caught up in her quest. Ed blamed himself for spending so much time bonding with Jake before getting the DNA test done. He should have thought about Jake – they should both have thought about Jake. Why hadn't they? It wasn't fair on the poor kid.

'Will we go back to Canada now?' Jake asked Jody in a woeful voice.

Jody rubbed her face. 'I don't know, Jake. I suppose we should. We need to get in touch with your real father.'

'Do you know where he is?' Ed asked. He felt an irrational stab of jealousy. Some other guy, who might not even want to be Jake's father, for fuck's sakes, was going to get to hang out with this awesome kid instead of him.

Jody nodded. 'Yes. I used to work with him. He's still at the company, as far as I know. It's just a matter of a phone call.'

'At least you don't need a DNA test,' Ed said flatly.

Jody's face crumpled with misery. 'I guess not.'

Ed didn't think he could stand it. Some other guy was going to get to chuck a ball back and forth on a beach with Jake, play football in the park. Help Jake with his homework, tell him about girls, introduce him to beer.

Ed wasn't going to get to do any of this stuff. He had been shown an image of an amazing father–son relationship – he had even got to experience it for a while – and now it was being cruelly taken away from him. Ed hadn't known he wanted it, had never thought he would want to be a father, *could* be a good father.

The trouble was, now that Ed had experienced this with Jake, he almost couldn't see him doing it with his own child at some point. Which was absurd. Surely he could? But right now, such a thought was crucifying him. It was just something about Jake, something about this special little boy that had connected with Ed's heart. And Ed didn't know if such a feeling could ever be resurrected.

'So you'll go back to Canada then?' Ed repeated Jake's question, still holding on to Jake. The boy hadn't stopped weeping since he'd heard the news.

'I think it might be for the best,' Jody said, getting to her feet. Her voice cracked. 'I don't think it would be a good thing for you to see Jake all the time and vice versa. And I have to give his real – the other guy – a chance to be a father to Jake. I'm so sorry, Ed.'

Ed recoiled at the word 'real'. He had wanted so badly to be Jake's real dad. Instead, he had just been a temporary pretend dad with no rights whatsoever.

'I'm going to miss you so much,' Jake sobbed, holding on to Ed.

Ed felt Jake's little hands clutching at his shirt and almost lost it. 'Me too, dude. But hey, listen.' He dropped to his knees and put his hands on Jake's shoulders. 'You get to see all your friends again, ok? You get to go back to your old house and your old school.'

'I don't care about any of that stuff,' Jake shouted. 'I want to be with you.'

Ed knew he had to be brave to help Jake. 'I know. I want the same. But I'm not actually your dad, am I?' He let the tears trickle down his cheeks. 'I wanted it and you wanted it, but sometimes life doesn't work that way.'

'Life sucks,' Jake cried angrily.

'It does sometimes,' Ed agreed. 'It really does. But you're going to be ok. You have your mum and I bet this other guy will be over the moon to be your dad.' He squeezed Jake's shoulders. 'And I bet he'll be much better than me at football.'

Jake burst into tears again. Ed stayed on his knees and held him, running his hands over Jake's back. They stayed like that for ages, Jody giving them their moment. Ed put his hand on Jake's hair and inhaled the smell one last time. Nothing would ever smell as good as Jake's hair after a day on the beach. Ed wished he could bottle that smell so he could open the bottle every so often and inhale the essence of Jake. Take himself back to this moment – maybe the moments he had enjoyed just a few hours earlier – and feel the joy again.

Ed finally pulled back. 'Right. We need to man-up now. We've had a good cry, but it's time to pull ourselves together and get on with it. Agreed?'

'Agreed.' Jake sniffed.

'I'll speak to you before we leave,' Jody said to Ed, her eyes full of apology. 'And I can't say it enough. I'm so, so sorry.'

Ed nodded. He must look like a wreck, but he didn't care.

Jake took Jody's outstretched hand and started to walk off with her. Then he broke away and ran back to Ed.

'I love you,' he said in a strangled voice. 'Don't care if you're my dad or not.'

'I love you too,' Ed whispered. 'Bye, dude.'

Jake ran back to Jody, giving Ed a look over his shoulder. Ed watched them reach the edge of the beach, but his eyes were so blurred with tears, he missed them getting into the car and driving off. Had he waved? He hoped he had waved.

Ed stood on the beach for some time in the same spot, crying his eyes out. At some point, he noticed that the beach was becoming emptier and the sky a shade darker. Thrusting his hands into his pockets, he walked back to his car, not even realising he'd left his blanket and picnic bag behind.

Molly wandered around her house. It looked good. Good enough to sell. Which was exactly what she was going to do with it. She had de-cluttered and she had cleaned, she had added more accent colours and feminine touches. She had bought a spray which smelt of fresh linen and she had a candle that wafted coffee scent into the air. So she was basically armed with everything she needed to lure buyers into snapping up this property.

Sam had agreed to it, but then why wouldn't he? He wanted to cut himself off from all aspects of his old life, and the house he had shared with Molly was one of those things he wanted to be free of. The house – and Molly. He had given Molly a good sum of money for her share of the business and she had been hugely offended by it. She had put so much into the business with Sam it seemed cruel to be paid off in such a way. It was also ironic that Sam, the worrier about all things financial, had simply handed money over the way he had. It was as if he just wanted her to be out of his life.

But Molly had to admit that the money might come in useful later, when she needed more full-on care. As awful as that thought was, Molly knew she needed to be practical about her illness. One day she would need help and Sam's money – arguably, money she had also made – would assist with that. Sam was happily ensconced in some sterile little flat close to the office and Molly had no doubt he would quickly settle there and get his life back on track. It cut like a knife, but Molly was beginning to feel better about being without Sam. She had even spoken to a solicitor about divorce proceedings.

Molly wandered into her studio. It looked the tidiest it ever had, but that was fine because she wasn't painting at the moment. With the help of her neurological consultant, she was looking into some new drugs, drugs that might at least help with the stiffening. Because not being able to paint was affecting the quality of Molly's life to such an extent, she had focused on this as the main area to work on. And as she was no longer part of Sam's business, she needed something to do.

Impulsively, Molly called Sara. 'Can you come over? I need a chat.'

Sara didn't need telling twice. After arriving in a taxi with two bottles of wine she made herself comfortable on the sofa and started pouring.

'Shoot,' she said.

'Well, first of all, I have something to show you.' Molly held up the torn envelope she had found in Sam's things.

'What's that?'

'I don't know. It was in Sam's stuff and it's in Ed's handwriting.'

'How long have you had it?'

Molly shrugged. 'A few weeks, I guess. A month, maybe.'

'What? And you haven't read it yet?'

'Nope.'

'So bloody well read it! What are you waiting for?' Sara made a grab for it, but Molly held it up.

'I don't want to. I can't.'

'Why the hell not?'

'Because I feel disloyal.'

'Towards whom?' Sara was getting exasperated.

'Towards Ed, of course! Not Sam. Sam has been hiding something.' Molly turned the envelope over in her hands. 'I feel as though this is Pandora's Box or something. This is significant. If I read this, I feel as though something will shift and change.'

'Bloody hell, woman, you're killing me,' Sara moaned. 'I literally would not be able to not read that. Listen, what's going on? I'm so in the dark here, I wouldn't be able to find my way with an entire box of matches.'

Molly gazed out of the window and tried to explain. 'I-I miss Ed. With everything that's happened to me, I really miss Ed.' She turned back to Sara. 'You know I'm always taking the micky out of Ed for writing his memoirs?'

Sara nodded. 'The infamous novel. Does it even exist?'

'That's the thing. It actually does. I read it. It's about me and Ed.'

'No way.' Sara was agog.

Molly sighed. 'It's the most romantic thing I've ever read. I didn't quite get to the end, but what I read blew me away.'

'Wowzers. That's incredible.' Sara broke into a smile. 'Go and see Ed. Go and see him and tell him how moved you are by his book.'

'I can't. I-I just can't. He has feelings for Jody, I'm sure of it.'

'No he doesn't,' Sara scoffed. 'Look, I get it, Molly. We all want to be someone's first choice. But you always have been Ed's first choice, Molly. You must know that.'

'Not now Jake has come along.'

'Ok. But that doesn't mean Ed is into Jody. Why don't you bloody well ask him?'

Molly shook her head. 'Thing is, I feel strong right now, weirdly, really strong. Strong enough to know I don't want to be an afterthought for anyone any more. Maybe it's time to go it alone,' she finished, looking solemnly at Sara.

'Blimey,' said Sara. 'Well, I'm glad I brought two bottles of wine over. Are you seriously saying that you might have a chance to finally get with Ed and you have changed your mind?'

Molly's mouth twisted. 'I don't know if I have a chance with him. But after Sam . . . and if Ed has feelings for Jody . . . I don't know . . .'

'Lordy.' Sara topped their wine glasses up. 'That's epic.'

It's not, Molly thought. It's not remotely epic. It's the most tragic thing ever. But it's how I feel. Maybe time had just ran out as far as she and Ed were concerned. Maybe this was one mishap too many.

Not every love story had a happy ending, Molly acknowledged sadly. She and Ed had missed their timing so many times, it wasn't surprising it was just too late to make things work. It was heartbreaking, but Molly really couldn't see how she and Ed could ever make it work now.

It was actually three days before Ed got in touch with Molly. Every time he had tried, he'd started crying. And that wouldn't do. Finally, he got himself together and he headed over to Molly's house.

'Ed.' Molly's eyes widened as soon as she saw him. 'What's happened?'

Ed fell into her arms and Molly held his shuddering body. 'Ed, talk to me. What's happened?'

Ed shook his head, his shoulders heaving. 'I-I can't . . .'

'It's Jake.' Realisation dawned on Molly. 'He's not yours.'

'No,' Ed managed, clinging on to her for dear life.

'Oh fucking hell,' Molly said, squeezing him tighter. 'That's so fucking unfair.'

She held him and held him. Ed didn't let go. He couldn't. After what seemed like an age, he was finally spent. He eased himself out of Molly's arms and fell into an armchair.

'Shit. I've literally cried for about three hours,' Ed said, wiping his nose. 'I must look like a complete wreck.'

'Pretty much. Wine?'

'Yes, please. Don't bother with a glass. Just bring me a bucket and I'll put my head in it.'

'Right you are.' Molly came back with the largest glass she could find and glugged wine into it. 'Drink. I know I'm always on at you not to get pissed, but this is a time to get royally pissed.'

'Cheers,' Ed said, clinking his glass with hers. He started crying again. 'I love that kid. I bloody love him.'

'I know,' Molly soothed, putting her wine glass down to stroke Ed's hair. 'I know you do. And you were a great dad to him for a while.'

'I was, right? I really tried hard at it. I was responsible, I got a job. I played, I helped with homework. I would have disciplined.' Ed lay back in the armchair. 'And now he's going back to Canada.'

'Oh no. That's terrible.'

Molly sat on the edge of the chair and rubbed Ed's arm.

'It's the worst,' Ed agreed. He started crying again.

Molly wanted to make everything better. She wanted to tell him how she felt about him, how she had always felt about him. But it wasn't the right time. Not now, when Ed was dealing with this terrible blow. His next words shocked her.

'And it's upset Jody as well.' Ed wiped his nose.

'Jody?'

'Yes. She's devastated. Utterly devastated. She so wanted me to be Jake's dad.'

Molly nodded. 'I can understand why she's upset.' Her heart thumped.

'I am too. I really wanted to be Jake's dad. I wanted to be there for him. For Jody.'

'Right.' Molly's stomach slid. He had feelings for Jody. Ed was in love with Jody.

'I just hated seeing her looking so destroyed by the results.' Ed rubbed at his eyes. They were stinging as though he had rubbed sea water into them. 'We'd developed this really great relationship.'

'Of course,' Molly said numbly. 'You thought you were both Jake's parents.'

'Right. And that we could be parents together, you know?' Ed sniffed and put his head back against the chair. 'I actually thought we were doing a pretty good job of it too.'

Molly sat down opposite him. 'So Jake and Jody are going back to Canada?'

'Yes,' Ed nodded. Abruptly, he started to cry again. 'I can't bear it. I can't bear the thought of them leaving.'

'This is so horrible for you,' Molly managed. 'I . . . I wish I could make it better.'

Ed wept into his hands. 'That kid . . . God, but he got to me. He's such a brilliant little boy. I don't think my heart can take this. Jake . . . Jody . . . this is just so shit.'

Molly hugged him. She couldn't not. He needed a cuddle. And he had come to her for that. Despite her own broken heart, Molly held Ed until he passed out from wine and sheer exhaustion. Curling up next to him, Molly drifted off into a fitful sleep.

In the early hours, Ed woke up. Leaning over, he stroked Molly's hair. God, she looked beautiful. And she was

313

always there for him. Ed thought about Jake and his heart clenched again. But it just wasn't meant to be. Jake wasn't his. Some other guy was his father and there was nothing Ed could do about it.

Ed had wanted to speak to Molly about her reading his novel. But this wasn't the right time. How could he talk to her about something as important as that when he was still dealing with this bombshell?

No. Molly would have to wait. Just a little bit longer. Ed had an idea of what he was going to do to convince her of his feelings. He just hoped he hadn't blown it, that it wasn't too late. That would be unthinkable.

Molly and Ed

June 2010
'Another beer?'

'Don't mind if I do.'

'There you go.' Ed opened a beer with a hiss and handed it to Boyd. 'What do you think of my new pad then? It just shows you; I would never have found this place if me and Nicki hadn't split up.' He felt a pang. He had missed Nicki a bit after they had split up a few years ago. They were fearfully ill-suited, but they had got used to one another. They had been good friends. But now Saskia was in his life, and it couldn't be better.

'It's fantastic,' Boyd said, glancing round the garden appreciatively. 'Moving a bit further out bought you much more space.'

'And this garden.'

'It's a great garden. Oh, bugger it!' Boyd spilt beer all over his shirt. 'Honestly, Ed. Do not ever have bloody children. They keep you awake all night long, the little

315

sods, and then you can't function properly.' He rubbed ineffectually at his shirt. 'Look at that. Helen bought me this shirt for my birthday.'

'Here.' Ed tossed him a tea towel. 'I'm sure Helen will forgive you. Isn't she due to drop another one at any minute?' He lay back in his deckchair and turned his face to the sun.

'Don't remind me,' Boyd grumbled. 'Number five is on its way. Five children.' He smiled good-naturedly, clearly delighted in spite of his moaning. 'I have my mobile phone at the ready.' He held up the latest model, a swanky-looking thing. Boyd always did want the very best technology could offer. 'I actually think it would do you good to have kids, Ed.'

'Do you?' Ed raised his eyebrows and put his sunglasses on. 'I'm not sure I'm cut out for it. It's enough responsibility having a dog. Fingal, fetch!' He took a ball from under his deckchair and tossed it down the garden. He had acquired Fingal when he was an eight-week-old puppy – an adorable, sleek ball of brown fur and excitable yelps. It had mostly been for company, but also because Ed was being a big girl's blouse now that he lived in the sticks. Fingal was a great guard dog and Ed had slept so much better since he got him.

'I do love a chocolate Lab, but why the hell did you call him Fingal?' Boyd frowned.

'It's an Oscar Wilde thang.'

Dear Boyd. Great literature was lost on him. Still, who knew that one of Oscar Wilde's middle names was Fingal? Molly, sure, but not many other people.

'You're great with that dog, Ed. I'm sure you'd be just as good with kids.'

Ed made a snorting sound. 'Hardly the same thing! Look, you're a wonderful dad, Boyd. A natural. But I'm crap with kids. Seriously.'

'You can't really know that until you actually become a father,' Boyd said reasonably, almost tipping his deck-chair up as he settled himself. 'I was crap with other people's kids. Your own are very different. With your own, you feel comfortable about beating them senseless, ha ha.'

Ed smiled. He was pleased for Boyd. He had done well for himself. Not only had he made some excellent financial decisions (which Ed had also benefited from), he was happily married to Helen who patently adored him. And unlike other parents Ed knew, Boyd and Helen seemed to genuinely enjoy being around their gaggle of somewhat unruly children. They lived in a self-consciously nouveau riche house which would look like a show home if it wasn't obliterated by toys, tiny clothes and little brightly coloured tables and chairs that Ed always seemed to trip over when he visited. But it was a lovely home.

Homely, Ed thought to himself. That sounded ridiculous, but it *was* homely. Comfortable, messy, warm. That said, Ed wasn't sure he envied Boyd as such. Boyd seemed extremely content, so he was probably doing better than Ed in that sense, but Ed knew himself. He wasn't sure a crowd of kids and a home in suburbia would be his idea of heaven.

He glanced at Boyd fondly. His friend had developed a slight paunch – well, more than a paunch, if Ed were to be brutal. Boyd was receding a tad, his exposed forehead turning pink in the sun, but he had plenty of laughter lines. Or were they stress lines? Ed wasn't sure. Providing for five children must be a financial drain, however well Boyd was doing.

'So how's the novel coming along?'

Ed dreaded that question. But he had made a rod for his own back. Since telling all and sundry of his silly plans to write a book, he had since read countless website articles about aspiring writers that all very clearly suggested *not* telling *anyone* about said novel until it was published. Or, at very least, until an agent had been secured, as apparently that was the way to go. These days publishers would only consider writers who were represented by an agent, who had already sifted through the shite of the slush pile.

'The novel is . . . it's not going so well,' Ed confessed, wincing at the admission. He rubbed Fingal's ears.

'Why not?'

'Oh, I don't know. It's complicated.'

Ed shifted awkwardly in his deckchair. That wasn't strictly true. He knew why it was so hard to finish his novel. It was because it was about Molly. And his friendship – relationship – with Molly had taken so many twists and turns over the years, sometimes it was tough writing about it. Sometimes it hurt.

Ed sighed. Since that New Year's Eve at Nigel and Sukie's a few years ago, Ed had done his best to steer clear of Molly. It had been a concerted effort. Which hadn't been as difficult as expected because Molly seemed to be steering well clear of him as well. Ed guessed that, like him, she felt it to be the best course of action. Clearly they had missed their window and despite whatever spark they seemed to have between them, Molly was married to Sam and that was that.

Ed envied Molly her relationship with Sam. That was what *he* needed. A proper relationship. Someone to love. Someone who could banish Molly from sight – someone Ed could well and truly fall for. His relationship with Nicki had been a non-starter, but Saskia . . . She was good for him. He felt settled with her. She was a beautiful girl, but she was also a lot of fun. They were constantly laughing and even if they didn't always enjoy the same books and music, they had plenty of shared interests to keep them talking incessantly. Quite simply, their relationship worked.

Ed moodily lit a cigarette. He and Molly were now friends of the distant variety. They slipped in and out of each other's lives when they couldn't avoid it, meeting at social functions, bumping into each other in town now and again. They were always pleased to see each other and Ed always wanted to arrange to meet Molly somewhere for coffee or dinner, but something always stopped him. Pride, for one thing. Molly didn't ever look as though she was trying to stop herself from asking *him* to meet up. And Ed supposed the other part of it was self-preservation. It was absurd to think that the person who made his life brighten by virtue of her presence also had the ability to make it feel sharply lacking.

'Is it that complicated, Ed?' Boyd threw him an astute glance. 'I can't imagine that writing a book is that different to any other job, really. Don't you simply need to get your head down and get on with it?' His face jerked apologetically. 'I mean, I'm no expert, obviously. I get that it's a creative process – that you need to have inspiration flowing and all that. But I just wonder if it's one of those things that requires hard graft. Fingers on a typewriter, pen to paper – whatever.'

Ed drained his beer and blew smoke into the air. 'You are actually spot-on, Boyd. I guess I'm just making excuses.' He sat up, feeling a curl of fire in his stomach. 'I should get this book written. I actually think the stuff I've written so far is pretty good.'

'Well, there you go then. I know you don't need to work as such – and believe me, that can be a real firework up your backside,' Boyd grimaced at this point. 'But still, it's what you've always wanted to do. Maybe it's time.'

Ed nodded. 'It is, it is. You speak such sense, Middleton.' He got up. 'Let's have some more beers. See if you can sort the rest of my life out.'

'Ah, speaking of which, I have a proposition for you.' Boyd handed over his empty bottle and passed a hand over his burning pate gingerly. 'Ouch. Might need some factor twenty on my bonce.'

'Proposition?'

'Yes. I have an investment opportunity for you.' Boyd tapped his nose. 'A biggie. You'd need a massive wodge of capital to get on board, but I think we can manage that, don't you?'

Ed shrugged. He didn't pay a great deal of attention to his investments. Boyd unofficially acted as his financial advisor/accountant most of the time and all Ed knew was that he received a steady trickle of cash into his current account each month. He didn't get involved; he trusted Boyd implicitly.

'Just let me know where I need to sign and we'll sort the money out.'

'Excellent, excellent. I think this could make us a fortune, Ed.'

'Splendid.'

'By the way, I really like Saskia,' Boyd commented. 'Gorgeous girl.'

'Isn't she?' And she really was. Long, blond hair, pale skin and a sylph-like body. Lovely eyes.

'Where's she been hiding?'

'She's been living in the States with her boyfriend,' Ed explained. 'Ex-boyfriend, obviously. But she's from round here originally.'

'I have a good feeling about this one, Edison,' Boyd said with a wink. 'She's an absolute cracker. Maybe I'll be best man at *your* wedding one day.'

'Yeah, yeah.' Ed strolled towards the house, doubtful of such an occurrence. Open mind, he reminded himself.

'And don't forget my factor twenty,' Boyd yelled. 'I'm burning like a bitch here.'

Ed grinned. He really was very fond of Boyd.

'Sam. I just want you to talk to me.'

'Molly.' Sam placed his mobile phone carefully on the table. 'Are we really going to talk about children again?' He ran his hand through his hair. 'I have so much work here . . .'

'Oh screw the work!' Molly leapt up from her chair. 'Sam, there is more to life than work.'

Sam stared at her. 'I know that. Do you think I don't know that?'

Molly felt tears coming to her eyes, but she dashed them away. This was an emotive issue and she wasn't sure she was really rowing with Sam about having children. It was an issue between them, but it wasn't the only issue, by any means.

'Is this really about having kids?' Sam asked gently.

'I don't know. I just don't know any more.'

Molly sank down into her chair and gazed out of the window. They were eating dinner at the huge desk they shared in their office, the way they often did. Even at the weekends. Thai noodles with chicken and peanut sauce from the takeaway shop on the corner, where the owners knew their names and the three different orders they more or less rotated. And wine. Molly seemed to be drinking an awful lot of wine recently.

Work was so plentiful, Molly and Sam practically lived at the office, popping home to shower and change before coming back and wading through paperwork and projects. They had taken on another four members of staff over the past year to help with the workload, but it hardly seemed to have made a dent.

Molly had wondered for a while if Sam kept the staff levels down because he liked to be in control, but she realised now it was quite simply because he loved his work so much, he wanted to be involved in every aspect of it. But this was Sam's company. And as much as Molly enjoyed being busy and as much as she loved what they did, it wasn't *hers*. She and Sam were partners, they were husband and wife, but Molly couldn't shake off the feeling that she was working for Sam. That this was all for him. Nothing seemed to be hers or about her. Which sounded utterly ridiculous. Molly wasn't even sure she knew what she was getting at, so how the hell was Sam supposed to understand?

'Do you need some time off?' Sam said, his face crumpled with concern. 'I'm so worried about you, Molls. I want to help. I really want to help. But I'm floundering.'

So am I, thought Molly. I've been floundering for months.

She wasn't sure what the problem was – why she had suddenly started questioning her life. But something felt off-kilter – something wasn't sitting right. Molly had latched on to the issue of having children, had grabbed on to the idea that Sam didn't ever want them, and was running with it. But she wasn't sure she was ready for children herself. Or if she ever wanted them, really. It was such a big decision. But if the issue making her stomach tighten and her head constantly ache *wasn't* about having babies, then what was it?

Sam reached across the table and took her hand. 'I'll hire some more staff,' he said decisively. 'We can afford it. We have enough work for another two or three designers.'

Molly wanted to cry. Sam was trying so hard to please her. He was always trying to please her. And that made her feel terrible. Sam was so supportive, and she wasn't sure she was the same for him. She worked all the same hours – they were side by side day in, day out – but it always seemed to be Sam trying to lift her, trying to keep her happy. Who was doing that for him?

'I'm so sorry,' Molly mumbled. 'I really don't know what's wrong with me. But it's not just about having kids. I'm pretty sure it's not that.'

Sam got up, stood behind her chair and put his arms around her shoulders. 'You're stressed. Stressed up to the eyeballs. You need a break.'

'A holiday?' Molly said hopefully.

'Well.' Sam removed his arms and sat on the edge of the desk. 'Maybe not a holiday, but definitely a few days away here and there.'

'Sam, we haven't had a holiday in years. I want to visit places with you. I want to go to Italy, to France. To a Caribbean island. To the Bahamas. Vegas. Anywhere. Just anywhere.'

'I know, I know.' Sam looked contrite. 'That all sounds amazing. And you deserve a holiday, you really do.'

'We deserve one, not just me.'

Molly was beginning to feel exasperated again. Sometimes it felt as though Sam, as supportive as he was, almost martyred himself when it came to holidays and time off and having a balanced life. It was as if he was a machine some of the time, as if he just never needed to step away. Molly slopped more wine into her glass and downed it rapidly. Sam was so selfless at times. So focused on work. Sam would do anything to make her happy. To do what she wanted to do. Well, as long as it didn't take him away from work.

Sheesh, Molly thought to herself. It was like going round and round in circles. More and more she found herself standing in front of travel agents, gazing wistfully at pictures of Mauritius, Mexico, the Seychelles. She yearned to be on a beach somewhere, to feel the seductive glow of sun on her body. To slop about in flip-flops with a cocktail in her hand, the scent of coconut sun lotion under her nose. Molly found herself craving it. But why didn't Sam want that? Why didn't he want to stretch out next to her in the sun? Why didn't he want to take a break from work? Work was great – invigorating, exciting – but surely nothing compared to some sunshine, some time together that didn't involve being hunched over a desk?

'We will go on holiday,' Sam assured Molly, watching her top her wine glass up again. 'Maybe in December. Perhaps we can have Christmas away.'

Molly frowned. 'What about Dad? I can't leave him on his own, can I?'

'I forgot about your dad. Sorry.' Sam sat down again. 'Ok, Molly. It was just an idea.'

Molly immediately felt like a bitch. And very, very guilty. She often felt guilty around Sam and she couldn't for the life of her figure out why.

I wish I could speak to Ed, Molly thought to herself. She sat up straight and sipped her wine. Where had that come from? She did her very best not to think about Ed. Since that New Year's Eve some years back, Molly had forced herself to step away from Ed. Clearly they couldn't be friends. There was a spark between them and every so often, whatever had gone on before, it flared up. And it was dangerous. Molly knew it was dangerous for her to be around Ed. She didn't ever look at another man with any kind of intent. Not one. It was just Ed. She had a weakness for him, which she could only blame on their history. Staying away from him was the best option. And she proved that to herself every time they accidentally bumped into one another. Molly found herself desperate to sneak into his arms. To spend more time with him. And she simply couldn't do it any more.

Molly couldn't shake off the feeling that she had compromised herself in some way. That she had lost herself.

'I wish I could make you happy,' Sam said suddenly and with an air of melancholy.

'You do make me happy!' Molly was astonished. 'Why would you say such a thing?'

'Molly.' Sam swallowed. 'You look so unhappy sometimes. You don't enjoy work the way I do. You – you drink too much.'

'I drink too much?' Molly flushed.

'You do. A bit.' Sam shrugged. 'I don't mind. It's just I wonder why you do it.'

Molly bristled. Who was Sam to question her drinking habits? She had to relax somehow, for heaven's sakes! She didn't ever go on holiday, she worked most weekends and she had nothing else to focus on. So what if she had the odd glass of wine in the evenings?

'Well. I'm sorry if my drinking offends you.' Molly knew she sounded childish. And to underline that point, she deliberately filled her wine glass again and drained it. What on earth was wrong with her?

'It doesn't offend me.' Sam narrowed his eyes. 'But you don't need to make a point here, Molly.'

'Don't I?' Molly airily waved a hand. 'If it doesn't offend you, I might just drink another few bottles.' She stood up and opened the cupboard. 'We have many a great vintage in here, don't we? Presents from clients and all sorts.' Molly pulled a bottle out. 'Look at this one! That's probably worth thousands.'

'Ok. I think this is getting out of hand now.' Sam pushed his noodles to one side and pulled his work towards him.

'Well, yes, we don't want anything to interfere with work, do we?' Molly was beginning to dislike herself intensely. Apart from enjoying his work rather too much, what had Sam done that was so terrible?

'Why don't you go home?' Sam's voice was clipped. 'I can cover this.'

'Home? I can't even remember what it looks like.'

'A walk then?' Sam suggested with a grimace. 'Whatever works best. I just don't want to do this any more. If we carry on, I'm going to lose my temper and this is going to get really ugly.'

On cue, his phone started ringing. Not even looking at her, Sam answered it, his face breaking into a smile as he suavely started doing business.

Molly watched him slip effortlessly into work mode. How could he do that? How could he be mid row and just go straight back to making money, even when someone called him at a bad moment?

Feeling utterly superfluous, Molly grabbed her bag, shoved the wine bottle into it and left the office. She started to walk but, perversely, she didn't want to do what Sam suggested. In fact, she wanted to do the opposite. What *wouldn't* he want her to do?

Hailing a cab, Molly slid in and gave an address she had stored on her phone but had never yet had cause to use. Fifteen minutes later, she found herself outside Ed's house. Not even giving herself time to think, Molly paid the driver and headed up the driveway. This was, by far, the nicest house Ed had ever owned. It was almost in the countryside, and she knew it had a lovely garden because he had told her about it one time they had bumped into each other.

'Molly!'

Ed looked shocked to see her, Molly decided. Shocked but happy, maybe? She wasn't sure.

'Sorry to just turn up,' she said breathlessly. 'I-I . . .' She wasn't sure what to say. What the hell was she doing there? 'I bring wine?' she said eventually, tugging the bottle out of the bag.

'Well, then you are very welcome,' Ed said, standing back and grandly sweeping his hand. 'Come on in.'

'You're very bronzed,' she commented, setting her bag down on the hall table.

'I've been out in the garden all day with Boyd. We got completely plastered and I sent him home in a cab twenty minutes ago.' Ed grinned. 'Burnt to a crisp, the poor lad. I'd run out of factor twenty. Come on through, we can sit in the conservatory.'

Molly stifled a laugh. Ed with a conservatory? She never thought she'd see the day. She was so used to him having little bedsits and flats that he wasn't overly fussed about, it was strange to see him in a lovely little house with all the mod cons.

'And don't you laugh about me having a conservatory, Molls,' Ed said, giving her a sideways glance. 'I know what you're like for taking the piss.'

Molly shook her head. 'I wasn't going to say a word, Edison. Not. A. Word.'

'Cheeky wench,' Ed said, knowing exactly what she was thinking.

He took a good look at Molly while she was nosing round his conservatory. She looked good, but something was a bit off. She was wearing a summer dress that showed off an expanse of leg, only lightly tanned, but Ed assumed she spent most of her time working in the office, so it made sense. Her hair was loose and her face was mostly free of make-up. But she looked stressed out. Her mouth was tight and her shoulders were hunched. Something was up.

'What's wrong, Molls?' Ed gently removed the bottle of wine from Molly's taut fingers.

'What's wrong? Oh, I don't know.' Molly threw herself into a wicker chair. 'Ouch. Thought that would be comfier. Open that would you? Please?'

'Sure.'

Ed slowly unscrewed the top, took two glasses out of the cupboard and poured red wine into both. He handed one to Molly. Then watched her down it.

He knelt down by her chair. 'Molly. Talk to me. What's wrong? I've barely seen you in months and here you are on my doorstep, complete with wine. Looking like you've been hit by a bus or something.'

Molly stared at Ed. He looked impossibly good-looking and lovely. Tanned and relaxed. Dressed in his usual crumpled shirt and shorts combo, his cigarettes tucked in his top pocket. None of the adverts about the hideousness of smoking had affected Ed one way or another; he was a maverick when it came to such things. And annoyingly, smoke smelt sexy on him, even though Molly wasn't exactly a fan.

'Talk to me,' Ed said, taking her hand. It felt cold in his, despite the heat outside. It was odd how it always seemed to fit his so perfectly. 'I hate seeing you like this.'

'And I hate feeling like this. I bloody well hate it.'

Molly slopped more wine into her glass and jerkily drank it. She didn't know what was wrong with her exactly, but she couldn't pull herself out of her negative mindset.

'Come here.' Ed pulled her into his arms. 'Cry. Scream. Shout. Talk to me. Don't talk to me. Anything. I'm here.'

That was it. Molly burst into tears. She sobbed and sobbed and sobbed into Ed's shoulder. In between gasps, she told him about the row with Sam. She knew she wasn't making any sense whatsoever, but she just kept talking and talking and talking.

Ed held Molly. And listened. He wasn't sure what the problem was because everything that was coming out was so garbled, but he realised Molly was suffering a crisis. She felt trapped, suffocated. She maybe wanted kids but that wasn't what this was really about. She was tired. She needed a break – a proper holiday, most likely. She had lost herself. Sam was wonderful, a good husband and very supportive. He worked too much, but he was kind, thoughtful.

Ed fought with himself as he held her. God, but he was weak as far as she was concerned. Here she was, bawling her eyes out, clearly in a terrible state and yet he welcomed having her in his arms. It was like some

330

sort of illness, for goodness' sakes. He wondered if there was one person in the world for everyone – one person who had the ability to render another into a state of utterly gorgeous disarray.

Whoever he had been in a relationship with over the years, long-term or short-lived, he had been consumed by thoughts of Molly. His mind flitted to her constantly, in a variety of ways. Sometimes in an innocent, 'friend' capacity – along the lines of 'I totally need to tell Molly about that' – and sometimes in a rather less noble fashion, which involved beltingly lustful thoughts that really shouldn't rear their head when he was doing his best to commit to someone else.

For fuck's sakes, Ed thought to himself. This has to stop.

'I've soaked your shoulder,' Molly mumbled, pulling back.

'Not to worry. This shirt needs a good wash to be honest.'

'Lovely.'

'I live on my own. No one cares.' Right on cue, Fingal bounded up. 'Well, alright. Not quite on my own.' Ed reached down and patted Fingal's neck.

'Oh, he's adorable!' Molly was momentarily distracted. 'Ed, you didn't say you had a dog.'

'I've only had him for a few months. Fingal, meet Molly. Molly – Fingal.'

'Fingal? How cool. A nod to Oscar.'

'I knew you'd get that. Anyway, he's a wonderful guard dog. I'm only confessing this because it's you, but I was having trouble sleeping in this place on my own.'

'Big girl's blouse,' Molly said.

'I know, right? So embarrassing. But Fingal keeps me company. And he barks at pretty much everything. Bats, mice, frogs.'

'So not much more sleep, then?' Molly giggled then frowned. She was beginning to feel rather queasy.

'Not so much,' Ed agreed with a grin. 'But at least I know a burglar won't come in and bugger me senseless. Not until Fingal's had a good go at him.'

'I think a burglar would be more likely to want to lift your TV than bugger you senseless,' Molly said sensibly.

She watched Ed petting Fingal. *Ed, Ed, Ed.* Whenever things went wrong in her life, she seemed to turn to Ed. Not to Sam, to Ed. It was a pattern she couldn't seem to break. Was she using Ed? Surely not. He was her friend. Her best friend, if she was honest. Molly barely saw any of her friends any more; she worked such long hours, she couldn't fit her social life around them. Jody had gone off to Canada and, apart from Sara, Ed was the one person who remained constant. Even if he had been absent for much of the past few years.

Molly felt a sob rising in her throat again. She grabbed her wine and drank it down quickly.

Ed watched her, feeling panicked. He hated people drinking like this. It reminded him of his mother. But he knew he had to be gentle with Molly in this mood.

'Are you off again? Fingal, cuddle Molly. That's an order.'

Fingal obliged by jumping up on to Molly's lap. She laughed and cried and cuddled him. He curled up on her lap and she bit her lip, looking at Ed.

'Sleep with me.' Her heart pounded in her chest. But her gaze was unwavering.

Ed felt his stomach drop. Right before his groin kicked into life. 'What? What the fuck, Molly?'

'You heard me.'

'You're drunk.'

'No, I'm not. Not that drunk anyway. I just asked you to sleep with me.'

Ed's heart was going like a jackhammer. He wanted her. She looked eminently desirable, even with a tear-stained face, rosy cheeks from all the wine and eyes that were full of utter misery.

'Well, what about it, Ed?'

Molly had never been so bold in her life before. And she wasn't entirely sure where she had found the courage to say such a thing to Ed. All she knew was that in this moment, it felt right. Not because she was angry with Sam, but because, for her sins, she wanted Ed. Badly.

'You're angry with Sam.' Ed moved closer. Fingal's head popped up and he sought Ed's hand with his wet nose.

'I'm not. I mean, I am, but that's not the reason for this. Kiss me immediately.'

'Oh fuck.' Ed leant in and kissed her. She tasted of wine, sexiness and just – Molly. There was nothing better.

She kissed him back ardently. She felt Fingal jump off her lap and she wound her arms around Ed's neck. 'Kiss me again,' she whispered. 'Make me feel like that again.'

Ed obliged. He knew it was wrong, but he couldn't help himself. He knew he had to stop in a second, because in spite of Molly's protestations, she was drunk. Ed knew she was drunk. And there was no way he was sleeping with her, even though every fibre of his being yearned to tear her clothes off and consume her. It was going to be the hardest thing he had ever done, saying no to her and he was going to do it in a minute. He was. He most definitely was. But just a few seconds longer with her mouth on his . . .

'Hang on.' Molly stopped kissing Ed for a second. God. That was some wave of nausea. It passed. 'Come back here.'

Ed drew back. 'Er, no. Wait there.' He disappeared for a minute, returning with a glass of water, a towel and a bucket.

'What's all that for?'

'I'm your mate,' Ed said, moving her to the sofa. He knelt down and placed the bucket in front of him. He laid the towel on her lap. 'I've seen all this before. You're about to puke, Molls. Into the bucket please and then you can have some water.'

'I am absolutely, most definitely not going to be sick.' Molly put a hand to her mouth. 'Oh God. Ed. Hold my hair . . .'

She leant over and heaved into the bucket. Repeatedly. It was as though she simply couldn't stop her stomach from bringing everything up. Molly felt Ed's hand holding her hair at the nape of her neck and she started crying again. God, what a bloody mess.

'Thai noodles,' she said, wiping the back of her mouth.

'Yes, I got that, thank you,' Ed said, looking squeamish. 'I'm not that great with vomit, Molls. Are you done?'

'I think so.' She shakily sipped the water he offered,

grateful when he disappeared with the bucket. What an idiot she was. Now she was going to have to apologise to Ed for being such a brazen hussy.

'No need to apologise,' Ed said breezily when he returned. 'Drink does terrible things to a person. It's forgotten already.'

Molly rubbed her eyes. Meeting Ed's, she thought about his words. Did she want him to forget about her proposition? She knew he should and that he was being an absolute gent suggesting such a thing. But Molly wasn't sure.

Love me, Ed, she thought to herself. Just love me. Kiss me, make love to me, make all of this go away. I don't know if I love Sam any more. But I think I love you. I think I've always loved you. Please, Ed. Please.

Ed swallowed, trying to get his thoughts together. Before the vomiting incident, he had been raging inside, ready to pounce. Ready to behave in a very ungentlemanly fashion, yanking Molly's clothes off and familiarising himself with her glorious body.

It always felt like he was making a play for Molly, but she had made the move this time. But she had rowed with Sam. She was in a mess. She didn't really mean that she wanted him that way – she just wanted some escapism. Ed's heart sank. If only Molly really wanted him, the way he wanted her. If she had, Ed knew his life would all fall into place.

'I think you should get some sleep,' he said firmly, grabbing a fleece blanket from the back of the sofa. 'Does Sam know where you are? Shall I call him?'

Sam. It was as though Ed had thrown cold water all

over her. 'Um. Yes. I mean, no. He doesn't know where I am. Yes, please, to calling him.'

Molly lay down on the sofa. Ed didn't want her. She had offered herself to him on a plate and he had said no. Was it because she'd been sick? Surely not. It had to be more than that. So maybe he wasn't in love with her, after all. He had had the chance to spend the night with her again after all these years and he had turned her down. They were clearly just friends; nothing more. Molly wanted to cry all over again. She also felt thoroughly exhausted.

Ed pulled the fleece over her. Leaving the room briefly, he called Sam and reassured him that Molly was perfectly safe and sleeping off the booze. Sam sounded stilted but seemed happy enough that Molly was safe. Returning to the conservatory, Ed found Fingal curled up on Molly's body, Molly's arm around him. She was out for the count and so was Fingal.

'Good boy,' Ed whispered, sitting down on the floor in front of the sofa. 'You keep Molly warm.'

He spent much of the night watching Molly sleep. Wishing things were different, that he could turn time back so they could be together. So they could have been together for all of these years. Boyfriend and girlfriend, husband and wife. But it just wasn't meant to be. Him and Molly weren't meant to be.

Ed slept fitfully on the floor, then woke early and went outside for a cigarette. He was joined by Fingal, who leapt around joyously when Ed flung a ball for him. Ed had a long hard think. About himself, but particularly about Molly. He alighted on something and wondered if he had hit the nail on the head. If Molly was anything like him – and she most assuredly was – Ed was pretty sure he had come up with the answer Molly had been searching for. He fed Fingal and put the kettle on. And the coffee machine, for good measure. He peered into the fridge, pleased to find a pack of bacon and some sausages.

Expecting Molly to be awake when he returned, Ed was surprised to find her still curled up in a ball, her little hand tucked under her face. He put a mug of coffee down on the table and tenderly tucked a strand of hair behind her ear. They both had to move on. He needed to keep his life on track and so did she. And they needed each other, but it had to be a friendship and nothing more. No more drunken kisses, no more blurred lines.

Ed's phone beeped and he took it out of his pocket. It was a text from Saskia.

Can't stop thinking about you. Life's too short . . . think we should make this more formal. Or something. Call me if you want to talk about it.

Life *was* too short. And Ed wasn't into funny messages or signs. But this was a sign. This text from Saskia, the timing of it, the content, was a sign.

'Hey.' Molly woke up and stretched. 'Was that my phone?'

'No, it was mine. How are you feeling?'

'Crappy. My head hurts. I'm embarrassed. And I smell of sick.'

'Apart from that?'

'Apart from that, I'm bloody marvellous.' She smiled.

Ed sat on the coffee table in front of her. 'Ok, I've been thinking. Don't make a joke, cheeky wench. Right. I reckon it's about time you and I stopped pissing about and did what we're meant to be doing. What we always said we'd do.'

Molly yawned and sat up. 'What do you mean?'

Ed handed her the mug of coffee. 'Do you remember that talk under the stars, the first time we met?'

'Er, yes. We were pontificating about being artists and writers.'

'We were. And that's what we are meant to be.'

'Is it?'

Ed nodded fervently. 'It is. So, I think we need to just get on with it. I need to finish my bloody novel – and I'm going to – and you need to paint again.'

'Paint again?' Molly let out a bitter laugh. 'And when shall I do that?'

'That's up to you to sort out. But you need to paint. It's who you are.'

'I haven't painted for years.' Molly sipped the coffee. 'God, that's good.'

Ed took out a cigarette. 'You need to. You need to paint. I need to write and you need to paint. Sam will let you have the time to do it – you said it yourself; he'll do anything to make you happy. Painting makes you happy. He loves working so let him work.'

'As simple as that,' Molly said, hearing the sarcastic tone to her voice.

'If you want it to be,' Ed said earnestly. 'Why not?'

Molly considered. Painting. Just the thought made her stomach fire up and her mind conjure possibilities and visions and colours. Get back to painting. What a thought. Molly wondered what Sam would say if she dared to suggest such a thing. Would he care? Would he mind if she took time off work? He was already planning to employ more staff – maybe she could duck out and do some painting. Just one day a week. Maybe two. Two days. Two whole days of painting. What utter bliss that would be.

Molly couldn't believe she had gone for so long without doing the thing she loved. She had allowed herself to get so caught up in Sam's work, she had lost herself. This wasn't about babies at all. It was about painting, about her getting back to her roots – back to who she really was.

'I'm right, aren't I? You need to paint again?'

'Yes, you smug bastard. I need to paint again.' Molly met Ed's eyes. How did he know her this well? How had he managed to alight on this when Sam, who had been married to her for so many years, had missed it?

'So I'll finish my novel. You'll get back to painting.' Ed stood up and turned to Molly. 'And we'll draw a line under everything. You'll be happy with Sam and I'll – well, I'll be alright.'

'Have you met someone?' Molly felt her insides coil up slightly.

'It's that girl, Saskia,' Ed said. 'Do you remember her from the New Year's Eve party? I might have a good feeling about her.'

Molly was engulfed by a wave of jealousy so strong, she almost repeated last night's vomiting incident. She gulped down some more coffee. It didn't matter if Ed had met someone, it didn't matter. Because she was married to Sam. And Ed deserved to be happy.

'But, I need you in my life,' Ed said soberly. 'I need you, Molly. As my friend. Ok? No blurred lines. You're my very good friend and I need to be able to go out to coffee with you. And dinner. Just now and again.'

'Yes. I-I want the same.'

Molly could feel tears coming again. Don't you dare, she told herself sternly. Don't you bloody dare. The thought of never putting her mouth on Ed's again was crushing. But it was wrong. It was wrong because of Sam. And because Ed had met someone else.

'Great.' Ed felt emotional. He knew he had to get out of the room before he disgraced himself. 'Then that's settled. The artist and the writer. Best friends. Finally happy.'

'Yes.'

Molly felt both elated and deflated all at once. But he was right. So right. It was how it had to be.

'Ok then.' Ed plastered a jaunty smile on his face. 'Bacon and sausage sandwiches for breakfast?'

'Perfect,' Molly said.

Out in the kitchen, Ed fired up the oven he had barely used and clutched the edge of the worktop. He was going to finish his novel. And maybe Saskia would be the one to make him happy. It was right. Life made sense. Which didn't explain why, yet again, his heart felt like it had been squashed by a coffee grinder – it should be used to it by now.

Pulling himself together, Ed put some bacon on the grill and started frying up some sausages. It was time. Time for something new.

Now

It was early evening and Molly was pouring herself a glass of wine. She had had several viewers for the house and three couples seemed really interested. Molly hadn't actually found a new place for herself yet, but she would worry about that later. She could always rent somewhere if she needed to.

There was a knock at the door. She answered it, surprised to see Sara. 'What are you doing here at this time of night?'

'I've come to meddle in your life,' Sara grinned, coming in.

'What?'

'Ed sent me.'

'Ed?' Molly decided she really should stop repeating everything Sara was saying.

'Yes. I have a formal invitation for you. Have a read.' Sara handed an envelope over.

Molly opened the envelope. It contained a stiff, white card. On it, Ed had written:

Please join me for some pretentious stargazing. Location: Maplethorpe Beach. Time: 7pm. Please, Molly. Have so much to tell you. Wrap up warm; it's freezing! Ed x

'What's this?'

'I think it's Ed being romantic,' Sara said, throwing herself on to Molly's sofa. 'I think it's Ed wanting to tell you how he feels about you.'

Molly stared at the card. 'But . . . Ed has feelings for Jody.'

'Does he? Do you know that for sure? Did you ask him?'

'Well, no. But he was so gutted about Jake, I assumed there had to be more to it.'

Sara pulled a face. 'No. I think that was just Ed being gutted about Jake. But why didn't you check with him?'

'I don't think I had the guts to hear the answer if it was bad news,' Molly confessed. 'I literally couldn't take it, Sara. Not with everything else – Sam . . . my illness.'

'I get that.' Sara shot her a sympathetic glance. 'But I think this is all going to be alright, Molly. You and Ed. Maybe it's finally time for you to be together.'

Molly started shaking. 'I'm scared, Sara, and I don't know why.'

'Because this is the biggest thing ever. You and Ed. It's everything.' Sara squeezed Molly's hand. 'Listen, I don't know for sure, ok? I don't know what Ed has up his sleeve. But I know he wants to talk to you. And he was so worried you might not come, he sent me to convince you. Which has to be good, right?'

Molly nodded. Part of her wanted to go. Desperately. There was so much she wanted to say. She still hadn't read the letter she had found in Sam's things, but she wanted to ask Ed about it.

The other part of Molly – the vulnerable part that had been hurt countless times – wanted to stay well away. Going to the beach was putting herself out there and Molly felt that she had put herself out there so many times before with Ed. And each time had ended in disaster. Disasters which had left her heart splintered and sent her limping away, bruised and battered.

When she had told Sara that it might be time to go it alone, she had meant it. Molly felt strong alone. She felt strong without Sam and without Ed. She wasn't deliriously happy, but her heart was intact. She didn't feel vulnerable or scared or mistrustful.

Molly's phone alerted her to a text. It was Ed. Molly read it. It said:

Hope you received my invitation to join me at Maplethorpe Beach for some pretentious stargazing. Sara said she would get the invite to you. But just in case, this is me texting you with the same information because I am not taking any chances this time. Please join me, Molly. I have so much to say and I need to do it face to face. Ed x

Molly sank down on to the sofa. What should she do? Should she go? Or should she protect herself from Ed, barricade herself into her house, lock all the doors and make sure he couldn't get in and do any damage? Because Molly's heart ached. It felt bruised and punctured from the knocks it had received over the years.

They were not all Ed's fault, but still Molly felt each fracture and tear.

But this was Ed. *Ed*. Her friend. The friend who had been there through so many of the good – and the bad – times in her life. The friend who had rushed to her side when Molly's mother had died. Who had held her so tenderly when she had told him about her Parkinson's diagnosis. Who had loved her more deeply and more passionately than anyone else in her life.

'Go, Molly,' Sara urged. 'Be brave. Grab this chance. Find out what he has to say.'

Molly stood up, her legs trembling slightly. And this time, it had nothing whatsoever to do with her illness. The trouble was, she was already head over heels for Ed. It was already too late. It pretty much always had been. Molly pushed back the tears that were pricking her eyelids. It had always been Ed. Right from the first moment they'd met.

'I'm going,' she said decisively. 'I'm doing it.'

'Yay!' Sara looked delighted.

Grabbing the letter she'd found in Sam's things, Molly pulled on her warmest coat and jumped into her car. She drove to Maplethorpe Beach with her heart in her mouth. She had heard that expression before, but she had never known what it meant. Now she did.

Arriving at the beach, Molly headed for the spot they always went to, just to the right of the first beach hut.

She saw the spot immediately, it was lit up by a ring of what looked like tiny candles. Quite close to the shore, closer than Ed and Molly normally sat. Or perhaps the tide was in higher than usual, she wasn't sure.

Squinting, Molly saw Ed waving both his arms in the air, the great big idiot. Molly pulled on a woolly hat with a bear face and ears and drew her massive winter coat more closely around her. Making her way down towards Ed, she realised that what she had thought was a circle of candles was, in fact, a heart. Ed had made a heart out of candles. And he had put two deckchairs in the middle, an ice bucket with champagne in it and, obscurely, a stack of books.

'Molly.' Ed looked nervous. 'Love the hat.'

Molly smiled, her heart thumping like crazy. 'Immature, I know. But it makes me laugh.'

'It's adorable. Here. Take a seat.'

'Deckchairs. Good lord. We *are* going posh.' Molly eased herself into a deckchair carefully, aware that no one could really get into one of these with any degree of elegance.

'Oh, you have no idea.' Ed joined her, sitting clumsily in the other one. 'Oh, shit. These chairs have a mind of their own.'

'They really do,' Molly said, struggling to sit properly. There was a sudden silence and Molly realised Ed was staring at her.

'I have spent my life missing you,' Ed said quietly. 'My whole life.'

'H-have you?'

'Yes.' He started to say something, then stopped.

'What's with the books?' Molly picked one up and broke into a smile. *The Portrait of Dorian Gray.*

'Thought we could recreate the first night we met,' Ed said. 'Stargazing . . .' He peered at the sky. 'Well. It's not

345

the best night for stargazing, but I can see a few popping up here and there.'

'Do tell me about them,' Molly said, her mouth twitching. 'I hope you swotted up on them to impress me.'

'Wikipedia is a wondrous thing,' Ed commented. 'So, we have pretentious stargazing, books we can discuss – there's some about art there at the bottom.' He lifted the bottle of champagne. 'I couldn't remember what we were drinking that night but I suspect it was some fruity shit they don't sell any more. Or one of Mrs Middleton's lethal cocktails that made everyone go off their rockers.'

'What's all this in aid of, Ed?' Molly asked, turning to him. 'It's very sweet, but I'm not sure what it's about.'

'Oh, didn't I say?' Ed put the champagne down and took her hand. 'This is me putting myself out there. This is me showing you that the night we first met changed my life for ever. And that I have never really stopped loving you since that first night.' He nodded gravely. 'I have just loved you in a variety of different ways at different times in our lives.'

'Ed . . .'

'No, let me finish, please. I'm on a roll. I have loved you as a friend. I have loved you as a lover. Christ,' Ed groaned. 'You have no idea how often I've thought about that night, Molls. No idea. It has haunted me, comforted me, turned me on, and made me fall in love with you over and over again. Just the mere memory of it.'

Molly blushed. She knew exactly what Ed meant.

'But you know all this. You've read my novel. I know you did. So, you know. Deep down, you must have known it anyway, but it's there in black and white, Molls. I've put my entire heart into that novel. My heart, our love story . . . you and me.'

Molly started to cry. 'I can't believe you feel that way about me.' She sniffed. 'The thing is, I didn't actually get to the end. So I don't know what is supposed to happen.'

'Ah. Well. With the ending, I allowed myself to be completely self-indulgent. I wrote what I wanted to happen with us. I'll tell you about that in a minute.' Ed came out of his deckchair even more clumsily than he had got in it and ended up on his knees in front of her. 'As for not being able to believe that's how I feel about you, you must. It's how I've always felt.'

'But what about Jake? What about Jody?'

'I will always love Jake,' Ed said sincerely. 'Even though he's not mine, I will always have a special place for him in my heart. But Jody, no. Me and Jody – that was never a thing. I just felt connected to her because of Jake. I have never had feelings for her. Not in that way.'

Molly felt a rush of relief. 'But you know about the Parkinson's. I didn't think you really knew about it, but you do.' She was stricken with anxiety. 'How do I know you can cope? I thought Sam could and he ran a mile from me.'

'I'm not Sam,' Ed told her firmly, grabbing her hands. 'I love you, Molly. I love these hands, whether they shake or not. I love your beautiful face, however old it gets. I love, *love* your body. Every inch of it. And whatever happens to it, I will always, always love every inch of it. And most of all, I love your mind. And I surely don't need to say it, but whatever happens to it, I will love it until the end of my days.'

Molly was sobbing, great big tears splashing down on to her hands and on to Ed's hands. Everything he had just said to her was incredible. Stunning. Romantic. Gorgeous. But she had to know that Ed wasn't going to run away from her. Ed running away from her would kill her. It almost had once before.

'I will never run away from you,' Ed said solemnly. 'Never.'

'How do you do that? Read my mind?' Molly started laughing and crying at the same time. 'You've always been able to do it.'

Ed shrugged. 'I don't know. You read mine too. Not all the time, thank God – you'd be appalled at the things I think about when you come into my head.'

Molly blushed. 'Listen, Ed. About that . . .'

'Is this the thing about Parkinson's not being sexy?' Ed sighed and tightened his grip on her hands. 'Seriously, Molly. I repeat: I'm not Sam, ok? I don't know what his problem is, but I can assure you that I will fancy you until we are both old and grey with awful hair and . . . and saggy bits.'

'What a vision.' Molly was beginning to come undone. Ed always had this incredible way of making her come undone.

'I mean it,' Ed assured her. 'Molly, you've read my novel. And I wrote you a letter once . . . I wish you'd read it. I assume Sam must have destroyed it.'

'Is this it?' Molly drew the battered envelope out of her pocket.

'Oh my God,' Ed took it, stunned. 'Sam didn't destroy this?'

Molly shook her head. 'I guess not.'

'So you know everything.'

'I don't. I haven't read it.'

'What?' Ed was incredulous. 'How could you *not* have read it? You missed the end of the novel and you didn't read my letter either?'

Molly shrugged. 'Sara said the same thing. But honestly, Ed, I was scared. I still am. I know that whatever is contained in this letter will change everything – how I feel about Sam, how I feel about you.'

'Yes.' Ed nodded in agreement. 'But Molly, you already know me. This letter tells you some things you don't know about my past . . . the things I always wanted to tell you. But apart from that, it's just me. It's just me, telling you how I feel about you. Why I love you. Why you were the best – always the best – part of my life.'

Molly realised she was holding her breath and she let it out jerkily.

'And as for Sam, he's not the guy you thought he was anyway.' Ed put the letter into her hands. 'Reading this won't change your views on him, I swear. I guess he thought he was doing the right thing. He loved you. He was protecting you. I might have done the same in his shoes.'

Molly stared at the letter.

'Listen. Read it, don't read it. I could quote it word for word to you. Oh yes.' Ed nodded emphatically. 'I'll leave it up to you. But to go back to your other point, I guess me and Sam must be hard-wired a little differently. Or I just feel differently about you. Because I find you sexy whatever you're doing and whatever you're wearing. Do you think a few tremors and you forgetting where the bacon is are going to put me off?'

'I think it's a little more serious than that,' Molly said. She was starting to cry again now, petrified about the way she was going to deteriorate and how Ed might react to it.

Ed linked his fingers through hers. 'Well, of course it is, you silly thing,' he said gently. 'And I know that, Molly. I have reconciled myself to all the facts, to the reality of how this illness will affect you. And me. But it doesn't matter. Nothing matters if you're here with me. I've realised that since I met Jake. He stole my heart for a while and, to be fair, he'll always have a ruddy great chunk. But you – you're something else. You have the rest of it. You always have had. No one else has come close. I'm ready for you. For this. For us. I've always been ready, but trust me, I have never been more ready than I am now.'

Molly stared up at the sky, trying to tip the tears back into her eyes. 'But you do know what the future holds with a Parkinson's sufferer, Ed? It's not going to be pretty.'

'I don't care. Nothing will faze me. I promise you. You will always be pretty to me. Beautiful. Breathtaking. And I want to take care of you. I want to be here for you, always. I never want us to be apart again.'

'But you really do know, right?' Molly turned to him pointedly. 'This isn't a game, Ed. Sam ran away because he couldn't face the future. I-I won't always be like this. I might get all depressed and weird and do strange things. My body will let me down spectacularly at some point. Embarrassingly. I will fall over. I'll . . . fall. In all sorts of ways.'

'But I will catch you,' Ed said simply. 'I will never, ever, let you fall, Molly. Never.'

Molly caught her breath. She believed him. She did. 'Ed. Is this really going to happen between us after all this time?'

'I think it is, yes.'

'Bloody hell.' She wiped her face. 'I literally don't think I've felt as happy as this in a long time. The last time – if I'm being completely honest – was probably that night we spent together.'

Ed groaned. 'Don't remind me. But – that's the thing. We can do that whenever we want now. Blimey. What a thought. What an amazing thought. Shall we do that as much as possible? As soon as possible.'

Ed was rather disappointed in himself that he was getting so hot and bothered. But he couldn't help it; this was Molly. He had always felt this way about her. He loved her, he was in love with her, he liked her, he fancied her and he couldn't think of anyone he would rather be with.

Molly felt her breath quickening. Ed had always had a knack of making her blood rush. She had only ever felt this kind of passion with him. It used to make her feel guilty about Sam, but it didn't now.

'Cor, I can't wait. Can we cut this crap and go home right now please?'

'Ed, wait. What about kids?' Molly was panicking again. After Jake, surely Ed wanted kids?

'I honestly don't mind,' Ed told her. And he meant it. 'We can talk about it at some point. Or not. It doesn't matter. This is about me and you. I don't know if I could put myself through it after Jake anyway. Not unless you want to have them,' he added hurriedly. 'And if you do, I will put myself through it. I will put myself through anything.'

Molly finally relaxed. He was incredible. Awesome, she would have said, back when they first met. 'Ed. I think I really love you.'

'Good to know. I *know* I really love *you.*'

'Are you always going to try and outdo me like that?'

'Every chance I get,' Ed replied. 'Super-competitive over here. But that can be a very good thing, trust me. Is it time to go home and roll you into bed yet?'

'No. It's time for you to hold my hand, look at the stars and tell me again how much you love me.'

'Rightio. And then bed?'

'And then bed.'

Ed glanced at Molly. 'And this, Molly, is how my novel ended. With everything I'm ever going to need. You, me and the stars.'

Molly and Ed lay back, hands entwined, bodies tingling with anticipation, and gazed in a really rather pretentious manner at the stars twinkling above them.

The next day, Molly decided to read Ed's letter. And when she had, she knew she would go back and read it over and over again whenever she got scared. Whenever she worried that Ed might run away and leave her.

And Molly knew that she would come undone again, every time. But she would also know that she and Ed would always be entwined. And that was all Molly needed.

Dearest Molls,

I know it's old-fashioned to write letters – a 'lost art' if you will – but as you know, I'm all about words, Molly. Pretentious and then some. To say these words to your face would be better, I know, but somehow, I feel that here, on paper, it will be easier for me to be honest with you. That open book I've always wanted to be. The open book you have always wanted me to be.

So here it is. If you could please imagine me taking a deep breath, that would be marvellous. Because I am. Even writing this down, which has to be easier than saying it out loud, I am bracing myself. Because I haven't talked to anyone about this. A few people have happened upon this secret of mine accidentally, but there isn't anyone I have trusted with this before. You are the only person I have ever wanted to tell. And the reason I didn't? It wasn't because I didn't trust you. You are the only person in my life I truly trust. And I mean that. It is because I always want you to think the best of me, Molls. To see the best in me. You make me want to be this amazing person, even if, in reality, I am flawed and somewhat damaged.

I've now waffled on for so long, I need to take another breath. And now I'm saying it. My mum was an alcoholic. By which I don't mean that she liked one too many drinks now and again. I am talking about genuine alcoholism. The kind that comes with vomiting, bed wetting and falling down stairs. Mean tempers, unforgivable insults, suicide threats and duplicitous antics. Secrets, lies and deceit.

Why was she an alcoholic? I think it was mainly due to my dad. He walked out when I was fifteen. (Bit of a twat, my dad, just as aside. Poet, philanderer and prick – that's him sewn up.) So there was just me. Now, don't you feel sorry for me, Molls. Don't you dare. Because I wanted to look after her. I loved her. And I thought I could help her. But I couldn't; she was too far gone. And then she died. In fact, she took her own life. Last week. That night we were together. And I hate her a little bit for that. I can't believe I'm saying it, but it's true – I hate her for ruining something that, for me, was utter perfection.

And I mean that, Molly. It was perfection. You are perfection to me. You are my ultimate. The best person I could ever be with. My favourite person in the whole world. The person I am meant to live with. Die with. Probably annoy a bit with my smoking and my pestering you for snogs – and far more rude things – and my whining on endlessly about writing a book.

But you and me, Molls, we rocked the world off its hinges. Rudely, beautifully, and in ways I could never have imagined. And I know I sound like a stupid romantic idiot here (but dirty, yes . . . yes?) but that's how I feel. As if this – you and me – are the real thing. The real deal. Real, raw, beautiful, emotional, and anything else wondrous.

Please forgive me for leaving; I just need some

space. I couldn't bring all of that hatred back with me. But I have enclosed a plane ticket for you. To join me here, in Bermuda. And some directions to a beach. An incredible beach that immediately made me think of our beach. Join me so we can talk about everything. That night – that night, God, I can't stop thinking about it, about you. I feel as though I looked into your actual soul, Molly.

I'm in love with you. I want you in my life. You are the only thing that matters and you have always made me better. I am better with you and beside you. We have everything in front of us. A lifetime together, I hope. If you'll have me. I'm ready for you and I mean that. We are going to have that thing everyone talks about, that indescribable, indefinable thing that everyone wants to find.

And we have found it, Molls, because we have found one another. And that means we should never let each other go. Right? So let's do that. Never let each other go.

Here's to endless stargazing,

Yours (and I mean that), Ed x

Acknowledgements

I would like to thank lots of people, as ever, so do bear with me.

Thanks to the wonderful team at Avon/HarperCollins. Katy Loftus, for being such a fantastic editor (and friend) and for helping me through some tough times. I loved our brainstorming sessions – such an inspiration and they contributed hugely to shaping this novel into something very different. I am very sad to lose you but a huge thank you to Caroline Kirkpatrick for effortlessly stepping into Katy's shoes and for supporting me throughout the usual author anxieties.

Thanks to my fantastic agents Kate Burke and Diane Banks – always there for me, always cheering and supporting. I very much appreciate your loyalty and commitment.

To all my author pals (too many to mention) for carrying me through this novel . . . with writing stuff, as well as personal stuff.

To all my friends but special mentions for Jeni (still

keeping me sane from all those miles away), for Kate and Claire (the same sanity thing but at close quarters), all my EEB girls (do keep rearranging my novels wherever you go please, I love it) and my many mum friends, old and new.

To my parents – thank you for everything over the past year.

To Phoebe and Daisy, my gorgeous girls: lots and lots of love and thanks for just being there and making my life all kinds of ace.

Very special thanks to my incredible friends Chireal Shallow and Jo Murray-Dry . . . you know why.

This novel and the issues contained within it are very personal to me. I hope you all enjoy reading it and that it restores your faith in love, romance and friendship.

A Conversation with Ella Harper

• What inspired you to write The Years of Loving You?

I wanted to examine the whole idea of missed timing between friends – a guy and a girl who really should have ended up together at some point. Opportunities that arise that should draw two people together, but life gets in the way. Or something happens to prevent those two people getting together yet ultimately, they are still drawn to one another. Also, I wanted to explore the concept of male and female friendship and how that can last over a long period of time.

The issue of early onset Parkinson's wasn't inspired by anything in particular, although I used to be a huge Michael. J. Fox fan, so I might have drawn some inspiration from his incredible journey. I also wanted to look at how such a progressive illness would affect an otherwise healthy, vibrant person. The impact it might have on a relationship, which had otherwise been unchallenged until that point.

Ed's discovery that he might have fathered a son some years ago intrigued me as an idea, especially for a character who had very strong reasons for not wanting to bring a child into the world. And I loved the contrast to the scenes from the past that allowed the reader to get to know Ed and Molly intimately, whilst their current challenges played out, causing the two characters to collide both in the past and in the present day.

- Your novel is highly emotive. Do you draw from personal experience when writing?

I think there are always shades of my real life that find their way into my novels. But only shades. I also have a very over-active imagination! And often, I want to explore specific issues that interest me so my novels tend to be a combination of all of these elements threaded together: personal experience, reality, fiction, exploration.

- Your characters are so authentic. How do you get into their psyche?

When I really get to grips with my characters, I literally write as them, thinking the way they think, reacting the way I know they will react. When I first started out, I used to write huge character notes, detailing physical characteristics, music taste, perfume/aftershave worn, personal style, reading habits, preferred food...all sorts. These days, I have some of these elements in my head as a general background if relevant, but I am much more motivated by how my characters have got to where they are today, what drives them emotionally and how they will react to a given situation. As soon as I connect and have a clear picture, I write as if I am that character. I recognise elements of myself and my thoughts in my male characters as much as I do my female leads. Tiny fragments filter through – because I am in their psyche and vice versa.

- The Years of Loving You is a real tear-jerker. How do you switch off from your writing?

I often cry when writing an emotive scene. If something moves me, I react, even if I am writing it myself. So I can feel very emotional whilst writing, but I do tend to be able to switch off when I walk away from my desk. Writing is very much about being in the zone for me so I can fully immerse myself in it, but once out of that zone again, I can disconnect. However, when I re-read my work – editing, proof reading etc., I can confirm that I cry all over again when I reach a sad or emotional bit!

- Can you tell us a little about what you are writing next?

In my next novel, I want to explore friendships in more detail – male and female again, but in a group dynamic. I want to look at how people appear to others, what goes on behind closed doors, and the idea that people can be hiding deep-rooted issues or secrets, whilst seeming very together on the outside. This novel will have a fairly dramatic – but also enigmatic – start and the truth will slowly unravel in a series of scenes: flashbacks, current day and key events. I'm very excited about it!